THE
BLACK
ECHO

BOOKS BY MICHAEL CONNELLY

The Harry Bosch Novels

The Black Echo
The Black Ice
The Concrete Blonde
The Last Coyote
Trunk Music
Angels Flight
A Darkness More than Night
City of Bones
Lost Light
The Narrows
The Closers
Echo Park
The Overlook

Other Novels

The Poet
Blood Work
Void Moon
Chasing the Dime
The Lincoln Lawyer
The Scarecrow

Anthologies

Mystery Writers of America Presents Blue Religion:
New Stories about Cops, Criminals, and the Chase

Nonfiction

Crime Beat: A Decade of Covering Cops and Killers

MICHAEL CONNELLY

THE
BLACK
ECHO

GRAND CENTRAL
PUBLISHING

NEW YORK   BOSTON

Copyright © 1992 by Michael Connelly
All rights reserved. Except as permitted under the U.S. Copyright Act of 1976, no part of this publication may be reproduced, distributed, or transmitted in any form or by any means, or stored in a database or retrieval system, without the prior written permission of the publisher.

This edition is published in arrangement with St. Martin's Press.

Cover design by Diane Luger / George Cornell
Cover photo by Reza Estakhrian / Getty Images

Grand Central Publishing
Hachette Book Group
237 Park Avenue
New York, NY 10017
Visit our website at www.HachetteBookGroup.com

Grand Central Publishing is a division of Hachette Book Group, Inc.
The Grand Central Publishing name and logo is a trademark of Hachette Book Group, Inc.

Printed in the United States of America

First Printing: December 2002

20 19 18 17 16 15 14 13 12

ATTENTION CORPORATIONS AND ORGANIZATIONS:
Most HACHETTE BOOK GROUP books are available at quantity discounts with bulk purchase for educational, business, or sales promotional use. For information, please call or write:
Special Markets Department, Hachette Book Group
237 Park Avenue, New York, NY 10017
Telephone: 1-800-222-6747 Fax: 1-800-477-5925

*This is for W. Michael Connelly
and Mary McEvoy Connelly*

Acknowledgments

I WOULD LIKE TO THANK the following people for their help and support:

Many thanks to my agent, Philip Spitzer, and to my editor, Patricia Mulcahy, for all their hard work, enthusiasm and belief in this book.

Also, thanks to the many police officers who over the years have given me an insight into their jobs and lives. I also want to ackowledge Tom Mangold and John Pennycate, whose book *The Tunnels of Cu Chi* tells the reals story of the tunnel rats of the Vietnam War.

Last, I would like to thank my family and friends for their encouragement and unqualified support. And, most of all, I am indebted to my wife, Linda, whose belief and inspiration never waned.

Introduction

I have always been puzzled by our collective tendency to place American writing into categories, particularly when the categorical designation is not meant to be complimentary. William Burroughs once suggested that categorization was the vice of the professional journalist and, as a former news reporter myself, I think Burroughs was probably right.

The format of any news story demands brevity and simplicity, but since most subjects worth writing about are complex, the journalist usually gives up trying to pack an elephant into a phone booth and instead puts this rotund, unmanageable fellow under a circus tent.

Terms like "mystery" and to some degree "crime" fiction have connotations that may not be derogatory but are hardly laudable, at least not laudable in the way the categorical terms "literary" fiction and "metaphysical" poetry and, my all-time favorite, "metafiction" are used.

Academics do not teach James M. Cain, even though he is one of our best writers—his novel *Mildred Pierce* is arguably as good as any book Henry James wrote using a female protagonist. By the same token, I would suspect most academics would probably not want to call Robert Stone's

Dog Soldiers a crime novel, even though its subject is heroin smuggling and the moral insanity of a profligate society. Why not? You got me.

Perhaps books that win the National Book Award are automatically excluded from the crime-novel category.

Michael Connelly and I met by coincidence. Shortly after the acceptance of his first novel, *The Black Echo*, he came to a book signing of mine in Los Angeles and introduced himself. After we shook hands, he explained how he had found an agent for his manuscript. I had dedicated my novel *Heaven's Prisoners* to my agent, Philip Spitzer, whom I had met during a period when I could not sell ice water in the Sahara. Philip was driving a cab in Hell's Kitchen at night and running a one-man agency during the day. We became friends and business partners, and Philip kept my novels under submission for thirteen years, when nobody else in New York would touch me with a dung fork.

Michael read my dedication to my agent, one in which I indicated the level of personal commitment and faith that Philip had invested in my work during the many years of its rejection. Michael decided Philip was the agent for him and he sent off the manuscript of *The Black Echo*. As soon as Philip read it, he knew a writer of enormous talent and ability was about to arrive on the American literary scene.

Edna Buchanan and I both blurbed the jacket of Little, Brown's hardcover printing of *The Black Echo*. I'd like to quote my words as they originally appeared, because I think they apply as much today as they did then, and I'm also proud that my endorsement appeared on the jacket of this fine book:

"*The Black Echo* is one of the most authentic pieces of crime writing I've ever read. It is an extraordinary story, one that engages the reader on the first page and never lets go. The conclusion will leave you short of breath. When Connelly takes you into a tunnel beneath the earth, either in Los Angeles or Vietnam, you feel that you're entering a domain of moral darkness that only Joseph Conrad could adequately describe. It's hard to believe that this is Connelly's first novel. I'm convinced that his career will be a major one."

This novel will stand up against James M. Cain's. I think that is the highest compliment I can give any literary artist. Michael turns the City of Los Angeles into a protagonist, in the same fashion James Ellroy does. Every line in the book is written with the eye of someone who either understands or has lived the ethos of the characters. The cops, the street hustlers, the tunnel rats, the desperate souls who join hands around a community meal in a homeless shelter are flesh and blood. In an odd way, the reader feels that with just a small twist of the dial in the back of his head, he might have become one of them.

I have always maintained that this novel would be a classic, one that critics will refer back to when they talk about the evolution of crime writing. We forget sometimes that the genre begun by Edgar Allan Poe was actually a metaphor, at least for Poe, about the decay of Western civilization. James M. Cain once said that the premise of all his plots was the tragedy that befalls us when we eventually get what we want. Of course, he was writing about the materialism and consumerism that drives the American economy. In effect, he was saying the American dream is the American nightmare.

The American crime novel, in effect, has become the sociological novel that has its origins with Theodore Dreiser, John Dos Passos, John Steinbeck, and James T. Farrell. One doesn't have to be a student of Depression-era fiction to recognize the elements of naturalism in Connelly's work. The same authenticity and power are there. I think, in part, this comes from Connelly's background as a journalist, but it also comes from his passion about his subject.

Many years ago I listened to Nelson Algren give a talk on fiction writing to a group of young writers at the University of Missouri. One member of the audience asked him if news reporting was good work for someone who wanted to write novels. Algren replied that it could be a good learning experience, but that the work itself was fragmented and disconnected in nature and did not allow the mental continuity that every writer wishes in his workday.

Later, when I worked in an editorial room, I would remember those words.

Michael Connelly managed to write one of the best noir novels in American literature while he was a police reporter at the *Los Angeles Times*. How he did that is beyond me. I think the answer probably lies in the fact that he's a consummate pro.

I think you will enjoy this book. It's a milestone that is much larger in importance than itself. And I think that's what all great art tries to be.

James Lee Burke

Part I

Sunday, May 20

The boy couldn't see in the dark, but he didn't need to. Experience and long practice told him it was good. Nice and even. Smooth strokes, moving his whole arm while gently rolling his wrist. Keep the marble moving. No runs. Beautiful.

He heard the hiss of the escaping air and could sense the roll of the marble. They were sensations that were comforting to him. The smell reminded him of the sock in his pocket and he thought about getting high. Maybe after, he decided. He didn't want to stop now, not until he had finished the tag with one uninterrupted stroke.

But then he stopped—when the sound of an engine was heard above the hiss of the spray can. He looked around but saw no light save for the moon's silvery white reflection on the reservoir and the dim bulb above the door of the pump house, which was midway across the dam.

But the sound didn't lie. There was an engine approaching. Sounded like a truck to the boy. And now he thought he could hear the crunching of tires on the gravel access road that skirted the reservoir. Coming closer. Almost three in the morning and someone was coming. Why? The boy stood up and threw the aerosol can over the fence toward the water. He heard it chink down in the brush, short of the mark. He pulled the sock from his pocket and decided just one quick blow to give himself balls. He buried his nose in the sock and drew in heavily on the paint fumes. He rocked back on his heels, and his eyelids fluttered involuntarily. He threw the sock over the fence.

The boy stood his motorbike up and wheeled it across the road, back toward the tall grass and the bottlebrush and pine trees at the base of the hill. It was good cover, he thought, and he'd be able to see what was coming. The sound of the engine was louder now. He was sure it was just a few seconds away, but he didn't see the glow of headlights, This confused him. But it was too late to run.

He put the motorbike down in the tall brown grass and stilled the free-spinning front wheel with his hand. Then he huddled down on the earth and waited for whatever and whoever was coming.

Harry Bosch could hear the helicopter up there, some-where, above the darkness, circling up in the light. Why didn't it land? Why didn't it bring help? Harry was mov-ing through a smoky, dark tunnel and his batteries were dying. The beam of the flashlight grew weaker every yard he covered. He needed help. He needed to move faster. He needed to reach the end of the tunnel before the light was gone and he was alone in the black. He heard the chopper make one more pass. Why didn't it land? Where was the help he needed? When the drone of the blades fluttered away again, he felt the terror build and he moved faster, crawling on scraped and bloody knees, one hand holding the dim light up, the other pawing the ground to keep his balance. He did not look back, for he knew the enemy was behind him in the black mist. Unseen, but there. And closing in.

When the phone rang in the kitchen, Bosch immediately woke. He counted the rings, wondering if he had missed the first one or two, wondering if he had left the answering machine on.

He hadn't. The call was not picked up and the ringing didn't stop until after the required eight rounds. He absentmindedly wondered where that tradition had come from. Why not six rings? Why not ten? He rubbed his eyes and looked around. He was slumped in the living room chair again, the soft recliner that was the centerpiece of his meager furnishings. He thought of it as his watch chair. This was a misnomer, however, because he slept in the chair often, even when he wasn't on call.

Morning light cut through the crack in the curtains and slashed its mark across the bleached pine floor. He watched particles of dust floating lazily in the light near the sliding glass door. The lamp on the table next to him was on, and the TV against the wall, its sound very low, was broadcasting a Sunday-morning Jesus show. On the table next to the chair were the companions of insomnia: playing cards, magazines and paperback mystery novels—these only lightly thumbed and then discarded. There was a crumpled pack of cigarettes on the table and three empty beer bottles—assorted brands that had once been members of six-packs of their own tribe. Bosch was fully dressed, right down to a rumpled tie held to his white shirt by a silver 187 tie tack.

He reached his hand down to his belt and then around back to the area below his kidney. He waited. When the electronic pager sounded he cut the annoying chirp off in a second. He pulled the device off his belt and looked at the number. He wasn't surprised. He pushed himself out of the chair, stretched, and popped the joints of his neck and back. He walked to the kitchen, where the phone was on the counter. He wrote "Sunday, 8:53 A.M." in a notebook he took from his jacket pocket before dialing. After two rings a voice said, "Los Angeles Police Department, Hollywood Division. This is Officer Pelch, how can I help you?"

Bosch said, "Somebody could die in the time it took to get all that out. Let me talk to the watch sergeant."

Bosch found a fresh pack of cigarettes in a kitchen cabinet and got his first smoke of the day going. He rinsed dust out of a glass and filled it with tap water, then took two aspirins out of a plastic bottle that was also in the cabinet. He was swallowing the second when a sergeant named Crowley finally picked up.

"What, did I catch you in church? I rang your house. No answer."

"Crowley, what have you got for me?"

"Well, I know we had you out last night on that TV thing. But you're still catching. You and your partner. All weekend. So, that means you got the DB up at Lake Hollywood. In a pipe up there. It's on the access road to the Mulholland Dam. You know it?"

"I know the place. What else?"

"Patrol's out. ME, SID notified. My people don't know what they got, except a DB. Stiff's about thirty feet into this pipe there. They don't want to go all the way in, mess up a possible crime scene, you know? I had 'em page your partner but he hasn't called in. No answer at his phone either. I thought maybe the two of you was together or something. Then I thought, nah, he ain't your style. And you ain't his."

"I'll get ahold of him. If they didn't go all the way in, how they know it's a DR and not just some guy sleeping it off?"

"Oh, they went in a bit, you know, and reached in with a stick or something and poked around at the guy pretty good. Stiff as a wedding night prick."

"They didn't want to mess up a crime scene but then they go poking around the body with a stick. That's wonderful. These guys get in after they raised the college requirement, or what?"

"Hey, Bosch, we get a call, we've got to check it out. Okay? You want for us to transfer all our body calls directly to the homicide table to check out? You guys'd go nuts inside a week."

Bosch crushed the cigarette butt in the stainless steel sink, and looked out the kitchen window. Looking down the hill he could see one of the tourist trains moving between the huge beige sound studios in Universal City. A side of one of the block-long buildings was painted sky blue with wisps of white clouds; for filming exteriors when the natural L.A. exterior turned brown as wheat.

Bosch said, "How'd we get the call?"

"Anonymous to nine one one. A little after oh four hundred. Dispatcher said it came from a pay phone on the boulevard. Somebody out screwin' around, found the thing in the pipe. Wouldn't give a name. Said there was a stiff in the pipe, that's all. They'll have the tape down at the com center."

Bosch felt himself getting angry. He pulled the bottle of aspirin out of the cabinet and put it in his pocket. While thinking about the 0400 call, he opened the refrigerator and bent in. He saw nothing that interested him. He looked at his watch.

"Crowley, if the report came in at four A.M. why are you just getting to me now, nearly five hours later?"

"Look, Bosch, all we had was an anonymous call. That's it. Dispatcher said it was a kid, no less. I wasn't going to send one of my guys up that pipe in the middle of the night on information like that. Coulda been a prank. Coulda been an ambush. Coulda been anything, fer crissake. I waited till it got light out and things slowed down around here. Sent some of my guys over there at the end of shift. Speaking of end of shifts, I'm outta here. I've been waiting to hear from them and then from you. Anything else?"

Bosch felt like asking if it ever occurred to him that it would be dark in the pipe whether they went poking around at 0400 or 0800, but let it go. What was the use?

"Anything else?" Crowley said again.

Bosch couldn't think of anything, but Crowley filled the empty space.

"It's probly just some hype who croaked himself, Harry. No righteous one eighty-seven case. Happens all the time. Hell, you remember we pulled one out of that same pipe last year.... Er, well, that was before you came out to Hollywood.... So, see, what I'm saying is some guy, he goes into this same pipe—these transients, they sleep up there all the time—and he's a slammer but he shoots himself with a hot load and that's it. Checks out. 'Cept we didn't find him so fast that time, and with the sun and all beating on the pipe a couple days, he gets cooked in there. Roasted like a tom turkey. But it didn't smell as good."

Crowley laughed at his own joke. Bosch didn't. The watch sergeant continued.

"When we pulled this guy out, the spike was still in his arm. Same thing here. Just a bullshit job, a no-count case. You go out there, you'll be back home by noon, take a nap, maybe go catch the Dodgers. And then next weekend? Somebody else's turn in the barrel. You're off watch. And that's a three-day pass. You got Memorial Day weekend coming next week. So do me a favor. Just go out and see what they've got."

Bosch thought a moment and was about to hang up, then said, "Crowley, what did you mean you didn't find that other one so fast? What makes you think we found this one fast?"

"My guys out there, they say they can't smell a thing off this stiff other than a little piss. It must be fresh."

"Tell your guys I'll be there in fifteen minutes. Tell them not to fuck anymore with anything at my scene."

"They—"

Bosch knew Crowley was going to defend his men again but hung up before he had to hear it. He lit another cigarette as he went to the front door to get the *Times* off the step. He spread the twelve pounds of Sunday paper out on the kitchen counter, wondering how many trees died. He found the real estate supplement and paged through it until he saw a large display ad for Valley Pride Properties. He ran his finger down a list of Open Houses until be found one address and description marked CALL JERRY. He dialed the number.

"Valley Pride Properties, can I help you?"

"Jerry Edgar, please."

A few seconds passed and Bosch heard a couple of transfer clicks before his partner got on the line.

"This is Jerry, may I help you?"

"Jed, we just got another call. Up at the Mulholland Dam. And you aren't wearing your pager."

"Shit," Edgar said, and there was silence. Bosch could almost hear him thinking, I've got three showings today. There was more silence and Bosch pictured his partner on the other end of the line in a $900 suit and a bankrupt frown. "What's the call?"

Bosch told him what little he knew.

"If you want me to take this one solo, I will," Bosch said, "If anything comes up with Ninety-eight, I'll be able to cover it. I'll tell him you're taking the TV thing and I'm doing the stiff in the pipe."

"Yeah, I know you would, but it's okay, I'm on my way. I'm just going to have to find someone to cover for my ass first."

They agreed to meet at the body, and Bosch hung up. He turned the answering machine on, took two packs of cigarettes from the cabinet and put them in his sport coat pocket. He reached into another cabinet and took out the nylon holster that held his gun, a Smith & Wesson 9mm—satin finished, stainless steel and loaded with eight rounds of XTPs. Bosch thought about the ad he had seen once in a police magazine. Extreme Terminal Performance. A bullet that expanded on impact to 1.5 times its width, reaching terminal depth in the body and leaving maximum wound channels. Whoever had written it had been right. Bosch had killed a man a year earlier with one shot from twenty feet. Went in under the right armpit, exited below the left nipple, shattering heart and lungs on its way. XTP. Maximum wound channels. He clipped the holster to his belt on the right side so he could reach across his body and take it with his left hand.

He went into the bathroom and brushed his teeth without toothpaste: he was out and had forgotten to go by the store. He dragged a wet comb through his hair and stared at his red-rimmed, forty-year-old eyes for a long moment. Then he studied the gray hairs that were steadily crowding out the brown in his curly hair. Even the mustache was going gray. He had begun seeing flecks of gray in the sink when he shaved. He touched a hand to his chin but decided not to shave. He left his house then without changing even his tie. He knew his client wouldn't mind.

Bosch found a space where there were no pigeon droppings and leaned his elbows on the railing that ran along the top of the Mulholland Dam. A cigarette dangled from his lips, and he looked through the cleft of the hills to the city below. The sky was gunpowder gray and the smog was a form-fitted shroud over Hollywood. A few of the far-off towers in downtown poked up through the poison, but the rest of the city was under the blanket. It looked like a ghost town.

There was a slight chemical odor on the warm breeze and after a while he pegged it. Malathion. He'd heard on the radio that the fruit fly helicopters had been up the night before spraying North Hollywood down through the Cahuenga Pass. He thought of his dream and remembered the chopper that did not land.

To his back was the blue-green expanse of the Hollywood reservoir, 60 million gallons of the city's drinking water trapped by the venerable old dam in a canyon between two of the Hollywood Hills. A six-foot band of dried clay ran the length of the shoreline, a reminder that L.A. was in its fourth year of drought. Farther up the reservoir bank was a ten-foot-high chain-link fence that girded the entire shoreline. Bosch had studied this barrier when he first arrived and wondered if the protection was for the people on one side of the fence or the water on the other.

Bosch was wearing a blue jumpsuit over his rumpled suit. His sweat had stained through the underarms and back of both layers of clothing. His hair was damp and his mustache drooped. He had been inside the pipe. He could feel the slight, warm tickle of a Santa Ana wind drying the sweat on the back of his neck. They had come early this year.

Harry was not a big man. He stood a few inches short of six feet and was built lean. The newspapers, when they described him, called him wiry. Beneath the jumpsuit his muscles were like nylon cords, strength concealed by economy of size. The gray that flecked his hair was more partial to the left side. His eyes were brown-black and seldom betrayed emotion or intention.

The pipe was located above ground and ran for fifty yards alongside the reservoir's access road. It was rusted inside and out, and was empty and unused except by those who sought its interior as a shelter or its exterior as a canvas for spray paint. Bosch had had no clue to its purpose until the reservoir caretaker had volunteered the information. The pipe was a mud break. Heavy rain, the caretaker said, could loosen earth and send mud sliding off the hillsides and into the reservoir. The three-foot-wide pipe, left over from some unknown district project or boondoggle, had been placed in a predicted slide area as the reservoir's first and only defense. The pipe was held in place by half-inch-thick iron rebar that looped over it and was embedded in concrete below.

Bosch had put on the jumpsuit before going into the

pipe. The letters LAPD were printed in white across the back. After taking it out of the trunk of his car and stepping into it, he realized it was probably cleaner than the suit he was trying to protect. But he wore it anyway, because he had always worn it. He was a methodical, traditional, superstitious detective.

As he had crawled with flashlight in hand into the damp-smelling, claustrophobic cylinder, he felt his throat tighten and his heartbeat quicken. A familiar emptiness in his gut gripped him. Fear. But he snapped on the light and the darkness receded along with the uneasy feelings, and he set about his work.

Now he stood on the dam and smoked and thought about things. Crowley, the watch sergeant, had been right, the man in the pipe was certainly dead. But he had also been wrong. This would not be an easy one. Harry would not be home in time for an afternoon nap or to listen to the Dodgers on KABC. Things were wrong here. Harry wasn't ten feet inside the pipe before he knew that.

There were no tracks in the pipe. Or rather, there were no tracks that were of use. The bottom of the pipe was dusty with dried orange mud and cluttered with paper bags, empty wine bottles, cotton balls, used syringes, newspaper bedding—the debris of the homeless and addicted. Bosch had studied it all in the beam of the flashlight as he slowly made his way toward the body. And he had found no clear trail left by the dead man, who lay headfirst into the pipe. This was not right. If the dead man had crawled in of his own accord, there would be some indication of this. If he had been dragged in, there would be some sign of that, too. But there was nothing, and this deficiency was only the first of the things that troubled Bosch.

When he reached the body, he found the dead man's shirt—a black, open-collar crew shirt—pulled up over his head with his arms tangled inside. Bosch had seen enough dead people to know that literally nothing was impossible during the last breaths. He had worked a suicide in which a man who had shot himself in the head had then changed pants before dying, apparently because he did not want his body to be discovered soaked in human waste. But the shirt and the arms on the dead man in the pipe did not seem acceptable to Harry. It looked to Bosch as if the body had been dragged into the pipe by someone who had pulled the dead man by the collar.

Bosch had not disturbed the body or pulled the shirt away from the face. He noted that it was a white male. He detected no immediate indication of the fatal injury. After finishing his survey of the body, Bosch carefully moved over the corpse, his face coming within a half foot of it, and then continued through the pipe's remaining forty yards. He found no tracks and nothing else of evidentiary value. In twenty minutes he was back in the sunlight. He then sent a crime scene tech named Donovan in to chart the location of debris in the pipe and video the body in place. Donovan's face had betrayed his surprise at having to go into the pipe on a case he'd already written off as an OD. He had tickets to the Dodgers, Bosch figured.

After leaving the pipe to Donovan, Bosch had lit a cigarette and walked to the dam's railing to look down on the fouled city and brood.

At the railing he could hear the sound of traffic filtering up from the Hollywood Freeway. It almost sounded gentle from such a distance. Like a calm ocean. Down through the cleft of the canyon he saw blue swimming pools and Spanish tile roofs.

A woman in a white tank top and lime-green jogging shorts ran by him on the dam. A compact radio was clipped to her waistband, and a thin yellow wire carried sound to the earphones clamped to her head. She seemed to be in her own world, unaware of the grouping of police ahead of her until she reached the yellow crime scene tape stretched across the end of the dam. It told her to stop in two languages. She jogged in place for a few moments, her long blond hair clinging to sweat on her shoulders, and watched the police, who were mostly watching her. Then she turned and headed back past Bosch. His eyes followed her, and he noticed that when she went by the pump house she deviated her course to avoid something. He walked over and found glass on the pavement. He looked up and saw the broken bulb in the socket above the pump house door. He made a mental note to ask the caretaker if the bulb had been checked lately.

When Bosch returned to his spot at the railing a blur of movement from below drew his attention. He looked down and saw a coyote sniffing among the pine needles and trash that covered the earth below the trees in front of the dam. The animal was small and its coat was scruffy and completely missing some patches of hair. There were only a few of them left in the city's protected areas, left to scavenge among the debris of the human scavengers.

"They're pulling it out now," a voice said from behind. Bosch turned and saw one of the uniforms that had been assigned to the crime scene. He nodded and followed him off the dam, under the yellow tape, and back to the pipe.

•　•　•

A cacophony of grunts and heavy gasps echoed from the mouth of the graffiti-scarred pipe. A shirtless man, with his heavily muscled back scratched and dirty, emerged backward, towing a sheet of heavy black plastic on top of which lay the body. The dead man was still face up with his head and arms mostly obscured in the wrapping of the black shirt. Bosch looked around for Donovan and saw him stowing a video recorder in the back of the blue crime scene van. Harry walked over.

"Now I'm going to need you to go back in. All the debris in there, newspapers, cans, bags, I saw some hypos, cotton, bottles, I need it all bagged."

"You got it," Donovan said. He waited a beat and added, "I'm not saying anything, but, Harry, I mean, you really think this is the real thing? Is it worth busting our balls on?"

"I guess we won't know until after the cut."

He started to walk away but stopped.

"Look, Donnie, I know it's Sunday and, uh, thanks for going back in."

"No problem. It's straight OT for me."

The shirtless man and a coroner's technician were sitting on their haunches, huddled over the body. They both wore white rubber gloves. The technician was Larry Sakai, a guy Bosch had known for years but had never liked. He had a plastic fishing-tackle box open on the ground next to him. He took a scalpel from the box and made a one-inch-long cut into the side of the body, just above the left hip. No blood came from the slice. From the box he then removed a thermometer and attached it to the end of a curved probe. He stuck it into the incision, expertly though roughly turning it and driving it up into the liver.

The shirtless man grimaced, and Bosch noticed he had a blue tear tattooed at the outside corner of his right eye. It somehow seemed appropriate to Bosch. It was the most sympathy the dead man would get here.

"Time of death is going to be a pisser," Sakai said. He did not look up from his work. "That pipe, you know, with the heat rising, it's going to skew the temperature loss in the liver. Osito took a reading in there and it was eighty-one. Ten minutes later it was eighty-three. We don't have a fixed temp in the body or the pipe."

"So?" Bosch said.

"So I am not giving you anything here. I gotta take it back and do some calculating."

"You mean give it to somebody else who knows how to figure it?" Bosch asked.

"You'll get it when you come in for the autopsy, don't worry, man."

"Speaking of which, who's doing the cutting today?"

Sakai didn't answer. He was busy with the dead man's legs. He grabbed each shoe and manipulated the ankles. He moved his hands up the legs and reached beneath the thighs, lifting each leg and watching as it bent at the knee. He then pressed his hands down on the abdomen as if feeling for contraband. Lastly, he reached inside the shirt and tried to turn the dead man's head. It didn't move. Bosch knew rigor mortis worked its way from the head through the body and then into the extremities.

"This guy's neck is locked but good," Sakai said. "Stomach's getting there. But the extremities still have good movement."

He took a pencil from behind his ear and pressed the eraser end against the skin on the side of the torso. There was purplish blotching on the half of the body closest to the ground, as if the body were half full of red wine. It was post-mortem lividity. When the heart stops pumping, the blood seeks the low ground. When Sakai pressed the pencil against the dark skin, it did not blanch white, a sign the blood had fully clotted. The man had been dead for hours.

"The po-mo lividity is steady," Sakai said. "That and the rig makes me estimate that this dude's been dead maybe six to eight hours. That's going to have to hold you, Bosch, until we can work with the temps."

Sakai didn't look up as he said this. He and the one called Osito began pulling the pockets on the dead man's green fatigue pants inside out. They were empty, as were the large baggy pockets on the thighs. They rolled the body to one side to check the back pockets. As they did this, Bosch leaned down to look closely at the exposed back of the dead man. The skin was purplish with lividity and dirty. But he saw no scratches or marks that allowed him to conclude that the body had been dragged.

"Nothing in the pants, Bosch, no ID," Sakai said, still not looking up.

Then they began to gently pull the black shirt back over the head and onto the torso. The dead man had straggly hair that had more gray in it than the original black. His beard was unkempt and he looked to be about fifty, which made Bosch figure him at about forty. There was something in the breast pocket of the shirt and Sakai fished it out, looked at it a moment and then put it into a plastic bag held open by his partner.

"Bingo," Sakai said and handed the bag up to Bosch. "One set of works. Makes our jobs all a lot easier."

Sakai next peeled the dead man's cracked eyelids all the way open. The eyes were blue with a milky caul over them. Each pupil was constricted to about the size of a pencil lead. They stared vacantly up at Bosch, each pupil a small black void.

Sakai made some notes on a clipboard. He'd made his decision on this one. Then he pulled an ink pad and a print card from the tackle box by his side. He inked the fingers of the left hand and began pressing them on the card. Bosch admired how quickly and expertly he did this. But then Sakai stopped.

"Hey. Check it out."

Sakai gently moved the index finger. It was easily manipulated in any direction. The joint was cleanly broken, but there was no sign of swelling or hemorrhage.

"It looks post to me," Sakai said.

Bosch stooped to look closer. He took the dead man's hand away from Sakai and felt it with both his own, ungloved hands. He looked at Sakai and then at Osito.

"Bosch, don't start in," Sakai barked. "Don't be looking at him. He knows better. I trained him myself."

Bosch didn't remind Sakai that it was he who had been driving the ME wagon that dumped a body strapped to a wheeled stretcher onto the Ventura Freeway a few months back. During rush hour. The stretcher rolled down the Lankershim Boulevard exit and hit the back end of a car at a gas station. Because of the fiberglass partition in the cab, Sakai didn't know he had lost the body until he arrived at the morgue.

Bosch handed the dead man's hand back to the coroner's tech. Sakai turned to Osito and spoke a question in Spanish. Osito's small brown face became very serious and he shook his head no.

"He didn't even touch the guy's hands in there. So you

better wait until the cut before you go saying something you aren't sure about."

Sakai finished transferring the fingerprints and then handed the card to Bosch.

"Bag the hands," Bosch said to him, though he didn't need to. "And the feet."

He stood back up and began waving the card to get the ink to dry. With his other hand he held up the plastic evidence bag Sakai had given him. In it a rubber band held together a hypodermic needle, a small vial that was half filled with what looked like dirty water, a wad of cotton and a pack of matches. It was a shooter's kit and it looked fairly new. The spike was clean, with no sign of corrosion. The cotton, Bosch guessed, had only been used as a strainer once or twice. There were tiny whitish-brown crystals in the fibers. By turning the bag he could look inside each side of the matchbook and see only two matches missing.

Donovan crawled out of the pipe at that moment. He was wearing a miner's helmet equipped with a flashlight. In one hand he carried several plastic bags, each containing a yellowed newspaper, or a food wrapper or a crushed beer can. In the other he carried a clipboard on which he had diagramed where each item had been found in the pipe. Spiderwebs hung off the sides of the helmet. Sweat was running down his face and staining the painter's breathing mask he wore over his mouth and nose. Bosch held up the bag containing the shooter's kit. Donovan stopped in his tracks.

"You find a stove in there?" Bosch asked.

"Shit, he's a hype?" Donovan said. "I knew it. What the fuck are we doin' all this for?"

Bosch didn't answer. He waited him out.

"Answer is yes, I found a Coke can," Donovan said.

The crime scene tech looked through the plastic bags in his hands and held one up to Bosch. It contained two halves of a Coke can. The can looked reasonably new and had been cut in half with a knife. The bottom half had been inverted and its concave surface used as a pan to cook heroin and water. A stove. Most hypes no longer used spoons. Carrying a spoon was probable cause for arrest. Cans were easy to come by, easy to handle and disposable.

"We need the kit and the stove printed as soon as we can," Bosch said. Donovan nodded and carried his burden of plastic bags toward the police van. Bosch turned his attention back to the ME's men.

"No knife on him, right?" Bosch said.

"Right," Sakai said. "Why?"

"I need a knife. Incomplete scene without a knife."

"So what. Guy's a hype. Hypes steal from hypes. His pals probably took it."

Sakai's gloved hands rolled up the sleeves of the dead man's shirt. This revealed a network of scar tissue on both arms. Old needle marks, craters left by abscesses and infections. In the crook of the left elbow was a fresh spike mark and a large yellow-and-purplish hemorrhage under the skin.

"Bingo," Sakai said. "I'd say this guy took a hot load in the arm and, phssst, that was it. Like I said, you got a hype case, Bosch. You'll have an early day. Go get a Dodger dog."

Bosch crouched down again to look closer.

"That's what everybody keeps telling me," he said.

And Sakai was probably right, he thought. But he didn't want to fold this one away yet. Too many things didn't fit. The missing tracks in the pipe. The shirt pulled over the head. The broken finger. No knife.

"How come all the tracks are old except the one?" he asked, more of himself than Sakai.

"Who knows?" Sakai answered anyway. "Maybe he'd been off it awhile and decided to jump back in. A hype's a hype. There aren't any reasons."

Staring at the tracks on the dead man's arms, Bosch noticed blue ink on the skin just below the sleeve that was bunched up on the left bicep. He couldn't see enough to make out what it said.

"Pull that up," he said and pointed.

Sakai worked the sleeve up to the shoulder, revealing a tattoo of blue and red ink. It was a cartoonish rat standing on hind legs with a rabid, toothy and vulgar grin. In one hand the rat held a pistol, in the other a booze bottle marked XXX. The blue writing above and below the cartoon was smeared by age and the spread of skin. Sakai tried to read it.

"Says 'Force'—no, 'First.' Says 'First Infantry.' This guy was army. The bottom part doesn't make—it's another language. 'Non . . . Gratum . . . Anum . . . Ro—' I can't make that out."

"Rodentum," Bosch said.

Sakai looked at him.

"Dog Latin," Bosch told him. "Not worth a rat's ass. He was a tunnel rat. Vietnam."

"Whatever," Sakai said. He took an appraising look at the body and the pipe. He said, "Well, he ended up in a tunnel, didn't he? Sort of."

Bosch reached his bare hand to the dead man's face and pushed the straggly black and gray hairs off the forehead and away from the vacant eyes. His doing this without gloves made the others stop what they were doing and watch this unusual, if not unsanitary, behavior. Bosch paid no notice. He stared at the face for a long moment, not saying anything, not hearing if anything was said. In the moment that he realized that he knew the face, just as he knew the tattoo, the vision of a young man flashed in his mind. Rawboned and tan, hair buzzed short. Alive, not dead. He stood up and turned quickly away from the body.

Making such a quick, unexpected motion, he banged straight into Jerry Edgar, who had finally arrived and walked up to huddle over the body. They both took a step back, momentarily stunned. Bosch put a hand to his forehead. Edgar, who was much taller, did the same to his chin.

"Shit, Harry," Edgar said. "You all right?"

"Yeah. You?"

Edgar checked his hand for blood.

"Yeah. Sorry about that. What are you jumping up like that for?"

"I don't know."

Edgar looked over Harry's shoulder at the body and then followed his partner away from the pack.

"Sorry, Harry," Edgar said. "I sat there waiting an hour till somebody came out to cover me on my appointments. So tell me, what have we got?"

Edgar was still rubbing his jaw as he spoke.

"Not sure yet," Bosch said. "I want you to get in one of these patrol cars that has an MCT in it. One that works. See if you can get a sheet on a Meadows, Billy, er, make that William. DOB would be about 1950. We need to get an address from DMV."

"That's the stiff?"

Bosch nodded.

"Nothing, no address with his ID?"

"There is no ID. I made him. So check it out on the box. There should be some contact in the last few years. Hype stuff, at least, out of Van Nuys Division."

Edgar sauntered off toward the line of parked black-and-whites to find one with a mobile computer terminal mounted on the dashboard. Because he was a big man, his gait seemed slow, but Bosch knew from experience that Edgar was a hard man to keep pace with. Edgar was impeccably tailored in a brown suit with a thin chalk line. His hair was close cropped and his skin was almost as smooth and as black as an eggplant's. Bosch watched Edgar walk away and couldn't help but wonder if he had timed his arrival to be just late enough to avoid having to wrinkle his ensemble by stepping into a jumpsuit and crawling into the pipe.

Bosch went to the trunk of his car and got out the Polaroid camera. He then went back to the body, straddled it and stooped to take photographs of the face. Three would be enough, he decided, and he placed each card that was ejected from the camera on top of the pipe while the photo developed. He couldn't help but stare at the face, at the changes made by time. He thought of that face and the inebriated grin that creased it on the night that all of the First Infantry rats had come out of the tattoo parlor in Saigon. It had taken the burned-out Americans four hours, but they had all been made blood brothers by putting the same brand on their shoulders. Bosch remembered Meadows's joy in the companionship and fear they all shared.

Harry stepped away from the body while Sakai and

Osito unfolded a black, heavy plastic bag with a zipper running up the center. Once the body bag was unfolded and opened, the coroner's men lifted Meadows and placed him inside.

"Looks like Rip Van-fucking-Winkle," Edgar said as he walked up.

Sakai zipped the bag up and Bosch saw a few of Meadows's curling gray hairs had been caught in the zipper. Meadows wouldn't mind. He had once told Bosch that he was destined for the inside of a body bag. He said everybody was.

Edgar held a small notepad in one hand, a gold Cross pen in the other.

"William Joseph Meadows, 7-21-50. That sound like him, Harry?"

"Yeah, that's him."

"Well, you were right, we have multiple contacts. But not just hype shit. We've got bank robbery, attempted robbery, possession of heroin. We got a loitering right here at the dam a year or so ago. And he did have a couple hype beefs. The one in Van Nuys you were talking about. What was he to you, a CI?"

"No. Get an address?"

"Lives up in the Valley. Sepulveda, up by the brewery. Tough neighborhood to sell a house in. So if he wasn't an informant, how'd you know this guy?"

"I didn't know him—at least recently. I knew him in a different life."

"What does that mean? When did you know the guy?"

"Last time I saw Billy Meadows was twenty years ago, or thereabouts. He was—it was in Saigon."

"Yeah, that'd make it about twenty years." Edgar

walked over to the Polaroids and looked down at the three faces of Billy Meadows. "You know him good?"

"Not really. About as well as anybody got to know somebody there. You learned to trust people with your life, then when it's over you realize you didn't really even know most of them. I never saw him once I got back here. Talked to him once on the phone last year, that's all." "How'd you make him?"

"I didn't, at first. Then I saw the tattoo on his arm. That brought the face back. I guess you remember guys like him. I do, at least."

"I guess . . ."

They let the silence sit there awhile. Bosch was trying to decide what to do, but could only wonder about the co-incidence of being called to a death scene to find Mead-ows. Edgar broke the reverie.

"So you want to tell me what you've got that looks hinky here? Donovan over there looks like he's getting ready to shit his pants, all the work you're putting him through."

Bosch told Edgar about the problems, the absence of distinguishable tracks in the pipe, the shirt pulled over the head, the broken finger and that there was no knife.

"No knife?" his partner said.

"Needed something to cut the can in half to make a stove—if the stove was his."

"Could've brought the stove with him. Could have been that somebody went in there and took the knife after the guy was dead. If there was a knife."

"Yeah, could have been. No tracks to tell us anything."

"Well, we know from his sheet he was a blown-out junkie. Was he like that when you knew him?"

"To a degree. A user and seller."

"Well, there you go, longtime addict, you can't predict what they're going to do, when they're going to get off the shit or on it. They're lost people, Harry."

"He was off it, though—at least I thought he was. He's only got one fresh pop in his arm."

"Harry, you said you hadn't seen the guy since Saigon. How do you know whether he was off or on?"

"I hadn't seen him, but I talked to him. He called me once, last year sometime. July or August, I think. He'd been pulled in on another track marks beef by the hype car up in Van Nuys. Somehow, maybe reading newspapers or something—it was about the same time as the Dollmaker thing—he knew I was a cop, and he calls me up at Robbery-Homicide. He calls me from Van Nuys jail and asks if I could help him out. He would've only done, what, thirty days in county, but he was bottomed out, he said. And he, uh, just said he couldn't do the time this time, couldn't kick alone like that. . . ."

Bosch trailed off without finishing the story. After a long moment Edgar prompted him.

"And? . . . Come on, Harry, what'd you do?"

"And I believed him. I talked to the cop. I remember his name was Nuckles. Good name for a street cop, I thought. And then I called the VA up there in Sepulveda and I got him into a program. Nuckles went along with it. He's a vet, too. He got the city attorney to ask the judge for diversion. So anyway, the VA outpatient clinic took Meadows in. I checked about six weeks later and they said he'd completed, had kicked and was doing okay. I mean, that's what they told me. Said he was in the second level of maintenance. Talking to a shrink, group counseling. . . . I never talked to Meadows after that first call. He never called again, and I didn't try to look him up."

Edgar referred to his pad. Bosch could see the page he was looking at was blank.

"Look, Harry," Edgar said, "that was still almost a year ago. A long time for a hype, right? Who knows? He could have fallen off the wagon and kicked three times since then. That's not our worry here. The question is, what do you want to do with what we have here? What do you want to do about today?"

"Do you believe in coincidence?" Bosch asked.

"I don't know. I—"

"There are no coincidences."

"Harry, I don't know what you're talking about. But you know what I think? I don't see anything here that's screaming in my face. Guy crawls into the pipe, in the dark maybe he can't see what he's doing, he puts too much juice in his arm and croaks. That's it. Maybe somebody else was with him and smeared the tracks going out. Took his knife, too. Could be a hundred dif—"

"Sometimes they don't scream, Jerry. That's the problem here. It's Sunday. Everybody wants to go home. Play golf. Sell houses. Watch the ballgame. Nobody cares one way or the other. Just going through the motions. Don't you see that that's what they are counting on?"

"Who is 'they,' Harry?"

"Whoever did this."

He shut up for a minute. He was convincing no one, and that almost included himself. Playing to Edgar's sense of dedication was wrong. He'd be off the job as soon as he put in twenty. He'd then put a business card–sized ad in the union newsletter—"LAPD retired, will cut commission for brother officers"—and make a quarter million a year selling houses to cops or for cops in the San Fernando Valley or the Santa Clarita Valley or the Antelope Valley or whatever valley the bulldozers aimed at next.

"Why go in the pipe?" Bosch said then. "You said he lived up in the Valley. Sepulveda. Why come down here?"

"Harry, who knows? The guy was a junkie. Maybe his wife kicked him out. Maybe he croaked himself up there and his friends dragged his dead ass down here because they didn't want to be bothered with explaining it."

"That's still a crime."

"Yeah, that's a crime, but let me know when you find a DA that'll file it for you."

"His kit looked clean. New. The other tracks on his arm look old. I don't think he was slamming again. Not regularly. Something isn't right."

"Well, I don't know. . . . You know, AIDS and everything, they're supposed to keep a clean kit."

Bosch looked at his partner as if he didn't know him.

"Harry, listen to me, what I'm telling you is that he may have been your foxhole buddy twenty years ago but he was a junkie this year. You'll never be able to explain every action he took. I don't know about the kit or the tracks, but I do know that this does not look like one we should bust our humps on. This is a nine-to-fiver, week-ends and holidays excluded."

Bosch gave up—for the moment.

"I'm going up to Sepulveda," he said. "Are you coming. or are you going back to your open house?"

"I'll do my job, Harry," Edgar said softly. "Just because we don't agree on something doesn't mean I'm not gonna do what I'm paid to do. It's never been that way, never will be. But if you don't like the way I do business, we'll go see Ninety-eight tomorrow morning and see about a switch."

Bosch was immediately sorry for the cheap shot, but didn't say so. He said, "Okay. You go on up there, see if anybody's home. I'll meet you after I sign off on the scene."

Edgar walked over to the pipe and took one of the Polaroid photos of Meadows. He slipped it into his coat pocket, then walked down the access road toward his car without saying another word to Bosch.

After Bosch took off his jumpsuit and folded it away in the trunk of his car, he watched Sakai and Osito slide the body roughly onto a stretcher and then into the back of a blue van. He started over, thinking about what would be the best way to get the autopsy done as a priority, meaning by at least the next day instead of four or five days later. He caught up with the coroner's tech as he was opening the driver's door.

"We're outta here, Bosch."

Bosch put his hand on the door, holding it from opening enough for Sakai to climb in.

"Who's doing the cutting today?"

"On this one? Nobody."

"Come on, Sakai. Who's on?"

"Sally. But he's not going near this one, Bosch."

"Look, I just went through this with my partner. Not you, too, okay?"

"Bosch, you look. You listen. I've been working since six last night and this is the seventh scene I've been to. We got drive-bys, floaters, a sex case. People are dying to meet us, Bosch. There is no rest for the weary, and that means no time for what you think might be a case. Listen to your partner for once. This one is going on the routine schedule. That means we'll get to it by Wednesday, maybe Thursday. I promise Friday at the latest. And tox results is at least a ten-day wait, anyway. You know that. So what's your goddam hurry?"

"Are. Tox results *are* at least a ten-day wait."

"Fuck off."

"Just tell Sally I need the prelim done today. I'll be by later."

"Christ, Bosch, listen to what I'm telling you. We've got bodies on gurneys stacked in the hall that we already know are one eighty-sevens and need to be cut. Salazar is not going to have time for what looks to me and everybody else around here except you like a hype case. Cut and dried, man. What am I going to say to him that's going to make him do the cut today?"

"Show him the finger. Tell him there were no tracks in the pipe. Think of something. Tell him the DB was a guy who knew needles too well to've OD'd."

Sakai put his head back against the van's side panel and laughed loudly. Then he shook his head as if a child had made a joke.

"And you know what he'll say to me? He'll say that it doesn't matter how long he'd been spiking. They all fuck up. Bosch, how many sixty-five-year-old junkies do you see around? None of them go the distance. The needle gets them all in the end. Just like this guy in the pipe."

Bosch turned and looked around to make sure none of the uniforms were watching and listening. Then he turned back to Sakai's face.

"Just tell him I'll be by there later," he said quietly. "If he doesn't find anything on the prelim, then fine, you can stick the body at the end of the line in the hall, or you can park it down at the gas station on Lankershim. I won't care then, Larry. But you tell him. It's his decision, not yours."

Bosch dropped his hand from the door and stepped back. Sakai got in the van and slammed the door. He started the engine and looked at Bosch through the window for a long moment before rolling it down.

"Bosch, you're a pain in the ass. Tomorrow morning. It's the best I can do. Today is no way."

"First cut of the day?"

"Just leave us alone today, okay?"

"First cut?"

"Yeah. Yeah. First cut."

"Sure, I'll leave you alone, See you tomorrow, then."

"Not me, man. I'll be sleeping."

Sakai rolled the window back up and the van moved away. Bosch stepped back to let it pass, and when it was gone he was left staring at the pipe. It was really for the first time then that he noticed the graffiti. Not that he hadn't seen that the exterior of the pipe was literally covered with painted messages, but this time he looked at the individual scrawls. Many were old, faded together—a tableau of letters spelling threats either long forgotten or since made good. There were slogans: Abandon LA. There were names: Ozone, Bomber, Stryker, many others. One of the fresher tags caught his eye. It was just three letters, about twelve feet from the end of the pipe— *Sha*. The three letters had been painted in one fluid motion. The top of the S was jagged and then contoured, giving the impression of a mouth. A gaping maw. There were no teeth but Bosch could sense them. It was as though the work wasn't completed. Still, it was good work, original and clean. He aimed the Polaroid at it and took a photo.

Bosch walked to the police van, putting the exposure in his pocket. Donovan was stowing his equipment on shelves and the evidence bags in wooden Napa Valley wine boxes.

"Did you find any burned matches in there?"

"Yeah, one fresh one," Donovan said. "Burned to the end. It was about ten feet in. It's there on the chart."

Bosch picked up a clipboard on which there was a piece of paper with a diagram of the pipe showing the body location and where the other material taken from the pipe had been. Bosch noticed that the match was found about fifteen feet from the body. Donovan then showed him the match, sitting at the bottom of its own plastic evidence bag. "I'll let you know if it matches the book in the guy's kit," he said. "If that's what you're thinking."

Bosch said, "What about the uniforms? What'd they find?"

"It's all there," Donovan said, pointing to a wooden bin in which there were still more plastic evidence bags. These contained debris picked up by patrol officers who had searched the area within a fifty-yard radius of the pipe. Each bag contained a description of the location where the object had been found. Bosch took each bag out and examined its contents. Most of it was junk that would have nothing to do with the body in the pipe. There were newspapers, clothing rags, a high-heeled shoe, a white sock with dried blue paint in it. A sniff rag.

Bosch picked up a bag containing the top to a can of spray paint. The next bag contained the spray paint can. The Krylon label said it was Ocean Blue. Bosch hefted the bag and could tell there was still paint in the can. He carried the bag to the pipe, opened it and, touching the nozzle with a pen, sprayed a line of blue next to the letters *Sha*. He sprayed too much. The paint ran down the curved side of the pipe and dripped onto the gravel. But Bosch could see the colors matched.

He thought about that for a moment. Why would a graffiti tagger throw half a can of paint away? He looked at the writing on the evidence bag. It had been found near the edge of the reservoir. Someone had attempted to throw the can into the lake but came up short. Again he thought, Why? He squatted next to the pipe and looked closely at the letters. He decided that whatever the message or name was, it wasn't finished. Something had happened that made the tagger stop what he was doing and throw the can, the top and his sniff sock over the fence. Was it the police? Bosch took out his notebook and wrote a reminder to call Crowley after midnight to see if any of his people had cruised the reservoir during the A.M. watch.

But what if it wasn't a cop that made the tagger throw the paint over the fence? What if the tagger had seen the body being delivered to the pipe? Bosch thought about what Crowley had said about an anonymous caller reporting the body. A kid, no less. Was it the tagger who called? Bosch took the can back to the SID truck and handed it to Donovan.

"Print this after the kit and the stove," he said. "I think it might belong to a witness."

"Will do," Donovan said.

•   •   •

Bosch drove down out of the hills and took the Barham Boulevard ramp onto the northbound Hollywood Freeway. After coming up through the Cahuenga Pass he went west on the Ventura Freeway and then north again on the San Diego Freeway. It took about twenty minutes to go the ten miles. It was Sunday and traffic was light. He exited on Roscoe and went east a couple of blocks into Meadows's neighborhood on Langdon.

Sepulveda, like most of the suburban communities within Los Angeles, had both good and bad neighborhoods. Bosch wasn't expecting trimmed lawns and curbs lined with Volvos on Meadows's street, and he wasn't disappointed. The apartments were at least a decade past being attractive. There were bars over the windows of the bottom units and graffiti on every garage door. The sharp smell of the brewery on Roscoe wafted into the neighborhood. The place smelled like a 4 A.M. bar.

Meadows had lived in a U-shaped apartment building that had been built in the 1950s, when the smell of hops wasn't yet in the air, gangbangers weren't on the street corner and there was still hope in the neighborhood. There was a pool in the center courtyard but it had long been filled up with sand and dirt. Now the courtyard consisted of a kidney-shaped plot of brown grass surrounded by dirty concrete. Meadows had lived in an upstairs corner apartment. Bosch could hear the steady drone of the freeway as he climbed the stairs and moved along the walkway that fronted the apartments. The door to 7B was unlocked and it opened into a small living room–dining room–kitchen. Edgar was leaning against a counter, writing in his notebook. He said, "Nice place, huh?"

"Yeah," Bosch said and looked around. "Nobody home?"

"Nah. I checked with a neighbor next door and she hadn't seen anybody around since the day before yesterday. Said the guy that lived here told her his name was Fields, not Meadows. Cute, huh? She said he lived all by himself. Been here about a year, kept to himself, mostly. That's all she knew."

"You show her the picture?"

"Yeah, she made him. Didn't like looking at a picture of a dead guy, though."

Bosch walked into a short hallway that led to a bathroom and a bedroom. He said, "You pick the door?"

"Nah—it was unlocked. No shit, I knock a couple times and I'm fixing to get my pouch outta the car and finesse the lock when, for the hell of it, I try the door."

"And it opens."

"It opens."

"You talk to the landlord?"

"Landlady's not around. Supposed to be, but maybe she went out to eat lunch or score some horse. I think everybody I seen around here is a spiker."

Bosch came back into the living room and looked around. There wasn't much. A couch covered with green vinyl was pushed against one wall, a stuffed chair was against the opposite wall with a small color television on the carpet next to it. There was a Formica-topped table with three chairs around it in the dining room. The fourth chair was by itself against the wall. Bosch looked at an old cigarette-scarred coffee table in front of the couch. On it were an overloaded ashtray and a crossword puzzle book. Playing cards were laid out in an unfinished game of solitaire. There was a *TV Guide*. Bosch had no idea if Meadows smoked but knew that no cigarettes had been found on the body. He made a mental note to check on it later.

Edgar said, "Harry, this place was turned. Not just the door being open and all, but, I mean, there are other things. The whole place has been searched. They did a halfway decent job, but you can tell. It was rushed. Go check out the bed and the closet, you'll see what I mean. I'm gonna give the landlady another try."

Edgar left and Bosch walked back through the living room to the bedroom. Along the way he noted the smell of urine. In the bedroom, he found a queen-sized bed without a backboard pushed against one wall. There was a greasy discoloration on the white wall at about the level where Meadows would have leaned his head while sitting up in bed. Opposite the bed an old six-drawer dresser was against the wall. A cheap rattan night table with a lamp on it stood next to the bed. Nothing else was in the room, not even a mirror.

Bosch studied the bed first. It was unmade; with pillows and sheets in a pile in the center. Bosch noticed that a corner of one of the sheets was folded between the mattress and the box spring, in the midsection of the left side of the bed. The bed would not have been made that way, obviously. Bosch pulled the corner out from under the mattress and let it hang loosely off the side of the bed. He lifted the mattress as if to search underneath it, then lowered it back into place. The corner of the sheet was back between the mattress and the box spring. Edgar was right.

He next opened the six bureau drawers. What clothes there were—underwear, white and dark socks and several T-shirts—were neatly folded and seemed undisturbed. When he closed the bottom left drawer he noticed that it slid unevenly and would not close all the way. He pulled it all the way out of the bureau. Then he pulled another drawer completely out of the dresser. Then the rest. When he had all the drawers out he checked the underside of each to see if something was or had been taped to it. He found nothing. He put them back in but kept changing their order until each one slid easily into place and closed completely. When he was done the drawers were in a different order. The right order. He was satisfied that someone had pulled the drawers out to search beneath and behind them, and had then put them back in the wrong order.

He went into the walk-in closet. He found only a quarter of the available space used. On the floor were two pairs of shoes, a pair of black Reebok running shoes that were dirty with sand and gray dust, and a pair of laced work boots that looked as though they had been recently cleaned and oiled. There was more of the gray dust from the shoes in the carpet. He crouched down and pinched some between his fingers. It seemed like concrete dust. He took a small evidence bag from his pocket and put some of the granules into it. Then he put the bag away and stood up. There were five shirts on hangers, a single white button-down oxford and four long-sleeved black pullovers, like the one Meadows had been wearing. On hangers next to the shirts were two pairs of well-faded jeans and two pairs of black pajamas or karate-style pants. The pockets on all four pairs of pants had been turned inside out. A plastic laundry basket on the floor contained dirty black pants, T-shirts, socks and a pair of boxer shorts.

Bosch walked out of the closet and left the bedroom. He stopped in the hallway bathroom and opened the medicine cabinet. There was a half-used tube of toothpaste, a bottle of aspirin and a single, empty insulin syringe box. When he closed the cabinet, he looked at himself and saw weariness in his eyes. He smoothed his hair.

Harry walked back to the living room and sat on the couch, in front of the unfinished solitaire hand. Edgar came in.

"Meadows rented the place last July first," he said. "The landlady's back. It was supposed to be a month-to-month lease but he paid for eleven months up front. Four bills a month. That's nearly five grand in cash he put down. Said she didn't ask him for references. She just took the money. He lived—"

"She said he paid for eleven months?" Bosch interrupted. "Was it a deal, pay for eleven, get the twelfth free?"

"Nah, I asked her about that and she said no, it was him. That's just the way he wanted to pay. Said he'd move out June first, this year. That's—what—ten days from now? She said he told her he moved out here on some kind of job, she thinks from Phoenix. Said he was some kind of shift supervisor for the tunnel dig on the subway project downtown. She got the impression that's all his job would take, eleven months, and then he'd go back to Phoenix."

Edgar was looking in his notebook, reviewing his conversation with the landlady.

"That's about it. She ID'd him off the Polaroid, too. She also knew him as Fields. Bill Fields. Said he kept odd hours, like he was on a night shift or something. Said she saw him last week coming home one morning, getting dropped off from a beige or tan Jeep. No license number because she wasn't looking. But she said he was all dirty, that's how she knew he was coming home from work."

They were silent for a few moments, both thinking.

Bosch finally said, "J. Edgar, I have a deal for you."

"You got a deal for me? Okay, let me hear it."

"You go home now or back to your open house or whatever. I'll take this from here. I'll go pull the tape at the com center, go back to the office and start the paper going. I'll see if Sakai made next-of-kin notification; I think, if I remember right, that Meadows was from Louisiana. Anyway, I've got the autopsy skedded for tomorrow at eight. I'll take that, too, on my way in.

"Now, your end is tomorrow you finish up last night's TV thing and take it over to the DA. Shouldn't be any problems with it."

"So you're taking the end that's dipped in shit and letting me skate. The transvestite-offs-transvestite case is as cut and dried as they come. No pun intended."

"Yeah. There's one thing I'd also want. On your way in from the Valley tomorrow, stop by the VA in Sepulveda and see if you can talk them into letting you see Meadows's file. Might have some names that could help. Like I said before, he was supposedly talking to a shrink in the outpatient care unit and in one of those circle jerks. Maybe one of those guys was spiking with him, knows what happened here. It's a long shot, I know. If they give you a hard time, give me a call and I'll work on a search warrant."

"Sounds like a deal. But I'm worried about you, Harry. I mean, you and I haven't been partners too long, and I know you probably want to work your way back downtown to Robbery-Homicide, but I don't see the percentage in busting your balls on this one. Yeah, this place has been turned over, but that isn't the question. The question is why. And on the face of things, nothing really stirs me. It looks to me like somebody dumped Meadows down at the reservoir after he croaked and searched his place to find his stash. If he had one."

"Probably that's the way it was," Bosch said after a few moments. "But a couple things still bother me. I want to puzzle with it a little more until I'm sure."

"Well, like I said, no problem with me. You're giving me the clean end of the stick."

"I think I'm going to look around a little more. You go ahead, and I'll see you tomorrow when I get back in from the cut."

"Okay, partner."

"And Jed?"

"Yeah?"

"It's got nothing to do with getting downtown again."

Bosch sat alone, thinking, and scanning the room for secrets. His eyes eventually came down on the cards spread out before him on the coffee table. Solitaire. He saw that all four aces were up. He picked up the deck of remaining cards and went through it, peeling off three cards at a time. In the course of going through he came across the two and three of spades and the two of hearts. The game hadn't stalled. It had been interrupted. And never finished.

He became restless. He looked down into the green glass ashtray and saw that all the butts were nonfiltered Camels. Was that Meadows's brand or his killer's? He got up and walked around the room. The faint smell of urine hit him again. He walked back into the bedroom. He opened the drawers of the bureau and stared at their contents once more. Nothing turned in his mind. He went to the window and looked out at the back end of another apartment building across an alley. There was a man with a supermarket cart in the alley. He was poking through a

Dumpster with a stick. The cart was half full of aluminum cans. Bosch walked away and sat down on the bed and put his head back against the wall where the headboard should have been and the white paint was a dingy gray. The wall felt cool against his back.

"Tell me something," he whispered to no one.

Something had interrupted the card game and Meadows had died here, he believed. Then he was taken to the pipe. But why? Why not leave him? Bosch leaned his head back to the wall and looked straight across the room. It was at that moment that he noticed a nail in the wall. The nail was about three feet above the bureau and had been painted white along with the wall at some point a long time ago. That was why he hadn't noticed it before. He got up and went to look behind the bureau. In the three-inch space between it and the wall, he saw the edge of a fallen picture frame. With his shoulder, he pushed the heavy bureau away from the wall and picked up the frame. He stepped backward and sat on the edge of the bed studying it. The glass was cracked into an intricate spiderweb that had probably occurred when the frame fell. The damaged glass partially obscured an eight-by-ten black-and-white photograph. It was grainy and fading to a brownish yellow around the edges. The photo was more than twenty years old. Bosch knew this because between two cracks in the glass he saw his own, young face staring out and smiling.

Bosch turned the frame over and carefully bent back the tin prongs that kept the cardboard backing in place. As he was sliding the yellowed photo out, the glass finally gave way and the pieces dropped to the floor in shatters. He moved his feet away from the glass but didn't get up. He studied the photograph. There were no markings on front or back to tell where or when it had been taken. But he knew it must have been sometime in late 1969 or early 1970, because some of the men in the picture were dead after that.

There were seven of them in the photo. All tunnel rats. All shirtless and proudly displaying their T-shirt tan lines and tattoos, each man's dog tags taped together to keep them from jangling while they crawled through the tunnels. They had to have been in the Echo Sector of Cu Chi District, but Bosch could not tell or remember what village. The soldiers stood in a trench, positioned on both sides of a tunnel entrance no wider than the pipe in which Meadows would later be found dead. Bosch looked at himself and thought that his smile in the photograph was foolish. He was embarrassed by it now, in light of what was still to come after the moment was captured. Then he looked at Meadows in the photo and saw the thin smile and vacant stare. The others had always said Meadows would have a thousand-yard stare in an eight-by-eight room.

Bosch looked down at the glass between his feet and saw a pink piece of paper about the size of a baseball card. He picked it up by its edges and studied it. It was a pawn ticket from a shop downtown. The customer name on it was William Fields. It listed one item pawned: an antique bracelet, gold with jade inlay. The ticket was dated six weeks earlier. Fields had gotten $800 for the bracelet. Bosch slipped it into an evidence envelope from his pocket and stood up.

The trip downtown took an hour because of the traffic heading to Dodger Stadium. Bosch spent the time thinking about the apartment. It had been searched, but Edgar was right. It was a rush job. The pants pockets were the obvious tip. But the bureau drawers should've been put back in correctly, and the photo and the hidden pawn slip should not have been missed. What had been the hurry? He concluded it was because Meadows's body was in the apartment. It had to be moved.

Bosch exited on Broadway and headed south past Times Square to the pawnshop located in the Bradbury Building. Downtown L.A. was as quiet as Forest Lawn on most weekends, and he didn't expect to find the Happy Hocker open. He was curious and just wanted to drive by and take a look at the place before heading to the communications center. But when he drove past the storefront he saw a man outside with an aerosol can painting the word OPEN in black on a sheet of plywood. The board stood in place of the shop's front window. Bosch could see shards of glass on the dirty sidewalk below the plywood. He pulled to the curb. The spray painter was inside by the time he got to the door. He stepped through the beam of an electric eye, which sounded a bell from somewhere above all the musical instruments hanging from the ceiling.

"I'm not open, not Sundays," a man called from the back. He was standing behind a chrome cash register that was atop a glass counter.

"That's not what the sign you just painted says."

"Yes, but that is for tomorrow. People see boards over your windows they think you're out of business. I'm not out of business. I'm open for business, except for weekends. I just have a board out there for a few days. I painted OPEN so people will know, you see? Starting tomorrow."

"Do you own this business?" Bosch said as he pulled

his ID case out and flipped open his badge. "This will only take a couple minutes."

"Oh, police. Why din't you say? I been waiting all day for you police."

Bosch looked around, confused, then put it together.

"You mean the window? I'm not here about that."

"What do you mean? The patrol police said to wait for detective police. I waited. I been here since five A.M. this morning."

Bosch looked around the shop. It was filled with the usual array of brass musical instruments, electronic junk, jewelry and collectibles. "Look, Mr.—"

"Obinna. Oscar Obinna pawnshops of Los Angeles and Culver City."

"Mr. Obinna, detectives don't roll on vandalism reports on weekends. I mean, they might not even be doing that during the week anymore."

"What vandalism? This was a breakthrough. Grand robbery."

"You mean a break-in? What was taken?"

Obinna gestured to two glass counter cases that flanked the cash register. The top plate in each case had been smashed into a thousand pieces. Bosch walked up closer and could see small items of jewelry, cheap-looking earrings and rings, nestled among the glass. But he also saw velvet-covered jewelry pedestals, mirrored plates and wood ring pegs where pieces should have been but weren't. He looked around and saw no other damage in the store.

"Mr. Obinna, I can call the duty detective and see if anyone is going to come out today, and if so when they will be here. But that is not what I've come for."

Bosch then pulled out the clear plastic envelope with the pawn ticket in it. He held it up for Obinna to see.

"Can I see this bracelet please?" The moment he said it he felt a bad premonition come over him. The pawnbroker, a small, round man with olive skin and dark hair noodled over a bare cranium, looked at Bosch incredulously, his dark bushy eyebrows knitted together.

"You're not going to take the report on my cases?"

"No sir, I'm investigating a murder. Can you please show me the bracelet pawned on this ticket? Then I will call the detective bureau and find out if anyone is coming today on your break-in. Thank you for your cooperation."

"Aygh! You people! I cooperate. I send my lists each week, even take pictures for your pawn men. Then all I ask for is one detective to investigate a robbery and I get a man who says his job is murder. I been waiting now since five A.M. in the morning."

"Give me your phone. I'll get somebody over."

Obinna took the receiver off a wall phone behind one of the damaged counters and handed it across. Bosch gave him the number to dial. While Bosch talked to the duty detective at Parker Center, the shopkeeper looked up the pawn ticket in a logbook. The duty detective, a woman Bosch knew had not been involved in a field investigation during her entire career with the Robbery-Homicide Division, asked Bosch how he had been, then told him that she had referred the pawnshop break-in to the local station even though she knew there would be no detectives there today. The local station was Central Division. Bosch walked around the counter and dialed the detective bureau there anyway. There was no answer. While the phone rang on unanswered, Bosch began a one-sided conversation.

"Yeah, this is Harry Bosch, Hollywood detectives, I'm

just trying to check on the status of the break-in over at the Happy Hocker on Broadway. . . . He is. Do you know when? . . . Uh huh, uh huh. . . . Right, Obinna, O-B-I-N-N-A."

He looked over and Obinna nodded at the correct spelling.

"Yeah, he's here waiting. . . . Right . . . I'll tell him. Thank you."

He hung up the phone. Obinna looked at him, his bushy eyebrows arched.

"It's been a busy day, Mr. Obinna," Bosch said. "The detectives are out, but they'll get here. Shouldn't be too much longer. I gave the watch officer your name and told him to get 'em over here as soon as possible. Now, can I see the bracelet?"

"No."

Bosch dug a cigarette out of a package he pulled from his coat pocket. He knew what was coming before Obinna spread his arm across one of the damaged display cases.

"Your bracelet, it is gone," the pawnbroker said. "I looked it up here in my record. I see that I had it here in the case because it was a fine piece, very valuable to me. Now it is gone. We are both victims of the robber, yes?"

Obinna smiled, apparently happy to share his woe. Bosch looked into the glitter of sharp glass in the bottom of the case. He nodded and said, "Yes."

"You are a day late, detective. A shame."

"Did you say only these two cases were robbed?"

"Yes. A smash and grab. Quick. Quick."

"What time?"

"Police called me at four-thirty A.M. in the morning. That is the time of the alarm. I came at once. The alarm, when the window was smashed, the alarm went off. The officers found no one. They stayed until I came. Then I begin to wait for detectives that do not come. I cannot clean up my cases until they get here to investigate this crime."

Bosch was thinking of the time scheme. The body dumped sometime before the anonymous 911 call at 4 A.M. The pawnshop broken into about the same time. A bracelet pawned by the dead man taken. There are no co-incidences, he told himself.

"You said something about pictures. Lists and pictures for the pawn detail?"

"Yes, LAPD, that is true. I turn over lists of everything I take in to the pawn detectives. It is the law. I cooperate fully."

Obinna nodded his head and frowned mournfully into the broken display case.

"What about the pictures?" Bosch said.

"Yes, pictures. These pawn detectives, they ask me to take pictures of my best acquisitions. Help them better identify for stolen merchandise. It is not the law, but I say sure, I cooperate fully. I buy the Polaroid kind of camera. I keep pictures if they want to come and look. They never do. It's bullshit."

"You have a picture of this bracelet?"

Obinna's eyebrows arched again as he considered the idea for the first time.

"I think," he said, and then he disappeared through a black curtain in a doorway behind the counter. He came out a few moments later with a shoe box full of Polaroid photos with yellow carbon slips paper-clipped to them. He rustled through the photos, occasionally pulling one out, raising his eyebrows, and then sliding it back into place. Finally, he found what he wanted.

"Here. There it is."

Bosch took the photo and studied it.

"Antique gold with carved jade, very nice," Obinna said. "I remember it, top line. No wonder the shitheel that broke through my window took it. Made in the 1930s, Mexico . . . I gave the man eight hundred dollars. I have not often paid such a price for a piece of jewelry. I remember, very big man, he came here with the ring for the Super Bowl. Nineteen eighty-three. Very nice. I gave him one thousand dollars. He did not come back for it."

He held out his left hand to display the oversized gold ring, which seemed even larger on his small finger.

"The guy who pawned the bracelet, you remember him as well?" Bosch asked.

Obinna looked puzzled. Bosch decided that watching his eyebrows was like watching two caterpillars charging each other. He took one of the Polaroids of Meadows out of his pocket and handed it to the pawnbroker. He studied it closely.

"The man is dead," Obinna said after a moment. The caterpillars seemed to quiver with fear. "The man looks dead."

"I don't need your help for that," Bosch said. "I want to know if he pawned the bracelet."

Obinna handed the photo back. He said, "I think yes."

"He ever come in here and pawn anything else, before or after the bracelet?"

"No. I think I'd remember him. I'll say no."

"I need to take this," Bosch said, holding up the Polaroid of the bracelet. "If you need it back, give me a call."

He put one of his business cards on the cash register. The card was one of the cheap kind, with his name and phone number handwritten on a line. As he walked to the front door, crossing under a row of banjos, Bosch looked at his watch. He turned to Obinna, who was looking through the box of Polaroids again.

"Mr. Obinna, the watch officer, he said to tell you that if the detectives didn't get here in a half hour, you should go home and they will be by in the morning."

Obinna looked at him without saying a word. The caterpillars charged and collided. Bosch looked up and saw himself in the polished brass elbow of a saxophone that hung overhead. A tenor. Then he turned and walked out the door, heading to the com center to pick up the tape.

The watch sergeant in the com center beneath City Hall let Bosch record the 911 call off one of the big reel-to-reels that never stop rolling and recording the cries of the city. The voice of the emergency operator was female and black. The caller was male and white. The caller sounded like a boy.

"Nine one one emergency. What are you reporting?"

"Uh, uh—"

"Can I help you? What are you reporting?"

"Uh, yeah, I'm reporting you have a dead guy in a pipe."

"You said you are reporting a dead body?"

"Yeah, that's right."

"What do you mean a pipe, sir?"

"He is in a pipe up by the dam."

"What dam is that?"

"Uh, you know, where they got the water reservoir and everything, the Hollywood sign."

"Is that the Mulholland Dam, sir? Above Hollywood?"

"Yeah, that's it. You got it. Mulholland. I couldn't remember the name."

"Where is the body?"

"They have a big old pipe up there. You know, the one that people sleep in. The dead guy is in the pipe. He's there."

"Do you know this person?"

"No, man, no way."

"Is he sleeping?"

"Shit, no," The boy laughed nervously. "He's dead."

"How are you sure?"

"I'm sure. I'm just telling you. If you don't want to—"

"What is your name, sir?"

"What is this? What do you need my name for? I just saw it, I didn't do it."

"How am I to know this is a legitimate call?"

"Check the pipe, you'll know. I don't know what else to tell you. What's my name got to do with anything?"

"For our records, sir. Can you give me your name?"

"Uh, no."

"Sir, will you stay there until an officer arrives?"

"No, I'm already gone. I'm not there, man. I'm down—"

"I know, sir. I have a readout here that says you are at a pay phone on Gower near Hollywood Boulevard. Will you wait for the officer?"

"How—? Never mind, I gotta go now. You check it out. The body is there. A dead guy."

"Sir, we would like to talk—"

The line was disconnected. Bosch put the cassette tape in his pocket and headed out of the com center the way he had come in.

It had been ten months since Harry Bosch had been on the third floor at Parker Center. He had worked in RHD—the

Robbery-Homicide Division—for almost ten years, but never came back after his suspension and transfer from the Homicide Special squad to Hollywood detectives. On the day he got the word, his desk was cleared by two goons from Internal Affairs named Lewis and Clarke. They dumped his stuff on the homicide table at Hollywood Station, then left a message on his phone tape at home saying that's where he could find it. Now, ten months later, he was back on the hallowed floor of the department's elite detective squad, and he was glad it was Sunday. There would be no faces he knew. No reason to look away.

Room 321 was empty except for the weekend duty detective, whom Bosch didn't know. Harry pointed to the back of the room and said, "Bosch, Hollywood detectives. I have to use the box."

The duty man, a young guy with a haircut he had kept when he split the Marine Corps, had a gun catalog open on his desk. He looked back at the computers along the back wall as if to make sure they were still there and then back at Bosch.

"S'pose to use the one in your own division," he said.

Bosch walked by him. "I don't have the time to go out to Hollywood. I got an autopsy in twenty minutes," he lied.

"You know, I've heard of you, Bosch. Yeah. The TV show and all of that. You used to be on this floor. Used to."

The last line hung in the air like smog and Bosch tried to ignore it. As he went back to the computer terminals, he couldn't help but let his eyes wander over his old desk. He wondered who used it now. It was cluttered, and he noticed the cards on the Rolodex were crisp and unworn at the edges. New. Harry turned around and looked at the duty man, who was still watching him.

"This your desk when you aren't pulling Sundays?"

The kid smiled and nodded his head.

"You deserve it, kid. You're just right for the part. That hair, that stupid grin. You're going to go far."

"Just 'cause you got busted out of here for being a one-man army . . . Ah, fuck you, Bosch, you has-been."

Bosch pulled a chair on casters away from a desk and pushed it in front of the IBM PC sitting on a table against the rear wall. He hit the switch and in a few moments the amber-colored letters appeared on the screen: "Homicide Information Tracking Management Automated Network."

For a moment Bosch smiled at the department's unceasing need for acronyms. It seemed to him that every unit, task force and computer file had been christened with a name that gave its acronym the sound of eliteness. To the public, acronyms meant action, large numbers of manpower applied to vital problems. There was HIT-MAN, COBRA, CRASH, BADCATS, DARE. A hundred others. Somewhere in Parker Center there was someone who spent all day making up catchy acronyms, he believed. Computers had acronyms, even ideas had acronyms. If your special unit didn't have an acronym, then you weren't shit in this department.

Once he was in the HITMAN system, a template of case questions appeared on the screen and he filled in the blanks. He then typed in three search keys: "Mulholland Dam," "overdose" and "staged overdose." He then pushed the execute key. Half a minute later, the computer told him that a search of eight thousand homicide cases—about ten years' worth—stored on the computer's hard disk had come up with only six hits. Bosch called them up one by one. The first three were unsolved slayings of young women who were found dead on the dam in the early 1980s. Each was strangled. Bosch glanced quickly at the information and went on. The fourth case was a body found floating in the reservoir five years earlier. Cause of death was not drowning but otherwise unknown. The last two were drug overdoses, the first of which occurred during a picnic at the park above the reservoir. It looked pretty straightforward to Bosch and he went on. The last bit was a DB found in the pipe fourteen months earlier. Cause of death was later determined to be heart stoppage due to an overdose of tar heroin.

"Decedent known to frequent area of the dam and sleep in pipe," the computer readout said. "No further follow-up."

It was the death that Crowley, the Hollywood watch sergeant, had mentioned when he woke Bosch up that morning. Bosch pushed a key and printed out the information on the last death, though he didn't think it figured into his case. He signed off and shut down the computer, then he sat there a moment thinking. Without getting out of the chair he rolled over to another PC. He turned it on and fed his password in. He took the Polaroid out of his pocket, looked at the bracelet and typed in its description for a stolen property records search. This in itself was an art. He had to describe the bracelet the way he believed other cops would, cops who might be typing in descriptions of a whole inventory of jewelry taken in a robbery or burglary. He described the bracelet simply as "antique gold bracelet with carved jade dolphin design." He pressed the search key and in thirty seconds the computer screen said "No hit." He tried it again, typing "gold-and-jade bracelet" and then punching the search key. This time there were 436 hits. Too many. He needed to thin the herd. He typed "gold bracelet with jade fish" and pressed search. Six hits. That was more like it.

The computer said a gold bracelet with carved jade fish had turned up on four crime reports and two departmental bulletins that had been entered into the computer system since its development in 1983. Bosch knew that because of the immense duplication of records in any police department, all six entries could be and probably were from the same case or report of a missing or stolen bracelet. He called the abbreviated crime reports up on the computer screen and found that his suspicion was correct. The reports were generated by a single burglary in September at Sixth and Hill downtown. The victim was a woman named Harriet Beecham, age seventy-one, of Silver Lake. Bosch tried to place the location in his mind but could not think of what building or business was there. There was no summary of the crime on the computer; he would have to go to records and pull a hard copy. But there was a limited description of the gold-and-jade bracelet, and several other pieces of jewelry taken from Beecham. The bracelet Beecham reported lost could or could not have been the one that Meadows had pawned—the description was too vague. There were several supplementary report numbers given on the computer report and Bosch wrote them all down in his notebook. It seemed to him as he did this that Harriet Beecham's loss had generated an unusual amount of paper.

He next called up the information on the two bulletins. Both had come from the FBI, the first issued two weeks after Beecham had been burglarized. It was then reissued three months later when Beecham's jewelry had still not turned up. Bosch wrote down the bulletin number and turned off the computer. He went across the room to the robbery/commercial burglary section. On a steel shelf that ran along the back wall were dozens of black binders that held the bulletins and BOLOs from past years. Bosch took down the one marked September and began looking through it. He quickly realized that the bulletins were not in chronological order and weren't all issued in September. In fact, there was no order. He might have to look through all ten months since Beecham's burglary to find the bulletin he needed. He pulled an armful of the binders off the shelf and sat down at the burglary table. A few moments later he felt the presence of someone across the table from him.

"What do you want?" he said without looking up.

"What do I want?" the duty detective said. "I want to know what the fuck you are doing, Bosch. This isn't your place anymore. You can't just come in here like you're running the crew. Put that shit back on the shelf, and if you want to look through it come back down here tomorrow and ask, goddammit. And don't give me any bullshit about an autopsy. You've already been here a half hour."

Bosch looked up at him. He put his age at twenty-eight, maybe twenty-nine, even younger than Bosch had been when he had made it to Robbery-Homicide. Either standards had dropped or RHD wasn't what it was. Bosch knew it was actually both. He looked back down at the bulletin binder.

"I'm talking to you, asshole!" the detective boomed.

Bosch reached his foot up under the table and kicked the chair that was across from him. The chair shot out from the table and its backrest hit the detective in the crotch. He doubled over and made an *oomph* sound, grabbing the chair for support. Bosch knew he had his reputation going for him now. Harry Bosch: a loner, a fighter, a killer. C'mon kid, he was saying, do something. But the young detective just stared at Bosch, his anger and humiliation in check. He was a cop who could pull the gun but maybe not the trigger. And once Bosch knew that, he knew the kid would walk away.

The young cop shook his head, waved his hands like he was saying Enough of this, and walked back to the duty desk.

"Go ahead, write me up, kid," Bosch said to his back.

"Fuck you," the kid feebly returned.

Bosch knew he had nothing to worry about. IAD wouldn't even look at an officer-on-officer beef without a corroborating witness or tape recording. One cop's word against another's was something they wouldn't touch in this department. Deep down, they knew a cop's word by itself was worthless. That was why Internal Affairs cops always worked in pairs.

An hour and seven cigarettes later, Bosch found it. A photocopy of another Polaroid of the gold-and-jade bracelet was part of a fifty-page packet of descriptions and photos of property lost in a burglary at WestLand National Bank at Sixth and Hill. Now Bosch was able to place the address in his mind, and he remembered the dark smoked glass of the building. He had never been inside the bank. A bank heist with jewelry taken, he thought. It didn't make much sense. He studied the list. Almost every item was a piece of jewelry and there was too much there for a walk-in robbery. Harriet Beecham alone was listed as having lost eight antique rings, four bracelets, four earrings. Besides that, these were listed as burglary losses, not robbery losses. He looked through the Be on Lookout package for any kind of crime summary, but didn't find any. Just a bureau contact: Special Agent E. D. Wish.

Then he noticed in a block on the BOLO sheet that there were three dates noted for the date of the crime. A burglary over a three-day span during the first week of September. Labor Day weekend, he realized. Downtown banks are closed three days. It had to have been a safe-deposit caper. A tunnel job? Bosch leaned back and thought about that. Why hadn't he remembered it? A heist like that would have played in the media for days. It would have been talked about in the department even longer. Then he realized he had been in Mexico on Labor Day, and for the next three weeks. The bank heist had occurred while he was serving the one-month suspension for the Dollmaker case. He leaned forward, picked up a phone and dialed.

"*Times*, Bremmer."

"It's Bosch. Still got you working Sundays, huh?"

"Two to ten, every Sunday, no parole. So, what's up? I haven't talked to you since, uh, your problem with the Dollmaker case. How you liking Hollywood Division?"

"It'll do. For a while, at least." He was speaking low so the duty detective would not overhear.

Bremmer said, "Like that, huh? Well, I heard you caught the stiff up at the dam this morning."

Joel Bremmer had covered the cop shop for the *Times* longer than most cops had been on the force, including Bosch. There was not much he didn't hear about the department, or couldn't find out with a phone call. A year ago he called Bosch for comment on his twenty-two-day suspension, no pay. Bremmer had heard about it before Bosch. Generally, the police department hated the *Times*, and the *Times* was never short in its criticism of the department. But in the middle of that was Bremmer, whom any cop could trust and many, like Bosch, did.

"Yeah, that's my case," Bosch said. "Right now, it's nothing much. But I need a favor. If it works out the way it's looking, then it will be something you'd want to know about."

Bosch knew he didn't have to bait him, but he wanted the reporter to know there might be something later.

"What do you need?" Bremmer said.

"As you know, I was out of town last Labor Day on my extended vacation, courtesy of IAD. So I missed this one. But there was—"

"The tunnel job? You're not going to ask about the tunnel job, are you? Over here in downtown? All the jewelry? Negotiable bonds, stock certificates, maybe drugs?"

Bosch heard the reporter's voice go up a notch in urgency. He had been right, it had been a tunnel and the story had played well. If Bremmer was this interested, then it was a substantial case. Still, Bosch was surprised he had not heard of it after coming back to work in October.

"Yeah, that's the one," he said. "I was gone then, so I missed it. Ever any arrests?"

"No, it's open. FBI's doing it, last I checked."

"I want to look at the clips on it tonight. Is that all right?"

"I'll make copies. When are you coming?"

"I'll head over in a little while."

"I take it this has got something to do with this morning's stiff?"

"It's looking that way. Maybe. I can't talk right now. And I know the feebees have the case. I'll go see them tomorrow. That's why I want to see the clips tonight."

"I'll be here."

After hanging up the phone, Bosch looked down at the FBI photocopy of the bracelet. There was no doubt it was the piece that had been pawned by Meadows and was in Obinna's Polaroid. The bracelet in the FBI photo was in place on a woman's liver-spotted wrist. Three small carved fish swimming on a wave of gold. Bosch guessed it was Harriet Beecham's seventy-one-year-old wrist and the photo had probably been taken for insurance purposes. He looked over at the duty detective, who was still leafing through the gun catalog. He coughed loudly like he had seen Nicholson do in a movie once and at the same time tore the BOLO sheet out of the binder. The kid detective looked over at Bosch and then went back to the guns and bullets.

As he folded the BOLO sheet into his pocket, Bosch's electronic pager went off. He picked up the phone and called Hollywood Station, expecting to be told there was another body waiting for him. It was a watch sergeant named Art Crocket, whom everyone called Davey, who took the call.

"Harry, you still out in the field?" he said.

"I'm at Parker Center. Had to check on a few things."

"Good, then you're already near the morgue. A tech over there name of Sakai called, said he needs to see you."

"See me?"

"He said to tell you that something came up and they're doing your cut today. Right now, matter of fact."

It took Bosch five minutes to get over to County-USC Hospital and fifteen minutes to find a parking spot. The medical examiner's office was located behind one of the medical center buildings that had been condemned after the '87 earthquake. It was a two-story yellow prefab without much architectural style or life. As Bosch was going through the glass doors where the living people entered and into the front lobby, he passed a sheriff's detective he had spent some time with while working the Night Stalker task force in the early eighties.

"Hey, Bernie," Bosch said and smiled.

"Hey, fuck you, Bosch," Bernie said. "The rest of us catch ones that count, too."

Bosch stopped there a moment to watch the detective walk into the parking lot. Then he went in and to the right, down a government-green corridor, passing through two sets of double doors—the smell getting worse each time. It was the smell of death and industrial-strength disinfectant. Death had the upper hand. Bosch stepped into the yellow-tiled scrub room. Larry Sakai was in there, putting a paper gown over his hospital scrubs. He already had on a paper mask and booties. Bosch took a set of the same out of cardboard boxes on a stainless steel counter and started putting them on.

"What's with Bernie Slaughter?" Bosch asked. "What happened in here to piss him off?"

"You're what happened, Bosch," Sakai said without looking at him. "He got a call out yesterday morning. Some sixteen-year-old shoots his best friend. Up in Lancaster. Looks like accidental but Bernie's waiting on us to check the bullet track and powder stippling. He wants to close it. I told him we'd get to it late today, so he came in. Only we aren't going to get to it at all today. 'Cause Sally's got a bug up his ass about doing yours. Don't ask me why. He just checked the stiff out when I brought it in and said we'd do it today. I told him we'd have to bump somebody, and he said bump Bernie. But I couldn't get him on the line in time to stop him from coming in. So that's why Bernie's pissed. You know he lives all the way down to Diamond Bar. Long ride in for nothing."

Bosch had the mask, gown and booties on and followed Sakai down the tiled hall to the autopsy suite. "Then maybe he ought to be pissed at Sally, not me," he said.

Sakai didn't answer. They walked to the first table, where Billy Meadows lay on his back, naked, his neck braced against a short cut of two-by-four wood. There were six of the stainless steel tables in the room. Each had gutters running alongside its edges and drain holes in the corners. There was a body on each. Dr. Jesus Salazar was huddled over Meadows's chest with his back to Bosch and Sakai.

"Afternoon, Harry, I've been waiting," Salazar said, still not looking. "Larry, I'm going to need slides on this."

The medical examiner straightened up and turned. In his rubber-gloved hand he held what looked like a square plug of flesh and pink muscle tissue. He placed it in a steel pan, the kind brownies are cooked in, and handed it to Sakai. "Give me verticals, one of the puncture track, then two on either side for comparison."

Sakai took the pan and left the room to go to the lab. Bosch saw that the plug of meat had been cut from Meadows's chest, about an inch above the left nipple.

"What'd you find?" Bosch asked.

"Not sure yet. We'll see. The question is, What did you find, Harry? My field tech told me you were demanding an autopsy on this case today. Why is that?"

"I told him I needed it today because I wanted to get it done tomorrow. I thought that was what we had agreed on, too."

"Yes, he told me so, but I got curious about it. I love a good mystery, Harry. What made you think this was hinky, as you detectives say?"

We don't say it anymore, Bosch thought. Once it's said in the movies and people like Salazar pick it up, it's ancient.

"Just some things didn't fit at the time," Bosch said. "There are more things now. From my end, it looks like a murder. No mystery."

"What things?"

Bosch got out his notebook and started flipping through the pages as he talked. He listed the things he had noticed wrong at the death scene: the broken finger, the lack of distinct tracks in the pipe, the shirt pulled over the head.

"He had a hype kit in his pocket and we found a stove in the pipe, but it doesn't look right. Looks like a plant to me. Looks to me like the pop that killed him is in the arm there. Those other scars on his arms are old. He hasn't been using his arms in years."

"You're right about that. Aside from the one recent puncture in the arm, the groin area is the only area where punctures are fresh. The inside thighs. An area usually used by people going to great lengths to hide their addiction. But then again, this could have just been his first time back on the arms. What else you got, Harry?"

"He smoked, I'm pretty sure. There was no pack of cigarettes with the body."

"Couldn't somebody have taken them off the body? Before it was discovered. A scavenger?"

"True. But why take the smokes and not the kit? There's also his apartment. Somebody searched the place."

"Could have been someone who knew him. Someone looking for his stash."

"True again." Bosch flipped through a few more pages in the notebook. "The kit on the body had whitish-brown crystals in the cotton. I've seen enough tar heroin to know it turns the straining cotton dark brown, sometimes black. So it looks like it was some fine stuff, probably overseas, that was put in his arm. That doesn't go with the way he was living. That's uptown stuff."

Salazar thought a moment before saying, "It's all a lot of supposition, Harry."

"The last thing, though, is—and I am just starting to work on this—he was involved in some kind of caper."

Bosch gave him a brief synopsis of what he knew about the bracelet, its theft from the bank vault and then from the pawnshop. Salazar's domain was the forensic detail of the case. But Bosch had always trusted Sally and found that it sometimes helped to bounce other details of a case off him. The two had met in 1974, when Bosch was a patrolman and Sally was a new assistant coroner. Bosch was assigned guard duty and crowd control on East Fifty-fourth in South-Central where a firefight with the Symbionese Liberation Army had left a house burned to the ground and five bodies in the smoking rubble. Sally was assigned to see if there was a sixth—Patty Hearst—somewhere in the char. The two of them spent three days there, and when Sally finally gave up, Bosch had won a bet that she was still alive. Somewhere.

When Bosch was finished with the story about the bracelet, it seemed to have mollified Sally's worries about the death of Billy Meadows not being a mystery. He seemed energized. He turned to a cart on which his cutting tools were piled and rolled it next to the autopsy table. He switched on a sound-activated tape recorder and picked up a scalpel and a pair of regular gardening shears. He said, "Well, let's get to work."

Bosch moved back a few steps to avoid any spatter and leaned against a counter on which there was a tray full of knives and saws and scalpels. He noticed that a sign taped to the side of the tray said: To Be Sharpened.

Salazar looked down at the body of Billy Meadows and began: "The body is that of a well-developed Caucasian male measuring sixty-nine inches in length, weighing one hundred sixty-five pounds and appearing generally consistent with the stated age of forty years. The body is cold and unembalmed with full rigor and posterior dependent fixed lividity."

Bosch watched him start but then noticed the plastic bag containing Meadows's clothes on the counter next to the tool pan. He pulled it over and opened it up. The smell of urine immediately assaulted his nostrils, and he thought for a moment of the living room at Meadows's apartment. He pulled on a pair of rubber gloves as Salazar continued to describe the body.

"The left index finger shows a palpable fracture without laceration or petechial contusion or hemorrhage."

Bosch glanced over his shoulder and saw that Salazar was wiggling the broken digit with the blunt end of the scalpel as he spoke to the tape recorder. He concluded his external description of the body by mentioning the skin punctures.

"There are hemorrhagic puncture wounds, hypodermic type, on the upper inside thighs and interior side of the left arm. The arm puncture exudes a bloody fluid and appears to be most recent. No scabbing. There is another puncture, in the upper left chest, which exudes a small amount of bloody fluid and appears to be slightly larger than that caused by hypodermic puncture."

Salazar put his hand over the tape recorder's speaker and said to Bosch, "I'm having Sakai get slides of this chest puncture. It looks very interesting."

Bosch nodded and turned back to the counter and began spreading out Meadows's clothes. Behind him he heard Salazar using the shears to open up the dead man's chest.

The detective pulled each pocket out and looked at the lint. He turned the socks inside out and checked the inside lining of the pants and shirt. Nothing. He took a scalpel out of the To Be Sharpened pan and cut the stitches out of Meadows's leather belt and pulled it apart. Again nothing. Over his shoulder he heard Salazar saying, "The spleen weighs one hundred ninety grams. The capsule is intact and slightly wrinkled, and the parenchyma is pale purple and trabecular."

Bosch had heard it all hundreds of times before. Most of what a pathologist said into his tape recorder meant nothing to the detective who stood by. It was the bottom line the detective waited for: What killed the person on the cold steel table? How? Who?

"The gallbladder is thin walled," Salazar was saying. "It contains a few cc's of greenish bile with no stones."

Bosch shoved the clothes back into the plastic bag and sealed it. Then he dumped the leather work shoes Meadows had been wearing out of a second plastic bag. He noticed reddish-orange dust fall from inside the•shoes. Another indication the body had been dragged into the pipe. The heels had scraped on the dried mud at the bottom of the pipe, drawing the dust inside the shoes.

Salazar said, "The bladder mucosa is intact, and there

are only two ounces of pale yellow urine. The external genitalia and vagina are unremarkable."

Bosch turned around. Salazar had his hand on the tape recorder speaker. He said, "Coroner's humor. Just wanted to see if you were listening, Harry. You might have to testify to this one day. To back me up."

"I doubt it," Bosch said. "They don't like boring juries to death."

Salazar started the small circular saw that was used to open the skull. It sounded like a dentist's drill. Bosch turned back to the shoes. They were well oiled and cared for. The rubber soles showed only modest wear. Stuck in one of the deep grooves of the tread of the tight shoe was a white stone. Bosch pried it out with the scalpel. It was a small chunk of cement. He thought of the white dust in the rug in Meadows's closet. He wondered if the dust or the chunk from the shoe tread could be matched to the concrete that had guarded the WestLand Bank's vault. But if the shoes were so well cared for, could the chunk have been in the tread for nine months since the vault break-in? It seemed unlikely. Perhaps it was from his work on the subway project. If he actually had such a job. Bosch slipped the chunk of cement into a small plastic envelope and put it in his pocket with the others he had collected throughout the day.

Salazar said, "Examination of the head and cranial contents reveals no trauma or underlying pathological disease conditions or congenital anomalies. Harry, I'm going to do the finger now."

Bosch put the shoes back in their plastic bag and returned to the autopsy table as Salazar placed an X-ray of Meadows's left hand on a light window on the wall.

"See here, these fragments?" he said as he traced small,

sharp white spots on the negative. There were three of them near the fractured joint. "If this was an old break, these would, over time, have moved into the joint. There is no scarring discernible on the X-ray but I am going to take a look."

He went to the body and used a scalpel to make a T-incision in the skin on the top of the finger joint. He then folded the skin back and dug around with the scalpel in the pink meat, saying, "No . . . no . . . nothing. This was post, Harry. You think it could have been one of my people?"

"I don't know," Bosch said. "Doesn't look like it. Sakai said he and his sidekick were careful. I know I didn't do it. How come there's no damage to the skin?"

"That is an interesting point. I don't know. Somehow the finger was broken without the exterior being damaged. I can't answer that one. But it shouldn't have been too hard to do. Just grab the finger and yank down. Provided you have the stomach for it. Like so."

Salazar went around the table. He lifted Meadows's right hand and yanked the finger backward. He couldn't get the leverage needed and couldn't break the joint.

"Harder than I thought," he said. "Perhaps the digit was struck with a blunt object of some kind. One that did not blemish the skin."

When Sakai came in with the slides fifteen minutes later, the autopsy was completed and Salazar was sewing Meadows's chest closed with thick, waxed twine. He then used an overhead hose to spray debris off the body and wet down the hair. Sakai bound the legs together and the arms to the body with rope, to prevent them from moving during the different stages of rigor. Bosch noticed that the rope cut across the tattoo on Meadows's arm, across the rat's neck.

Using his thumb and forefinger, Salazar closed Meadows's eyes.

"Take him to the box," he said to Sakai. Then to Bosch, "Let's take a look at these slides. This seemed odd to me because the hole was bigger than your normal scag spike and its location, in the chest, was unusual.

"The puncture is clearly antemortem, possibly perimortem—there was only slight hemorrhaging. But the wound is not scabbed over. So we're talking shortly before, or even during death. Maybe the cause of death, Harry."

Salazar took the slides to a microscope that was on the counter at the back of the room. He chose one of the slides and put it on the viewing plate. He bent over to look and after half a minute finally said, "Interesting."

He then looked briefly at the other slides. When he was done, he put the first slide back on the viewing plate.

"Okay, basically, I removed a one-inch-square section of the chest where this puncture was located. I went into the chest about one and a half inches deep with the cut. The slide is a vertical dissection of the sample, showing the track of the perforation. Do you follow me?"

Bosch nodded.

"Good. It's kind of like slicing an apple open to expose the track of a worm. The slide traces the path of the perforation and any immediate impact or damage. Take a look."

Bosch bent to the eyepiece of the microscope. The slide showed a straight perforation about one inch deep, through the skin and into the muscle, tapering in width like a spike. The muscle's pink color changed to a dark brownish color around the deepest point of the penetration.

"What does it mean?" he asked.

"It means," said Salazar, "that the puncture was through the skin, through the fascia—that's the fibrous fat layer— and then directly into the pectoral muscle. You notice the deepening color of the muscle around the penetration?"

"Yes, I notice."

"Harry, that's because the muscle is burned there."

Bosch looked away from the microscope to Salazar. He thought he could make out the line of a thin smile beneath the pathologist's breathing mask.

"Burned?"

"A stun gun," the pathologist said. "Look for one that fires its electrode dart deep into the skin tissue. About three to four centimeters deep. Though in this case, it is likely the electrode was manually pressed deeper into the chest."

Bosch thought a moment. A stun gun would be virtually impossible to trace. Sakai came back into the room and leaned on the counter by the door, watching. Salazar collected three glass vials of blood and two containing yellowish liquid from the tool cart. There was also a small steel pan containing a brown lump of material that Bosch recognized from experience in this room as liver.

"Larry, here are the tox samples," Salazar said. Sakai took them and disappeared from the room again.

"You're talking about torture, electric shock," Bosch said.

"I would say it looks so," Salazar said. "Not enough to kill him, the trauma is too small. But possibly enough to get information from him. An electric charge can be very persuasive. I think there is ample history on that. With the electrode positioned in the subject's chest, he could probably feel the juice going right into his heart. He would have been paralyzed. He'd tell them what they wanted and then could only watch while they put a fatal dosage of heroin into his arm."

"Can we prove any of this?"

Salazar looked down at the tile floor and put his finger on his mask, and scratched his lip beneath it. Bosch was dying for a cigarette. He had been in the autopsy room nearly two hours.

"Prove any of it?" Salazar said. "Not medically. Tox tests will be done in a week. For the sake of argument, say they come back heroin overdose. How do we prove that someone else put it in his arm, not himself? Medically, we can't. But we can show that at the time of death or shortly before, there was a traumatic assault on the body in the form of electric shock. He was being tortured. After death there is the unexplained damage to the first digit of the left hand."

He rubbed the finger over his mask again and then concluded, "I could testify that this was a homicide. The totality of the medical evidence indicates death at the hands of others. But, for the moment, there is no cause. We wait for the tox studies to be completed and then we'll put our heads together again."

Bosch wrote a paraphrase of what Salazar had just said into his notebook. He would have to type it into his own reports.

"Of course," Salazar said, "proving any of this beyond a reasonable doubt to a jury is another matter. I would guess that, Harry, you have to find that bracelet and find out why it was worth torturing and killing a man for."

Bosch closed his notebook and started to pull off the paper gown.

The setting sun burned the sky pink and orange in the same bright hues as surfers' bathing suits. It was beautiful deception, Bosch thought, as he drove north on the Hollywood Freeway to home. Sunsets did that here. Made you forget it was the smog that made their colors so brilliant, that behind every pretty picture there could be an ugly story.

The sun hung like a ball of copper in the driver's-side window. He had the car radio tuned to a jazz station and Coltrane was playing "Soul Eyes." On the seat next to him was a file containing the newspaper clippings from Bremmer. The file was weighted down by a six-pack of Henry's. Bosch got off at Barham and then took Woodrow Wilson up into the hills above Studio City. His home was a wood-framed, one-bedroom cantilever not much bigger than a Beverly Hills garage. It hung out over the edge of the hill and was supported by three steel pylons at its midpoint. It was a scary place to be during earthquakes, daring Mother Nature to twang those beams and send the house down the hill like a sled. But the view was the trade-off. From the back porch Bosch could look northeast across Burbank and Glendale. He could see the purple-hued mountains past Pasadena and Altadena. Sometimes he could see the smoky loom-up and orange blaze of brush fires in the hills. At night the sound of the freeway below softened and the searchlights at Universal City swept the sky. Looking out on the Valley never failed to give Bosch a sense of power which he could not explain to himself. But he did know that it was one reason—the main reason—he bought the place and would never want to leave it.

Bosch had bought it eight years earlier, before the real estate boom got seriously endemic, with a down payment of $50,000. That left a mortgage of $1,400 a month, which he could easily afford because the only things he spent money on were food, booze and jazz.

The down payment money had come from a studio that gave it to him for the rights to use his name in a TV mini-series based on a string of murders of beauty shop owners in Los Angeles. Bosch and his partner during the investigation were portrayed by two midlevel TV actors.

His partner took his fifty grand and his pension and moved to Ensenada. Bosch put his down on a house he wasn't sure could survive the next earthquake but that made him feel as though he were prince of the city.

Despite Bosch's resolve never to move, Jerry Edgar, his current partner and part-time real estate man, told him the house was now worth three times what he had paid for it. Whenever the subject of real estate came up, which was often, Edgar counseled Bosch to sell and trade up. Edgar wanted the listing. Bosch just wanted to stay where he was.

It was dark by the time he reached the hill house. He drank the first beer standing on the back porch, looking out at the blanket of lights below. He had a second bottle while sitting in his watch chair, the file closed on his lap. He hadn't eaten all day and the beer hit him quickly. He felt lethargic and yet jumpy, his body telling him it needed food. He got up and went to the kitchen and made a pressed turkey sandwich that he brought back to the chair with another beer.

When he was finished eating be brushed the sandwich

crumbs off the file and opened it up. There had been four *Times* stories on the WestLand bank caper. He read them in the order of publication. The first was just a brief that had run on page 3 of the Metro section. The information had apparently been gathered on the Tuesday the break-in was discovered. At the time, the LAPD and the FBI weren't that interested in talking to the press or letting the public know what had happened.

AUTHORITIES PROBE BANK BREAK-IN

An undisclosed amount of property was stolen from the WestLand National Bank in downtown during the three-day holiday weekend, authorities said Tuesday.

The burglary, being investigated by the FBI and the Los Angeles Police Department, was discovered when managers of the bank located at the corner of Hill Street and Sixth Avenue arrived Tuesday and found the safe-deposit vault had been looted, FBI Special Agent John Rourke said.

Rourke said an estimate on the loss of property had not been made. But sources close to the investigation said more than $1 million worth of jewels and other valuables stored in the vault by customers of the bank was taken.

Rourke also declined to say how the burglars entered the vault but did say that the alarm system was not working properly. He declined to elaborate.

A spokesman for WestLand declined Tuesday to discuss the burglary. Authorities said there were no arrests or suspects.

Bosch wrote the name John Rourke in his notebook and went on to the next newspaper story, which was much longer. It had been published the day after the first and had been bannered across the top of the front page of the Metro section. It had a two-deck headline and was accompanied by a photograph of a man and woman standing in the safe-deposit vault looking down at a manhole-sized opening in the floor. Behind them was a pile of deposit boxes. Most of the small doors on the back wall were open. Bremmer's byline was on the story.

AT LEAST $2 MILLION TAKEN IN BANK TUNNEL JOB; BANDITS HAD HOLIDAY WEEKEND TO DIG INTO VAULT

The article expanded on the first story, filling in the detail that the perpetrators had tunneled into the bank, digging an approximately 150-yard line from a city storm main that ran under Hill Street. The story said an explosive device had been used to make the final break through the floor of the vault. According to the FBI, the burglars probably were in the vault through most of the holiday weekend, drilling open the individual safe-deposit boxes. The entry tunnel from the stormwater main to the vault was believed to have been dug during seven to eight weeks before the heist.

Bosch made a note to ask the FBI how the tunnel had been dug. If heavy equipment was used, most banks' alarms, which measured sound as well as earth vibrations, would have picked up the ground movement and sounded. Also, he wondered, why hadn't the explosive device set off alarms?

He looked then at the third article, published the day

after the second. This one wasn't written by Bremmer, though it still had been played on the front of Metro. It was a feature on the dozens of people lining up at the bank to see if their safe-deposit boxes were among those pried open and emptied. The FBI was escorting them into the vault and then taking their statements. Bosch scanned the story but saw the same thing over and over again: people angry or upset or both because they had lost items that they had placed in the vault because they believed it was safer than their homes. Near the bottom of the story Harriet Beecham was mentioned. She had been interviewed as she came out of the bank, and she told the reporter she had lost a lifetime's collection of valuables bought while traveling the world with her late husband, Harry. The story said Beecham was dabbing at her eyes with a lace handkerchief.

"I lost the rings he bought me in France, a bracelet of gold and jade from Mexico," Beecham said. "Whoever they were that did this, they took my memories."

Very melodramatic. Bosch wondered if the last quote had been made up by the reporter.

The fourth story in the file had been published a week later. By Bremmer, it was short and had been buried in the back of Metro, behind where they stuffed the Valley news. Bremmer reported that the WestLand investigation was being handled exclusively by the FBI. The LAPD provided initial backup, but as leads dried up, the case was left in the bureau's hands. Special Agent Rourke was quoted again in this story. He said agents were still on the case full-time but no progress had been made or suspects identified. None of the property taken from the vault, he said, had turned up.

Bosch closed the file. The case was too big for the bureau to slough off like a bank stickup. He wondered if Rourke had been telling the truth about the lack of suspects. He wondered if Meadows's name had ever come up. Two decades earlier Meadows had fought and sometimes lived in the tunnels beneath the villages of South Vietnam. Like all the tunnel fighters, he knew demolition work. But that was for bringing a tunnel down. Implosion. Could he have learned how to blow through the concrete-and-steel floor of a bank vault? Then Bosch realized that Meadows would not necessarily have needed to know how. He was sure the WestLand job had taken more than one person.

He got up and got another beer from the refrigerator. But before going back to the watch chair he detoured into the bedroom, where he pulled an old scrapbook out of the bottom drawer of the bureau. Back in the chair he drank down half the beer, then opened the book. There were bunches of photographs loose between the pages. He had meant to mount them but had never gotten around to it. He rarely even opened the book. The pages were yellowed and had gone to brown at the edges. They were brittle, much like the memories the photos evoked. He picked up each snapshot and examined it, at some point realizing that he had never mounted them on the pages because he liked the idea of holding each picture in his hands, feeling it.

The photographs were all taken in Vietnam. Like the picture found in Meadows's apartment, these were mostly in black and white. It was cheaper back then, getting black-and-white film developed in Saigon. Bosch was in some of the shots, but most were photos that he had taken with an old Leica his foster father had given him before he left. It was a peace gesture from the old man. He hadn't wanted Harry to go, and they had fought about it. So the camera was given. And accepted. But Bosch was not one to tell stories when he returned, and the snapshots were left spread through the pages of the scrapbook, never to be mounted, rarely to be looked at.

If there was a recurring theme of the photographs it was the smiling faces and the tunnels. In almost every shot, there were soldiers standing in defiant poses at the mouth of a hole they had probably just been in and conquered. To the outsider, the photos would appear strange, maybe fascinating. But to Bosch they were scary, like newspaper photos he had seen of people trapped in wrecked cars, waiting to be cut out by the firemen. The photos were of the smiling faces of young men who had dropped down into hell and come back to smile into the camera. Out of the blue and into the black is what they called going into a tunnel. Each one was a black echo. Nothing but death in there. But, still, they went.

Bosch turned a cracked page of the album and found Billy Meadows staring up at him. The photo had undoubtedly been taken a few minutes after the one Bosch had found at Meadows's apartment. The same group of soldiers. The same trench and tunnel. Echo Sector, Cu Chi District. But Bosch wasn't in this portrait because he had left the frame to snap the photo. His Leica had caught Meadows's vacant stare and stoned smile—his pale skin looked waxy but taut. He had captured the real Meadows, Bosch thought. He put the photo back in the page and turned to the next one. This one was of himself, no one else in the frame. He clearly remembered setting the camera down on a wooden table in a hootch and setting the timer. Then he moved into the frame. The camera had snapped as he was shirtless, the tattoo on his deeply tanned shoulder catching the falling sun through the window. Behind him, but out of focus, was the dark entrance to a tunnel lying uncovered on the straw floor of the hootch. The tunnel was blurred, forbidding darkness, like the ghastly mouth in Edvard Munch's painting *The Scream*.

It was a tunnel in the village they called Timbuk2, Bosch knew as he stared at the photo. His last tunnel. He was not smiling in the picture. His eyes were set in dark sockets. And neither was he smiling as he looked at it now. He held the photo in two hands, absentmindedly rubbing his thumbs up and down the borders. He stared at the photograph until fatigue and alcohol pulled him down into sleepy thought. Almost dreamlike. He remembered that last tunnel and he remembered Billy Meadows.

Three of them went in. Two of them came out.

The tunnel had been discovered during a routine sweep at a small village in E Sector. The village had no name on the recon maps, so the soldiers called it Timbuk2. The tunnels were turning up everywhere, so there weren't enough rats to go around. When the tunnel mouth was found under a rice basket in a hootch, the top sergeant didn't want to have to wait for a dust-off to land with fresh rats. He wanted to press on, but he knew he had to check the tunnel out. So the top made a decision like so many others in the war. He sent three of his own men in. Three virgins, scared as shit, maybe six weeks in country among them. The top told them not to go far, just set charges and come out. Do it fast, and cover each other's ass. The three green soldiers dutifully went down into the hole. Except a half-hour later, only two came out.

The two who made it out said that the three of them had separated. The tunnel branched into several directions and they split up. They were telling the top this when there was a rumble, and a huge cough of noise and smoke and dust belched from the tunnel mouth. The C-4 charges had detonated. The company loot came in then and said they wouldn't leave the zone without the missing man. The whole company waited a day for the smoke and dust to settle in the tunnel and then two tunnel rats were dropped during a dust-off—Harry Bosch and Billy Meadows. He didn't care if the missing soldier was dead, the lieutenant told them. Get him out. He wasn't going to leave one of his boys in that hole. "Go get 'im and bring 'im out here so we can get 'im a decent burial," the lieutenant said.

Meadows said, "We wouldn't leave any of our own in there, either."

Bosch and Meadows went down the hole then and found that the main entry led to a junction room where baskets of rice were stored and three other passageways began. Two of these had collapsed in the C-4 explosions. The third was still open. It was the one the missing soldier had taken. And that was the way they went.

They crawled through the darkness, Meadows in front, using their lights sparingly, until they reached a dead end. Meadows poked around the tunnel's dirt floor until he found the concealed door. He pried it open and they dropped down into another level of the labyrinth. Without saying a word, Meadows pointed one way and crawled off. Bosch knew he would go the other way. Each would be alone now, unless the VC were waiting ahead. Bosch's way was a winding passage that was as warm as a steam bath. The tunnel smelled damp and faintly like a latrine. He smelled the missing soldier before he saw him. He was dead, his body putrifying but sitting in the middle of the tunnel with his legs straight out and spread, the toes of his boots pointed upward. His body was propped against a stake planted in the floor of the tunnel. A piece of wire that cut an inch into his neck was wrapped around the stake and held him in place. Afraid of a booby trap, Bosch didn't touch him. He played the beam of his flasnlight over the neck wound and followed the trail of dried blood down the front of the body. The dead man wore a green T-shirt with his name stenciled in white on the front. Al Crofton, it said beneath the blood. There were flies mired in the crusted blood on his chest, and for a moment Bosch wondered how they found their way so far down. He dipped the light to the dead soldier's crotch and saw that it, too, was black with dried blood. The pants were torn open and Crofton looked as though he had been mauled by a wild animal. Sweat began to sting Bosch's eyes and his breathing became louder, more hurried than he wanted it to be. He was immediately aware of this but was also aware that he could do nothing to stop it. Crofton's left hand was palm up on the ground next to his thigh. Bosch put the light on it and saw the bloody set of testicles. He stifled the urge to vomit but could not prevent himself from hyperventilating.

He cupped his hands over his mouth and tried to slow his gasping for air. It didn't work. He was losing it. He was panicking. He was twenty years old and he was scared. The walls of the tunnel were closing tighter on him. He rolled away from the body and dropped the light, its beam still focused on Crofton. Bosch kicked at the clay walls of the tunnel and curled into a fetal position. The sweat in his eyes was replaced by tears. At first they came silently, but soon his sobs racked his entire body and his noise seemed to echo in all directions in the darkness, right to where Charlie sat and waited. Right to hell.

Part II
Monday, May 21

Bosch came awake in his watch chair about 4 A.M. He had left the sliding glass door open to the porch, and the Santa Ana winds were billowing the curtains, ghostlike, out across the room. The warm wind and the dream had made him sweat. Then the wind had dried the moisture on his skin like a salty shell. He stepped out onto the porch and leaned against the wood railing, looking down at the lights of the Valley. The searchlights at Universal were long since retired for the night and there was no traffic sound from the freeway down in the pass. In the distance, maybe from Glendale, he heard the whupping sound of a helicopter. He searched and found the red light moving low in the basin. It wasn't circling and there was no searchlight. It wasn't a cop. He thought then that he could smell the slight scent of malathion, sharp and bitter, on the red wind.

He went back inside and closed the sliding glass door. He thought about bed but knew there would be no more sleep this night. It was often this way with Bosch. Sleep would come early in the night but not last. Or it would not come until the arriving sun softly cut the outline of the hills in the morning fog.

He had been to the sleep disorder clinic at the VA in Sepulveda but the shrinks couldn't help him. They told him he was in a cycle. He would have extended periods of deep sleep trances into which torturous dreams invaded. This would be followed by months of insomnia, the mind reacting defensively to the terrors that awaited in sleep. Your mind has repressed the anxiety you feel over your part in the war, the doctor told him. You must assuage these feelings in your waking hours before your sleep time can progress undisturbed. But the doctor didn't understand that what was done was done. There was no going back to repair what had happened. You can't patch a wounded soul with a Band-Aid.

He showered and shaved, afterward studying his face in the mirror and remembering how unkind time had been to Billy Meadows. Bosch's hair was turning to gray but it was full and curly. Other than the circles under his eyes, his face was unlined and handsome. He wiped the remaining shaving cream off and put on his beige summer suit with a light-blue button-down oxford. On a hanger in the closet he found a maroon tie with little gladiator helmets on it that was not unreasonably wrinkled or stained. He pegged it in place with the 187 tie pin, clipped his gun to his belt and then headed out into the predawn dark. He drove into downtown for an omelet, toast and coffee at the Pantry on Figueroa. Open twenty-four hours a day since before the Depression. A sign boasted that the place had not gone one minute in that time without a customer. Bosch looked around from the counter and saw that at the moment he was personally carrying the record on his shoulders. He was alone.

The coffee and cigarettes got Bosch ready for the day. After, he took the freeway back up to Hollywood, passing a frozen sea of cars already fighting to get downtown.

Hollywood Station was on Wilcox just a couple of blocks south of the Boulevard, where most of its business came from. He parked at the curb out front because he was only staying awhile and didn't want to get caught in the back lot traffic jam at the change of watch. As he walked through the small lobby he saw a woman with a blackened eye, who was crying and filling out a report with the desk officer. But down the hall to the left the detective bureau was quiet. The night man must have been out on a call or up in the Bridal Suite, a storage room on the second floor where there were two cots, first come, first served. The detective bureau's hustle and bustle seemed to be frozen in place. No one was there, but the long tables assigned to burglary, auto, juvenile, robbery and homicide were all awash in paperwork and clutter. The detectives came and went. The paper never changed.

Bosch went to the back of the bureau to start a pot of coffee. He glanced through a rear door and down the back hallway where the lockup benches and the jail were located. Halfway down the hall to the holding tank, a young white boy with blond dreadlocks sat handcuffed to a bench. A juvie, maybe seventeen at most, Bosch figured. It was against California law to put them in a holding tank with adults. Which was like saying it might be dangerous for coyotes to be put in a pen with dobermans.

"What you looking at, fuckhead?" the boy called down the hall to Bosch.

Bosch didn't say anything. He dumped a bag of coffee into a paper filter. A uniform stuck his head out of the watch commander's office farther down the hall.

"I told you," the uniform yelled at the kid. "Once more and I'm going to go up a notch on the cuffs. Half hour and you won't feel your hands. Then how you going to wipe your ass in the john?"

"I guess I'll have to use your fuckin' face."

The uniform stepped into the hall and headed toward the kid, his hard black shoes making long, mean strides. Bosch shoved the filter bowl into the coffee machine and hit the brewing cycle switch. He walked away from the hallway door and over to the homicide table. He didn't want to see what happened with the kid. He dragged his chair away from his spot at the table and over to one of the community typewriters. The pertinent forms he needed were in slots on a rack on the wall above the machine. He rolled a blank crime scene report into the typewriter. Then he took his notebook out of his pocket and opened to the first page.

Two hours of typing and smoking and drinking bad coffee later, a bluish cloud hung near the ceiling lights over the homicide table and Bosch had completed the myriad forms that accompany a homicide investigation. He got up and made copies on the Xerox in the back hall. He noticed the dreadlock kid was gone. Then he got a new blue binder out of the office supplies closet—after finessing the door with his LAPD ID card—and hooked one set of the typed reports onto the three rings. The other set he hid in an old blue binder he kept in a file drawer and that was labeled with the name of an old unsolved case. When he was done, he reread his work. He liked the order the paperwork gave the case. On many previous cases he had made it a practice to reread the murder book each morning. It helped him draw out theories. The smell of the binder's new plastic reminded him of other cases and invigorated him. He was in the hunt again. The reports he had typed and placed in the murder book were not complete, though. On the Investigating Officer's Chronological Report he had left out several parts of his Sunday afternoon and evening. He neglected to type in the connection he had made between Meadows and the WestLand bank burglary. He also left out the visits to the pawnshop and to see Bremmer at the *Times*. There were no typed summaries of these interviews either. It was only Monday, day two. He wanted to wait until he had been to the FBI before committing any of that information to the official record. He wanted to know, exactly, what was going on first. It was a precaution he took on every case. He left the bureau before any of the other detectives had arrived for the day.

By nine Bosch had driven to Westwood and was on the seventeenth floor of the Federal Building on Wilshire Boulevard. The FBI waiting room was austere, the usual plastic-covered couches and scarred coffee table with old copies of the *FBI Bulletin* fanned across its fake wood-grain veneer. Bosch didn't bother to sit down or read. He stood before the sheer white curtains that covered the floor-to-ceiling windows and looked out at the panorama. The northern exposure offered a view that stretched from the Pacific eastward around the rim of the Santa Monica Mountains to Hollywood. The curtains served as a layer of fog over the smog. He stood with his nose almost touching the soft gauze fabric and looked down, across Wilshire, at the Veterans Administration Cemetery. Its white stones sprouted in the manicured grass like row after row of baby teeth. Near the cemetery's entrance a funeral was in progress, with a full honor guard at attention. But there wasn't much of a crowd of mourners. Farther north, at the top of a rise where there were no tombstones, Bosch could see several workers removing sod and using a backhoe to dig up a long slice of the earth. He checked their progress from time to time as he scanned the view, but he could not figure out what they were doing. The clearing was far too long and wide for a grave.

By ten-thirty the soldier's funeral was done but the cemetery workers were still toiling on the hill. And Bosch was still waiting at the curtain. A voice finally hit him from behind.

"All those graves. Such neat rows. I try never to look out the windows here."

He turned. She was tall and lithesome with brown wavy hair about to the shoulder with blond highlights. A nice tan and little makeup. She looked hard-shell and maybe a little weary for so early in the day, the way lady cops and hookers get. She wore a brown business suit and a white blouse with a chocolate-brown western bow. He detected the unsymmetrical curves of her hips beneath the jacket. She was carrying something small on the left side, maybe a Rugar, which was unusual. Bosch had always known female detectives to carry their weapons in their purses.

"That's the veterans cemetery," she said to him.

"I know."

He smiled, but not at that. It was that he had expected Special Agent E. D. Wish to be a man. No reason other than that was who most of the bureau agents assigned to the bank detail were. Women were part of the newer image of the bureau and weren't usually found in the heavy squads. It was a fraternity largely made up of dinosaurs and cast-outs, guys who couldn't or wouldn't cut

it in the bureau's hard-charging focus on white-collar, es-
pionage and drug investigations. The days of Melvin
Purvis, G-man, were just about over. Bank robbery
wasn't flashy anymore. Most bank robbers weren't professional thieves. They were hypes looking for a score
that would keep them going for a week. Of course, stealing from a bank was still a federal crime. That was the
only reason the bureau still bothered.

"Of course," she said. "You must know that. How can
I help you, Detective Bosch? I'm Agent Wish."

They shook hands, but Wish made no movement toward the door she had come through. It had closed and
the lock had snapped home. Bosch hesitated a moment
and then said, "Well, I've been waiting all morning to see
you. It's about the bank squad . . . One of your cases."

"Yes, that's what you told the receptionist. Sorry to
have kept you, but we had no appointment and I had another pressing matter. I wish you had called first."

Bosch nodded his understanding, but again there was
no movement toward inviting him in. This isn't working
right, he thought.

"Do you have any coffee back there?" he said.

"Uh . . . yes, I believe we do. But can we make this
quick? I'm really in the middle of something at the moment."

Who isn't, Bosch thought. She used a card key to open
the door and then pulled it open and held it for him. Inside, she led him down a corridor where there were plastic signs on the walls next to the doors. The bureau didn't
have the same affinity for acronyms as the police department. The signs were numbered—Group 1, Group 2 and
so on. As they went along, he tried to place her accent. It
had been slightly nasal but not like New York. Philadel-

phia, he decided, maybe New Jersey. Definitely not Southern California, never mind the tan that went with it.

"Black?" she said.

"Cream and sugar, please."

She turned and entered a room that was furnished as a small kitchen. There was a counter and cabinets, a four-cup coffeemaker, a microwave and a refrigerator. The place reminded Bosch of law offices he had been to to give depositions. Nice, neat, expensive. She handed him a styrofoam cup of black coffee and signaled for him to put in his own cream and sugar. She wasn't having any. If it was an attempt to make him uncomfortable, it worked. Bosch felt like an imposition, not someone who brought good news, a break in a big case. He followed her back into the hallway and they went through the next doorway, which was marked Group 3. It was the bank robbery-kidnap unit. The room was about the size of a convenience store. It was the first federal squad room Bosch had been in, and the comparison to his own office was depressing. The furniture here was newer than anything he had ever seen in any LAPD squad. There was actually carpet on the floor and a typewriter or computer at almost every desk. There were three rows of five desks and all of them but one were empty. A man in a gray suit sat at the first desk in the middle row, holding a phone to his ear. He didn't look up as Bosch and Wish walked in. Except for the background noise of a tactical channel coming from a scanner on a file cabinet in the back, the place could have passed for a real estate office.

Wish took a seat behind the first desk in the first row and gestured for Bosch to take the seat alongside it. This put him directly between Wish and Gray Suit on the phone. Bosch put his coffee down on her desk and began to figure right away that Gray Suit wasn't really on the phone, even though the guy kept saying "Uh huh, uh huh" or "Uh uh" every few moments or so. Wish opened a file drawer in her desk and pulled out a plastic bottle of water, some of which she poured into a paper cup.

"We had a two eleven at a savings and loan in Santa Monica, just about everybody's out on it," she explained as he scanned the almost empty room. "I was coordinating from here. That's why you had to wait out there. Sorry."

"No problem. Get him?"

"What makes you say it was a him?"

Bosch shrugged his shoulders. "Percentages."

"Well, it was two of them. One of each. And yes, we got them. They were in a stolen from Reseda reported yesterday. Female went in and took care of business. Male was the wheel. They took the 10 to the 405, then into LAX, where they left the car in front of a skycap at United. Then they took the escalator to the arrivals level, got on a shuttle bus to the Flyaway station in Van Nuys and then took a cab all the way back down to Venice. To a bank. We had an LAPD copter over them the whole time. They never looked up. When she went into the second bank we thought we were going to see another two eleven so we rushed her while she was waiting in line for a teller. Got him in the parking lot. Turns out she was just going to deposit the take from the first bank. An interbank transfer, the hard way. See some dumb people in this business, Detective Bosch. What can I do for you?"

"You can call me Harry."

"As I am doing what for you?"

"Interdepartmental cooperation," he said. "Kinda like you and our helicopter this morning."

• • •

Bosch drank some of his coffee and said, "Your name is on a BOLO I came across yesterday. Year-old case out of downtown. I'm interested in it. I work homicide out of Hollywood Div—"

"Yes, I know," Agent Wish interrupted.

"—ision."

"The receptionist showed me the card you gave. By the way, do you need it back?" That was a cheap shot. He saw his sad-looking business card on her clean green blotter. It had been in his wallet for months and its corners were curled up at the edges. It was one of the generic cards the department gave detectives who worked out in the bureaus. It had the embossed police badge on it and the Hollywood Division phone number but no name. You could buy yourself an ink pad and order a stamp and sit at your desk at the beginning of each week and stamp out a couple of dozen cards. Or you could just write your name on the line with a pen and not give out too many. Bosch had done the latter. Nothing the department could do could embarrass him anymore.

"No, you can keep it. By the way, you have one?"

In a quick, impatient motion, she opened the top middle drawer of the desk, took a card out of a little tray and put it down on the desk top next to the elbow Bosch had leaned there. He took another sip of coffee while glancing down at it. The E stood for Eleanor.

"So anyway you know who I am and where I come from," he began. "And I know a little bit about you. For instance, you investigated, or are investigating, a bank caper from last year in which the perps came in through the ground. A tunnel job. WestLand National."

He noticed her attention immediately pick up with

that, and even thought he sensed Gray Suit's breathing catch. Bosch had a line in the right water.

"Your name is on the bulletins. I am investigating a homicide I believe is related to your case and I want to know . . . basically, I want to know what you've got . . . Can we talk about suspects, possible suspects. . . . I think we might be looking for the same people. I think my guy might have been one of your perps."

Wish was quiet for a moment and played with a pencil she'd picked up off the blotter. She pushed Bosch's card around on the green square with the eraser end. Gray Suit was still acting like he was on the phone. Bosch glanced over at him and their eyes briefly connected. Bosch nodded and Gray Suit looked away. Bosch figured he was looking at the man whose comments had been in the newspaper articles. Special Agent John Rourke.

"You can do better than that, can't you, Detective Bosch?" Wish said. "I mean, you just walk in here and wave the flag of cooperation and you expect me to just open up our files."

She tapped the pencil three times on the desk and shook her head like she was disciplining a child.

"How about a name?" she said. "How about giving me some reason for the connection? We usually handle this kind of request through channels. We have liaisons that evaluate requests from other law enforcement agencies to share files and information. You know that. I think it might be best—"

Bosch pulled the FBI bulletin with the insurance photo of the bracelet out of his pocket. He unfolded it and laid it on the blotter. Then he took the pawnshop Polaroid out of the other pocket and also dropped that on the desk.

"WestLand National," he said, tapping a finger on the

bulletin. "The bracelet was pawned six weeks ago in a downtown shop. My guy pawned it. Now he's dead."

She kept her eyes on the Polaroid bracelet and Bosch saw recognition there. The case had stayed that much with her.

"The name is William Meadows. Found him in a pipe yesterday morning, up at the Mulholland Dam."

Gray Suit ended his one-sided conversation. He said, "I appreciate the information. I have to go, we're wrapping up a two eleven. Uh huh. . . . Thank you. . . . You too, good-bye now."

Bosch didn't look at him. He watched Wish. He thought he sensed that she wanted to look over at Gray Suit. Her eyes darted that way but then quickly went back to the photograph. Something wasn't right, and Bosch decided to jump back into the silence.

"Why don't we skip the bullshit, Agent Wish? As far as I can tell, you've never recovered a single stock certificate, a single coin, a single jewel, a single gold-and-jade bracelet. You've got nothing. So screw the liaison stuff. I mean, what is this? My guy pawned the bracelet; he ended up dead. Why? We have parallel investigations here, don't you think? More likely, the same investigation."

Nothing.

"My guy was either given that bracelet by your perps or he stole it from them. Or possibly, he was one of them. So, maybe the bracelet wasn't supposed to turn up yet. Nothing else has. And he goes and breaks the rules and pawns the thing. They whack him, then go to the pawnshop and steal it back. Whatever. The thing is, we are looking for the same people. And I need a direction to start in."

She remained silent still, but Bosch sensed a decision coming. This time he waited her out.

"Tell me about him," she finally said.

He told her. About the anonymous call. About the body. About the apartment that had been searched. About finding the pawn stub hidden behind the photo. And then going to the pawnshop to find the bracelet stolen. He didn't say that he had known Meadows.

"Anything else taken from the pawnshop, or just this bracelet?" she asked when he was done.

"Of course. Yes. But just as a cover for the real thing they wanted. The bracelet. Way I see it, Meadows was killed because whoever killed him wanted the bracelet. He was tortured before he was murdered because they wanted to know where it was. They got what they needed, killed him, then went and got the bracelet. Mind if I smoke?"

"Yes, I do. What could be so important about one bracelet? This bracelet is only a drop in the bucket of what was taken, of what hasn't ever turned up."

Bosch had thought of that and didn't have an answer. He said, "I don't know."

"If he was tortured as you say, why was the pawn ticket there for you to find? And why did they have to break into the pawnshop? You're suggesting that he told them where the bracelet was but didn't give up the ticket?"

Bosch had thought about this, too. He said, "I don't know. Maybe he knew they wouldn't let him live. So he only gave them half of what they needed. He kept something back. It was a clue. He left the pawn stub behind as a clue."

Bosch thought about the scenario. He had first begun

to put it together when rereading his notes and the reports he had typed. He decided it was time to play one more card.

"I knew Meadows twenty years ago."

"You knew this victim, Detective Bosch?" Her voice was louder now, accusatory. "Why didn't you say that when you first came in here? Since when does the LAPD allow its detectives to go around investigating the deaths of their friends?"

"I didn't say that. I said I knew him. Twenty years ago. And I didn't ask for the case. It was my turn in the bucket. I got the call out. It was . . ."

He didn't want to say coincidence.

"This is all very interesting," Wish said. "It is also irregular. We—I'm not sure we can help you. I think—"

"Look, when I knew him, it was with the U.S. Army, First Infantry in Vietnam. Okay? We were both there. He was what they called a tunnel rat. Do you know what that means? . . . I was one too."

Wish said nothing. She was looking down at the bracelet again. Bosch had totally forgotten about Gray Suit.

"The Vietnamese had tunnels under their villages," Bosch said. "Some were a century old. The tunnels went from hootch to hootch, village to village, jungle to jungle.

They were under some of our own camps, everywhere. And that was our job, the tunnel soldiers, to go down into those things. There was a whole other war under the ground."

Bosch realized that aside from a shrink and a circle group at the VA in Sepulveda he had never told anyone about the tunnels and what he did.

"And Meadows, he was good at it. As much as you

could like going down into that blackness with just a flashlight and a .45, well, he did. Sometimes we'd go down and it would take hours, and sometimes it would take days. And Meadows, well, he was the only one I ever knew over there that wasn't scared of going down there. It was life above ground that scared him."

She didn't say anything. Bosch looked over at Gray Suit, who was writing on a yellow tablet Bosch couldn't read. Bosch heard someone report on the tac channel that he was transporting two prisoners to the Metro lockup.

"So now twenty years later you've got a tunnel caper and I've got a dead tunnel fighter. He was found in a pipe, a tunnel. He had property from your caper." Bosch felt around in his pockets for his cigarettes, then remembered she had said no. "We have to work together on this one. Right now."

He knew by her face it hadn't worked. He emptied his coffee cup, ready for the door. He didn't look at Wish now. He heard Gray Suit pick up the phone again and punch a number out. He stared down at the residue of sugar in the bottom of his cup. He hated sugar in his coffee.

"Detective Bosch," Wish began, "I am sorry you had to wait in the hall so long this morning. I am sorry this fellow soldier you knew, Meadows, is dead. Whether it was twenty years ago or not, I am. I have sympathy for him, and you, and what you may have had to go through. . . . But I am also sorry that I can't help you at the moment. I will have to follow established protocol and talk to my supervisor. I will get back to you. As soon as possible. That is all I can do at the moment."

Bosch dropped the cup into a trash can next to her

desk and reached over to pick up the Polaroid and the bulletin page.

"Can we keep the photo here?" Agent Wish asked. "I need to show it to my supervisor."

Bosch kept the Polaroid. He got up and stepped in front of Gray Suit's desk. He held the Polaroid up to the man's face. "He's seen it," he said over his shoulder as he walked out of the office.

Deputy Chief Irvin Irving sat at his desk, brushing his teeth and working the muscles of his jaw into hard rubber balls. He was disturbed. And this clenching and gnashing of teeth was his habit when disturbed or in solitary, contemplative moods. As a result, the musculature of his jaw had become the most pronounced feature of his face. When looked at head-on, Irving's jawline was actually wider than his ears, which were pinned flat against his shaven skull and had a winglike shape to them. The ears and the jaw gave Irving an intimidating if not odd visage. He looked like a flying jaw, as though his powerful molars could crush marbles. And Irving did all he could to promote this image of himself as a fearsome junkyard dog who might sink his teeth into a shoulder or leg and tear out a piece of meat the size of a softball. It was an image that had helped overcome his one impediment as a Los Angeles policeman—his silly name—and could only aid him in his long-planned ascendancy to the chiefs office on the sixth floor. So he indulged the habit, even if it did cost him a new set of $2,000 molar implants every eighteen months.

Irving pulled his tie tight against his throat and ran his hand over his gleaming scalp. He reached to the intercom buzzer. Though he could have easily pushed the speaker button then and barked his command, he waited for his new adjutant's reply first. This was another of his habits.

"Yes, Chief?"

He loved hearing that. He smiled, then leaned forward until his great, wide jaw was inches from the intercom speaker. He was a man who did not trust that technology could do what it was supposed to do. He had to put his mouth to the speaker and shout.

"Mary, get me the jacket on Harry Bosch. It should be in the actives."

He spelled the first and last names for her.

"Right away, Chief."

Irving leaned back, smiled through clenched teeth but then thought he felt something out of alignment. He deftly ran his tongue over his left rear lower molar, searching for a defect in its smooth surface, maybe a slight fissure. Nothing. He opened the desk drawer and took out a small mirror. He opened his mouth and studied the back teeth. He put the mirror back and took out a pale blue Post-it pad and made a note to call for a dental checkup. He closed the drawer and remembered the time he had popped a fortune cookie into his mouth while dining with the city councilman from the Westside. The right rear lower molar had crumbled on the stale cookie. The junkyard dog decided to swallow the dental debris rather than expose the weakness to the councilman, whose confirmation vote he would someday need and expect. During the meal, he had brought to the councilman's attention the fact that his nephew, an LAPD motorman, was a closet homosexual. Irving mentioned that he was doing his best to protect the nephew and prevent his exposure. The department was as homophobic as a Nebraska church, and if the word leaked to the rank and file,

Irving explained to the councilman, the officer could forget any hope for advancement. He could also expect brutal harassment from the rest of L.A.'s finest. Irving didn't need to mention the consequences if a scandal broke publicly. Even on the liberal Westside, it wouldn't help a councilman's mayoral ambitions.

Irving was smiling at the memory when Officer Mary Grosso knocked and then walked into the office with a one-inch-thick file in her hand. She placed it on Irving's glass-topped desk. There was nothing else on its gleaming surface, not even a phone.

"You were right, Chief. It was still in the actives files."

The deputy chief in charge of the Internal Affairs Division leaned forward and said, "Yes, I believe I did not have it transferred to archives because I had a feeling we had not seen the last of Detective Bosch. Let me see, that would be Lewis and Clarke, I believe."

He opened the file and read the notations on the inside of the jacket.

"Yes. Mary, will you have Lewis and Clarke come in, please."

"Chief, I saw them in the squad. They were getting ready for a BOR. I'm not sure which case."

"Well, Mary, they will have to cancel the Board of Rights—and please do not talk to me in abbreviations. I am a slow-moving, careful policeman. I do not like shortcuts. I do not like abbreviations. You will learn that. Now, tell Lewis and Clarke I want them to delay the hearing and report to me forthwith."

He flexed his jaw muscles and held them, hard as tennis balls, at their full width. Grosso scurried from the office. Irving relaxed and paged through the file, reacquainting himself with Harry Bosch. He noted Bosch's military record and his fast advance through the department. From patrol to detectives to the elite Robbery-Homicide Division in eight years. Then the fall: administrative transfer last year from Robbery-Homicide to Hollywood homicide. Should have been fired, Irving lamented as he studied the entries on Bosch's career chronology.

Next, Irving scanned the evaluation report on a psychological given Bosch the year before to determine if he should be allowed to return to duty after killing an unarmed man. The department psychologist wrote:

> Through his war and police experiences, most notably including the aforementioned shooting resulting in fatality, the subject has to a high degree become desensitized to violence. He speaks in terms of violence or the aspect of violence being an accepted part of his day-to-day life, for all of his life. Therefore, it is unlikely that what transpired previously will act as a psychological deterrent should he again be placed in circumstances where he must act with deadly force in order to protect himself or others. I believe he will be able to act without delay. He will be able to pull the trigger. In fact, his conversation reveals no ill effects at all from the shooting, unless his sense of satisfaction with the outcome of the incident—the suspect's death—should be deemed inappropriate.

Irving closed the file and tapped it with a manicured nail. He then picked a strand of long brown hair—Officer Mary Grosso's, he presumed—off the glass desk top and dropped it into a wastebasket next to the desk. Harry

Bosch was a problem, he thought. A good cop, a good detective—actually, Irving grudgingly admired his homicide work, particularly his affinity for serial slayers. But in the long run, the deputy chief believed, outsiders did not work well inside the system. Harry Bosch was an outsider, always would be. Not part of the LAPD Family. And now the worst had come to Irving's attention. Bosch had not only left the family but appeared to be engaged in activities that would hurt the family, embarrass the family. Irving decided that he would have to move swiftly and surely. He swiveled in his chair and looked out the window at City Hall across Los Angeles Street. Then his gaze dropped, as it always did, to the marble fountain in front of Parker Center, the memorial to officers killed in the line of duty. There was family, he thought. There was honor. He clenched his teeth powerfully, triumphantly. Just then the door opened.

Detectives Pierce Lewis and Don Clarke strode into the office and presented themselves. Neither spoke. They could have been brothers, They shared close-cropped brown hair, the arms-splayed build of weight lifters, conservative gray silk suits. Lewis's had a thin charcoal stripe; Clarke's maroon. Each man was built wide and low to the ground for better handling. Each had a slightly forward tilt to his body, as if he were wading out to sea, crashing through breakers with his face.

"Gentlemen," said Irving, "we have a problem—a priority problem—with an officer who has come across our threshold before. An officer you two worked with some degree of success before."

Lewis and Clarke glanced at each other and Clarke allowed himself a small, quick smile. He couldn't guess who it could be, but he liked going after repeaters. They were so desperate.

"Harry Bosch," Irving said. He waited a moment to let the name sink in, then said, "You need to take a little ride up to Hollywood Division. I want to open a one point eighty-one on him right away. Complainant will be the Federal Bureau of Investigation."

"FBI?" Lewis said. "What did he do with them?"

Irving corrected him for using the abbreviation for the bureau and told them to sit down in the two chairs in front of his desk. He spent the next ten minutes recounting the telephone call he had received minutes earlier from the bureau.

"The bureau says it is too coincidental," he concluded. "I concur. He may be dirty in this, and the bureau wants him off the Meadows case. At the very least, it appears he intervened to help this suspect, his former military comrade, avoid a jail term last year, possibly so he could accomplish this bank burglary. Whether Bosch knew this, or if there was further involvement in the crime, I do not know. But we are going to find out what Detective Bosch is up to."

Irving delayed here to drive home his point with a full jaw flex. Lewis and Clarke knew better than to interrupt. Irving then said, "This opportunity opens the door for the department to do what it was unable to accomplish before with Bosch. Eliminate him. You will report directly to me. Oh, and I want Bosch's supervisor, a Lieutenant Pounds, copied with your daily reports. On the quiet. But you will do more than copy me. I want telephonic reports twice daily, morning and evening."

"We're on our way," Lewis said as he stood up.

"Aim high, gentlemen, but be careful," Irving counseled them. "Detective Harry Bosch is no longer the celebrity he once was. But, nevertheless, do not let him slip away."

Bosch's embarrassment at being unceremoniously dismissed by Agent Wish had turned to anger and frustration as he rode down the elevator. It was like a physical presence in his chest that jumped into his throat as the stainless steel cell descended. He was alone, and when the pager on his belt started to chirp, he let it go on for its allotted fifteen seconds rather than turn it off. He swallowed his anger and embarrassment and formed it into resolve. As he stepped out of the elevator car, he looked down at the phone number on the pager's digital display. An 818 area code—the Valley, but he didn't recognize the number. He stepped to a pod of pay phones in the courtyard in front of the Federal Building and dialed the number. Ninety cents, an electronic voice said. Luckily he had the loose change. He dumped it in and the call was picked up on a half ring by Jerry Edgar.

"Harry," he began without a hello, "I'm still up here at the VA and I'm getting the runaround, man. They don't have any files on Meadows. They say I have to go through D.C. or I gotta get a warrant. I tell them I know there is a file, you know, on account of what you told me. I say, 'Look, if I was to get a search warrant, can you look and make sure you know where this file is?' And so they're lookin' for a while and what they finally come out saying is, yes, they had a file but it's gone. Guess who came and got it with a court order last year?"

"The FBI."

"You know something I don't know?"

"I haven't exactly been sitting on my ass. They say when the bureau took it or why?"

"They weren't told why. FBI agent just came in with the warrant and took it. Checked it out last September and hasn't brought it back since. Didn't give a reason. The Fucking-B-I doesn't have to.'

Bosch was quiet while he thought about this. They knew all along. Wish knew about Meadows and the tunnels and everything else he had just told her. It had all been a show.

"Harry, you there?"

"Yeah, listen, did they show you a copy of the paperwork or know the name of the agent?"

"No, they couldn't find the subpoena receipt and nobody remembered the agent's name, except that she was a woman."

"Take this number where I'm at. Go back to them in records and ask for another file, just see if it's there. My file."

He gave Edgar the pay phone number, his date of birth, social security number and his full name, spelling out his real first name.

"Jesus, that's your first name?" Edgar said. "Harry for short. How'd your momma come up with that one?"

"She had a thing about fifteenth-century painters. It goes with the last name. Go check on the file, then call me back. I'll wait here."

"I can't even pronounce it, man."

"Rhymes with 'anonymous.' "

"Okay, I'll try that. Where you at, anyway?"

"A pay phone. Outside the FBI."

Bosch hung up before his partner could ask any questions. He lit a cigarette and leaned on the phone booth while watching a small group of people walking in a circle on the long green lawn in front of the building. They were holding up homemade signs and placards that protested a proposal to open new oil leases in Santa Monica Bay. He saw signs that said Just Say No to Oil and Isn't the Bay Polluted Enough? and United States of Exxon and so on.

He noticed a couple of TV news crews on the lawn filming the protest. That was the key, he thought. Exposure. As long as the media showed up and put it on the six o'clock news, the protest was a success. A sound-bite success. Bosch noticed that the group's apparent spokesman was being interviewed on camera by a woman he recognized from Channel 4. He also recognized the spokesman but he wasn't sure from where. After a few moments of watching the man's ease during the interview in front of the camera, Bosch placed him. The guy was a TV actor who used to play a drunk on a popular situation comedy that Bosch had seen once or twice. Though the guy still looked like a drunk, the show wasn't on anymore.

Bosch was on his second cigarette, leaning on the phone booth and beginning to feel the heat of the day, when he looked up at the glass doors of the building and saw Agent Eleanor Wish walking through. She was looking down and digging a hand through her purse and hadn't noticed him. Quickly and without analyzing why, he ducked behind the phones and, using them as a shield, moved around them as she walked by. It was sunglasses she had been looking for in the purse. Now she had them on as she walked past the protestors without even a glance in their direction. She headed up Veteran Avenue to Wilshire Boulevard. Bosch knew the federal garage was under the building. Wish was walking in the opposite direction. She was going somewhere nearby. The phone rang.

"Harry, they have your file, too. The FBI. What's going on?"

Edgar's voice was urgent and confused. He didn't like waves. He didn't like mysteries. He was a straight nine-to-five man.

"I don't know what's going on, they wouldn't tell me," Bosch replied. "You head into the office. We'll talk there. If you get there before me, I want you to make a call over to the subway project. Personnel. See if they had Meadows working there. Try under the name Fields, too. Then just do the paper on the TV stabbing. Like we said. Keep your end of our deal. I'll meet you there."

"Harry, you told me you knew this guy, Meadows. Maybe we should tell Ninety-eight it's a conflict, that we ought to turn the case over to RHD or somebody else on the table."

"We'll talk about it in a little while, Jed. Don't do anything or talk to anybody about it till I get there."

Bosch hung up the phone and walked off toward Wilshire. He could see Wish already had turned east toward Westwood Village. He closed the distance between them, crossed to the other side of the street and followed behind. He was careful not to get too close, so that his reflection would not be in the shop windows she was looking in as she walked. When she reached Westwood Boulevard she turned north and crossed Wilshire, coming to Bosch's side of the street. He ducked into a bank lobby. After a few moments he went back out on the sidewalk and she was gone. He looked both ways and then trotted up to the corner. He saw her a half block up Westwood, going into the village.

Wish slowed in front of some shop windows and came to a stop in front of a sporting goods store. Bosch could see female manikins in the window, dressed in lime-green running shorts and shirts. Last year's fad on sale today. Wish looked at the outfits for a few moments and then headed off, not stopping until she was in the theater district. She turned into Stratton's Bar & Grill.

Bosch, on the other side of the street, passed the restaurant without looking and went up to the next corner. He stood in front of the Bruin, below the old theater's marquee, and looked back. She hadn't come out. He wondered if there was a rear door. He looked at his watch. It was a little early for lunch but maybe she liked to beat the crowd. Maybe she liked to eat alone. He crossed the street to the other corner and stood below the canopy of the Fox Theater. He could see through the front window of Stratton's but didn't see her. He walked through the parking lot next to the restaurant and into the rear alley. He saw a public access door at the back. Had she seen him and used the restaurant to slip away? It had been a long while since he had been on a one-man tail, but he didn't think she had made him. He headed down the alley and went in the back door.

Eleanor Wish was sitting alone in the row of wooden booths along the restaurant's right wall. Like any careful cop she sat facing the front door, so she didn't see Bosch until he slid onto the bench across from her and picked up the menu she had already scanned and dropped on the table.

He said, "Never been here, anything good?"

"What is this?" she said, surprise clearly showing on her face.

"I don't know, I thought you might want some company."

"Did you follow me? You followed me."

"At least I'm being up front about it. You know, you made a mistake back at the office. You played it too cool. I walk in with the only lead you've had in nine months and you want to talk about liaisons and bullshit. Something wasn't right but I couldn't figure out what. Now I know."

"What are you talking about? Never mind, I don't want to know."

She made a move to slide out of the booth, but Bosch reached across the table and firmly put his hand on her wrist. Her skin was warm and moist from the walk over. She stopped and turned and smoked him with brown eyes so angry and hot they could have burned his name on a tombstone.

"Let go," she said, her voice tightly controlled but carrying enough of an edge to suggest she could lose it. He let go.

"Don't leave. Please." She lingered a moment and he worked quickly. He said, "It's all right. I understand the reasons for the whole thing, the cold reception back there, everything. I have to say it actually was good work, what you did. I can't hold it against you."

"Bosch, listen to me, I don't know what you are talking about. I think—"

"I know you already knew about Meadows, the tunnels, the whole thing. You pulled his military files, you pulled mine, you probably pulled files on every rat that made it out of that place alive. There had to have been something in the WestLand job that connected to the tunnels back there."

She looked at him for a long moment and was about to speak, when a waitress approached with a pad and pencil.

"For now, just one coffee, black, and an Evian. Thank you," Bosch said before Wish or the waitress could speak. The waitress walked away, writing on the pad.

"I thought you were a cream-and-sugar cop," Wish said.

"Only when people try to guess what I am."

Her eyes seemed to soften then, but only a bit.

"Detective Bosch, look, I don't know how you know what you think you know, but I am not going to discuss the WestLand case. It is exactly as I said at the bureau. I can't do it. I am sorry. I really am."

Bosch said, "I guess maybe I should resent it, but I don't. It was a logical step in the investigation. I would've done the same. You take anybody who fit the profile—tunnel rat—and sift them through the evidence."

"You're not a suspect, Bosch, okay? So drop it."

"I know I'm not a suspect." He gave a short, forced burst of laughter. "I was serving a suspension down in Mexico and can prove it. But you already know that. So for me, fine, I'll drop it. But I need what you have on Meadows. You pulled his files back in September. You must have done a workup on him. Surveillance, known associates, background. Maybe . . . I bet you even pulled him in and talked to him. I need it all now—today, not in three, four weeks when some liaison puts a stamp on it."

The waitress came back with the coffee and water. Wish pulled her glass close but didn't drink.

"Detective Bosch, you are off the case. I'm sorry. I shouldn't be the one to tell you. But you're off. You go back to your office and you'll find out. We made a call after you left."

He was holding his coffee with two hands, elbows on the table. He carefully put the cup down on the saucer, in case his hands began to shake.

"What did you do?" Bosch asked.

"I'm sorry," Eleanor Wish said. "After you left, Rourke —the guy you shoved the picture in front of?— he called the number on your card and talked to a Lieutenant Pounds. He told him about your visit today and suggested there was a conflict, you investigating a friend's death. He said some other things and—"

"What other things?"

"Look, Bosch, I know about you. I'll admit we pulled your files, we checked you out. Hell, but to do that, all we had to do was read the newspapers back then. You and that Dollmaker thing. So I know what you have been through with the internal people, and this isn't going to help, but it was Rourke's decision. He—"

"What other things did he tell?"

"He told the truth. He said both your name and Meadows's had come up in our investigation. He said you both knew each other. He asked that you be taken off the case. So all of this doesn't matter."

Bosch looked off, out of the booth.

"I want to hear you answer," he said. "Am I a suspect?"

"No. At least you weren't until you walked in this morning. Now, I don't know. I'm trying to be honest. I mean, you have to look at this from our standpoint. One guy we looked at last year comes in and says he is investigating the murder of another guy we looked very hard at. This first guy says, 'Let me see your files.' "

She didn't have to tell him as much as she had. He knew this and knew she was probably going out on a limb saying anything at all. For all the shit he had just stepped in or been put in, Harry Bosch was beginning to like cold, hard Eleanor Wish.

"If you won't tell me about Meadows, tell me one thing about myself. You said I was looked at and then dropped. How'd you clear me? You go to Mexico?"

"That and other things." She looked at him a moment before going on. "You were cleared early on. At first we got excited. I mean, we look through the files of people with tunnel experience in Vietnam and there sitting on the top was the famous Harry Bosch, detective superstar, a couple books written about his cases. TV movie, a spin-off series. And the guy the newspapers just happened to have been filled with, the guy whose star crashed with a one-month suspension and transfer from the elite Robbery-Homicide Division to . . ." She hesitated.

"The sewer." He finished it for her.

She looked down into her glass and continued.

"So, right away Rourke started figuring that maybe that's how you spent your time, digging this tunnel into the bank. From hero to heel, this was your way to get back at society, something crazy like that. But when we backgrounded you and asked around quietly, we heard you went to Mexico for the month. We sent someone down to Ensenada and checked it out. You were clear. Around then we also had gotten your medical files from the VA up at Sepulveda—oh, that's it, that's who you checked with this morning, isn't it?"

He nodded. She continued.

"Anyway, in the medical there were the psychiatrist's reports . . . I'm sorry. This seems like such an invasion."

"I want to know."

"The therapy for PTS. I mean, you are completely functional. But you have infrequent manifestation of post-traumatic stress in forms of insomnia and other things, claustrophobia. A doctor even wrote once that you wouldn't go into a tunnel like that, never again. Anyway, we put a profile of you through our behavioral sciences lab in Quantico. They discounted you as a suspect, said it was unlikely that you would cross the line for something like financial gain."

She let all of that sink in a few moments.

"Those VA files are old," Bosch said. "The whole story is old. I'm not going to sit here and present a case for why I should be a suspect. But that VA stuff is old. I haven't seen a shrink, VA or otherwise, in five years. And as far as that phobia shit goes, I went into a tunnel to look at Meadows yesterday. What do you think your shrinks in Quantico would write about that?"

He could feel his face turn red with embarrassment. He had said too much. But the more he tried to control and hide it, the more blood rushed into his face. The wide-hipped waitress chose that moment to come back and freshen his coffee.

"Ready to order?" she said.

"No," Wish said without taking her eyes off Bosch. "Not yet."

"Hon, we have a big lunch crowd come in here, and we're going to need the table for people what want to eat. I make my living off the hungry ones. Not the ones too angry to eat."

She walked away with Bosch thinking that waitresses

were probably better observers of human behavior than most cops. Wish said, "I am sorry about all of this. You should have let me get up when I first wanted to."

The embarrassment was gone but the anger was still there. He wasn't looking out of the booth anymore. He was looking right at her.

"You think you know me from some papers in a file? You don't know me. Tell me what you know."

"I don't know you. I know about you," she said. She stopped a moment to gather her thoughts. "You are an institutional man, Detective Bosch. Your whole life. Youth shelters, foster homes, the army, then the police. Never leave the system. One flawed societal institution after another."

She sipped some water and seemed to be deciding whether to go on. She did. "Hieronymus Bosch. . . . The only thing your mother gave you was the name of a painter dead five hundred years. But I imagine the stuff you've seen would make the bizarre stuff of dreams he painted look like Disneyland. Your mother was alone. She had to give you up. You grew up in foster homes, youth halls. You survived that and you survived Vietnam and you survived the police department. So far, at least. But you are an outsider in an insider's job. You made it to RHD and worked the headline cases, but you were an outsider all along. You did things your way and eventually they busted you out for it."

She emptied her glass, seemingly to give Bosch time to stop her from continuing. He didn't.

"It only took one mistake," she said. "You killed a man last year. He was a killer himself but that didn't matter. According to the reports, you thought he was reaching under a pillow on the bed for a gun. Turned out he was reaching for his toupee. Almost laughable, but IAD found a witness who said she told you beforehand that the suspect kept his hair under the pillow. Since she was a street whore, her credibility was in question. It wasn't enough to bounce you, but it cost you your position. Now you work Hollywood, the place most people in the department call the sewer."

Her voice trailed off. She was finished. Bosch didn't say anything, and there was a long period of silence. The waitress cruised by the booth but knew better than to speak to them.

"When you get back to the office," he finally began, "you tell Rourke to make one more call. He got me off the case, he can get me back on."

"I can't do it. He won't do it."

"Yes, he'll do it, and tell him he has until tomorrow morning to do it."

"Or what? What can you do? I mean, let's be honest. With your record, you'll probably be suspended by tomorrow. As soon as Pounds got off the phone with Rourke he probably called IAD, if Rourke didn't do it himself."

"Doesn't matter. Tomorrow morning I hear something, or tell Rourke he'll be reading a story in the *Times* about how an FBI suspect in a major bank heist, a subject of FBI surveillance no less, was murdered right under the bureau's nose, taking with him the answers to the celebrated WestLand tunnel caper. All the facts might not be right or in the correct order, but it will be close enough. More important than that, it will be a good read. And it'll make waves all the way to D.C. It'll be embarrassing and it'll also be a warning to whoever did Meadows. You'll never get them then. And Rourke will always be known as the guy who let them get away."

She looked at him, shaking her head as if she were above this whole mess. "It's not my call. I'll have to go back to him and let him decide what to do. But if it was me, I'd call your bluff. And I will tell you straight out that's what I'll tell him to do."

"It's no bluff. You've checked me out, you know I'll go to the media and the media will listen to me and like it. Be smart. You tell him it's no bluff. I'll have nothing to lose by doing it. He'll have nothing to lose by bringing me in."

He began to slide out of the booth. He stopped and threw a couple of dollar bills on the table.

"You've got my file. You know where you can reach me."

"Yes, we do," she said, and then, "Hey, Bosch?"

He stopped and looked back at her.

"The street whore, was she telling the truth? About the pillow?"

"Don't they all?"

Bosch parked in the lot behind the station on Wilcox and smoked right up until he reached the rear door. He killed the butt on the ground and went in, leaving behind the odor of vomit that wafted from the mesh windows at the rear of the station holding tank. Jerry Edgar was pacing in the back hall waiting for him.

"Harry, we've got a forthwith from Ninety-eight."

"Yeah, what about?"

"I don't know, but he's been coming out of the glass box every ten minutes looking for you. You got your beeper and the Motorola turned off. And I saw a couple of the IAD silks up from downtown go in there with him a while ago."

Bosch nodded without saying anything comforting to his partner.

"What's going on?" Edgar blurted. "If we've got a story, let's get it straight before we go in there. You've had experience with this shit, not me."

"I'm not sure what's going on. I think they're kicking us off the case. Me, at least." He was very nonchalant about the whole thing.

"Harry, they don't bring IAD in to do that. Something's on, and, man, I hope whatever you did, you didn't fuck me up, too."

Edgar immediately looked embarrassed.

"Sorry, Harry, I didn't mean it that way."

"Relax. Let's go see what the man wants."

Bosch headed toward the detective squad room. Edgar said he'd cut through the watch office and then come in from the front hall so it wouldn't look like they had collaborated on a story. When Bosch got to his desk, the first thing he noticed was that the blue murder book on the Meadows case was gone. But he also noticed that whoever had taken it had missed the cassette tape with the 911 call on it. Bosch picked up the cassette and put it in his coat pocket just as Ninety-eight's voice boomed out of the glass office at the head of the squad room. He yelled just one word: "Bosch!" The other detectives in the squad room looked around. Bosch got up and slowly walked toward the glass box, as the office of Lieutenant Harvey "Ninety-eight" Pounds was called. Through the windows he could see the backs of two suits sitting in there with Pounds. Bosch recognized them as the two

IAD detectives who had handled the Dollmaker case. Lewis and Clarke.

Edgar came into the squad through the front hallway just as Bosch passed and they walked into the glass box together. Pounds sat dull-eyed behind his desk. The men from Internal Affairs did not move.

"First thing, no smoking, Bosch, you got that?" Pounds said. "In fact, the whole squad stunk like an ash-tray this morning. I'm not even going to ask if it was you."

Department and city policy outlawed smoking in all community-shared offices such as squad rooms. It was okay to smoke in a private office if it was your office or if the office's occupant allowed visitors to smoke. Pounds was a reformed smoker and militant about it. Most of the thirty-two detectives he commanded smoked like junkies. When Ninety-eight wasn't around, many of them would go into his office for a quick fix, rather than have to go out to the parking lot, where they'd miss phone calls and where the smell of piss and puke migrated from the rear windows of the drunk tank. Pounds had taken to locking his office door, even on quick trips up the hall to the station commander's office, but anybody with a letter opener could pop the door in three seconds. The lieutenant was constantly returning and finding his office space fouled by smoke. He had two fans in the ten-by-ten room and a can of Glade on the desk. Since the frequency of the fouling had increased with the reassignment of Bosch from Parker Center to Hollywood detectives, Ninety-eight Pounds was convinced Bosch was the major offender. And he was right, but he had never caught Bosch in the act.

"Is that what this is about?" Bosch asked. "Smoking in the office?"

"Just sit down," Pounds snapped.

Bosch held his hands up to show there were no cigarettes between his fingers. Then he turned to the two men from Internal Affairs.

"Well, Jed, it looks like we might be off on a Lewis and Clarke expedition here. I haven't seen the great explorers on the move since they sent me on a no-expense-paid vacation to Mexico. Did some of their finest work on that one. Headlines, sound bites, the whole thing. The stars of Internal Affairs."

The two IAD cops' faces immediately reddened with anger.

"This time, you might do yourself a favor and keep your smart mouth shut," Clarke said. "You're in serious trouble, Bosch. You get it?"

"Yeah, I get it. Thanks for the tip. I got one for you, too. Go back to the leisure suit you used to wear before you became Irving's bendover. You know, the yellow thing that matched your teeth. The polyester does more for you than the silk. In fact, one of the guys out there in the bullpen mentioned that the ass end of that suit is getting shiny, all the work you do riding a desk."

"All right, all right," Pounds cut in. "Bosch, Edgar, sit down and shut up for a minute. This—"

"Lieutenant, I didn't say one thing," Edgar began. "I—"

"Shut up! Everybody! Shut up a minute," Pounds barked. "Jesus Christ! Edgar, for the record, these two are from Internal Affairs, if you didn't already know, Detectives Lewis and Clarke. What this is—"

"I want a lawyer," Bosch said.

"Me too, I guess," added Edgar.

"Oh, bullshit," Pounds said. "We are going to talk about this and get some things straight, and we aren't bringing any Police Protective League bullshit into it. If you want a lawyer, you get one later. Right now you are going to sit here, the both of you, and answer some questions. If not, Edgar, you are going to be bounced out of that eight-hundred-dollar suit and back into uniform, and Bosch, shit, Bosch, you'll probably go down for the count this time."

For a few moments there was silence in the small room, even though the tension among the five men threatened to shatter the windows. Pounds looked out at the squad room and saw about a dozen detectives acting as if they were working but who were actually trying to pick up whatever they could through the glass. Some had been attempting to read the lieutenant's lips. He got up and lowered a set of venetian blinds over the windows. He rarely did this. It was a signal to the squad that this was big. Even Edgar showed his concern, audibly exhaling. Pounds sat back down. He tapped a long fingernail on the blue plastic binder that lay closed on his desk.

"Okay, now let's get down to it," he began. "You two guys are off the Meadows case. That's number one. No questions, you're done. Now, from the top, you are going to tell us anything and everything."

At that, Lewis snapped open a briefcase and pulled out a cassette tape recorder. He turned it on and put it on Pounds's spotless desk.

Bosch had been partnered with Edgar only eight months. He didn't know him well enough to know how he would take this kind of bullying, or how far he could hold out against these bastards. But he did know him well enough to know he liked him and didn't want him to get jammed up. His only sin in this whole thing was that he had wanted Sunday afternoon off to sell houses.

"This is bullshit," Bosch said, pointing to the recorder.

"Turn that off," Pounds said to Lewis, pointing to the recorder, which was actually closer to him than to Lewis. The Internal Affairs detective stood up and picked up the recorder; He turned it off, hit the rewind button and replaced it on the desk.

After Lewis sat back down Pounds said, "Jesus Christ, Bosch, the FBI calls me today and tells me they've got you as a possible suspect in a goddam bank heist. They say this Meadows was a suspect in the same job, and by virtue of that you should now be considered a suspect in the Meadows kill. You think we aren't going to ask questions about that?"

Edgar was exhaling louder now. He was hearing this for the first time.

"Keep the tape off and we'll talk," Bosch said. Pounds contemplated that for a moment and said, "For now, no tape. Tell us."

"First off, Edgar doesn't know shit about this. We made a deal yesterday. I take the Meadows case and he goes home. He does the wrap-up on Spivey, the TV stabbed the night before. This FBI stuff, the bank job, he doesn't know for shit. Let him go."

Pounds seemed to make a point of not looking at Lewis or Clarke or Edgar. He'd make this decision on his own. It produced a slight glimmer of respect in Bosch, like a candle set out in the eye of a hurricane of incompetence. Pounds opened his desk drawer and pulled out an old wooden ruler. He fiddled with it with both hands. He finally looked at Edgar.

"That right, what Bosch says?"

Edgar nodded.

"You know it makes him look bad, like he was trying to keep the case for himself, conceal the connections from you?"

"He told me he knew Meadows. He was up front all the way. It was a Sunday. We weren't going to get anybody to come out and take it off us on account of him knowing the guy twenty years ago. Besides, most of the people who end up dead in Hollywood the police have known one way or the other. This stuff about the bank and all, he must've found out after I left. I'm finding it all out sitting here."

"Okay," Pounds said. "You got any of the paper on this one?"

Edgar shook his head.

"Okay, finish up what you've got on the—what did you call it?—Spivey, yeah, the Spivey case. I'm assigning you a new partner. I don't know who, but I'll let you know. Okay, go on, that's all."

Edgar let out one more audible breath and stood up.

Harvey "Ninety-eight" Pounds let things settle in the room for a few moments after Edgar left. Bosch wanted a cigarette badly, even to just hold one unlit in his mouth. But he wouldn't show them such a weakness.

"Okay, Bosch," Pounds said. "Anything you want to tell us about all this?"

"Yeah. It's bullshit."

Clarke smirked. Bosch paid no mind. But Pounds gave the IAD detective a withering look that further increased his stock of respect with Bosch.

"The FBI told me today I was no suspect," Bosch said.

"They looked at me nine months ago because they looked at anybody around here who'd worked the tunnels in Vietnam. They found some connection to the tunnels back there. Simple as that. It was good work, they had to check out everybody, So they looked at me and went on. Hell, I was in Mexico—thanks to these two goons—when the bank thing went down. The FBI just—"

"Supposedly," Clarke said.

"Shove it, Clarke. You're just angling for a way to take your own vacation down there, at taxpayers' expense, checking it out. You can check with the bureau and save the money."

Bosch then turned back to Pounds and adjusted his chair so his back was to the IAD detectives. He spoke in a low voice to make it clear he was talking to Pounds, not them. "The bureau wants me off it because, one, I threw a curve at 'em when I showed up there today to ask about the bank caper. I mean, I was a name from the past, and they panicked and called you. And two, they want me off the case because they probably fucked it up when they let Meadows skate last year. They blew their one chance at him and don't want an outside department to come in and see that or to break the thing they couldn't break for nine months."

"No, Bosch, that's what's bullshit," Pounds said. "This morning I received a formal request from the assistant special agent in charge who runs their bank squad, a guy named—"

"Rourke."

"You know him. Well, he asked that—"

"I be removed from the Meadows case forthwith. He says I knew Meadows, who just happened to be the prime suspect in the bank job. He ends up dead and I'm on the case. Coincidence? Rourke thinks not. I'm not sure myself."

"That's what he said. So that's where we start. Tell us about Meadows, how you knew him, when you knew him, don't leave one thing out."

Bosch spent the next hour telling Pounds about Meadows, the tunnels, the time Meadows called after almost twenty years and how Bosch got him into VA Outreach in Sepulveda without ever seeing him. Just phone calls. At no time did Bosch address the IAD detectives or acknowledge that they were even in the room.

"I didn't make it a secret that I knew him," he said at the end. "I told Edgar. I walked right in and told the FBI. You think I would have done that if I was the one who did Meadows? Not even Lewis and Clarke are that dumb."

"Well, then, Jesus Christ, Bosch, why didn't you tell me?" Pounds boomed. "Why isn't it in the reports in this book? Why do I have to hear it from the FBI? Why does Internal Affairs have to hear it from the FBI?"

So Pounds hadn't made the call to IAD. Rourke had. Bosch wondered if Eleanor Wish had known that and had lied, or if Rourke called out the goons on his own. He hardly knew the woman—he didn't know the woman—but he found himself hoping she hadn't lied to him.

"I only started the reports this morning," Bosch said. "I was going to bring them up to date after seeing the FBI. Obviously, I didn't get the chance."

"Well, I'm saving you the time," Pounds said. "It's been turned over to the FBI."

"What has? The FBI has no jurisdiction over this. This is a murder case."

"Rourke said they believe the slaying is directly related to their ongoing investigation of the bank job. They will include this in their investigation. We will assign our own case officer through an interdepartmental liaison. If and when the time comes to charge someone in the murder, the appointed officer will take it to the DA for state charges."

"Christ, Pounds, there is something going on. Don't you see that?"

Pounds put the ruler back in the drawer and closed it.

"Yes, something is going on. But I don't see it your way," he said. "That's it, Bosch. That's an order. You are off. These two men want to talk to you and you are on a desk till Internal Affairs is finished with its investigation."

He was quiet a moment before beginning again in a solemn tone. A man unhappy with what be had to say.

"You know, you were sent out here to me last year and I could have put you anywhere. I could have put you on the goddam burglary table, handling fifty reports a week, just buried you in paper. But I didn't. I recognized your skills and put you on homicide, what I thought you wanted. They told me last year that you're good but you don't stay in the lines. Now I see they were right. How this will hurt me, I don't know. But I'm not worrying about what's best for you anymore. Now, you can either talk to these guys or not. I don't really care. But that's it. We're done, you and me. If somehow you ride this one out, you better see about getting a transfer, because you won't be on my homicide table anymore."

Pounds picked up the blue binder off his desk and stood up. As he headed out of the office he said, "I have to get somebody to take this over to the bureau. You men can have the office as long as you need it."

He closed the door and was gone. Bosch thought about

it and decided he really couldn't fault Pounds for what he had said, or done. He took out a cigarette and lit it.

"Hey, no smoking, you heard the man," Lewis said.

"Fuck off," Bosch said.

"Bosch, you're dead," Clarke said. "We're going to toast your ass right this time. You aren't the hero you once were. No PR problems this time. Nobody's going to give a shit about what happens to you."

Then he stood up and turned the tape recorder back on. He recited the date, the names of the three men present and the Internal Affairs case number assigned to the investigation. Bosch realized the number was about seven hundred higher than the case number from the internal investigation nine months earlier that sent him to Hollywood. Nine months, and seven hundred other cops have been through the bullshit wringer, he thought. One day there will be no one left to do what it says on the side of every patrol car, to serve and protect.

"Detective Bosch"—Lewis took over then in a modulated, calm tone—"we would like to ask you questions regarding the investigation of the death of William Mcadows. Will you tell us of any past association with or knowledge you had of the decedent."

"I refuse to answer any questions without an attorney present," Bosch said. "I cite my right to representation under California's Policeman's Bill of Rights."

"Detective Bosch, the department administration does not recognize that aspect of the Policeman's Bill of Rights. You are commanded to answer these questions, and if you do not you will be subject to suspension and possible dismissal. You—"

"Can you loosen these handcuffs, please?" Bosch said.

"What?" Lewis cried out, losing his calm, confident tone.

Clarke stood up and went to the tape recorder and bent over it.

"Detective Bosch is not handcuffed and there are two witnesses here who can attest to that fact," he said.

"Just the two that cuffed me," Bosch said. "And beat me. This is a direct violation of my civil rights. I request that a union rep and my attorney be present before we continue."

Clarke rewound the tape and turned the recorder off. His face was almost purple with anger as he carried it back to his partner's briefcase. It was a few moments before words came to either one of them.

Clarke said, "It's going to be a pleasure to do you, Bosch. We'll have the suspension papers on the chief's desk by the end of the day. You'll be assigned to a desk at Internal Affairs where we can keep an eye on you. We'll start with CUBO and work our way up from there, maybe even to murder. Either way, you're done in the department. You're over."

Bosch stood up and so did the two IAD detectives. Bosch took a last drag on his cigarette, dropped it on the floor in front of Clarke and stepped on it, grinding it into the polished linoleum. He knew they would clean it up rather than let Pounds know they had not controlled the interview or the interviewee. He stepped between them then, exhaled the smoke and walked out of the room without saying a word. Outside, he heard Clarke's barely controlled voice call out.

"You stay away from the case, Bosch!"

• • •

Avoiding the eyes that followed him, Bosch walked through the squad room and dropped into his seat at the homicide table. He looked across at Edgar, who was seated at his own space.

"You did good," Bosch said. "You should come out all right."

"What about you?"

"I'm off the case and those two assholes are going to put paper in on me. I've got the afternoon and that's about it before I get the ROD."

"God damn."

The deputy chief in charge of IAD had to sign off on all Relieved of Duty orders and temporary suspensions. Stiffer penalties had to be recommended to a police commission subcommittee for approval. Lewis and Clarke would go for a temporary ROD, for conduct unbecoming an officer, or CUBO, as it was known. Then they'd work on something stiffer to take to the commission. If the deputy chief signed an ROD on Bosch, he would have to be notified according to union regs. That meant in person or in a tape-recorded phone conversation. Once notification was made, Bosch could be assigned to a desk at IAD in Parker Center or to his home until the conclusion of the investigation. But as they had just promised, Lewis and Clarke would go for assignment to IAD. That way they could put him on display like a trophy.

"You need anything from me on Spivey?" he asked Edgar.

"No. I'm set. I'm gonna start typing it up if I can get a machine."

"Did you happen to check like I asked on Meadows's job on the subway project?"

"Harry, you . . ." Edgar must have thought better of

saying what he wanted to say. "Yeah, I checked it out. For what it's worth, they said they haven't had anyone named Meadows on the job. There is a Fields, but he's black and he was at work today. And Meadows probably wasn't working under any other name because they aren't running a midnight shift. The project is ahead of schedule, if you can believe that shit." Edgar then called out, "I got dibs on the Selectric."

"No way," called back an autos detective named Minkly. "I'm on deck with that one."

Edgar started looking around for another candidate. Late in the day, the typewriters in the office were like gold. There were a dozen machines for thirty-two detectives: that was if you included the manual jobs and the electrics with nervous tics like moving borders or jumpy space bars.

"Okay then," Edgar called out. "I got dibs after you, Mink." Then Edgar lowered his voice and turned to Bosch. "Who you think he'll put me with?"

"Pounds? I don't know." It was like guessing who your wife would marry after you punched the time clock for the last time. Bosch wasn't all that interested in speculating who would be partnered with Edgar. He said, "Listen, I have to do some things."

"Sure, Harry. You need any help, anything from me?" Bosch shook his head and picked up the phone. He called his lawyer and left a message. It usually took three messages before the guy would call back, and Bosch made a note to call again. Then he turned his Rolodex, got a number and called the U.S. Armed Services Records Archive in St. Louis. He asked for a law enforcement clerk and got a woman named Jessie St. John. He put in a priority request for copies of all of Billy Meadows's military records. Three days, St. John said. He hung up thinking that he would never see the records. They'd come but he wouldn't be in this office, at this table, on this case. Next he called Donovan at SID and learned there had been no latent prints on the needle kit found in Meadows's shirt pocket and only smears on the can of spray paint. The light-brown crystals found in the straining cotton in the kit came back as 55 percent pure heroin, Asian blend. Bosch knew that most heroin dealt on the street and shot into the vein was about 15 percent pure. Most of it was tar heroin made by Mexicans. Somebody had given Meadows a very hot shot. In Harry's mind, that made the tox tests he was waiting for a formality. Meadows had been murdered.

Nothing else from the crime scene was of much use, except Donovan mentioned that the freshly burned match found in the pipe was not torn from the matchbook in Meadows's kit. Bosch gave Donovan the address of Meadows's apartment and asked him to send a team out to process it. He said to check the matches in an ashtray on the coffee table against the book in the kit. Then he hung up, wondering if Donovan would send somebody before word spread that Bosch was off the case or suspended.

The last call he made was to the coroner's office. Sakai said he had made next-of-kin notification. Meadows's mother was still alive and was reached in New Iberia, Louisiana. She had no money to send for him or bury him. She hadn't seen him in eighteen years. Billy Meadows would not be going home. L.A. County would have to bury him.

"What about the VA?" Bosch asked. "He was a veteran."

"Right. I'll check it out," Sakai said and hung up.

Bosch got up and took a small portable tape recorder from one of his drawers in the file cabinets. The bank of files ran along the wall behind the homicide table. He slipped the recorder into his coat pocket with the 911 tape and walked out of the squad room through the rear hallway. He went past the lockup benches and the jail, down to the CRASH office. The tiny office was more crowded than the detective bureau. Desks and files for five men and a woman were crammed into a room no bigger than a second bedroom in a Venice apartment. Down one wall of the room was a row of four-drawer file cabinets. On the opposite wall was the computer and teletype. In between were three sets of two desks pushed side by side. The back wall had the usual map of the city with black lines detailing the eighteen police divisions. Above the map were the Top 10: color eight-by-tens of the ten top assholes of the moment in Hollywood Division. Bosch noticed one was a morgue shot. The kid was dead but still made the list. Now that's an asshole, he thought. And above the photos, black plastic letters spelled out Community Resources Against Street Hoodlums.

Only Thelia King was in, sitting in front of the computer. That was what Bosch wanted. Also known as The King, which she hated, and Elvis, which she didn't mind, Thelia King was the CRASH computer jockey. If you wanted to trace a gang lineage or were just looking for a juvie floating somewhere around Hollywood, Elvis was the one to see. But Bosch was surprised she was alone. He looked at his watch. Just after two, too early for the gang troops to be on the street.

"Where's everybody at?"

"Hey, Bosch," she said, looking away from the screen.

"Funerals. We got two different gangs, and I mean warring tribes, planting homeboys in the same cemetery today up in the Valley. They got all hands up there to make sure things stay cool."

"And so why aren't you out there with the boys?"

"Just got back from court. So, before you tell me why you are here, Harry, why don't you tell me what happened in Ninety-eight Pounds's office today?"

Bosch smiled. Word traveled faster through a police station than it did on the street. He gave her an abbreviated account of his time in the barrel and the expected battle with IAD.

"Bosch, you take things too seriously," she said. "Why don't you get yourself an outside gig? Something to keep yourself sane, moving in the flow. Like your partner. Too bad that sucker's married. He's making three times selling houses on the side what we make bustin' heads fulltime. I need a gig like that."

Bosch nodded. But too much going with the flow is heading us into the sewer, he thought but didn't say. Sometimes he believed that he took things just right and everybody else didn't take them seriously enough. That was the problem. Everybody had an outside gig.

"What do you need?" she said. "I better do it now before they put your paper through. After that, you'll be a leper 'round here."

"Stay where you are," he said, and then he pulled over a chair and told her what he needed from the computer.

The CRASH computer had a program called GRIT, an acronym within an acronym, this one for Gang-Related Information Tracking. The program files contained the vitals on the 55,000 identified gang members and juvenile offenders in the city. The computer also tied in with the gang computer at the sheriff's department, which had about 30,000 of its own gangbangers on file. One part of the GRIT program was the moniker file. This stored references to offenders by their street names and could match them with real names, DOBs, addresses, and so on. All monikers that came to police attention through arrests or shake cards—field interrogation reports—were fed into the computer program. It was said the GRIT file had more than 90,000 monikers in it. You just needed to know which keys to push. And Elvis did.

Bosch gave her the three letters he had. "I don't know if that's the whole thing or a partial," he said. "I think it's a partial."

She typed in the commands to open the GRIT files, put in the letters S-H-A and hit the prompt key. It took about thirteen seconds. A frown creased Thelia King's ebony face. "Three hundred forty-three hits," she announced. "You might be hidin' out here a while, Hon."

He told her to eliminate the blacks and Latinos. The 911 tape sounded white to him. She pressed more keys, then the computer screen's amber letters recomposed the list.

"That's better, nineteen hits," King said.

There was no moniker that was just the three letters, Sha. There were five Shadows, four Shahs, two Sharkeys, two Sharkies and one each of Shark, Shabby, Shallow, Shank, Shabot and Shame. Bosch thought quickly about the graffito he had seen on the pipe up at the dam. The jagged S, almost like a gaping mouth. The mouth of a shark?

"Pull up the variations on Shark," he said.

King hit a couple of keys and the top third of the screen filled with new amber letters. Shark was a Valley boy. Limited contact with police; he had gotten probation and graffiti clean-up after he was caught tagging bus benches along Ventura Boulevard in Tarzana. He was fifteen. It wasn't likely he would have been up at the dam at three o'clock on a Sunday morning, Bosch guessed. King pulled the first Sharkie up on the screen. He was currently in a Malibu fire camp for juvenile offenders. The second Sharkie was dead, killed in a gang war between the KGB—Kids Gone Bad—and the Vineland Boyz in 1989. His name had not yet been purged from the computer records.

When King called up the first Sharkey the screen filled with information and a blinking word at the bottom said "More." "Here's a regular troublemaker," she said. The computer report described Edward Niese, a male white, seventeen years of age, known to ride a yellow motorbike, tag number JVN138, and who had no known gang affiliation but used Sharkey as a graffiti tag. A frequent runaway from his mother's home in Chatsworth. Two screens of police contacts with Sharkey followed. Bosch could tell by the location of each arrest or questioning that this Sharkey was partial to Hollywood and West Hollywood when he ran away. He scanned to the bottom of the second screen, where he saw a loitering arrest three months earlier at the Hollywood reservoir.

"This is him," he said. "Forget the last kid. Hard copy?"

She pushed keys to print the computer file and then pointed to the wall of file cabinets. He went over and opened the N drawer. He found a file on Edward Niese and pulled it. Inside was a color booking photo. Sharkey was blond and seemed small in the picture. He had the look of hurt and defiance that was as common as acne on teenagers' faces these days. But Bosch was struck by a familiarity about the face. He couldn't place it. He turned the photo over. It was dated two years earlier. King handed him the computer printout and he sat down at one of the empty desks to study it and the contents of the file.

The most serious offenses the boy who called himself Sharkey had committed—and been caught at—were shoplifting, vandalism, loitering and possession of marijuana and speed. He had been held once—twenty days—at Sylmar Juvenile Hall after one of the drug arrests but later released on home probation. All the other times he was popped he was immediately released to his mother. He was a chronic runaway from home and a throwaway from the system.

There was not much more in the file than was on the computer. A little elaboration on the arrests was all. Bosch shuffled through the papers until he found the report on the loitering charge. It went to pretrial intervention and was dismissed when Sharkey agreed to go home to his mother and stay there. That apparently didn't last long. There was a report that the mother had reported him missing to his probation officer two weeks later. According to these records, he had not been picked up yet.

Bosch read the investigating officer's summary on the loitering arrest. It said:

I/O interviewed Donald Smiley, a caretaker at the Mulholland Dam, who said at 7 A.M. this date he went into the pipe situated alongside the reservoir access road to clear it of debris. Smiley found the boy asleep on a bed made of newspapers. The boy was dirty and incoherent when roused. Subject appeared to be under the influence of narcotics. Police were called and I/O responded. The arrestee stated to I/O that he had been sleeping there regularly because his mother did not want him at home. I/O determined the subject was a reported runaway and took him into custody this date, suspicion of loitering.

Sharkey was a creature of habit, Bosch thought. He was arrested at the dam two months ago, but had gone back there to sleep Sunday morning. He looked through the rest of the papers in the file for indications of other habits that would help Bosch find him. From a three-by-five shake card, Bosch learned that Sharkey had been stopped and questioned but not arrested on Santa Monica Boulevard near West Hollywood in January. Sharkey was lacing up new Reeboks and the officer, believing he might have just lifted them, asked Sharkey to produce a receipt. He did and that would have been that. But when the boy pulled the receipt out of a leather pouch on his motorbike, the officer noticed a plastic bag in there and asked to see that as well. The bag contained ten photographs of Sharkey. He was naked in each and stood in different poses, fondling himself in some, his penis erect in others. The officer took the photos and destroyed them, but noted on the shake card that he would alert the sheriff's station in West Hollywood that Sharkey was hustling photos to homosexuals on Santa Monica Boulevard.

That was it. Bosch closed the file but kept the photo of Sharkey. He thanked Thelia King and left the small office. He was walking through the station's rear hallway, past the lockup benches, when he placed the familiarity in the photo. The hair was longer now and in dreadlocks, the defiance crowding out the hurt in the face, but

Sharkey had been the kid who was cuffed to the juvie bench early that morning. Bosch felt sure of it. Thelia had missed it on the computer search because the arrest had not yet been logged in. Bosch cut into the watch commander's office, told the lieutenant what he was looking for and was led to a box labeled A.M. Watch. Bosch looked through the reports stacked in the box until he found the paperwork on Edward Niese.

Sharkey had been picked up at 4 A.M. loitering near a newsstand on Vine. A patrol officer thought he was hustling. After he grabbed him he ran a computer check and learned he was a runaway. Bosch checked the day's arrest sheet and learned the kid had been held until 9 A.M., when his probation officer came and got him. Bosch called the PO at Sylmar Juvenile Hall but learned that Sharkey had already been arraigned before a juvenile court referee and was released to the custody of his mother.

"And that's his biggest problem," the PO said. "He'll be gone by tonight, back on the street. I guarantee it. And I told the ref that, but he wasn't going to book the kid into the monkey house just 'cause he was caught loitering and his mother happens to be a telephone whore."

"A what?" Bosch asked.

"It should be in the file. Yeah, while Sharkey's on the street, dear old mom is at home telling guys on the phone how she's gonna piss in their mouths and put rubber bands on their dicks. Advertises in skin mags. She gets forty bucks for fifteen minutes. Takes MasterCard, Visa, puts 'em on hold while she checks on another line to make sure the number is valid and they got credit. Anyway, she's been doing it, near as I can tell, five years now. Edward's formative years were listening to this shit. I mean, no wonder the kid's a scammer and runner. What do you expect?"

"How long ago did he leave with her?"

"'Bout noon. You want to catch him there, you better go. You got the address?"

"Yeah."

"And Bosch, one thing: Don't be expecting no whore when you get there. His mom, she doesn't look like the part she plays on the phone, if you know what I mean. Her voice might do the job but her looks would scare a blind man."

Bosch thanked him for the warning and hung up. He took the 101 out to the Valley and then the 405 north to the 118 and west. He got off in Chatsworth and drove into the rocky bluffs at the top corner of the Valley. There was a condominium community built on what he knew was once a movie ranch. It had been one of the places Charlie Manson and his crew used to hide out. Parts of one member of that crew's body were supposedly still missing and buried around there someplace. It was near dusk when Bosch got there. People were off work and getting home. A lot of traffic on the development's thin roads. A lot of closing doors. A lot of calls to Sharkey's mother. Bosch was too late.

"I have no time to talk to more police," Veronica Niese said when she answered the door and looked at the badge. "As soon as I get him home he is out the door again. I don't know where he goes. You tell me. That's your job. I have three calls waiting, one long distance. I gotta go."

She was in her late forties, fat and wrinkled. She obviously wore a wig and the dilation of her eyes did not match. She had the dirty-socks smell of a speed addict.

Her callers were better off with their fantasies, with just a voice with which to construct a body and face.

"Mrs. Niese, I'm not looking for your son for something he did. I need to talk to him because of something he saw. He could possibly be in danger."

"Oh, bullshit. I've heard that line before."

She closed the door and he just stood there. After a few moments he could hear her on the phone, and he thought it was a French accent but couldn't be sure. He could only make out a few of the sentences but they made him blush. He thought about Sharkey and realized he wasn't really a runaway, because there was nothing here to run away from. He left the doorstep and went back to the car. That would be it for the day. And he was out of time. Lewis and Clarke must have paper out on him by now. He'd be assigned to a desk at IAD by morning. He drove back to the station and signed out. Everyone was already gone and there were no messages on his desk, not even from his lawyer. On the way home he stopped by the Lucky and bought four bottles of beer, a couple from Mexico, a lager from England called Old Nick and a Henry's.

He expected to find a message from Lewis and Clarke on his phone tape when he got home. He wasn't wrong, but the message was not what he expected.

"I know you're there, so listen," said a voice Bosch recognized as Clarke's. "They can change their mind but they can't change ours. We'll see you around."

There were no other messages. He played Clarke's message over three times. Something had gone wrong for them. They must have been called off. Could his lame threat to the FBI to go to the media have worked? Even as he thought the question, he doubted the answer was yes.

So then, what happened? He sat down in the watch chair and began drinking the beers, the Mexicans first, and looking through the war scrapbook he had forgotten to put away. When he had opened it Sunday night he had opened a dark memory. He now found himself entranced by it, the distance of time having faded the threat as well as the photos. Sometime after dark the phone rang and Harry picked it up before the tape machine.

"Well," said Lieutenant Harvey Pounds, "the FBI now thinks they might have been too harsh. They've reassessed and want you back in. You are to aid their investigation in any way they request. That comes down from administration, Parker Center."

Pounds's voice betrayed his astonishment at the reversal.

"What about IAD?" Bosch asked.

"Nothing filed on you. Like I said, the FBI is backing away, so is IAD. For now."

"So I am back in."

"You're back in. Not my choice. Just so you know, they went over me, because I told them to blow it out their collective asses. Something about this stinks, but I guess that will have to wait for later. For now, you are on detached assignment. You are working with them until further notice."

"What about Edgar?"

"Don't worry about Edgar. He's not your concern anymore."

"Pounds, you act like you did me a favor putting me on the homicide table when they kicked me out from Parker Center. I did you the favor, man. So if you're looking for apologies from me, you aren't getting any."

"Bosch, I'm not looking for anything from you. You

fucked yourself. Only problem with that is that you may have fucked me in the process. If it was up to me, you wouldn't be near this case. You'd be checking pawnshop lists."

"But it isn't up to you, is it?"

He hung up before Pounds could reply. He stood there thinking for a few moments and his hand was still on the phone when it rang again.

"Rough day, right?" Eleanor Wish said.

"I thought it was somebody else."

"Well, I guess you've heard."

"I heard."

"You'll be working with me."

"How come you called off the dogs?"

"Simple, we want to keep the investigation out of the papers."

"There's more to it."

She didn't say anything but she didn't hang up. Finally, he thought of something to say.

"Tomorrow, what do I do?"

"Come see me in the morning. We'll go from there."

Bosch hung up. He thought about her, and about how he didn't know what was going on. He didn't like it, but he couldn't walk away now. He went into the kitchen and took the bottle of Old Nick from the refrigerator.

Lewis stood with his back to the passing traffic, using his wide body to block the sound from intruding into the pay phone.

"He starts with the FBI—er, the bureau, tomorrow morning," Lewis said. "What do you want us to do?"

Irving didn't answer at first. Lewis envisioned him on the other end of the line, jaw worked into a clench. Popeye face, Lewis thought and smirked. Clarke walked over from the car then and whispered, "What's so funny? What did he say?"

Lewis batted him away and made a don't-bother-me face at his partner.

"Who was that?" Irving asked.

"It was Clarke, sir. He's just anxious to know our assignment."

"Did Lieutenant Pounds talk to the subject?"

"Yes sir," Lewis said, wondering if Irving was taping the call. "The lieutenant said the, uh, subject has been told he is to work with the F—the bureau. They are consolidating the murder and the bank investigations. He is working with Special Agent Eleanor Wish."

"What's his scam . . . ?" Irving said, though no reply was expected, or offered by Lewis. There was silence on the phone line for a while because Lewis knew better than to interrupt Irving's thoughts. He saw Clarke approaching the phone booth again and he waved him away and shook his head as if he were dealing with an impetuous child. The doorless phone booth was at the bottom of Woodrow Wilson Drive, next to the Barham Boulevard crossing over the Hollywood Freeway. Lewis heard the sound of a semi thunder by on the freeway and felt warm air blow into the booth. He looked up at the lights of the houses on the hillside and tried to pinpoint which one came from Bosch's stilt house. It was impossible to tell. The hill looked like a giant, fat Christmas tree with too many lights.

"He must have some kind of leverage on them," Irving finally said. "He's muscled his way into it. I'll tell you what your assignment is. You two stay on him. Not so he knows. But stay with him. He is up to something. Find out what. And build your one point eighty-one case along the way. The Federal Bureau of Investigation may have withdrawn its complaint, but we will not back off."

"What about Pounds, you still want him copied?"

"That is Lieutenant Pounds, Detective Lewis. And yes, copy him your daily surveillance log. That will be enough for him."

Irving hung up without another word.

"Very good, sir," Lewis said to the dead phone. He didn't want Clarke to know he had been slighted. "We'll stay with it. Thank you, sir. Good night."

Then he, too, hung up, privately embarrassed that his commander had not deemed it necessary to say good night to him. Clarke quickly walked up.

"So?"

"So we pick him up again tomorrow morning. Bring your piss bottle."

"That's it? Just surveillance?"

"At this time."

"Shit. I want to search that fucker's house. Break some stuff. He's probably got the shit from that heist sitting up there."

"If he was involved, I doubt he would be so stupid. We sit back, for now. If he's dirty on this, we'll see."

"Oh, he's dirty. Don't worry."

"We'll see."

Sharkey sat on the concrete block wall that fronted a parking lot on Santa Monica Boulevard. He closely watched the lighted front of the 7-Eleven across the Street, checking out who was coming and who was going. Mostly tourist trade and couples. No singles yet.

None that fit the bill. The boy called Arson sauntered over and said, "This ain't going nowhere, budro."

Arson's hair was red and waxed into spiky flames. He wore black jeans and a dirty black T-shirt. He was smoking a Salem. He wasn't stoned but he was hungry. Sharkey looked at him and then past him to where the third boy, the one known as Mojo, sat on the ground near the bikes. Mojo was shorter and wider, with his black hair slicked back in a knob behind his head. Acne scars marked his face forever as sullen.

"Give it a few more minutes," Sharkey said.

"I want to eat, man," Arson said.

"Well, what do you think I'm trying to do? We all want to eat."

"Maybe we could see how Bettijane's doing," Mojo said. "She'll have made enough for us to eat."

Sharkey looked over at him and said, "You two go ahead. I'm staying till I score. I'm gonna eat."

As he said this he watched a maroon Jaguar XJ6 pull into the convenience store's lot.

"How about the guy in the pipe?" Arson asked. "You think they found him yet? We could go up there and check him out, see if there is any bread. I don't know why you didn't have the balls to do it last night, Shark."

"Hey, you go up there by yourself and check it out if you want," Sharkey said. "See who has balls then."

He hadn't told them that he had called 911 about the body. That would be harder for them to forgive than his fear of going into the pipe. A lone man got out of the Jaguar. He looked like late thirties, brush cut, baggy white slacks and shirt, sweater draped around his shoulders. Sharkey saw no one waiting in the car.

"Hey, check out the Jag," he said. The other two looked over at the store. "This is it. I'm going."

"We'll be here," Arson said.

Sharkey got off the wall and trotted across the boulevard. He watched the Jag's owner through the windows of the store. He had an ice cream in his hand and was looking at the magazine rack. His eyes were constantly on the prowl as he looked at the other men in the store. Sharkey was encouraged as he saw the man head toward the counter to pay for the ice cream. He squatted against the front of the store, the grille of the Jag four feet away.

When the man came out, Sharkey waited for their eyes to lock and the man to smile before he spoke up.

"Hey, mister?" he said as he got up. "I was wondering if you could do me a favor?"

The man looked around the parking lot before answering.

"Sure. What do you need?"

"Well, I was wondering if you might go in and get me a beer. I'll give you the money and all. I just want a beer. To relax, you know?"

The man hesitated. "I don't know . . . that would be illegal, wouldn't it? You're not twenty-one. I could get in trouble."

"Well," Sharkey said with a smile, "do you have any beer at home? Then you wouldn't have to be buying it. Just giving somebody a beer ain't no crime."

"Well . . ."

"I wouldn't stay long. We could probably relax each other a little bit, you know?"

The man took another look around the parking lot. No one was watching. Sharkey thought he had him now.

"Okay," he said. "I can take you back here later if you want."

"Sure. That'd be cool."

They drove east on Santa Monica to Flores and then south a couple of blocks to a townhouse development. Sharkey never turned around or tried to look in the mirrors. They would be back there. He knew it. There was a security gate on the outside of the property which the man had a key for and pulled closed behind them. Then they went into his townhouse.

"My name is Jack," the man said. "What can I get you?"

"I'm Phil. Do you have any food? I'm kind of hungry, too." Sharkey looked around for the security intercom, and the button that would unlatch the gate. The apartment was mostly light-colored furniture on an off-white deep pile carpet. "Nice place."

"Thanks. Let me see what I have. If you want to wash your clothes, we can get that done, too, while you are here. I don't do this very often, you know. But when I can help someone I try."

Sharkey followed him into the kitchen. The security console was on the wall next to the phone. When Jack opened the refrigerator and bent down to look in, Sharkey pushed the button that opened the gate outside. Jack didn't notice.

"I have tuna fish. And I can make a salad. How long have you been on the street? I'm not going to call you Phil. If you don't want to tell me your real name, that's fine."

"Um, tuna fish would be good. Not too long."

"Are you clean?"

"Yeah, sure. I'm okay."

"We'll take precautions."

It was time. Sharkey stepped backward into the hall. Jack looked up from the refrigerator, a plastic bowl in his hand, his mouth slightly ajar. Sharkey thought there was a look of recognition in his face, like he knew what was about to happen. Sharkey twisted the dead bolt and opened the door. Arson and Mojo walked in.

"Hey, what is this?" Jack said, though there was no confidence in his voice. He rushed into the hall and Arson, who was the biggest of all four of them, hit him with a fist on the bridge of his nose. There was a sound like a pencil breaking, and the plastic bowl of tuna fish clumped to the ground. Then there was a lot of blood on the off-white carpet.

Part III

Tuesday, May 22

Eleanor Wish called again Tuesday morning while Harry Bosch was fiddling with his tie in front of the bathroom mirror. She said she wanted to meet at a coffee shop in Westwood before taking him into the bureau. He had already had two cups of coffee but said he'd be there. He hung up, fastened the top button on his white shirt and pulled the tie snugly to his neck. He couldn't remember the last time he had paid such attention to the details of his appearance.

When he got there, she was in one of the booths along the front windows. She had both hands on the water glass in front of her and looked content. There was a plate pushed off to the side that had the paper wrapping from a muffin on it. She gave him a short courtesy smile as he slid in and waved a hand at a waitress.

"Just coffee," Bosch said.

"You already ate?" Wish said when the waitress went away.

"Uh, no. But I'm fine."

"You don't eat much, I can tell."

Said more like a mother than a detective.

"So, who's going to tell me about it? You or Rourke?"

"Me."

The waitress put down a cup of coffee. Bosch could hear four salesmen in the next booth dickering over the table's breakfast bill. He took a small swallow of hot coffee.

"I would like the FBI's request for my help put on paper, signed by the senior special agent in charge of the Los Angeles office." She hesitated a moment, put her glass down and looked directly at him for the first time. Her eyes were so dark they betrayed nothing about her. At their corners, he saw just the beginning of a gentle web of lines in the tan skin.

At the line of her chin there was a small, white crescent scar, very old and almost unnoticeable. He wondered if the scar and the lines bothered her, as he believed they would most women. Her face seemed to him to have a slight sadness cast in it, as if a mystery carried inside had worked its way outside. Perhaps it was fatigue, he thought. Nevertheless, she was an attractive woman. He figured her age for early thirties.

"I think that can be arranged," she said. "Any other demands before we get to work?"

He smiled and shook his head no.

"You know, Bosch, I got your murder book yesterday and read through it last night. For what you had there, and for one day's work, it was very good work, Most other detectives, that body'd still be in the waiting line at the morgue and listed as probable accidental OD."

He said nothing.

"Where should we begin on it today?" she asked.

"I've got some things working that weren't in the book yet. Why don't you tell me about the bank burglary first?

I need the background. All I know is what you put out to the papers and on the BOLOs. You bring me up, then I'll take it from there, tell you about Meadows." The waitress came and checked his cup and her glass. Then Eleanor Wish told the story of the bank heist. Bosch thought of questions as she went along, but he tried to note them in his head to ask afterward. He sensed that she marveled at the story, the planning and execution of the caper. Whoever they were, the tunnelers, they had her respect. He found himself almost jealous.

"Beneath the streets of L.A.," she said, "there are more than four hundred miles of storm lines that are wide enough and tall enough to drive a car through. After that, you've got even more tributary lines. Eleven hundred more miles that you could walk or at least crawl through.

"This means anybody can go under and, if they know the way, get close to any building they want to in the city. And it is not that difficult to find the way. The plans for the whole network are public record, on file with the county recorder's office. Anyway, these guys used the drainage system to get to WestLand National."

He had already figured as much but didn't bother to say. She said the FBI believed there were at least three underground men and then at least one on top to act as lookout, provide other necessary functions. The topsider probably communicated with them by radio, except possibly near the end because of the danger that radio waves might set off the explosive detonators.

The underground men made their way through the drainage system on Honda all-terrain vehicles. There was a drive-in entrance to the storm sewer system at a wash in the Los Angeles River basin northeast of downtown. They drove in there, probably under cover of darkness, and following recorder's maps, made their way through the tunnel network to a spot under Wilshire Boulevard in downtown, about 30 feet below and 150 yards west of WestLand National. It was a two-mile trip.

An industrial drill with a twenty-four-inch circle bit, probably diamond-tipped, was attached to a generator on one of the ATVs and used to cut a hole through the six-inch concrete wall of the stormwater tunnel. From there the underground men began to dig.

"The actual break-in to the vault occurred on Labor Day weekend," Wish said. "We think they must have begun the tunnel three or four weeks earlier. They'd only work nights. Go in, dig some and be back out by dawn. The DWP has inspectors that routinely go through the system looking for cracks and other problems. They work days, so the perps probably didn't risk it."

"What about the hole they cut in the side, wouldn't the water and power people have seen that?" asked Bosch, who immediately became annoyed with himself for asking a question before she was done.

"No," she said. "These guys thought of everything. They had a piece of plywood cut in a circle twenty-four inches wide. They coated it with concrete—we found it there after. We think that when they left each morning, they put this in the hole, and then each time they'd caulk around the edges with more concrete. It would look like a pipeline from a storm drain that had been capped off. That's pretty common down there. I've been. You see capped lines all over the place. The twenty-four inches is a standard size. So this would have looked normal. It doesn't get noticed and the perps just come back the next night, go back in and dig a little farther toward the bank."

She said the tunnel was dug primarily with hand

tools—shovels, picks, drills powered off the generator on the ATV. The tunnelers probably used flashlights but also candles. Some of them were found still burning in the tunnel after the robbery was discovered. They were propped in small indentations cut in the walls.

"That ring a bell?" Wish asked.

He nodded.

"We figure they made about ten to twenty feet of progress a night," she said. "We found two wheelbarrows in the tunnel, after. They had been cut in half and disassembled to fit through the twenty-four-inch hole and then strapped back together to be used during the digging. It must have been one or two of the perps' jobs to make runs back out of the tunnel and to dump the dirt and debris from the dig into the main drainage line. There is a steady flow of water on the floor of the line, and it would have washed the dirt away, eventually, to the river wash. We figure that on some nights their topside partner opened fire hydrants up on Hill to get more water flowing down there."

"So they had water down there, even in a drought."

"Even in a drought . . ."

Wish said that when the thieves finally dug their way under the bank, they tapped into the bank's own underground electric and telephone lines. With downtown a ghost town on weekends, the bank branch was closed on Saturdays. So on Friday, after business hours, the thieves bypassed the alarms. One of the perps had to be a bellman. Not Meadows, he was probably the explosives man.

"The funny thing was, they didn't need a bellman," she said. "The vault's sensor alarm had repeatedly been going off all week. These guys, with their digging and their drills, must have been tripping the alarms. Four straight nights the cops are called out along with the manager. Sometimes three times in one night. They don't find anything and begin to think it's the alarm. The sound-and-movement sensor is off balance. So the manager calls the alarm company and they can't get anybody out until after the holiday weekend, you know, Labor Day. So this guy, the manager—"

"Turns the alarm off." Bosch finished for her.

"You got it. He decides he isn't going to get called out each night during the weekend. He's supposed to go down to the Springs to his time-share condo and play golf. He turns the alarms off. Of course, he no longer works for WestLand National."

Under the vault, the bandits used a water-cooled industrial drill, which was bolted upside down to the underside of the vault slab, to bore a two-and-a-half-inch hole through the five feet of concrete and steel. FBI crime scene analysts estimated that took five hours, and only if the drill didn't overheat. Water to cool it came from a tap into an underground water main. They used the bank's water.

"After they got the hole drilled, they packed it with C-4," she said. "Ran the wire down through their tunnel and out into the drainage tunnel. They popped it from there."

She said LAPD emergency-response records showed that at 9:14 A.M. on that Saturday, alarms were reported at a bank across the street from WestLand National and a jewelry store a half-block away.

"We figure that was the detonation time," Wish said. "Patrol was sent out, looked around and didn't find anything, decided the alarms were probably triggered by an earthquake tremor and left. Nobody bothered to check

WestLand National. Its alarm hadn't made a peep. They didn't know that it had been turned off."

Once into the vault, they didn't leave, she said. They worked right through the three-day weekend, drilling the locks on the deposit boxes, pulling the drawers and emptying them.

"We found empty food cans, potato chip bags, freeze-dried food packets, you know, survival store stuff," Wish said. "It looks like they stayed there, maybe slept in shifts. In the tunnel there was a wide part, it was like a small room. Like a sleeping room, we think. We found the pattern from a sleeping bag impressed on the dirt floor. We also found impressions in the sand left by the stocks of M-16s—they brought automatic weapons with them. They weren't planning on surrendering if things went wrong."

She let him think about that a few moments and then continued. "We estimate they were in the vault sixty hours, maybe a few more. They drilled four hundred and sixty-four of the boxes. Out of seven fifty. If there were three of them, then that's about a hundred and fifty-five boxes each. Subtract about fifteen hours for rest and eating over the three days they were in there, and you've got each man drilling three, four boxes an hour."

They must have had a time limit, she said. Maybe three o'clock or thereabouts Tuesday morning. If they quit drilling by then, it gave them plenty of time to pack up and get out. They took the loot and their tools and backed out. The bank manager, with a fresh Palm Springs tan on his face, discovered the heist when he opened the vault for business Tuesday morning.

"That's it in a nutshell," she said. "Best thing I've seen or heard of since I've been in the job. Only a few mistakes. We've found out a lot about how they did it but not much about who did it. Meadows was as close as we ever got, and now he's dead. That photograph you showed me yesterday. Of the bracelet? You were right, it's the first thing that's ever turned up from one of those boxes that we know of."

"But now it's gone."

Bosch waited for her to say something but she was done.

"How'd they pick the boxes to drill?" he asked.

"It looks random. I have a video at the office I'll show you. But it looks like they said, 'You take that wall, I'll take this one, you take that one,' and so on. Some boxes right next to others that were drilled were left untouched. Why, I don't know. Didn't look like a pattern. Still, we had losses reported in ninety percent of the boxes they drilled. Mostly untraceable stuff. They chose well."

"How did you come up with three of them?"

"We figured it would take at least that many to drill that many boxes. Plus, that's how many ATVs there were."

She smiled and he bit. "Okay, how'd you know about the ATVs?"

"Well, there were tracks in the mud in the drainage line and we identified them from tires. We also found paint, blue paint, on the wall on one of the curves of the drainage line. One of them had slid on the mud and hit the wall. The paint lab in Quantico came up with the model year and make. We hit all the Honda dealers in Southern California until we came up with a purchase of three blue ATVs at a dealership in Tustin, four weeks before Labor Day. Guy paid cash and loaded them on a trailer. Gave a phony name and address.

"What was it?"

"The name? Frederic B. Isley, as in FBI. It would come up again. We once showed the salesman some six-packs that included Meadows's, yours and a few other people's photos but he couldn't make anybody as Isley."

She wiped her mouth on a napkin and dropped it on the table. He could see no lipstick on it.

"Well," she said, "I've had enough water for a week. Meet me back at the bureau and we'll go over what we've got and what you've got on the Meadows thing. Rourke and I think that is the way to go. We've exhausted all leads on the bank job, been banging against the wall. Maybe the Meadows case will bring us the break we need."

Wish picked up the tab, Bosch put down the tip.

They took their separate cars to the Federal Building. Bosch thought about her as he drove and not the case. He wanted to ask her about that little scar on her chin and not how she connected the WestLand tunnelers to Vietnam tunnel rats. He wanted to know what gave the sweet sad look to her face. He followed her car through a neighbor-hood of student apartments near UCLA and then across Wilshire Boulevard. They met at the elevator in the park-ing garage of the Federal Building.

"I think this will be best if you basically just deal with me," she said as they rode up alone. "Rourke—You and Rourke did not start off well and—"

"We didn't even start off," Bosch said.

"Well, if you would give him the chance you would see he is a good man. He did what he thought was right for the case."

The elevator doors spread apart on the seventeenth floor, and there was Rourke.

"There you two are," he said. He put his hand out to Bosch, who took it without much conviction. Rourke introduced himself.

"I was just going down for coffee and a roll," he said. "Care to join me?"

"Uh, John, we just came from a coffee shop," Wish said. "We'll meet you back up here."

Bosch and Wish were now outside the elevator and Rourke was inside. The assistant special agent in charge just nodded his head, and the door closed. Bosch and Wish headed into the office.

"He's a lot like you in a way—been through the war and all," she said. "Give him a try. You're not going to help things if you don't thaw out."

He let it go by. They walked down the hall to the Group 3 squad and Wish pointed to a desk behind hers. She said it was empty since the agent who used it had been transferred to Group 2, the porno squad. Bosch put his briefcase on the desk and sat down. He looked around the room. It was much more crowded than the day before. About a half-dozen agents were at desks and three more were in the back standing around a file cabinet where there was a box of doughnuts. He noticed a television and VCR on a rack in the back of the office. It hadn't been there the day before.

"You said something about a video," he said to Wish.

"Oh, yes. I'll get that set up and you can watch while I answer a few phone messages on other things."

She took a videotape out of a drawer in her desk and they walked to the back of the squad. The gang of three quietly moved away with their doughnuts, alarmed by the presence of an outsider. She set the tape up and left him there to watch alone.

The video, obviously shot with a hand-held camera, was a bouncy, unprofessional walk-through of the thieves' trail. It began in what Bosch surmised was the storm sewer, a square tunnel that curved away into a darkness the camera's strobe couldn't reach. Wish had been right, it was large. A truck could have driven down it. A small stream of water moved slowly down the center of the concrete floor. There was mold and algae on the floor and the lower part of the walls, and Bosch could almost smell the dampness. The camera panned down to the grayish-green floor. There were tire tracks in the slime. The next video scene was the entrance to the thieves' tunnel, a cleanly cut hole in the sewer wall. A pair of hands moved into the picture holding the plywood circle Wish said had been used to cover the hole during the day. The hands moved further into the screen, then a head of dark hair. It was Rourke. He was wearing a dark jumpsuit with white letters across the back. FBI. He held the plywood up to the hole. It was a perfect fit.

The video jumped then, and the scene was now from inside the thieves' tunnel. It was eerie for Bosch to watch, and brought back memories of the hand-dug tunnels he had crawled through in Vietnam. This tunnel curved to the right. Surreal lighting flickered from candles set every twenty feet or so in notches dug into the wall. After curving for what he judged was about sixty feet, the tunnel turned sharply to the left. It then followed a straight-away for almost a hundred feet, candles still flickering from the walls. The camera finally came to a dead end where there was a pile of concrete rubble, twisted pieces of steel rebar and plating. The camera panned up to a gaping hole in the ceiling of the tunnel. Light poured down from the vault above. Rourke stood up there in his jumpsuit, looking down at the camera. He dragged a finger across his neck and the picture cut again. This time the camera was inside the vault, a wide-angle shot of the entire room. As in the newspaper photo Bosch had seen, hundreds of safe-deposit box doors stood open. The boxes lay empty in piles on the floor. Two crime scene techs were dusting the doors for fingerprints. Eleanor Wish and another agent were looking up at the steel wall of box doors and writing in notebooks. The camera panned down to the floor and the hole to the tunnel below. Then the tape went black. He rewound it, brought it back and put it on her desk.

"Interesting," he said. "I saw a few things I had seen before. In the tunnels over there. But nothing that would have made me start looking at tunnel rats in particular. What was the lead to Meadows, people like me?"

"First off, there was the C-4," she said. "Alcohol, Tobacco, and Firearms sent a team out to go through the concrete and steel from the blast hole. There were trace elements of the explosive. The ATF guys ran some tests and came up with C-4. I'm sure you know it. It was used in Vietnam. Tunnel rats used it especially to implode tunnels. The thing is, you can get much better stuff now, with more compressed impact area, easier handling and detonation. It's even cheaper. Also less dangerous to handle and easier to get ahold of. So we figured—I mean the ATF lab guy figured—the reason C-4 was used was because the user was comfortable with it, had used it before. So right off we thought it would be a Vietnam-era vet.

"Another corollary to Vietnam was the booby traps. We think that before they went up into the vault to start drilling, they wired the tunnel to protect their rear. We sent an ATF dog through as a precaution, you know, to make sure there wasn't any more live C-4 lying around. The animal got a reading—indicated explosives—in two places in the tunnel. The midway point and at the entrance cut in the wall of the storm line. But there was nothing there anymore. The perps took it with them. But we found peg holes in the floor of the tunnel and snippets of steel wire at both spots—like the leftover stuff when you are cutting lengths with a wire cutter."

"Tripwires," Bosch said.

"Right. We're thinking they had the tunnel wired for intruders. If anybody had come in from behind to take them, the tunnel would have gone up. They'd've been buried under Hill Street. At least, the tunnelers took the explosives out with them when they left. Saved us stumbling across them."

"But an explosion like that probably would've killed the tunnelers along with the intruders," Bosch said.

"We know. These guys just weren't taking chances. They were heavily armed, fortified and ready to go down. Succeed or suicide. . . .

"Anyway, we didn't narrow it down specifically to tunnel rats possibly being involved until somebody caught something when we were going over the tire tracks in the main sewer line. The tracks were here and there, no complete trail. So it took us a couple days to track them from the tunnel back to the entrance at the river wash. It wasn't a straight shot. It's a labyrinth down there. You had to know your way. We figured these guys weren't sitting there on their ATVs with a flashlight and a map every night."

"Hansel and Gretel? They left crumbs along the way?"

"Sort of. The walls down there have a lot of paint on them. You know, DWP marks, so they know where they are, what line is going where, dates of inspection and so forth. With all the paint on them, some look like the side of a 7-Eleven in an East L.A. barrio. So we figured the perps marked the way. We walked the trail and looked for reoccurring marks. There was only one. Kind of a peace sign, without the circle. Just three quick slash marks."

He knew the mark. He'd used it himself in tunnels twenty years ago. Three quick slashes on a tunnel wall with a knife. It was the symbol they'd used to mark their way, so they could find the way out again.

Wish said, "One of the cops there that day—this was before LAPD turned the whole thing over to us—one of the robbery guys said he recognized it from Vietnam. He wasn't a tunnel rat. But he told us about them. That's how we connected it. From there, we went to the Department of Defense and the VA and got names. We got Meadows's. We got yours. Others."

"How many others?"

She pushed a six-inch stack of manila files across her desk.

"They're all here. Have a look if you want."

Rourke walked up then.

"Agent Wish has told me about the letter you requested," he said. "I have no problem with it. I roughed out something and we'll try to get Senior Special Agent Whitcomb to sign it sometime today."

When Bosch didn't say anything Rourke went on.

"We may have overreacted yesterday, but I hope I've set everything straight with your lieutenant and your Internal Affairs people." He gave a smile a politician would envy. "And by the way, I wanted to tell you I admire your record. Your military record. Myself, I served three tours. But I never went down into any of those ghastly tunnels. I was over there, though, till the very end. What a shame."

"What was the shame, that it ended?"

Rourke eyed him a long moment, and Bosch saw red spread across his face from the point where his dark eyebrows knitted together. Rourke was a very pale man with a sallow face that gave the impression he was sucking on a sourball. He was a few years older than Bosch. They were the same height but Rourke had more weight on his frame. To the bureau's traditional uniform of blue blazer and light-blue button-down shift, he had added a red power tie.

"Look, detective, you don't have to like me, that's fine," Rourke said. "But, please, work with me on this. We want the same thing."

Bosch gave in for the time being.

"What is it that you want me to do? Tell me exactly. Am I just along for the ride or do you really want my work?"

"Bosch, you are supposedly a top-notch detective. Show us. Just follow your case. Like you said yesterday, you find who killed Meadows and we find who ripped off WestLand. So, yes, we want your best work. Proceed as you normally would but with Special Agent Wish as your partner."

Rourke walked away and out of the squad. Bosch figured he must have his own office somewhere off the quiet hallway. He turned to Wish's desk and picked up the stack of files. He said, "Okay then, let's go."

•   •   •

Wish signed out a bureau car and drove while Bosch looked through the stack of military files on his lap. He noticed his own was on top. He glanced at some of the others and recognized only Meadows's name.

"Where to?" Wish asked as she pulled out of the garage and took Veteran Avenue up to Wilshire.

"Hollywood," he said. "Is Rourke always such a stiff?"

She turned east and smiled one of those smiles that made Bosch wonder whether she and Rourke had something going on.

"When he wants," she said. "He's a good administrator, though. He runs the squad well. Always has been the leader type, I guess. I think he said he was in charge of a whole outfit or something when he was with the army. Over there in Saigon."

No way there was anything between them, he thought then. You don't defend your lover by calling him a good administrator. There was nothing there.

"He's in the wrong business for administrating," Bosch said. "Go up to Hollywood Boulevard, the neighborhood south of the Chinese theater."

It would take fifteen minutes to get there. He opened the top file—it was his own—and began looking through the papers. Between a set of psychiatric evaluation reports he found a black-and-white photo, almost like a mug shot, of a young man in uniform, his face unlined by age or experience.

"You looked good in a crew cut," Wish said, interrupting his thoughts. "Reminded me of my brother when I saw that."

Bosch looked at her but didn't say anything. He put the photo down and went back to roaming through the documents in the file, reading snatches of information about a stranger who was himself.

Wish said, "We were able to find nine men with Vietnam tunnel experience living in Southern California. We checked them all out. Meadows was the only one we really moved up to the level of suspect. He was a hype, had the criminal record. He also had a history of working in tunnels even after he came back from the war." She drove in silence for a few minutes while Bosch read. Then she said, "We watched him a whole month. After the burglary."

"What was he doing?"

"Nothing that we could tell. He might have been doing some dealing. We were never sure. He'd go down to Venice to buy balloons of tar about every three days. But it looked like it was for personal consumption. If he was selling, no customers ever came. No other visitors the whole month we watched. Hell, if we could prove he was selling, we would have popped him and then had something decent to scam him with when we talked about the bank job."

She was quiet again for a moment, then in a tone that Bosch thought was meant more to convince herself than him said, "He wasn't selling."

"I believe you," he said.

"You going to tell me what we're looking for in Hollywood?"

"We're looking for a wit. A possible witness. How was Meadows living during the month you watched? I mean, moneywise. How'd he get money to go down to Venice?"

"Near as we could tell, he was on welfare and had a VA disability check. That's it."

"Why did you call it off after a month?"

"We didn't have anything, and we weren't even sure he had anything to do with it. We—"

"Who pulled the plug?"

"Rourke did. He couldn't—"

"The administrator."

"Let me finish. He couldn't justify the cost of continued surveillance without any results. We were going on a hunch, nothing more. You're just looking at it from hindsight. But it had been almost two months since the robbery. There was nothing there that pointed to him. In fact, we were just going through the motions after a while. We thought whoever it really was, they were in Monaco or Argentina. Not scoring balloon hits of tar heroin on Venice beach and living in a tramp apartment in the Valley. At the time, Meadows didn't make sense. Rourke called the watch. But I concurred. I guess now we know we fucked up. Satisfied?"

Bosch didn't answer. He knew Rourke had been correct in calling the watch. Nowhere is hindsight better than in cop work. He changed the subject.

"Why that bank, did you ever think about that? Why WestLand National? Why not a Wells Fargo or a vault in a Beverly Hills bank? Probably more money in the banks over in the Hills anyway. You said these underground tunnels go all over the place."

"They do. I don't know the answer to that one. Maybe they picked a downtown bank because they wanted a full three days to open the boxes and they knew downtown banks aren't open Saturdays. Maybe only Meadows and his friends know the answer. What are we looking for in this neighborhood? There was nothing in your reports about a possible witness. Witness to what?"

They were in the neighborhood. The street was lined

with run-down motels that had looked depressing the day they were finished being built. Bosch pointed out one of these, the Blue Chateau, and told her to park. It was as depressing as all the others on the street. Concrete block, early fifties design. Painted light blue with darker blue trim that was peeling. It was a two-story courtyard building with towels and clothes hanging out of almost every open window. It was a place where the interior would rival the exterior as an eyesore, Bosch knew. Where runaways crowded eight or ten to a room, the strongest getting the bed, the others the floor or the bathtub. There were places like this on many of the blocks near the Boulevard. There always had been and always would be.

As they sat in the fed car looking at the motel Bosch told her about the half-finished paint scrawl he had found on the pipe at the reservoir and the anonymous 911 caller. He told her he believed the voice went with the paint. Edward Niese, AKA Sharkey.

"These kids, the runaways, they form street cliques," Bosch said as he got out of the car. "Not exactly like gangs. It's not a turf thing. It's for protection and business. According to the CRASH files, Sharkey's crew has been hanging out at the Chateau here for the last couple of months."

As Bosch closed the car door, he noticed a car pull to the curb a half-block up the street. He took a quick glance at it but didn't recognize the car. He thought he could see two figures in it, but it was too far away for him to be sure, or to tell if it was Lewis and Clarke. He headed up a flagstone walkway to an entrance hallway below a broken neon sign for the motel office.

In the office Bosch could see an old man sitting behind a glass window with a slide tray at its base. The man was reading the day's green sheet from Santa Anita. He didn't pull his eyes away until Bosch and Wish were at the window.

"Yes, officers, what can I do for you?"

He was a worn-out old man whose eyes had quit caring about anything but the odds on three-year-olds. He knew cops before they flipped their buzzers. And he knew to give them what they wanted without much fuss.

"Kid named Sharkey," Bosch said. "What's the room?"

"Seven, but he's gone. I think. His motorbike usually sets there in the hall when he's around. There's no bike there. He's gone. Most probably."

"Most probably. Anybody else in seven?"

"Sure. Somebody's always around."

"First floor?"

"Yup."

"Back door or window?"

"Both. Sliding door on the back. Very expensive to replace."

The old man reached over to the key rack and took a key off a hook marked 7. He slid it into the tray beneath the window between him and Bosch.

Detective Pierce Lewis found a receipt from an automatic teller machine in his wallet and used it to pick his teeth. His mouth tasted as though there was still a piece of breakfast sausage in there somewhere. He slid the paper card in and out between his teeth until they felt clean. He made a smacking, unsatisfied sound with his mouth.

"What?" Detective Don Clarke said. He knew his partner's behavioral nuances. The teeth picking and lip smacking meant something was bothering him.

"I think he made us, is all," Lewis said after flipping the card out the window into the street. "That little look he threw down the street when they got out of the car. He was very quick, but I think he made us."

"He didn't make us. If he did, he woulda come charging down here to start up a commotion or something. That's how they do it. Make a commotion, file a lawsuit. He'd've had the Police Protective League up our ass by now. I'm telling you, cops are the last to notice a tail."

"Well . . . I guess," Lewis said.

He let it go for the moment. But he stayed worried. He didn't want to mess up this job. He'd had Bosch by the balls once before and the guy skated because Irving, that flying jaw, had pulled Lewis and Clarke back. But not this time, Lewis silently promised himself. This time he goes down.

"You taking notes?" he asked his partner. "What do you think they're doing in that dump?"

"Looking for something."

"You're shitting me. You really think so?"

"Jeez, who put the pencil up your ass today?"

Lewis looked away from the Chateau to Clarke, who had his hands folded on his lap and his seat back at a sixty-degree angle. With his mirrored glasses shielding his eyes, it was impossible to tell if he was awake or not.

"Are you taking notes or what?" Lewis said loudly.

"If you want notes, whyn't you takin' 'em?"

"Because I'm driving. That's always the deal. You don't want to drive, you gotta write and take the pictures. Now, write something down so we have something to show Irving. Otherwise he'll write up a one eighty-one on us and forget about Bosch."

"That's one *point* eighty-one. Let's not take shortcuts, even in our language."

"Fuck off."

Clarke snickered and took a notebook out of his inside coat pocket and a gold Cross pen from his shirt pocket. When Lewis was satisfied that notes were being taken and looked back at the motel, he saw a teenage boy with blond dreadlocks circle twice in the road on a yellow motorbike. The boy pulled up next to the car Lewis had just watched Bosch and the FBI woman get out of. The boy shaded his eyes and looked through the driver's-side window into the car.

"Now, what's this?" Lewis said.

"Some kid," Clarke said after looking up from his notes. "He's looking for a stereo to snatch. If he makes a move, what are we going to do? Blow the surveillance to save some asshole's tape deck?"

"We aren't going to do anything. And he's not going to make a move: He sees the Motorola two-way. He knows it's a cop car. He's backing away now."

The boy revved the bike and did another two circles in the street. As the bike circled, he kept his eyes on the front of the motel. He then cruised through the side parking lot and back out onto the street. He stopped behind an old Volkswagen bus that was parked at the curb and shielded him from the motel. He seemed to be watching the entrance to the Chateau through the windows of the beat-up old bus. He did not notice the two IAD men in the car parked a half-block behind him.

"Come on kid, get going," Clarke said. "I don't want to have to call out patrol on you. Fucking delinquent."

"Use the Nikon and get his picture," Lewis said. "You never know. Something might happen and we'll need it.

And while you're at it, get the number off the motel sign. We'll have to call later and see what Bosch and the FBI girl were doing."

Lewis could have easily picked the camera up off the seat himself and taken the photos, but that would set a dangerous precedent that could harm the delicate balance of the rules of surveillance. The driver drives. The rider writes—and does all such related work.

Clarke dutifully picked up the camera, which was equipped with a telephoto lens, and took the photos of the boy on the bike.

"Get one with the bike's plate," Lewis said.

"I know what I am doing," Clarke said as he put the camera down.

"Did you get the motel number? We'll have to call."

"I got it. I'm writing it down. See? What's the big deal? Bosch is prolly in there knocking off a piece. A nice federal piece. Maybe when we call we find out they rented a room."

Lewis watched to make sure Clarke wrote down the number on the surveillance log.

"And maybe we don't," Lewis said. "They just met and, anyway, I doubt he'd be so stupid. They've got to be in there looking for somebody. A wit maybe."

"But there was nothing about any witness in the murder book."

"He held it back. That's Bosch. That's how he works."

Clarke didn't say anything. Lewis looked back down the street to the Chateau. He then noticed that the kid was gone. There was no sign of the motorbike.

Bosch waited a minute to give Eleanor Wish time to get behind the Chateau to watch the sliding door on the back of room 7. He bent and held his ear to the door and thought he heard a rustling sound and an occasional word mumbled. There was someone in the room. When it was time, he knocked heavily on the door. He heard the sound of movement—fast steps on carpet—from the other side of the door, but no one answered. He knocked again and waited, then heard a girl's voice.

"Who is it?"

"Police," Bosch said. "We want to talk to Sharkey."

"He's not here."

"Then I guess we want to talk to you."

"I don't know where he is."

"Open the door, please."

He heard more noise, like someone banging into furniture. But nobody opened the door. Then he heard a rolling sound, a glass door sliding open. He put the key in the doorknob and opened the door in time to catch a glimpse of a man going through the back doorway and jumping off the porch to the ground. It wasn't Sharkey. He heard Wish's voice outside, ordering the man to stop.

Bosch took a quick inventory of the room. An entrance hall with closet to the left, bathroom to the right, both empty except for some clothes on the closet floor. Two large double beds pushed up against opposite walls, a dresser with a mirror on the wall above it, a yellow-brown carpet worn flat on the pathways around the beds and to the bathroom. The girl, blond-haired, small, maybe seventeen years old, sat on the front edge of one of the beds with a sheet around her. Bosch could see the outline of a nipple pressing out against the dingy, once-white cloth. The room smelled like cheap perfume and sweat.

"Bosch, you all right in there?" Wish called from outside. He could not see her because of a sheet hung like a curtain over the sliding door.

"Okay. You?"

"Okay. What have we got?"

Bosch walked to the sliding door and looked out. Wish stood behind a man who had his arms extended and his hands on the motel's back wall. He was about thirty, with the sallow skin of a man who just did a month in county lockup. His pants were open in the front. His plaid shirt was buttoned incorrectly. And he stared straight down to the ground with the bug-eyed look of a man who had no explanation but needed one badly. Bosch was momentarily struck by the man's apparent decision to button his shirt before his pants.

"He's clean," she said. "Looks a little winded, though."

"Looks like soliciting sex with a minor if you want to spend the time with it. Otherwise kick him loose."

He turned to the girl on the bed.

"No bullshit, how old are you and what did he pay? I'm not here to bust you."

She thought it over a moment. Bosch never took his eyes off hers.

"Almost seventeen," she said in a bored monotone. "He didn't pay me anything. He said he would, but he didn't get to that yet."

"Who's in charge of your crew, Sharkey? Didn't he ever tell you to get the money first?"

"Sharkey ain't always around. And how'd you get his name?"

"Heard it around. Where is he today?"

"I tol' you, I don't know."

The plaid-shirted man came into the room through the

front door followed by Wish. His hands were cuffed be-hind him.

"I am going to book him. I want to. This is sick. She looks—"

"She told me she was eighteen," Plaid Shirt said.

Bosch walked up to him and pulled open his shirt with a finger. There was a blue eagle with its wings spreading across his chest. In its talons it carried a dagger and a Nazi swastika. Beneath that it said One Nation. Bosch knew that meant the Aryan Nation, the white supremacist prison gang. He let the shirt fall back into place.

"Hey, how long you been out?" he asked.

"Hey, come on, man," Plaid Shirt said. "This is bull-shit. She pulled me in from the street. And let me at least button my goddam pants. This is bullshit."

"Give me my money, fucker," the girl said.

She jumped from the bed, the sheet falling to the floor, and lunged naked at the john's pants pockets.

"Get her off me, get her off," he called out as he squirmed to avoid her hands. "See, you see! She should be going, not me."

Bosch moved in and separated the two and pushed the girl back to the bed. He moved behind the man and said to Wish, "Give me your key."

She made no move, so he reached into his own pocket and got out his own cuff key. One size fits all. He un-locked the cuffs and walked Plaid Shirt over to the room's front door. He opened it and pushed him through. In the hallway the man stopped to button his pants, which gave Bosch the opportunity to put his foot on his butt and push. "Get out of here, short eyes," he said as the man stumbled down the hall. "This is your lucky day."

The girl was wrapped in the dirty sheet again when

Bosch went back into the room. He looked at Wish and saw anger in her eyes. He knew it wasn't just for the man in the plaid shirt. Bosch looked at the girl and said, "Get your clothes, go into the bathroom and get dressed." When she didn't move, he said, "Now! Let's go!"

After she grabbed up some clothes from the floor next to the bed and walked to the bathroom, letting the sheet fall to the ground, Bosch turned to Wish.

"We've got too much else to do," he began. "You would have spent the rest of the afternoon getting her statement and booking that guy. In fact, it's a state beef, so I would've had to book him. And it's a flopper; can go felony or misdemeanor. And one look at that girl and the DA would have gone misdee if he filed it at all. It wasn't worth it. It's the life down here, Agent Wish."

She looked at him with smoldering eyes, the same eyes he had seen when he had gripped her wrist to keep her from leaving the restaurant.

"Bosch, I had decided it was worth it. Don't ever do that again."

They stood there trying to outstare each other until the girl came out of the bathroom. She wore faded jeans that were split at the knees and a black tank top. No shoes, and Bosch noticed her toenails were painted red. She sat on the bed without saying anything.

"We need to find Sharkey," Bosch said.

"About what? You got a cigarette?"

He pulled out a pack of cigarettes and shook one out for her. He gave her a match and she lit it herself.

"About what?" she said again.

"About Saturday night," Wish said curtly. "We do not want to arrest him. We do not want to hassle him. We only want to ask him a few questions."

"What about me?" the girl said.

"What about you?" Wish said.

"Are you going to hassle me?"

"You mean are we going to turn you over to Division of Youth Services, don't you?" Bosch looked at Wish to try to gauge a reaction. He got no reading. He said, "No, we won't call DYS if you help us. What's your name? Your real name."

"Bettijane Felker."

"All right, Bettijane, you don't know where Sharkey is? All we want to do is talk to him."

"All I know is that he's working."

"What do you mean? Where?"

"Boytown. He's probably taking care of business with Arson and Mojo."

"Those the other guys in the crew?"

"Right."

"Where in Boytown did they say they were going?"

"They didn't. They just go where the queers are, I guess. You know."

The girl either couldn't be more specific or wouldn't be. Bosch knew it didn't matter. He had the addresses from the shake cards and knew he'd find Sharkey somewhere on Santa Monica Boulevard.

"Thank you," he said to the girl and started heading toward the door. He was halfway down the hall before Wish came out of the room, walking after him at a brisk, angry pace. Before she said anything he stopped at a pay phone in the hallway by the office. He took out a small phone book he always carried, looked up the number for DYS and dialed. He was put on hold for two minutes before an operator transferred him to an automated tape line on which he reported the date and time and the location of Bettijane Felker, suspected runaway. He hung up wondering how many days it would be before they got the message and how many days after that it would be before they got to Bettijane.

They were all the way into West Hollywood on Santa Monica Boulevard and she was still hot. Bosch had tried to defend himself but realized there was no chance. So he sat there quietly and listened.

"It's a matter of trust, that's all," Wish said. "I don't care how long or short we work together. If you are going to keep up the one-man army stuff, there will never be the trust we need to succeed."

He stared at the mirror on the passenger's side, which he had adjusted so he could watch the car that had pulled away from the curb and followed them from the Blue Chateau. He was sure now it was Lewis and Clarke. He had seen Lewis's huge neck and crew cut behind the wheel when the car had pulled up within three car lengths at a traffic signal. He didn't tell Wish they were being followed. And if she had noticed the tail, she hadn't said so. She was too involved in other things. He sat there watching the tail car and listening to her complaints about how badly he had handled things.

Finally he said, "Meadows was found Sunday. Today is Tuesday. It is a fact of life in homicide that the odds, the likelihood, of solving a homicide grow longer as each day on the calendar flips by. And so, I'm sorry. I did not think it would help us to waste a day booking some asshole who was probably baited into a motel room by a hooker sixteen years old going on thirty. I also did not think it would be worth waiting for DYS to come out to pick up the girl because I would bet a paycheck that DYS already knows that girl and knows where she is, if they want her. In short, I wanted to get on with it, leave other people's jobs to other people and do my job. And that meant doing what we are doing now. Slow down up here at Ragtime. It's one of the spots I got off the shake cards."

"We both want to solve this, Bosch. So don't be so goddam condescending, as if you have this noble mission and I am just along for the ride. We are both on it. Don't forget it."

She slowed in front of the open-air café, where pairs of men sat in white wrought-iron chairs at glass-top tables, drinking iced tea with slices of orange hooked on the rim of beveled glasses. A few of the men looked at Bosch and then looked away uninterested. He scanned the dining area but didn't see Sharkey. As the car cruised past, he looked down the side alley and saw a couple of young men hanging around, but they were too old to be Sharkey.

They spent the next twenty minutes driving around gay bars and restaurants, keeping mostly on Santa Monica, but did not see the boy. Bosch watched as the Internal Affairs car kept pace, never more than a block back. Wish never said anything about them. But Bosch knew that law officers were usually the last to notice a surveillance because they were the last to ever think they might be followed. They were the hunters, not the prey.

Bosch wondered what Lewis and Clarke were doing. Did they expect that he would break some law or cop rule with an FBI agent in tow? He began to wonder if the two IAD detectives weren't just hotdogging on their own time. Maybe they wanted him to see them. Some kind of a psych-out. He told Wish to pull to a curb in front of Barnie's Beanery and he jumped out to use the pay phone near the old bar's screen door. He dialed the Internal Affairs nonpublic number, which he knew by heart, having had to call in twice a day when he was put on home duty the year before while they investigated him. A woman, the desk officer, answered the phone.

"Is Lewis or Clarke there?"

"No, sir, they're not. Can I take a message?"

"No thanks. Uh, this is Lieutenant Pounds, Hollywood detectives. Are they just out of the office? I need to check a point with them."

"I believe they are code seven till P.M. watch."

He hung up. They were off duty until four. They were scamming, or Bosch had simply kicked them too hard in the balls this time and now they were going after him on their own time. He got back in the car and told Wish he had checked his office for messages. It was as she merged the car back into traffic that he saw the yellow motorbike leaning on a parking meter about a half block from Barnie's. It was parked in front of a pancake restaurant.

"There," he said and pointed. "Go on by and I'll get the number. If it's his, we'll sit on it."

It was Sharkey's bike. Bosch matched the plate to his notes from the kid's CRASH file. But there was no sign of the boy. Wish drove around the block and parked in the same spot in front of Barnie's that they had been in before.

"So, we wait," she said. "For this kid you think might be a witness."

"Right. It's what I think. But two of us don't need to waste the time. You can leave me here if you want. I'll go in the beanery, order a pitcher of Henry's and a bowl of chili and watch from the window."

"That's all right. I'm staying."

Bosch settled back for a wait. He took out his cigarettes but she nailed him before he got one out of the pack.

"Have you heard of the draft risk assessment?" she asked.

"The what?"

"Secondhand cigarette smoke. It's deadly, Bosch. The EPA came out last month, officially. Said it's a carcinogen. Three thousand people are getting lung cancer a year from passive smoking, they call it. You are killing yourself and me. Please don't."

He put the cigarettes back in his coat pocket. They were quiet as they watched the bike, which was chain-locked to the parking meter. Bosch took a few glances at the sideview mirror but didn't see the IAD car. He glanced over at Wish, too, whenever he thought she wasn't looking. Santa Monica Boulevard steadily got crowded with cars as the apex of rush hour approached. Wish kept her window closed to cut down on the carbon monoxide. It made the car very hot.

"Why do you keep staring at me?" she asked about an hour into the surveillance.

"At you? I didn't know that I was."

"You were. You are. You ever have a female partner before?"

"Nope. But that's not why I would be staring. If I was."

"Why then? If you were."

"I'd be trying to figure you out. You know, why you are here, doing this. I always thought, I mean at least I heard, that the bank squad over at the FBI was for dinosaurs and fuckups, the agents too old or too dumb to use a computer or trace some white-collar scumbag's assets through a paper trail. Then, here you are. On the heavy squad. You're no dinosaur, and something tells me you're no fuckup. Something tells me you're a prize, Eleanor."

She was quiet a moment, and Bosch thought he saw the trace of a smile play on her lips. Then it was gone, if it had been there at all.

"I guess that is a backhanded compliment," she said. "If it is, thank you. I have my reasons for choosing where I am with the bureau. And believe me, I do get to choose. As far as the others in the squad, I would not characterize any of them as you do. I think that attitude, which, by the way, seems to be shared by many of your fellow—"

"There's Sharkey," he said.

A boy with blond dreadlocks had come through a side alley between the pancake shop and a mini-mall. An older man stood with him. He wore a T-shirt that said The Gay 90s Are Back! Bosch and Wish stayed in the car and watched. Sharkey and the man exchanged a few words and then Sharkey took something from his pocket and handed it over. The man shuffled through what looked like a stack of playing cards. He took a couple of cards and gave the rest back. He then gave Sharkey a single green bill.

"What's he doing?" Wish asked.

"Buying baby pictures."

"What?"

"A pedophile."

The older man headed off down the sidewalk and Sharkey walked to his motorbike. He hunched over the chain and lock.

"Okay," Bosch said, and they got out of the car.

•   •   •

That would be enough for today, Sharkey thought. Time to kick. He lit a cigarette and bent over the seat of his motorbike to work the combination on the Master lock. His dreads flopped down past his eyes and he could smell some of the coconut stuff he had put in his hair the night before at the Jaguar guy's house. That was after Arson had broken the guy's nose and the blood got everywhere. He stood up and was about to wrap the chain around his waist when he saw them coming. Cops. They were too close. Too late to run. Trying to act like he hadn't yet seen them, he quickly made a mental list of everything in his pockets. The credit cards were gone, already sold. The money could have come from anywhere, some of it did. He was cool. The only thing they'd have would be the queer guy's identification if they had a lineup. Sharkey was surprised the guy had made a report. No one ever had before.

Sharkey smiled at the two approaching cops, and the man held up a tape recorder. A tape recorder? What was this? The man hit the play button and after a few seconds Sharkey recognized his own voice. Then he recognized where it had come from. This wasn't about the Jaguar guy. This was about the pipe.

Sharkey said, "So?"

"So," said the man, "we want you to tell us about it."

"Man, I didn't have anything to do with it. You ain't going to put that—Hey! You're the guy from the police station. Yeah, I saw you there the next night. Well, you ain't going to get me to say I did that shit up there."

"Take it down a notch, Sharkey," the man said. "We know you didn't do it. We just want to know what you saw, is all. Lock your bike up again. We'll bring you back."

The man gave his name and the woman's. Bosch and Wish. He said she was FBI, which really confused things. The boy hesitated, then stooped and locked the bike again.

Bosch said, "We just want to take a ride over to Wilcox to ask you some questions, maybe draw a picture."

"Of what?" Sharkey asked.

Bosch didn't answer; he just gestured with his hand to come along and then pointed up the block at a gray Caprice. It was the car Sharkey had seen in front of the Chateau. As they walked, Bosch kept his hand on Sharkey's shoulder. Sharkey wasn't as tall as Bosch yet, but they shared the same wiry build. The boy wore a tie-dyed shirt of purple and yellow shades. Black sunglasses hung around his neck on orange string. The boy put them on as they approached the Caprice.

"Okay, Sharkey," Bosch said at the car. "You know the procedure. We've got to search you before you go in the car. That way we won't have to cuff you for the ride. Put everything on the hood."

"Man, you said I was no suspect," Sharkey protested. "I don't have to do this."

"I told you, procedure. You get it all back. Except the pictures. We can't do that."

Sharkey looked first at Bosch and then Wish, then he started putting his hands in the pockets of his frayed jeans.

"Yeah, we know about the pictures," Bosch said.

The boy put $46.55 on the hood along with a pack of cigarettes and book of matches, a small penknife on a key chain and a deck of Polaroid photos. They were photos of Sharkey and the other guys in the crew. In each, the model was naked and in various stages of sexual arousal. As Bosch shuffled through them, Wish looked over his shoulder and then quickly looked away. She picked up the pack of cigarettes and looked through it, finding a single joint among the Kools.

"I guess we have to keep that, too," Bosch said.

They drove to the police station on Wilcox because it was rush hour and it would have taken them an hour to get to the Federal Building in Westwood. It was after six by the time they got into the detective bureau, and the place was deserted, everybody having gone home. Bosch took Sharkey into one of the eight-by-eight interview rooms. There was a small, cigarette-scarred table and three chairs in the room. A handmade sign on one wall said No Sniveling! He sat Sharkey down in the Slider—a wooden chair with its seat heavily waxed and a quarter-inch of wood cut off the bottom of the front two legs. The incline was not enough to notice, but enough that the people who sat in the chair could not get comfortable. They would lean back like most hard cases and slowly slide off the front. The only thing they could do was lean forward, right into the face of their interrogator. Bosch told the boy not to move, then stepped outside to plan a strategy with Wish, shutting the door. She opened the door after he closed it.

She said, "It's illegal to leave a juvenile in a closed room unattended."

Bosch closed the door again.

"He isn't complaining," he said. "We've got to talk. What's your feel for him? You want him, or you want me to take it?"

"I don't know," she said.

That settled it. That was a no. An initial interview with a witness, a reluctant witness at that, required a skillful blend of scamming, cajoling, demanding. If she didn't know, she didn't go.

"You're supposed to be the expert interrogator," she said in what seemed to Bosch to be a mocking voice. "According to your file. I don't know if that's using brains or brawn. But I'd like to see how it's done."

He nodded, ignoring the jab. He reached into his pocket for the boy's cigarettes and matches.

"Go in and give him these. I want to go check my desk for messages and set up a tape." When he saw the look on her face as she eyed the cigarettes, he added, "First rule of interrogation: make the subject think he is comfortable. Give 'im the cigarettes. Hold your breath if you don't like it."

He started to walk away but she said, "Bosch, what was he doing with those pictures?"

So that was what was bothering her, he thought. "Look. Five years ago a kid like him would have gone with that man and done who knows what. Nowadays, he sells him a picture instead. There are so many killers—diseases and otherwise—these kids are getting smart. It's safer to sell your Polaroids than to sell your flesh."

She opened the door to the interview room and went in.

Bosch crossed the squad room and checked the chrome spike on his desk for messages. His lawyer had finally called back. So had Bremmer over at the *Times*, though he had left a pseudonym they had both agreed on earlier.

Bosch didn't want anybody snooping around his desk to know the press had called.

Bosch left the messages on the spike, took out his ID card and went to the supply closet and slipped the lock. He opened a new ninety-minute cassette and popped it into the recorder on the bottom shelf of the closet. He turned on the machine and made sure the backup cassette was turning. He set it on record and watched to make sure both tapes were rolling. Then he went back down the hallway to the front desk and told a fat Explorer Scout who was sitting there to order a pizza to be delivered to the station.

He gave the kid a ten and told him to bring it to the interview room with three Cokes when it came.

"What do you want on it?" the kid asked.

"What do you like?"

"Sausage and pepperoni. Hate anchovies."

"Make it anchovies."

Bosch walked back to the detective bureau. Wish and Sharkey were silent when he walked back into the small interview room, and he had the feeling they had not been talking much. Wish had no feel for the boy. She sat to Sharkey's right. Bosch took the seat on his left. The only window was a small square of mirrored glass in the door. People could look in but not out. Bosch decided to be up front with the boy from the start. He was a kid, but he was probably wiser than most of the men who had sat on the Slider before him. If he sensed deceit, he would start answering questions in one-syllable words.

"Sharkey, we are going to tape this because it might help us later to go over it," Bosch said. "Like I said, you are not a suspect, so you don't have to worry about what you say, unless of course you're going to say you did it."

"See what I mean?" the boy protested. "I knew you'd get around to saying that and putting on the tape. Shit, I been in one of these rooms before, you know."

"That's why we aren't bullshitting you. So let's say it once for the record. I'm Harry Bosch, LAPD, this is Eleanor Wish, FBI, and you are Edward Niese, AKA Sharkey. I want to start by—"

"What's this shit? Was that the president what got dragged in that pipe? What's the FBI doing here?"

"Sharkey!" Bosch said loudly. "Cool it. It's just an exchange program. Like when you used to go to school and the kids would come from France or someplace. Think like she's from France. She's just kinda watching and learning from the pros." He smiled and winked at Wish. Sharkey looked over at her and smiled a little, too. "First question, Sharkey, let's get it out of the way so we can get to the good stuff. Did you do the guy up at the dam?"

"Fuck no. I see—"

"Wait a minute, wait a minute," Wish broke in. She looked at Bosch. "Can we go outside a moment?"

Bosch got up and walked out. She followed, and this time she closed the interview room door.

"What are you doing?" he said.

"What are *you* doing? Are you going to read that kid his rights, or do you want to taint this interview from the start?"

"What are you talking about? He didn't do it. He isn't a suspect. I'm just asking him questions because I'm trying to establish an interrogation pattern."

"We don't know he isn't the killer. I think we should give him his rights."

"We read him his rights and he is going to think we think he's a suspect, not a witness. We do that and we might as well go in there and talk to the walls. He won't remember a thing."

She walked back into the interview room without another word. Bosch followed and picked up where he had left off, without saying anything about anybody's rights.

"You do the guy in the pipe, Sharkey?"

"No way, man. I seen him, that's all. He was already dead."

The boy looked to his right at Wish as he said this. Then he pulled himself up in his chair.

"Okay, Sharkey," Bosch said, "By the way, how old are you, where you from, tell me a couple of things like that."

"Almost eighteen, man, then I'm free," the boy said, looking at Bosch. "My mom lives up in Chatsworth, but I try not to live with—man, you already got all of this in one of your little notebooks."

"You a faggot, Sharkey?"

"No way, man," the boy said, staring hard at Bosch. "I sell them pictures, big fucking deal. I ain't one of 'em."

"You do more'n sell pictures to them? You roll a few when you get the chance? Bust 'em up, take their money. Who's going to file a complaint? Right?"

Now Sharkey looked back over to Wish and raised an open hand. "I don't do that shit. I thought we're talking about the dead guy."

"We are, Sharkey," Bosch said. "I just want to figure out who we're dealing with here, is all. Take it from the top. Tell us the story. I got pizza coming and there's more cigarettes. We got the time."

"It won't take any time. I din't see anything, except the body in there. I hope there's no anchovies."

He said this looking at Wish while pulling himself up in the chair. He had established a pattern in which he would look at Bosch when he was telling the truth, at Wish when he was shading it or outright lying. Scammers always play to the women, Bosch thought.

"Sharkey," Bosch said, "if you want we can take you up to Sylmar and have 'em hold you overnight. We can start again in the morning, maybe when you're memory's a little—"

"I'm worried about my bike back there, might get stole."

"Forget the bike," Bosch said, leaning into the boy's personal space. "We aren't spoiling you, Sharkey, you haven't told us anything yet. Start the story, then we'll worry about the bike."

"Okay, okay. I'll tell you everything."

The boy reached for his cigarettes on the table and Bosch pulled back and got out one of his own. The leaning in and out of his face was a technique Bosch had learned while spending what seemed like ten thousand hours in these little rooms. Lean in, invade that foot and a half that is all theirs, their own space. Lean back when you get what you want. It's subliminal. Most of what goes on in a police interrogation has nothing to do with what is said. It is interpretation, nuance. And sometimes what isn't said. He lit Sharkey's cigarette first. Wish leaned back in her chair as they exhaled the blue smoke.

"You wanna smoke, Agent Wish?" Bosch said.

She shook her head no.

Bosch looked at Sharkey and a knowing look passed between them. It said, You and me, sport. The boy smiled. Bosch nodded for him to start his story and he did. And it was a story.

"I go up there to crash sometimes," Sharkey said. "You know? When I don't find anybody to help me out with some motel money or nothing. Sometimes the room at my crew's motel is too crowded. I gotta get out. So I go up there, sleep in the pipe. It stays warm most the night. Not bad. So anyway, it was one of those nights. So I went up there—"

"What time was this?" Wish asked.

Bosch gave her a look that said, Cool it, ask the questions after the story is out. The kid had been going pretty good.

"Musta been pretty late," Sharkey answered. "Three, maybe four o'clock. I don't have a watch. And so I went up there. And I went in the pipe and I saw the guy that was dead. Just laying there. I climbed out and split. I wasn't going to stay in there with a dead guy. When I got down the hill I called you guys, nine one one."

He looked back from Wish to Bosch.

"That's it," he said. "Can I get a ride back to my bike?"

No one answered, so Sharkey lit another cigarette and pulled himself up in the chair.

"That's a nice story, Edward, but we need the whole thing," Bosch said. "We also need it right."

"Whaddaya mean?"

"I mean it sounds like it was made up by a moron, is what I mean. How'd you see the body in there?"

"I had a flashlight," he explained to Wish.

"No you didn't. You had matches, we found one." Bosch leaned forward until his face was only a foot from the boy's. "Sharkey, how do you think we knew it was you that called? You think the operator just recognized your voice? 'Oh, that's old Sharkey. He's a good kid, calling us about the body.' Think, Sharkey. You signed your name—or at least half of it on the pipe up there. We got your prints off a half a can of paint. And we know you only crawled halfway in the pipe. That's when you got scared and got out. You left tracks."

Sharkey stared forward, his eyes slightly lifted toward the mirrored window on the door.

"You knew the body was there before you went in. You

saw somebody drag it into the pipe, Sharkey. Look at me now and tell me the real story."

"Look, I didn't see nobody's face. It was too dark, man," the boy said to Bosch. Eleanor let out a breath. Bosch felt like telling her that if she thought the boy was a waste of time she could leave.

"I was hiding," Sharkey said. "'Cause, see, at first I thought they were after me or something. I had nothin' to do with this. Why you dragging me down, man?"

"We got a man dead, Edward. We've got to find out why. We don't care about faces. That's fine. Tell us what you did see, and then you're no longer in it."

"That'll be it?"

"That'll be it."

Bosch leaned back then and lit his second cigarette.

"Well, yeah, I was up there and I wasn't too tired yet so I was doing my paint thing and I heard a car coming. Like holy shit. And what was weird was that I heard it before I saw it. 'Cause the guy has no lights on. So, man, I hauled ass and hid in the bushes on the hill right by there, you know, right by the pipe, right by where I hide my bike, you know, while I'm sleeping."

The boy was becoming more animated, using his hands and nodding his head and looking mostly at Bosch now.

"Shit, I thought those guys were coming for me, like somebody had called the cops on account of me being up there spraying a scrip or something. So like I hid. In fact, when they got there a guy gets out and says to the other guy he smells paint. But it turns out they didn't even see me. They just stopped by the pipe 'cause of the body. And only it wasn't a car, either. It was a Jeep."

"You get a license plate number?" Wish said.

"Let him tell it," Bosch said without looking at her.

"No, I didn't get a fuckin' plate. Shit, their lights were off and it was too dark. So anyway, there was three of them, if you count the dead guy. One guy gets out, he was the driver, and he pulls the dead guy right out of the back, from underneath a blanket or something. Opened a little back door those Jeeps got and drug the guy onto the ground. It was total horror, man. I could tell it was real, you know, a real dead body, just kinda by the way it fell on the ground. Like a dead guy. It made a noise like a body. Not like on TV. But what you'd expect, like, 'Oh no, that's a body he drug out of there,' or something. Then he drug it into the pipe. The other guy wouldn't help him. He stayed in the Jeep. So the first dude, he did it by hisself."

Sharkey took a deep drag on his cigarette and then killed it in the tin ashtray, which was already full of ash and old butts. He exhaled through his nose and looked at Bosch, who just nodded for him to continue. The boy pulled himself up in the seat.

"Um, I stayed there and the guy came out of the pipe after a minute. No longer than that. He looked around when he came out but didn't see me. He went over to a bush near where I was hiding and tore off a branch. Then he went back inside the pipe for a while. And I could hear him in there sweeping or something with the branch. Then he came out and they left. Oh, and uh, he started to back up and the reverse light went on, you know. He took it out of gear like real quick. Then I heard him say something about they couldn't go backward 'cause of the light. They might get seen. So then they went forward, you know, without lights. They drove down the road and across the dam and around the other side of the lake. When they went by that little house on the dam they bashed the light bulb. I saw it go out. I stayed hidden till I couldn't hear the engine anymore. Then I come out."

Sharkey stopped the story for a beat and Wish said, "I'm sorry, can we open the door, get some of this smoke out of here?"

Bosch reached over and pulled the door open without getting up or trying to hide his annoyance. "Go on, Sharkey," was all he said.

"So when they were gone I went over to the pipe and yelled in to the guy. You know, 'Hey, in there' and 'Are you all right,' stuff like that. But nobody answered. So I leaned my bike down on the ground so the light would go in there and I crawled in a little bit. I also lighted a match like you say. And I could see him in there and he looked dead and all. I was going to check but it was too creepy. I got out. I went down the hill and I called the cops. That's all I did, and that's the whole thing."

Bosch figured the boy was going to rob the body but got scared halfway in. That was okay though. The boy could keep that as his secret. Then he thought of the branch taken from the bush and used by the man Sharkey had seen to obliterate the tracks and drag marks in the pipe. He wondered why the uniform cops hadn't come across either the discarded branch or the broken bush during the crime scene search. But he didn't dwell on it long, because he knew the answer. Sloppiness. Laziness. It wasn't the first time things had been missed and wouldn't be the last.

"We're going to go check on that pizza," Bosch said, and he stood up. "We'll only be a couple of minutes."

Outside the interview room Bosch checked his anger and said, "My fault. We should have talked more about how we wanted to do it before we heard his story. I like to hear what they have to say first, then ask questions. It was my fault."

"No problem," Wish said curtly. "He doesn't seem that valuable anyway."

"Maybe." He thought a moment. "I was thinking of going back in and talking a little more to him, maybe bring an Identikit in. And if he doesn't get any better at remembering things we could hypnotize him."

Bosch had no way of knowing what her reaction to the last suggestion would be. He offered it in an offhand manner, half hoping it would slip by unnoticed. California courts had ruled that hypnotizing a witness taints that witness's later court testimony. If they hypnotized Sharkey, he could never be a witness in any court case that could arise from the Meadows investigation.

Wish frowned.

"I know," Bosch. said. "We'd lose him in court. But we might never get to court with what he's given us now. You just said yourself he's not that valuable."

"I just don't know whether we should close the door on his usefulness now. So early in the investigation."

Bosch walked over to the interview room door and looked through the one-way glass at the boy. He was smoking another cigarette. He put it down on the ashtray and stood up. He looked at the door window, but Bosch knew he couldn't see out. The boy quickly and quietly switched his chair with the one Wish had been using. Bosch smiled and said, "He's a smart kid. There might be more there that we won't get unless we put him under. I think it's worth the chance."

"I didn't know you were one of LAPD's hypnotists. I must have missed that in your file."

"I'm sure there's a lot you missed," Bosch replied. After a few moments, he said, "I guess I'm one of the last around. After the Supreme Court shot it down the department quit training people. There was only one class of us. I was one of the youngest. Most of the others have retired."

"Anyway," she said, "I don't think we should do it yet. Let's talk to him some more, maybe wait a couple days before we waste him as a witness."

"Fine. But in a couple days who knows where a kid like Sharkey will be?"

"Oh, you're resourceful. You found him this time. You can do it again."

"You want to take a shot in there?"

"No, you're doing okay. As long as I can jump in now, whenever I think of something."

She smiled and he smiled and they went back into the interview room, which smelled of smoke and sweat. Bosch left the door open again to air it out. Wish didn't have to ask.

"No food?" Sharkey said.

"Still on the way," Bosch said.

Bosch and Wish took Sharkey through his story two more times, picking up small details along the way. They did it as a team. Partners, exchanging knowing looks, surreptitious nods, even smiles. A few times Bosch noticed Wish slipping in her chair and thought he saw a smile play on Sharkey's boyish face. When the pizza came he protested the anchovies but still ate three-quarters of the pie and downed two of the Cokes. Bosch and Wish passed.

Sharkey told them the Jeep that Meadows's body came in was dirty white or beige. He said there was a seal on the side door but he could not describe it. Perhaps this was so it would look like a DWP vehicle, Bosch thought. Maybe it was a DWP vehicle. Now he definitely wanted to hypnotize the boy, but he decided not to bring it up again. He'd wait for Wish to come around, to see that it had to be done.

Sharkey said the one who stayed behind in the Jeep as the body was dragged into the pipe didn't say a word the whole time the boy watched. This person was smaller than the driver. Sharkey described seeing only a slightly built form; a whisper of a silhouette against what little light there was from the moon above the reservoir perimeter's thick stand of pine.

"What did this other guy do?" Wish asked.

"Just watched, I guess. Like a lookout. He didn't even do the driving. I guess he was in charge or something."

The boy got a better look at the driver but not enough to describe a face, or to make a drawing with the facial templates in the Identikit that Bosch had brought into the interview room. The driver had dark hair and was white. Sharkey couldn't, or wouldn't, be any more exact in his description. He had worn matching dark shirt and pants, maybe overalls. Sharkey said that he also wore some kind of equipment belt or carpenter's apron. Its dark tool pockets hung empty at the hips and flapped like an apron at his waist. This was curious to Bosch, and he asked Sharkey several questions, coming at it from different angles but getting no better description.

After an hour they were finished. They left Sharkey in the smoky room while they conferred outside again. Wish said, "All we have to do now is find a Jeep with a blanket in the back. Do a microanalysis and match hairs. Only must be a couple million white or beige Jeeps in the state.

You want me to put out a BOLO, or you want to handle it?"

"Look. Two hours ago we had nothing. Now we've got a lot. If you want, let me hypnotize the kid. Who knows, we might get a license plate, a better description of the driver, maybe he'll remember a name spoken or be able to describe the seal on the door."

Bosch held his hands out palms up. His offer was out, but she had already turned it down. And she did again.

"Not yet, Bosch. Let me talk to Rourke. Maybe tomorrow. I don't want to rush into that and possibly have it come back on us as a mistake. Okay?"

He nodded and dropped his hands.

"So what now?" she said.

"Well, the kid's eaten. Why don't we get him squared away and then you and I get something to eat? There's a place—"

"I can't," she said.

"—on Overland I know."

"I already have plans for tonight. I'm sorry. Maybe we can make it another night."

"Sure." He walked over to the interview room door and looked through the glass. Anything to avoid showing his face to her. He felt foolish for trying to move so quickly with her. He said, "If you have to get going, go ahead. I'll get him in a shelter or something for the night. We don't both have to waste our time with it."

"You sure?"

"Yeah. I'll take care of him. I'll get a patrol unit to take us. We'll get his bike on the way. I'll have 'em drop me by my car."

"That's nice. I mean about you getting his bike and taking care of him."

"Well, we made a deal with him, remember?"

"I remember. But you care about him. I watched how you handled him. You see some of yourself there?"

He turned away from the glass to look at her.

"No, not especially," he said. "He's just another wit that has to be interviewed. You think he's a little bastard now, wait another year, wait till he's nineteen or twenty, if he makes it. He'll be a monster then. Preying on people. This isn't the last time he'll be sitting in that room. He'll be in and out of there his whole life till he kills somebody or they kill him. It's Darwin's rules; survival of the fittest, and he's fit to survive. So no, I don't care about him. I'm putting him in a shelter because I want to know where he is in case we need him again. That's all."

"Nice speech, but I don't think so. I know a little bit about you, Bosch. You care, all right. The way you got him dinner and asked him—"

"Look, I don't care how many times you read my file. You think that means you know about me? I told you, that's bullshit."

He had come up close to her, until his face was only a foot from hers. But she looked away from him, down at her notebook, as if what she had written there might have something to do with what he was saying.

"Look," he said, "we can work this together, maybe even find out who killed Meadows if we get a few more breaks like the one with the kid today. But we won't really be partners and we won't really know each other. So maybe we shouldn't act like we do. Don't tell me about your little brother with a crew cut and how he looks the way I did, because you don't know how I was. A bunch of papers and pictures in a file don't say anything about me."

She closed the notebook and put it in her purse. Then

she finally looked up at him. There was a knocking from inside the interview room. Sharkey was looking at himself in the mirrored window of the door. But they both ignored him and Wish just drilled Bosch with her eyes.

"You always get this way when a woman turns you down for dinner?" she asked calmly.

"That's got nothing to do with it and you know it."

"Sure. I know it." She started to walk away, then said, "Let's say nine A.M., we meet at the bureau again?"

He didn't answer and then she did walk away, toward the squad room door. Sharkey pounded on his door again, and Bosch looked over and saw the boy picking the acne on his face in the door's mirror. Wish turned once more before she was out of the room.

"I wasn't talking about my little brother," she said. "He was my big brother, actually. And I was talking about a long time ago. About the way he looked when I was a little girl and he was going away for a while, to Vietnam."

Bosch didn't look at her. He couldn't. He realized what was coming.

"I remember how he looked then," she said, "because it was the last time I saw him. It sticks with you. He was one of the ones that didn't come back."

She walked out.

Harry ate the last slice of pizza. It was cold and he hated anchovies and he felt he deserved it that way. Same for the Coke, which was warm. Afterward, he sat at the homicide table and made calls until he found an empty bed, rather, an empty space, in one of the no-questions-asked shelters near the Boulevard. At Home Street Home they didn't try to send runaways back to where they came from. They knew in most cases home was a worse nightmare than the streets. They just gave the children a safe place to sleep and then tried to send them off to any place but Hollywood.

He checked out an unmarked car and drove Sharkey to his motorbike. It would not fit in the trunk, so Bosch made a deal with the boy. Sharkey would ride the bike to the shelter and Bosch would follow. When the boy got there and got checked in, Bosch would give him back his money and wallet and cigarettes. But not the Polaroids and the joint. Those went into the trash. Sharkey didn't like it but he did it. Bosch told him to hang around the shelter a couple of days, though he knew the boy would probably split first thing in the morning.

"I found you once. If I need to, I can do it again," he said as the boy locked his bike up outside the home.

"I know, I know," Sharkey said.

It was an idle threat. Bosch knew that he had found Sharkey when the boy didn't know he was being looked for. It would be a different story if he wanted to hide. Bosch gave the boy one of his cheap business cards and told him to give a call if he thought of anything that would help.

"That would help you or me?" Sharkey asked.

Bosch didn't answer. He got back in the car and drove back to the station on Wilcox, watching the mirror for signs of a tail. He didn't see any. After checking the car in he went to his desk and picked up the FBI files. He went to the watch office, where the night lieutenant called one of his patrol units in to give Bosch a lift to the Federal Building. The patrol officer was a young cop with a quarter-inch hairdo. Asian. Bosch had heard around the station that he was called Gung Ho. They rode in silence the whole twenty ninutes to the Federal Building.

Harry got home by nine. The red light on his phone machine was blinking but there was no message, just the sound of someone hanging up. He turned on the radio for the Dodgers game, but then he turned it off, tired of hearing people talk. He put CDs by Sonny Rollins, Frank Morlan, and Branford Marsalis into the stereo and listened to the saxophone instead. He spread the files out on the table in the dining room and turned the cap on a bottle of beer. Alcohol and jazz, he thought as he swallowed. Sleeping with your clothes on. You're a cliché cop, Bosch. An open book. And no different from the dozen other fools who must hit on her every day. Just stick to the business in front of you. And don't hope for anything else. He opened the file on Meadows, carefully reading every page, whereas before, in the car with Wish, he had only skimmed.

Meadows was an enigma to Bosch. A pillhead, a heroin user, but a soldier who had re-upped to stay in Vietnam. Even after they took him out of the tunnels, he stayed. In 1970, after two years in the tunnels, he was assigned to a military police unit attached to the American embassy in Saigon. Never saw enemy action again but stayed right up to the end. After the treaty and pullout of 1973, he got a discharge and stayed on again, this time as one of the civilian advisers attached to the embassy. Everybody was going home, but not Meadows. He didn't leave until April 30, 1975, the day of the fall of Saigon. He was on a helicopter and then a plane ferrying refugees out of the country, on their way to the United States. That was his last government assignment: security on the massive refugee transport to the Philippines and then to the States.

According to the records, Meadows stayed in Southern California after coming back. But his skills were limited to military police, tunnel killer, and drug dealer. There was an LAPD application in the file that was marked rejected. He failed the drug test. Next in the file was a National Criminal Intelligence Computer sheet that showed Meadows's record. His first arrest, for possession of heroin, was in 1978. Probation. The next year, he was popped again, this time for possession with intent to sell. He pleaded it out to simple possession and got eighteen months at Wayside Honor Rancho. He did ten of them. The next two years were marked by frequent arrests on marks beefs—fresh needle tracks being a misdemeanor good for sixty days in county lockup. It looked like Meadows was riding the revolving door at county until 1981, when he went away for some substantial time. It was for attempted robbery, a federal beef. The NCIC printout didn't say if it was bank robbery, but Bosch figured it had to be to bring the feds in.

The sheet said Meadows was sentenced to four years at Lompoc and served two.

He wasn't out but a few months before he was picked up for a bank robbery. They must have had him cold. He pleaded guilty and took five years back to Lompoc. He would have been out in three but two years into the sentence he was busted in an escape attempt. He got five more years and was transferred to Terminal Island.

Meadows was paroled from TI in 1988. All those years in stir, Bosch thought. He never knew, never heard from him. What would he have done if he had heard? He thought about that for a moment. It probably changed Meadows more than the war. He was paroled to a halfway house for Vietnam vets. The place was called Charlie Company and was on a farm north of Ventura, about forty miles from Los Angeles. He stayed there nearly a year.

After that there were no further contacts, according to Meadows's sheet. The marks beef that had prompted Meadows to call Bosch a year earlier had never been processed. It wasn't on the sheet. No other known contact with police upon his release from prison.

There was another sheet in the package. This one was handwritten and Bosch guessed it was Wish's clean, legible hand. It was a work and home history. Gathered from records searches of Social Security and DMV records, the entries ran vertically down the left side of the paper. But there were gaps. Time periods unaccounted for. Meadows had worked for the Southern California Water District when he first came back from Vietnam. He was a pipeline inspector. He lost the job after four months for excessive tardiness and sick-outs. From there he must have tried his hand at dealing heroin, because the next lawful employment was not listed until after he got out of Wayside in 1979. He went to work for DWP as an underground inspector—storm drainage division. Lost the job six months later for the same reasons as with the water district. There were a few other sporadic employments. After he left Charlie Company he caught on with a gold mining company in the Santa Clarita Valley for a few months. Nothing else.

There were almost a dozen home addresses listed. Most of them were apartments in Hollywood. There was a house in San Pedro, prior to the 1979 bust. If he was dealing at the time, he was probably getting it at the port in Long Beach, Bosch thought. The San Pedro address would have been convenient.

Bosch also saw that he had lived in the Sepulveda apartment since leaving Charlie Company. There was nothing else in the file about the halfway house or what Meadows did there. Bosch found the name of Meadows's parole officer on the copies of his six-month evaluation reports.

Daryl Slater, worked out of Van Nuys. Bosch wrote it down in the notebook. He also wrote down the address of Charlie Company. He then spread the arrests sheet, the work and home history, and the parole reports out in front of him. On a new piece of paper he began to write out a chronology beginning with Meadows being sent to federal prison in 1981.

When he was done, many of the gaps were closed. Meadows served a total of six and a half years in the federal pen. He was paroled in early 1988, when he was sponsored by the Charlie Company program. He spent ten months in the program before moving to the apartment in Sepulveda. Parole reports showed he secured a job as a drill operator in the gold mine in the Santa Clarita Valley. He completed parole in February 1989 and he quit his job a day after his PO signed him off. No known employment since, according to the Social Security Administration. IRS said Meadows hadn't filed a return since 1988.

Bosch went into the kitchen and got a beer out and made a ham and cheese sandwich. He stood by the sink eating and drinking and trying to organize things about the case in his head. He believed that Meadows had been scheming from the time he walked out of TI, or at least Charlie Company. He'd had a plan. He worked legitimate jobs until he cleared parole, and then he quit and the plan was set into action. Bosch felt sure of it. And he felt that it was therefore likely that, at either the prison or the halfway house, Meadows had hooked up with the men who had burglarized the bank with him. And then killed him.

The doorbell rang. Bosch checked his watch and saw it was eleven o'clock. He walked to the door and looked through the peephole and saw Eleanor Wish staring at him. He stepped back, glanced at the mirror in the entrance hall and saw a man with dark, tired eyes looking back at him. He smoothed his hair and opened the door.

"Hello," she said. "Truce?"

"Truce. How'd you know where I—never mind. Come in."

She was wearing the same suit as earlier, hadn't been home yet. He saw her notice the files and paperwork on the card table.

"Working late," he said. "Just looking over some things in the file on Meadows."

"Good. Um, I happened to be out this way and I just wanted, I just came by to say that we . . . Well, it's been a rough week so far. For both of us. Maybe tomorrow we can start this partnership over."

"Yes," he said. "And, listen, I'm sorry for what I said earlier . . . and I'm sorry about your brother. You were trying to say something nice and I. . . . Can you stay a few minutes, have a beer?"

He went to the kitchen and got two fresh bottles. He handed her one and led her through the sliding door to the porch. It was cool out, but there was a warm wind occasionally blowing up the side of the dark canyon. Eleanor Wish looked out at the lights of the Valley. The spotlights from Universal City swept the sky in a repetitive pattern.

"This is very nice," she said. "I've never been in one of these. They're called cantilevers?"

"Yes."

"Must be scary during an earthquake."

"It's scary when the garbage truck drives by."

"So how'd you end up in a place like this?"

"Some people, the ones down there with the spotlights, gave me a bunch of money once to use my name and my so-called technical advice for a TV show. So I didn't have anything else to do with it. When I was growing up in the Valley I always wondered what it would be like to live in one of these things. So I bought it. It used to belong to a movie writer. This is where he worked. It's pretty small, only one bedroom. But that's all I'll ever need, I guess."

She leaned on the railing and looked down the slope into the arroyo. In the dark there was only the dim outline of the live oak grove below. He also leaned over, and absentmindedly peeled bits of the gold foil label off his beer bottle and dropped them. The gold glinted in the darkness as it fluttered down out of sight.

"I have questions," he said. "I want to go up to Ventura."

"Can we talk about it tomorrow? I didn't come up to go over the files. I've been reading those files for almost a year now."

He nodded and stayed quiet, deciding to let her get to whatever it was that brought her. After some time she said, "You must be very angry about what we did to you, the investigation, us checking you out. Then what happened yesterday. I'm sorry."

She took a small sip from her bottle and Bosch realized he had never asked if she wanted a glass. He let her words hang out there in the dark for a few long moments.

"No," he finally said. "I'm not angry. The truth is, I don't really know what I am."

She turned and looked at him. "We thought you'd drop it when Rourke made trouble for you with your lieutenant. Sure, you knew Meadows, but that was a long time ago. That's what I don't get. It's not just another case for you.

But why? There must be something more. Back in Viet-nam? Why's it mean so much to you?"

"I guess I have reasons. Reasons that have nothing to do with the case."

"I believe you. But whether I believe you is not the point. I'm trying to know what's going on. I need to know."

"How's your beer?"

"It's fine. Tell me something, Detective Bosch."

He looked down and watched a little piece of the printed foil disappear in the black.

"I don't know," he said. "Actually I do know and I don't. I guess it goes back to the tunnels. Shared experience. It's nothing like he saved my life or I saved his. Not that easy. But I feel something is owed. No matter what he did or what kind of fuckup he became after. Maybe if I had done more than make a few calls for him last year. I don't know."

"Don't be silly," she said. "When he called you last year he was well into this caper. He was using you then. It's like he's using you now, even though he's dead."

He'd run out of label to peel. He turned around and leaned his back on the railing. He fumbled a cigarette out of his pocket with one hand, put it in his mouth but didn't light it.

"Meadows," he said and shook his head at the memory of the man. "Meadows was something else. . . . Back then, we were all just a bunch of kids, afraid of the dark. And those tunnels were so damn dark. But Meadows, he wasn't afraid. He'd volunteer and volunteer and volunteer. Out of the blue and into the black. That's what he said going on a tunnel mission was. We called it the black echo. It was like going to hell. You're down there and you could smell your own fear. It was like you were dead when you were down there."

They had gradually turned so that they were facing each other. He searched her face and saw what he thought was sympathy. He didn't know if that's what he wanted. He was long past that. But he didn't know what he wanted.

"So all of us scared little kids, we made a promise. Every time anybody went down into one of the tunnels we made a promise. The promise was that no matter what happened down there, nobody would be left behind. Didn't matter if you died down there, you wouldn't be left behind. Because they did things to you, you know. Like our own psych-ops. And it worked. Nobody wanted to be left behind, dead or alive. I read once in a book that it doesn't matter if you're lying beneath a marble tombstone on a hill or at the bottom of an oil sump, when you're dead you're dead.

"But whoever wrote that wasn't over there. When you're alive but you're that close to dying, you think about those things. And then it does matter. . . . And so we made the promise."

Bosch knew he hadn't explained a thing. He told her he was going to get another beer. She said she was fine. When he came back out she smiled at him and said nothing.

"Let me tell you a story about Meadows," he said. "See, the way they worked it was, they'd assign a couple, maybe three of us tunnel rats to go out with a company. So when they'd come across a tunnel, we'd zip on down, check it out, mine it, whatever."

He took a long pull on the fresh beer.

"And so once, this would have been in 1970, Meadows and me were tagging at the back of a patrol. We were in a VC stronghold and, man, it was just riddled with tunnels.

Anyway, we were about three miles from a village called Nhuan Luc when we lost a point man. He got—I'm sorry, you probably don't want to hear this. With your brother and all."

"I do want to hear. Please."

"So this point got shot by a sniper who was in a spider hole. That was what they called the little entrances to a tunnel network. So somebody took out the sniper and then me and Meadows had to go down the hole to check it out. We went down, and right away we had to split up. This was a big network. I followed one line one way and he went the other. We had said we'd go for fifteen minutes, set charges with a twenty-minute delay, then head back, setting more along the way. . . . I remember I found a hospital down there. Four empty grass mats, a cabinet of supplies, all just sitting in the middle of this tunnel. I remember I thought, Jesus Christ, what's going to be around the bend, a drive-in movie or something? I mean these people had dug themselves in. . . . Anyway, there was a little altar, and there was incense burning. Still burning. I knew then that they were still in there somewhere, the VC, and it scared me. I set a charge and hid it behind the altar, and then I started back as fast as I could. I set two more charges along the way, timing everything so it would all go off at once. So I get back to the drop-in point, you know, the original spider hole, and no Meadows. I waited a few minutes and it's getting close. You don't want to be down there when the C-4 goes. Some of those tunnels are a hundred years old. There was nothing I could do, so I climbed out. He wasn't up top either."

He stopped to drink some beer and think about the story. She watched intently but didn't prod him.

"A few minutes later my charges went off and the tunnel, at least the part I had been in, came down. Whoever was in there was dead and buried. We waited a couple hours for the smoke and dust to settle. We hooked a Mighty Mite fan up and blew air down the entry shaft, and then you could see smoke being pushed out and coming up out of the air vents, and other spider holes all around the jungle.

"And when it was clear, me and another guy went in to find Meadows. We thought he was dead, but we had the promise; no matter what, we were going to get him out and send him home. But we didn't find him. Spent the rest of the day down there looking, but all we found were dead VC. Most of them had been shot, some had cut throats. All of them had ears slashed off. When we came up, the top told us we couldn't wait anymore. We had orders. We pulled out, and I had broken the promise."

Bosch was staring blankly out into the night, seeing only the story he was telling.

"Two days later, another company was in the village, Nhuan Luc, and somebody found a tunnel entrance in a hootch. They get their rats to check it out, and they aren't in that tunnel more than five minutes when they find Meadows. He was just sitting like Buddha in one of the passageways. Out of ammo. Talking gibberish. Not making sense, but he was okay. And when they tried to get him to come up with them, he didn't want to. They finally had to tie him up and put a rope on him and have the patrol up there pull him out. Up in the sunlight they saw he was wearing a necklace of human ears. Strung with his tags."

He finished the beer and walked in off the balcony. She followed him to the kitchen, where he got a fresh bottle. She put her half-finished bottle on the counter.

"So that's my story. That was Meadows. He went to

Saigon for some R and R but he came back. He couldn't stay away from the tunnels. After that one, though, he was never the same. He told me that he just got mixed up and lost down there. He just kept going in the wrong direction, killing anything he came across. The word was that there were thirty-three ears on his necklace. And somebody asked me once why Meadows let one of the VC keep an ear. You know, accounting for the odd number. And I told him that Meadows let them all keep an ear."

She shook her head. He nodded his.

Bosch said, "I wish I had found him that time I went back in to look. I let him down."

They both stood for a while looking down at the kitchen floor. Bosch poured the rest of his beer down the sink.

"One question about Meadows's sheet and then no more business," he said. "He got jammed up at Lompoc on an escape attempt. Then sent to TI. You know anything about that?"

"Yes. And it was a tunnel. He was a trusty and he worked in the laundry. The gas dryers had underground vents going out of the building. He dug beneath one of them. No more than an hour a day. They said he had probably been at it at least six months before it was discovered, when the sprinklers they use in the summer on the rec field softened the ground and there was a cave-in."

He nodded his head. He figured it had been a tunnel.

"The two others that were in on it," she said. "A drug dealer and a bank robber. They're still inside. There's no connection to this."

He nodded again.

"I think I should go now," she said. "We have a lot to do tomorrow."

"Yeah. I have a lot more questions."

"I'll try to answer them if I can."

She passed closely by him in the small space between the refrigerator and counter and moved out into the hallway. He could smell her hair as she went by. An apple scent, he thought. He noticed that she was looking at the print hanging on the wall opposite the mirror in the hallway. It was in three separate framed sections and was a print of a fifteenth-century painting called *The Garden of Delights*. The painter was a Dutchman.

"Hieronymus Bosch," she said as she studied the nightmarish landscape of the painting. "When I saw that was your full name I wondered if—"

"No relation," he said. "My mother, she just liked his stuff. I guess 'cause of the last name. She sent that print to me once. Said in the note that it reminded her of L.A. All the crazy people. My foster parents . . . they didn't like it, but I kept it for a lot of years. Had it hanging there as long as I've had this place."

"But you like to be called Harry."

"Yeah, I like Harry."

"Good night, Harry. Thanks for the beer."

"Good night, Eleanor. . . . Thanks for the company."

Part IV

Wednesday, May 23

B y 10 A.M. they were on the Ventura Freeway, which cuts across the bottom of the San Fernando Valley and out of the city. Bosch was driving and they were going against the grain of traffic, heading northwest, toward Ventura County, and leaving behind the blanket of smog that filled the Valley like dirty cream in a bowl.

They were heading to Charlie Company. The FBI had only done a cursory check on Meadows and the prison outreach program the year before. Wish said she had thought its importance was minimal because Meadows's stay had ended nearly a year before the tunnel caper. She said the bureau had requested a copy of Meadows's file but had not checked the names of other convicts who were part of the program at the same time as Meadows. Bosch thought this was a mistake. Meadows's work record indicated the bank caper was part of a long-range plan, he told Wish. The bank burglary might have been hatched at Charlie Company.

Before leaving, Bosch had called Meadows's parole officer, Daryl Slater, and was given a rundown on Charlie Company. Slater said the place was a vegetable farm owned and operated by an army colonel who was retired and born again. He contracted with the state and federal prisons to take early release cases, the only requirement being that they be Vietnam combat veterans. That wasn't too difficult a bill to fill, Slater said. As in every other state in the country, the prisons in California had high populations of Vietnam vets. Gordon Scales, the former colonel, didn't care what crimes the vets had been convicted of, Slater said. He just wanted to set them right again. The place had a staff of three, including Scales, and held no more than twenty-four men at a time. The average stay was nine months. They worked the vegetable fields from six to three, stopping only for lunch at noon. After the workday there was an hour-long session called soul talk, then dinner and TV. Another hour of religion before lights-out. Slater said Scales used his connections in the community to place the vets in jobs when they were ready for the outside world. In six years, Charlie Company had a recidivist record of only 11 percent. A figure so enviable that Scales got a favorable mention in a speech by the president during his last campaign swing through the state.

"The man's a hero," Slater said. "And not 'cause of the war. For what he did after. When you get a place like that, moving maybe thirty, forty cons through it a year, and only one in ten gets his ass in a jam again, then you are talking about a major success. Scales, he has the ear of the federal and state parole boards and half the wardens in this state."

"Does that mean he gets to pick who goes to Charlie Company?" Bosch asked.

"Maybe not pick, but give final approval to, yes," the

PO said. "But the word on this guy is out. His name is known in every and any cellblock where you got a vet doing time. These guys come to him. They send letters, send Bibles, make phone calls, have lawyers get in contact. All to get Scales to sponsor them."

"Is that how Meadows got there?"

"Far as I know. He was already heading there when he was assigned to me. You'd have to call Terminal Island and have them check their files. Or talk to Scales."

Bosch filled Wish in on the conversation while they were on the road. Otherwise, it was a long ride and there were long periods of silence. Bosch spent much of the time wondering about the night before. Her visit. Why had she come? After they crossed into Ventura County his mind came back to the case, and he asked her some of the questions he had come up with the night before while reviewing the files.

"Why didn't they hit the main vault? At WestLand there were two vaults. Safe-deposit and then the bank's main vault, for the cash and the tellers' boxes. The crime scene reports said the design of both vaults was the same. The safe-deposit vault was bigger but the armoring in the floor was the same. So it would seem that Meadows and his partners could just as easily have tunneled to the main vault, gotten in and taken whatever was there and gotten out. No need to risk spending a whole weekend inside. No need to pry open safe-deposit boxes either."

"Maybe they didn't know they were the same. Maybe they assumed the main vault would be tougher."

"But we are assuming they had some knowledge of the safe-deposit vault's structure before they started on this. Why didn't they have the same knowledge of the other vault?"

"They couldn't recon the main vault. It's not open to the public. But we think one of them rented a box in the safe-deposit vault and went in to check it out. Used a phony name, of course. But, see, they could check out one vault and not the other. Maybe that's why."

Bosch nodded and said, "How much was in the main vault?"

"Don't know offhand. It should have been in the reports I gave you. If not, it's in the other files back at the bureau."

"More, though. Right? There was more cash in the main vault than what, the two or three million in property they got from the boxes."

"I think that is probably right."

"See what I'm saying? If they had hit the main vault the stuff would have been laying around in stacks and bags. Right there for the taking. It would have been easier. There probably would have been more money for less trouble."

"But, Harry, we know that from hindsight. Who knows what they knew going in? Maybe they thought there was more in the boxes. They gambled and lost."

"Or maybe they won."

She looked over at him.

"Maybe there was something there in the boxes that we don't even know about. That nobody reported missing. Something that made the safe-deposit vault the better target. Made it worth more than the main vault."

"If you're thinking drugs, the answer is no. We thought of that. We had the DEA bring around one of their dogs and he went through the broken boxes. Nothing. No trace of drugs. He then sniffed around the boxes the thieves hadn't gotten to and he got one hit. On one of the small ones."

She laughed for a moment and said, "So then we drilled this box the dog went nuts over and found five grams of coke in a bag. This poor guy who kept his coke stash at the bank got busted just because somebody happened to tunnel into the same vault."

Wish laughed again, but it seemed to be a little forced to Bosch. The story wasn't that funny. "Anyway," she said, "the case against the guy was kicked by an assistant U.S. attorney because he said it was a bad search. We violated the guy when we drilled his box without a warrant."

Bosch exited the freeway into the town of Ventura and headed north. "I still like the drug angle, despite the dog," he said after a quarter hour of silence. "They aren't infallible, those dogs. If the stuff was packed in there right and the thieves got it, there may not have been a trace. A couple of those boxes with coke in them and the caper starts being worth their while."

"Your next question will be about the customer lists, right?" she said.

"Right."

"Well, we did a lot of work on that. We checked everybody, right down to tracing purchases of things they said were in the boxes. We didn't find who did the job, but we probably saved the bank's insurance companies a couple million in paying for things that were reported stolen but never really existed."

He pulled into a gas station so he could take out a map book from under the seat and figure out the way to Charlie Company. She continued to defend the FBI investigation.

"The DEA looked at every name on the boxholder list and drew a blank. We ran the names through NCIC. We got a few hits but nothing serious, mostly old stuff." She gave another one of those short fake laughs. "One of the holders of one of the bigger boxes had a kiddy porn conviction from the seventies. Served a deuce at Soledad. Anyway, after the bank job he was contacted and he reported nothing was taken, said he had recently emptied his box.

But they say these pedophiles can never part with their stuff, their photos and films, even letters written about kids. And there was no record at the bank of him going into the box in the two months before the burglary. So we figured that the box was for his collection. But, anyway, that had nothing to do with the job. Nothing we turned up did."

Bosch found the way on the map and pulled out of the service station. Charlie Company was in grove country. He thought about her story about the pedophile. Something about it bothered him. He rolled it around in his head but couldn't get to it. He let it drift and went on to another question.

"Why was nothing ever recovered? All that jewelry and bonds and stocks, and nothing ever turns up except for a single bracelet. Not even any of the other worthless things that were taken."

"They are sitting on it until they think they are clear," Wish said. "That's why Meadows was smoked. He went out of line and pawned the bracelet before he should have, maybe before everyone agreed they were clear. They found out he'd sold it. He wouldn't say where, so they buzzed him until he told them. Then they killed him."

"And by coincidence, I get the call."

"It happens."

"There is something in that story that doesn't work," Bosch said. "We start out with Meadows getting juiced, tortured, right? He tells them what they want, they put the hot load in his arm and they go get the bracelet from the pawnshop, okay?"

"Okay."

"But, see, it doesn't work. I've got the pawn slip. It was hidden. So he didn't give it to them, and they had to go break in the shop and take the bracelet, covering the scam by also taking a lot of other junk. So if he didn't give them the pawn slip, how'd they know where the bracelet was?"

"He told them, I guess," Wish said.

"I don't think so. I don't see him giving up one and not the other. He had nothing to gain from holding back the slip. If they got the name of the shop out of him, they would've gotten the slip."

"So, you're saying he died before he told them anything. And they already knew where the bracelet was pawned."

"Right. They worked him to get the ticket, but he wouldn't give it up, wouldn't break. They killed him. Then they dump the body and roll his place. But they still don't find the pawn stub. So they hit the pawnshop like third-rate burglars. The question is, if Meadows didn't tell them where he had sold the bracelet and they didn't find the stub, how did they know where it was?"

"Harry, this is speculation on top of speculation."

"That's what cops do."

"Well, I don't know. Could have been a lot of things. They could have had a tail on Meadows 'cause they didn't trust him and could have seen him go into the pawnshop. Could've been a lot of things."

"Could've been they had somebody, say a cop, who saw the bracelet on the monthly pawn sheets and told them. The sheets go to every police department in the county."

"I think that kind of speculation is reckless."

They were there. Bosch braked the car at a gravel entranceway below a wooden sign with a green eagle painted on it and the words Charlie Company. The gate was open and they drove down a gravel road with muddy irrigation ditches running along both sides. The road split the farmland, with tomatoes on the right and what smelled like peppers on the left. Up ahead there was a large aluminum-sided barn and a sprawling ranch-style house. Behind these Bosch could see a grove of avocado trees. They drove into a circular parking area in front of the ranch house and Bosch cut the engine.

A man wearing a white apron that was as clean as his shaven head came to the screen at the front door.

"Mr. Scales here?" Bosch asked.

"Colonel Scales, you mean? No, he is not. It's almost time for chow, though. He'll be coming in from the fields then."

The man did not invite them to come in out of the sun, and so Bosch and Wish went back and sat in the car. A few minutes later a dusty white pickup truck drove up. It had an eagle inside a large letter C painted on the driver's door. Three men got out of the cab and six more piled out of the back. They moved quickly toward the ranch house. They ranged in age from late thirties to late forties. They wore military green pants and white T-shirts soaked with sweat. No one wore a bandanna or sunglasses or had his sleeves rolled up. No one's hair was longer than a quarter inch. The white men were burned brown like stained wood. The driver, wearing the same uniform but at least ten years older than the rest, slowed to a stop and let the others go inside. As he approached, Bosch put him on the early side of his sixties, but a guy who was almost as solid as he had been in his twenties. His hair, what could be seen of it against his gleaming skull, was white and his skin was like walnut. He was wearing work gloves.

"Help you?" he asked.

"Colonel Scales?" Bosch said.

"That's right. You police?"

Bosch nodded and made introductions. Scales didn't seem too impressed, even with the FBI being mentioned.

"You remember about seven, eight months ago the FBI asked you for some information on a William Meadows, who spent some time here?" Wish asked.

"Sure I do. I remember every time you people call up or come around asking about one of my boys. I resent it, so I remember it. You want more information on Billy? Is he in some trouble?"

"Not anymore," Bosch said.

"What's that supposed to mean?" Scales said. "Sounds like you're saying he's dead."

"You didn't know?" Bosch said.

"'Course I didn't. Tell me what happened to him."

Bosch thought he saw genuine surprise and then a flashing hint of sadness cross Scales's face. The news had hurt.

"He was found dead three days ago in L.A. A homicide. We think it is related to a crime he took part in last year, that you may have heard about from the FBI's previous contact."

"The tunnel thing? At that bank in L.A.?" he asked. "I know what I was told by the FBI. That's it."

"That's fine," Wish said. "What we need from you is more complete information about who was here when Meadows was. We went over this ground before, but we are rechecking, looking for anything that might help. Will you cooperate with us?"

"I always cooperate with you people. I don't like it because half the time I think you got your wires crossed. Most of my boys, when they leave here, they don't get mixed up again. We have a good record here. If Meadows did what you're saying he did, he is the rarity."

"We understand that," she said. "And this will be strictly confidential."

"O'right then, come into my office and you can ask your questions."

As they went through the front door Bosch saw two long tables in what was probably once the ranch house's living room. About twenty men sat before plates of what looked like chicken-fried steaks and mounds of vegetables. Not one looked at Eleanor Wish. That was because they were silently saying grace, their heads down, eyes closed and hands folded. Bosch could see tattoos on almost every arm. When they stopped their prayer a chorus of forks struck home on the plates. A few of the men took the time then to look at Eleanor approvingly. The man in the apron who had come to the screen door earlier now stood in the doorway of the kitchen.

"Colonel, are you eating with the men today, sir?" he called.

Scales nodded and said, "I'll be through in a few minutes."

They went down a hallway and through the first door into an office that was supposed to be a bedroom. It was crowded by a desk with a top the size of a door. Scales pointed to two chairs in front of it and Bosch and Wish sat down, while he took the upholstered job behind the desk.

"Now, I know exactly what I am required by law to give you and what I don't have to even speak to you about. But I am inclined to do more, if it will help and we have an understanding. Meadows—I sort of knew he would end up as you say he did. I prayed to the Good Lord to guide him, but I knew. I will help you. No one should take a life in a civilized world. No one at all."

"Colonel," Bosch began, "we appreciate your help. I want you to know, first off, that we know what kind of job you are doing bere. We know you have the respect and encouragement of both state and federal authorities. But our investigation of Meadows's death leads us to conclude he was involved in a conspiracy with other men who had the same skills as he and—"

"You are saying they are vets," Scales cut in. He was filling a pipe with tobacco from a canister on the desk.

"Possibly. We have not identified them yet, so we don't know it for a fact. But if that is the case, there would seem a possibility that the players in the conspiracy may have met here. I stress the word "may." Therefore, there are two things we want from you. A look at any records you still have on Meadows and a list of every man that was here during the ten months he was."

Scales was tamping his pipe and seemingly paying no attention to what had just been said. Then he said, "No problem on his records—he's dead. On the other, I suppose I should call my lawyer just to make sure I can do that. We run a good program here. And vegetables and money from the state and the feds don't cover it. I get out the soapbox and make the rounds. We rely on the tithings of the community, civic organizations, things like that. Bad publicity will dry that money up faster than a Santa Ana wind. I help you, I risk that. The other risk is the loss in the faith of the men who come here for a new start. See, most of those men that were here back when Meadows was, they've gone on to new lives. They aren't criminals anymore. If I'm handing out their names to every cop that comes around, then that doesn't look too good for my program, does it?"

"Colonel Scales, we don't have time for lawyers to look this over," Bosch said. "We are on a murder case, sir. We need this information. You know we can get it if we go to the state and federal correctional departments, but that might take longer than your lawyer. We can also get it with a subpoena, but we thought mutual cooperation would be best. We are much more inclined to tread lightly if we have your cooperation."

Scales didn't move and again didn't seem to be listening. A curl of blue smoke swirled like a ghost out of his pipe bowl.

"I see," he finally said. "Then I'll just get those files, won't I?" He stood up then and went to a row of beige file cabinets that lined the wall behind his desk. He went to one drawer and after a short search pulled out a thin manila file. He dropped it on his desk near Bosch. "That's the file on Meadows, there," he said. "Now let's see what else we can find here."

He went to the first drawer, which had no marking in

the card slot on front. He looked through files without taking any out. Then he chose one and sat down with it.

"You are free to look through that file and I can copy anything you need from it," Scales said. "This one is my master flow chart of people through here. I can make you a list of any people Meadows could have met here. I assume you will need DOBs and PINs?"

"That would help, thank you," Wish said.

It took only fifteen minutes to look through Meadows's file. He had started a correspondence with Scales a year before his release from TI. He had the backing of a chaplain and an intake counselor who knew him because he had been assigned to maintenance at the prison's intake and placement office. In one of the letters Meadows had described the tunnels he had been into in Vietnam and how he had been drawn to their darkness.

"Most of the other guys were scared to go down there," he wrote. "I wanted to go. I didn't know why then, but I think now that I was testing my limits. But the fulfillment I received from it was false. I was as hollow as the ground we fought on. The fulfillment I now have is in Jesus Christ and knowing He is with me. If given the chance, and with His guidance, I can make the right choices this time and leave these bars forever behind. I want to go from hollow ground to hallowed ground."

"Tacky but sincere enough, I guess," Wish said.

Scales looked up from the desk, where he was writing names, birth dates and prison identification numbers on a sheet of yellow paper. "He was sincere," he said in a voice that suggested there was no other way about it. "When Billy Meadows left here, I thought, I believed, he was ready for the outside and that he had shed past alliances with drugs and crime. It becomes obvious that he fell back into that temptation. But I doubt you two will find what you are looking for here. I give you these names but they won't help you."

"We'll see," Bosch said. Scales went back to writing, and Bosch watched him. He was too consumed by his faith and loyalty to see he might have been used. Bosch believed Scales was a good man but one who might be too quick to see his beliefs and hopes in someone else, perhaps someone like Meadows.

"Colonel, what do you get out of all this?" Bosch asked.

This time he put his pen down, adjusted his pipe in his set jaw and folded his hands together on the desk. "It's not what I get. It's what the Lord gets." He picked up the pen again, but then another thought came to him. "You know, these boys were destroyed in many ways when they got back. I know, it's an old story and everybody's heard it, everybody's seen the movies. But these guys have had to live it. Thousands came back here and literally marched off to the prisons. One day I was reading about that and I wondered what if there hadn't been any war and these boys never went anywhere. They just stayed in Omaha and Los Angeles and Jacksonville and New Iberia and wherever. Would they still have ended up in prison? Would they be homeless, wandering mental cases? Drug addicts?

"For most of them, I doubt that. It was the war that did it to them, that sent them the wrong way." He took a long drag on the dead pipe. "So all I do, with the help of the earth and a few prayer books, is try to put back inside what the Vietnam experience took out. And I'm pretty good at it. So I'm giving you this list, letting you take a look at that file there. But don't hurt what we've got here.

You two have a natural suspicion of what goes on here, and that's fine. It's healthy for people in your position. But be careful with what is good here. Detective Bosch, you look the right age, were you over there?"

Bosch nodded and Scales said, "Then you know." He went back to finishing the list. Without looking up he said, "You two join us for lunch? Freshest vegetables in the county on our table."

They declined and stood up to go after Scales handed Bosch the list with the twenty-four names he had come up with. As Bosch turned to the office door he hesitated and said, "Colonel, do you mind me asking what other vehicles you have on the farm? I saw the pickup."

"We don't mind you asking, because we have nothing to hide. We got two more pickups like that, two John Deeres and a four-wheel-drive vehicle."

"What kind of four-wheel-drive vehicle?"

"It's a Jeep."

"And what color?"

"It's white. What's going on?"

"Just trying to clear up something. But I guess the Jeep would have the Charlie Company seal on the side, like the pickup?"

"That's right. All our vehicles are marked. When we go into Ventura we're proud of what we've accomplished. We want people to know where the vegetables are coming from."

Bosch didn't look at the names on the list until he was in the car. He didn't recognize any, but he noticed that Scales had written the letters PH after eight of the twenty-four names.

"What's that mean?" Wish asked as she leaned over and looked at the list also.

"Purple Heart," Bosch said. "One more way to say be careful, I guess."

"What about the Jeep?" she said. "He said it was white. It has a seal on the side."

"You saw how dirty the pickup was. A dirty white Jeep, it could have looked beige. If it's the right Jeep."

"He just doesn't seem right. Scales. He seems legit."

"Maybe he is. Maybe it's the people he lends his Jeep to. I didn't want to press it with him until we know more."

He started the car and they headed down the gravel road to the gate. Bosch rolled his window down. The sky was the color of bleached jeans and the air was invisible and clean and smelled like fresh green peppers. But not for long, Bosch thought. We go back into the nastiness now.

On the way back to the city Bosch cut off the Ventura Freeway and headed south through Malibu Canyon to the Pacific. It would take longer to get back, but the clean air was addictive. He wanted it for as long as possible.

"I want to see the list of the victims," he said after they had made their way through the winding canyon and the hazy blue surface of the ocean could be seen ahead. "This pedophile you mentioned earlier. Something about that story bothered me. Why would they take the guy's collection of kiddie porno?"

"Harry, come on, you are not going to suggest that was a reason, that these guys tunneled for weeks and then blasted into a bank vault to steal a collection of kiddie porn?"

"Of course not. But that's why it raises the question. Why'd they take the stuff?"

"Well, maybe they wanted it. Maybe one was a pedophile and he liked it. Who knows?"

"Or maybe it was all part of a cover. Take everything from every box they drilled to hide the fact that what they were really after was one box. You know, sort of blur the picture by hitting dozens of boxes. But all along the target was something in only one of the boxes. Same principle with the pawnshop break-in: take a lot of jewelry to cover they only wanted the bracelet.

"But with the vault, they wanted something that wouldn't be reported stolen afterward. Something that couldn't be reported stolen because it would get the owner into some kind of jam. Like with the pedophile. When his stuff got stolen what could he say? That's the sort of thing the tunnelers were after, but something more valuable. Something that would make hitting the safe-deposit vault more attractive than hitting the main vault.

"Something that would make killing Meadows a necessity when he endangered the whole caper by pawning the bracelet."

She was quiet. Bosch looked over at her, but behind her sunglasses she was unreadable.

"Sounds to me like you are talking about drugs again," she said after a while. "And the dog said no drugs. The DEA found no connections on our list of customers."

"Maybe drugs, maybe not. But that's why we should look at the boxholders again. I want to look at the list for myself. Want to see if anything rings a bell with it. The people who reported no losses, they are the ones that I want to start with."

"I'll get the list. We've got nothing else going anyway."

"Well, we've got these names from Scales to run

down," Bosch said. "I was thinking that we'd pull mugs and take 'em to Sharkey."

"Worth a try, I guess. More like just going through the motions."

"I don't know. I think the kid is holding something. I think he maybe saw a face that night."

"I left a memo with Rourke about the hypnosis. He'll probably get back to us on that today or tomorrow."

They took the Pacific Coast Highway around the bay. The smog had been blown inland and it was clear enough to see Catalina Island out past the whitecaps. They stopped at Alice's Restaurant for lunch, and since it was late there was an open table by a window. Wish ordered an iced tea and Bosch had a beer.

"I used to come out to this pier when I was a kid," Bosch told her. "They'd take a busload of us out. Back then, they had a bait shop out on the end. I'd fish for yellowtail."

"Kids from DYS?"

"Yeah. Er, no. Back then it was called DPS. Department of Public Services. Few years back they finally realized they needed a whole department for the kids, so they came up with DYS."

She looked out the restaurant window and down along the pier. She smiled at his memories and he asked where hers were.

"All over," she said. "My father was in the military. Most I ever spent in one place was a couple years. So my memories aren't really of places. They're people."

"You and your brother were close?" Bosch said.

"Yes, with my father gone a lot. He was always there. Until he enlisted and went away for good."

Salads were put down on the table and they ate a little

bit and small-talked a little bit and then sometime between when the waitress picked up the salad plates and put down the lunch plates she told her brother's story.

"Every week he'd write me from over there and every week he said he was scared, wanted to come home," she said. "It wasn't something he could say to our father or mother. But Michael wasn't the type. He should never have gone. He went because of our father. He couldn't let him down. He wasn't brave enough to say no to him, but he was brave enough to go over there. It doesn't make sense. Have you ever heard anything so dumb?"

Bosch didn't answer because he had heard similar stories, his own included. And she seemed to stop there. She either didn't know what had happened to her brother over there or didn't want to recount the details.

After a while she said, "Why'd you go?"

He knew the question was coming but in his whole life he had never been able to truthfully answer it, even to himself.

"I don't know. No choice, I guess. The institutional life, like you said before. I wasn't going to college. Never really thought about Canada. I think it would have been harder to go there than to just get drafted and go to Vietnam. Then in sixty-eight I sort of won the draft lottery. My number came up so low I knew I was going to go. So I thought I'd outsmart 'em by joining, thought I'd write my own ticket."

"And so?"

Bosch laughed a little in the same phony way she had laughed before. "I got in, went through basic and all the bullshit and when it came time to choose something, I picked the infantry. I still have never figured out why. They get you at that age, you know? You're invincible.

Once I got over there I volunteered for a tunnel squad. It was kind of like that letter Meadows wrote to Scales. You want to see what you've got. You do things you'll never understand. You know what I mean?"

"I think so," she said. "What about Meadows? He had chances to leave and he never did, not till the very end. Why would anybody want to stay if they didn't have to?"

"There were a lot like that," Bosch said. "I guess it wasn't usual or unusual. Some just didn't want to leave that place. Meadows was one of them. It might have been a business decision, too."

"You mean drugs?"

"Well, I know he was using heroin while he was there. We know he was using and selling afterward when he got back here. So maybe when he was over there he got involved in moving it and he didn't want to leave a good thing. There is a lot that points to it. He was moved to Saigon after they took him out of the tunnels. Saigon would have been the place to be, especially with embassy clearance like he had as an MP. Saigon was sin city. Whores, hash, heroin, it was a free market. A lot of people jumped into it. Heroin would have made him some nice money, especially if he had a plan, a way to move some of the stuff back here."

She pushed pieces of red snapper she wasn't going to eat around on her plate with a fork.

"It's unfair," she said. "He didn't want to come back. Some boys wanted to come home but never got the chance."

"Yes. There was nothing fair about that place."

Bosch turned and looked out the window at the ocean. There were four surfers in bright wet suits riding on the swells.

"And after the war you joined the cops."

"Well, I kicked around a little and then joined the department. It seemed most of the vets I knew, like what Scales said today, were going into the police departments or the penitentiaries."

"I don't know, Harry. You seem like the loner type. A private eye, not a man who has to take orders from men he doesn't respect."

"There are no more private operators. Everybody takes orders. . . . But all this stuff about me is in the file. You know it all."

"Not everything about somebody can be put down on paper. Isn't that what you said?"

He smiled as a waitress cleared the table. He said, "What about you? What's your story with the bureau?"

"Pretty simple, really. Criminal justice major, accounting minor, recruited out of Penn State. Good pay, good benefits, women highly sought and valued. Nothing original."

"Why the bank detail? I thought the fast track was antiterrorism, white-collar stuff, maybe even drugs. But not the heavy squad."

"I did the white-collar stuff for five years. I was in D.C., too, the right place to be. The thing is, the emperor had no clothes. It was all deadly, deadly boring stuff." She smiled and shook her head. "I realized I just wanted to be a cop. So, that's what I became. I transferred to the first good street unit that had an opening. L.A. is the bank robbery capital of the country. When an opening came up here, I called in my markers and got the transfer. Call me a dinosaur, if you want."

"You are too beautiful for that."

Despite her dark tan, Bosch could tell the remark em-

barrassed her. It embarrassed him, too, just sort of slipping out like that.

"Sorry," he said.

"No. No, that was nice. Thank you."

"So, are you married, Eleanor?" he said and then he
turned red, immediately regretting his lack of subtlety.
She smiled at his embarrassment.

"I was. But it was a long time ago."

Bosch nodded. "You don't have anything . . . what
about Rourke? You two seemed . . ."

"What? Are you kidding?"

"Sorry."

They laughed together then, and followed it with
smiles and a long, comfortable silence.

After lunch they walked out on the pier to the spot
where Bosch had once stood with rod and reel. There was
no one fishing. Several of the buildings at the end of the
pier were abandoned. There was a rainbow sheen on top
of the water near one of the pylons. Bosch also noticed
the surfers were gone. Maybe all the kids are in school,
Bosch thought. Or maybe they don't fish here anymore.
Maybe no fish make it this far into the poisoned bay.

"I haven't been here in a long time," he said to
Eleanor. He leaned on the pier railing, his elbows on
wood scarred by a thousand bait knives. "Things
change."

It was midafternoon by the time they got back to the Federal Building. Wish ran the names and prisoner identification numbers Scales had given them through the NCIC
and state department of justice computers and ordered
mug shots photo-faxed from various prisons in the state.
Bosch took the list of names and called U.S. military

archives in St. Louis and asked for Jessie St. John, the same clerk he had dealt with on Monday. She said the file on William Meadows that Bosch had asked for was already on the way. Bosch didn't tell her he already had seen the FBI's copy of it. Instead, he talked her into calling up the new names he had on her computer and giving him the basic service biography of each man. He kept her past the end of shift at five o'clock in St. Louis, but she said she wanted to help.

By five o'clock L.A. time Bosch and Wish had twenty-four mug shots and brief criminal and military service sketches of the men to go with them. Nothing jumped off Wish's desk and hit either of them over the head. Fifteen of the men had served in Vietnam at some point during the period Meadows was there. Eleven of these were U.S. Army. None were tunnel rats, though four were First Infantry along with Meadows on his first tour. There were two others who were MPOs in Saigon.

They focused on the NCIC records of the six soldiers who were First Infantry or military police. Only the MPOs had bank robbery records. Bosch shuffled through the mug shots and pulled those two out. He stared at the faces, half expecting to get confirmation from the hardened, disinterested looks they gave the camera. "I like these two," he said.

Their names were Art Franklin and Gene Delgado. They both had Los Angeles addresses. In Vietnam, they spent their tours in Saigon assigned to separate MP units. Not the embassy unit that Meadows was attached to. But, still, they were in the city. Both of them had been discharged in 1973. But as with Meadows, they stayed on in Vietnam as civilian military advisers. They were there until the end, April 1975. There was no question in

Bosch's mind. All three men—Meadows, Franklin and Delgado—knew each other before they met at Charlie Company in Ventura County.

Stateside after 1975, Franklin got jammed up on a series of robberies in San Francisco and went away for five years. He went down on a federal rap of bank robbery in Oakland in 1984 and was at TI at the same time as Meadows. He was paroled to Charlie Company two months before Meadows left the program. Delgado was strictly a state offender; three pops for burglaries in L.A., for which he was able to get by on county lockup time, then an attempted bank robbery in Santa Ana in 1985. He was able to plead in state court under an agreement with federal prosecutors. He went up to Soledad, getting out in 1988 and arriving at Charlie Company three months ahead of Meadows. He left Charlie Company a day after Franklin arrived.

"One day," Wish said. "This means all three were together there at Charlie Company only one day."

Bosch looked at their photos and the accompanying descriptions. Franklin was the larger one. Six foot, 190, dark hair. Delgado was lean, five-six and 140. Dark hair, too. Bosch stared at the photos of the big man and the small man, and was thinking about the descriptions of the men in the Jeep that had dumped Meadows's body.

"Let's go see Sharkey," he said after a while.

He called Home Street Home and was told what he knew they were going to tell him: Sharkey was gone. Bosch tried the Blue Chateau and a tired old voice told him that Sharkey's crew had moved out at noon. His mother hung up on Bosch after she determined he was not a customer.

It was near seven. Bosch told Wish they would have to

go back to the street to find him. She said she'd drive. They spent the next two hours in West Hollywood, mostly in the Santa Monica Boulevard corridor. But there was no sign of Sharkey or his motorbike locked to a parking meter. They flagged down a few sheriffs cruisers and told them who they were looking for, but not even the extra eyes helped. They parked at the curb by the Oki Dog, and Bosch was thinking that maybe the boy had gone back to his mother's house and she had hung up the phone to protect him.

"You want to take a ride up to Chatsworth?" he asked.

"As much as I'd like to see this witch you told me Sharkey has for a mother, I was thinking more along the lines of calling it a day. We can find Sharkey tomorrow. How about that dinner we didn't have last night?"

Bosch wanted to get to Sharkey, but he also wanted to get to her. She was right, there was always tomorrow.

"Sounds good to me," he said. "Where you feel like going?"

"My place."

Eleanor Wish lived in a rent-controlled townhouse she subleased two blocks from the beach in Santa Monica. They parked at the curb in front, and as they went in she told Bosch that although she lived close by, if he wanted to actually see the ocean he had to walk out onto her bedroom balcony, lean over and look sharply to the right down Ocean Park Boulevard. A slice of the Pacific could then be seen between two condominium towers that guarded the shoreline. From that angle, she mentioned, he could also see into her next-door neighbor's bedroom. The neighbor was a has-been television actor turned small-time dope dealer who had a never-ending procession of women through the bedroom. It kind of took away from the view, she said. She told Bosch to have a seat in the living room while she got dinner started. "If you like jazz, I have a CD over there I just bought but haven't had time to listen to," she said.

He walked over to the stereo, which was stacked on shelves next to a set of bookcases, and picked up the new disk. It was Rollins's *Falling in Love with Jazz*, and inside Harry smiled because he had it at home. It was a warm connection. He opened the case, put the music on and began to look around the living room. There were pastel throw rugs and light-colored coverings on the furniture. Architecture books and home magazines were spread on a glass-topped coffee table in front of a light-blue couch. The place was very neat. A framed cross-stitch canvas on the wall next to the front door said Welcome To This Home. Small letters stitched in its corner said EDS 1970, and Bosch wondered about the last letter.

He made another one of those psychic connections with Eleanor Wish when he turned around and looked at the wall above the couch. Framed in black wood was a print of Edward Hopper's *Nighthawks*. Bosch didn't have the print at home but he was familiar with the painting and from time to time even thought about it when he was deep on a case or on a surveillance. He had seen the original in Chicago once and had stood in front of it studying it for nearly an hour. A quiet, shadowy man sits alone at the counter of a street-front diner. He looks across at another customer much like himself, but only the second man is with a woman. Somehow, Bosch identified with it, with that first man. I am the loner, he thought. I am the nighthawk. The print, with its stark dark hues and shadows, did not fit in this apartment, Bosch realized. Its darkness clashed with the pastels. Why did Eleanor have it? What did she see there?

He looked around the rest of the room. There was no TV. There was just the music on the stereo and the magazines on the table and the books on the lawyer's shelves against the wall across from the couch. He stepped over and looked through the glass panes and browsed the collection. The top two shelves were mostly high-brow Book-of-the-Month offerings descending into crime fiction by writers like Crumley and Willeford and others. He had read some of them. He opened the glass door and pulled out a book called *The Locked Door*. He'd heard of the book but had never seen it to buy. He opened the cover to see how old it was and he solved the mystery of the last letter on the needlework. On the first page, printed in ink, it said Eleanor D. Scarletti—1979. She must have kept her husband's name after the divorce, Bosch thought. He put the book back and closed the case.

The books on the bottom two rows of the bookcase ranged from true crime to historical studies of the Vietnam War to FBI manuals. There was even an LAPD homicide investigation textbook. Many of these books Bosch had read. One of them he was even in. It was a book the *Times* reporter Bremmer had written about the so-called Beauty Shop Slasher. A guy named Harvard Kendal, the slasher killed seven women in one year in the San Fernando Valley. They were all beauty shop owners or employees. He cased the shops, followed the victims home and killed them by cutting their throats with a sharpened nail file. Bosch and his partner at the time connected Kendal through a license plate number the seventh victim had written on a pad in the salon the night before she was murdered. They never figured out why she had done it, but the detectives suspected she had seen Kendal watching the shop from his van. She wrote the tag number down as a precaution but then didn't take the precaution of not going home alone. Bosch and his partner traced the tag to Kendal and found out he had spent five years in Folsom for a series of beauty shop arsons near Oakland in the 1960s.

They later discovered his mother had worked as a manicurist in a beauty shop when he was a boy. She had practiced her craft on young Kendal's nails, and the shrinks figured he never got over it. Bremmer had gotten a best-seller out of it. And when Universal made a movie of the week out of it, the studio paid Bosch and his partner for the use of their names and technical assistance. The money doubled when a cop series spun off the movie. His partner quit the department and moved to Ensenada. Bosch stayed on, investing his stake in the stilt house on the hill that looked down on the studio that paid him the money. Bosch always found an unexplainable symbiosis in that.

"I read that book before your name ever came up in this. It wasn't part of the research."

Eleanor had come out of the kitchen with two glasses of red wine. Harry smiled.

"I wasn't going to accuse you of anything," he said. "Besides, it isn't about me. It's about Kendal. The whole thing was luck, anyway. But they still made a book and TV show about it. Whatever it is in there, it smells good."

"You like pasta?"

"I like spaghetti."

"That's what we're having. I made a big pot of sauce Sunday. I love to spend an entire day in the kitchen, not thinking about anything else. I find it's good therapy for stress. And it lasts and lasts. All I have to do is warm it up and boil some noodles."

Bosch sipped his wine and looked around some more. He still hadn't sat down but was feeling very comfortable with her. A smile played across his face. He gestured toward the Hopper print. "I like it. But why something so dark?"

She looked at the print and crinkled her brow as if this were the first time she had considered it.

"I don't know," she said. "I've always liked that painting. Something there grabs me. The woman is with a man. So that isn't me. So I guess if it's anyone, it would be the man sitting with his coffee. All alone, kind of watching the two that are together."

"I saw it in Chicago once," Bosch said. "The original. I was out there on an extradition and had about an hour to kill until I could pick up the body. So I went into the Art Institute and it was there. I spent the whole hour looking at it. There's something about it—like you said. I can't remember the case or who I was bringing back here. But I remember that painting."

They sat at the table talking for nearly an hour after the food was gone. She told him more about her brother and her difficulty getting over the anger and loss. Eighteen years later she was still working it out, she said. Bosch told her that he was still working things out, too. He still dreamed of the tunnels from time to time, but more often he battled insomnia instead. He told her how mixed up he was when he got back, how thin the line was, the choice, between what he had done afterward and what Meadows did. It could have been different, he said, and she nodded, seeming to know that was true.

Later, she asked about the Dollmaker case and his fall from Robbery-Homicide. It was more than curiosity. He sensed that something important rode on what he told her. She was making a decision about him.

"I guess you know the basics," he began. "Somebody was strangling women, mostly prostitutes, then painting over their faces with makeup. Pancake, red lipstick, heavy rouge on the cheeks, sharp black eyeliner. The same thing every time. The bodies were bathed, too. But we never said it looked like he was making them into dolls. Some asshole—I think it was a guy named Sakai over at the coroner's—leaked that the makeup was the common denominator. Then this Dollmaker stuff started playing in the press. I think Channel 4 was the first to come up with that name. It took off from there. To me, it looked more like a mortician's work. But the truth is we weren't doing too good. We didn't have a handle on the guy until he was into double figures.

"Not much physical evidence. The victims were all dumped in random locations, all over the Westside. We knew from fiber evidence on a couple of the bodies that the guy probably wore a rug or some kind of hair disguise, fake beard or something. The women that were taken off the stroll, we were able to isolate times and places of their last trick. We went to the hourly motels and got nothing. So we figured the guy was picking them up in a car and then taking them somewhere else, maybe to his home or some kind of safe place he used as a killing pad. We started watching the Boulevard and other hot spots the pros work, and we must've busted up three hundred tricks before we got the break. This whore name of Dixie McQueen calls up the task force one morning, early, and says she just escaped from the Dollmaker and is there a reward if she gives him up. Well, we were getting calls like that every week. I mean, eleven murdered women and people are coming out of the woodwork with clues that aren't really clues. It's panic city."

"I remember," Wish said.

"But Dixie was different. I was working the late shift in the task force offices that day and I caught the call. I went and talked to her. She told me that this john she'd picked up on Hollywood near Spa Row, you know, near the Scientology mansion, took her to this garage apartment in Silver Lake. She said that while the guy was getting naked she wanted to use the toilet. So she goes in and while she's running the water she looks through the cabinet below the sink, probably to see if there is anything worth lifting. But she sees all these little bottles and compacts and all this women's stuff. She looks at it all and she just puts it all together. Just like that. Bingo; this has to be the guy. So she gets a case of total creeps and bails out. She comes out of the bathroom and the guy's in the bed. She just hauls ass through the front door.

"The thing is, we hadn't put out all the stuff about the makeup. Or, actually, the asshole that was the media leak didn't put out everything. See, we knew that the guy was keeping the victims' stuff. They were found with their purses but there were no cosmetics—you know, lipstick, compacts, things like that. So when Dixie told me about what was in the bathroom cabinet she got my attention. I knew she was legit.

"And that is the point where I screwed up. It was three A.M. by the time I was done talking to Dixie. Everybody on the task force had gone home and I was left there thinking that this guy might realize Dixie made him and clear out. So I went there alone. I mean, Dixie went with me to show me the place, but then she never left the car. Once we were there, I saw a light on above the garage, which was behind this rundown house off of Hyperion. I called for patrol backup, and while I'm waiting I see the guy's shadow going back and forth across the window. Something tells me he is getting ready to bug out and take all the stuff from the cabinet with him. And we had no evidence from the eleven bodies. We needed the stuff that was in the bathroom cabinet. The other consideration was, what if he has someone up there? You know, a replacement for Dixie. So I went up. Alone. You know the rest."

Wish said, "You went in without a warrant and shot him when he was reaching under the pillow on the bed. You later told the shooting team that you believed it was an emergency situation. There had been enough time for him to go out and get another prostitute. You said that gave you the authority to come through the door without a warrant. You said you fired because you believed the suspect was reaching for a weapon. It was one shot, upper torso from fifteen or twenty feet, if I remember the report. But the Dollmaker was alone, and under the pillow was only his toupee."

"Only his rug," Bosch said. He shook his head like a Monday-morning quarterback. "The shooting team cleared me. We connected him to two of the bodies through the hair from the toupee, and the makeup in the bathroom was traced to eight of the victims. There was no doubt. It was him. I was clear, but then the shooflies started in on it. A Lewis and Clarke expedition. They ran down Dixie and got her to sign a statement saying she told me beforehand that he put his hair under the pillow. I don't know what they used against her, but I can imagine. IAD's always had a hard-on for me. They don't like anybody who's not a hundred percent part of the family. Anyway, the next thing I know they are bringing departmental charges against me. They wanted to fire me and take Dixie to a grand jury to get criminal charges. It was like there was blood in the water and two fat white sharks."

He stopped there but Eleanor continued. "The IAD detectives misjudged things, though, Harry. They didn't realize that public opinion would be with you. You were known in the newspapers as the cop who broke the Beauty Shop Slasher and Dollmaker cases. A character in a TV show. They couldn't take you down without a lot of public scrutiny and embarrassment for the department."

"Someone reached down from above them and put a stop to the grand jury move," Bosch said. "They had to settle for a suspension and my demotion to Hollywood homicide."

Bosch had his fingers on the stem of his empty wine glass and was absentmindedly turning the glass on the table.

"Some settlement," he said after a while. "And those two IAD sharks are still swimming around out there, waiting for the kill."

They sat silently for a while then. He was waiting for her to ask the question she had asked once before. Had the whore lied? She never asked it, and after a while she just looked at him and smiled. And he felt as if he had just passed the test. She started gathering the plates off the table. Bosch helped her in the kitchen and when the work was done, they stood close, drying their hands on the same dish towel, and lightly kissed. Then, as if following the same secret signals, they pressed themselves against each other and kissed with the kind of hunger lonely people have.

"I want to stay," Bosch said after momentarily breaking away.

"I want you to stay," she said.

Arson's stoned eyes were shiny and reflected the neon night. He sucked hard on the Kool and held the precious smoke in. The cigarette had been dipped in PCP. A smile cracked across his face as the jet streams of smoke escaped his nostrils. He said, "You're the only shark I ever heard of being used as bait. Get it?"

He laughed and took another deep drag before handing the cigarette to Sharkey, who waved it away because he'd had enough. Mojo took it then.

"Yeah, I'm getting tired of this shit," Sharkey said. "You take a turn for once."

"Chill out, man, you're the only one can get away with it, man. Mojo and me, man, we just don't play the part good as you. Besides, we got our part. You ain't big enough to pound these faggots."

"Well, whyn't we do the 7-Eleven again?" Sharkey said. "I don't like this not knowing who it is. I like it at the 7-Eleven. We pick our meat, they don't pick me."

"No way," Mojo spoke up then. "We go back there, we don't know if that last guy reported it to the sheriffs or not. We have to stay clear a there awhile. They're probly watching the place from the same parking lot we did."

Sharkey knew they were right. He just thought that being out on Santa Monica on the queer stroll was getting too close to the real thing. Next thing, he guessed, the two dopers will not feel like charging in. They'll want him to go through with it, get the money that way. That was when he would split these guys, he knew.

"Okay," he said, stepping off the curb. "Don't fuck me up."

He started to cross the street. Arson yelled after him, "BMW or better!"

As if I need to be told, Sharkey thought. He walked a half block toward La Brea and then leaned against the door of a closed print shop. He was still a half block from Hot Rod's, an adult bookstore that offered twenty-five-cent all-male peeps. But he was close enough to catch the eye of somebody walking out. If the eye was looking. He looked back the other way and saw the glow of the joint in the darkness of the driveway where Arson and Mojo sat on their bikes.

Sharkey hadn't been standing there ten minutes when a car, a new Grand Am, pulled to the curb and the electric window glided down. Sharkey was going to blow this one off, remembering BMW or better, until he saw the glint of gold and stepped closer. His adrenaline kicked up a notch. The wrist the driver had draped over the steering wheel was adorned with a Rolex Presidential. If it was real, Arson knew where they could get $3,000 for it. A grand apiece, not to mention what else the meat might have at home or in his wallet. Sharkey looked the man over. The guy looked like a straight, a businessman. Dark hair, dark suit. Mid-forties, not too big. Sharkey might even be able to take him alone. The man smiled at Sharkey and said, "Hey, howya doin'?"

"Not bad. What's up?"

"Oh, I don't know. Just out for a ride. You want to take a ride?"

"Where to?"

"No place special. I know a place we can go. Be alone."

"You got a hundred dollars on you?"

"No, but I've got fifty dollars for night baseball."

"Pitching or catching?"

"I'm a pitcher. And I brought my own glove."

Sharkey hesitated and glanced toward the driveway where he had seen the glow from the Kool. It was gone now. They must be ready to move. He looked back at the watch.

"That's cool," he said, and got in the car.

The car headed west past the alley driveway. Sharkey held himself from looking, but he thought he heard the revving and popping sound of their bikes. They were following.

"Where we going?" he asked.

"Uh, I can't go home with you, my friend. But I know a place we can go. Nobody will bother us."

"Cool."

They stopped at the light at Flores, which made Sharkey think of the guy from the other night. They were near his place. Arson was hitting harder, it seemed. This would have to stop soon or they would kill someone. He hoped the man with the Rolex would give it up peaceably. There was no telling what those two would do. Stoked on PCP, they would be ready for battle and blood.

Suddenly the car lurched through the intersection. Sharkey noticed the light was still red.

"What's going on?" he said sharply.

"Nothing. I'm tired of waiting, is all."

Sharkey thought there would be nothing suspicious about looking back now. He turned and saw only cars waiting back at the intersection. No motorbikes. Those bastards, he thought. He felt a dampness beginning on his scalp and the first tremblings of fear. The car turned right after Barnie's Beanery and up the hill to Sunset. Then they went east to Highland and the man with the Rolex steered north again.

"Have we been together before?" the man asked. "You seem familiar. I don't know, maybe we've just seen each other around."

"No, I've never—I don't think so."

"Look at me."

"What?" Sharkey said, startled by the question and the man's sharp tone. "Why?"

"Look at me. You know me? Have you seen me before?"

"What is this, a credit card commercial? I said no, man."

The man turned the car off the street into the east parking lot of the Hollywood Bowl. It was deserted. He drove quickly and without saying another word to the darkened north end. Sharkey thought, If this is your quiet little spot, then that ain't no real Rolex you got on your wrist, pal.

"Hey, what are we doing, man?" Sharkey said. He was thinking of a way to bail out of this. He was pretty sure Arson and Mojo, stoned as they were, were lost. He was alone with this guy and he wanted to scratch it.

"The bowl is closed," Rolex said. "But I got a key to the dressing rooms, see? We just take the tunnel under Cahuenga and then near where it comes up, there is a little walkway we take back around. There won't be anyone around. I work there. I know."

For a moment, Sharkey considered trying to take the guy alone, then decided he couldn't do it. Unless there was a way of taking him by surprise. He would see. The man turned the car engine off and opened his door. Sharkey opened his own door, got out and looked across the dark expanse of the empty parking lot. He was looking for the two lights of the motorbikes, but there weren't any. I'll take this guy out on the other side, he decided. He would make his move. Either hit and run, or just run.

They headed toward the sign that said Pedestrian Expressway. There was a concrete outbuilding with an open doorway and then stairs. As they walked down the whitewashed steps, the man with the Rolex put his hand on Sharkey's shoulder and then clamped it on the back of his neck in a fatherly manner. Sharkey could feel the cold metal of the watch's wristband.

The man said, "You sure we don't know each other, Sharkey? Maybe seen each other?"

"No, man, I'm telling you, I haven't been with you."

They were about halfway through the tunnel when Sharkey realized he hadn't told the man his name.

Part V

Thursday, May 24

It had been a long time for him. And in Eleanor's bedroom, Harry Bosch was clumsy in the way of a man who is overly self-conscious and out of practice. As with most first times he had had, it wasn't good. She directed him with her hands and whispers. And afterward he felt like apologizing but didn't. They held each other and lightly dozed, the smell of her hair in his face. The same apple scent he had encountered in his kitchen the night before. Bosch was infatuated with her and wanted to breathe the smell of her hair every minute. After a while he kissed her awake and they made love again. This time he needed no directions and she didn't need her hands. When they were done, Eleanor whispered to him, "Do you think you can be alone in this world and not be lonely?"

He didn't answer at first, and she said, "Are you alone or are you lonely, Harry Bosch?"

He thought about that for some time, while her fingers gently traced the tattoo on his shoulder.

"I don't know what I am," he finally whispered. "You

get so used to things the way they are. And I've always been alone. I guess that makes me lonely. Until now."

They smiled in the dark and kissed, and soon he heard her deep, sleeping breaths. Much later, Bosch got up from the bed, pulled on his pants and went out on the balcony to smoke. On Ocean Park Boulevard there was no traffic and he could hear the ocean's noise from nearby. The lights were out in the apartment next door. They were out everywhere except on the street. He could see that the jacaranda trees along the sidewalk were shedding their flowers. They had fallen like a violet snow on the ground and the cars parked along the curb. Bosch leaned on the railing and blew smoke into the cool night wind.

When he was on his second cigarette he heard the door behind him slide open and then felt her hands come around his waist as she embraced him from behind.

"What's wrong, Harry?"

"Nothing, just thinking. You better watch out. Carcinogen alert. You ever heard of the draft risk easement?"

"Assessment, Harry, not easement. What are you thinking about? Is this how it is most nights for you?"

Bosch turned around in her arms and kissed her forehead. She was wearing a short robe of pink silk. He rubbed his thumb up and down the nape of her neck. "Almost no night is like this. I just couldn't sleep. I guess I was thinking about a lot of things."

"About us?" She kissed his chin.

"I guess."

"And?"

He brought his hand around to her face and traced the outline of her jaw with his fingers.

"I was wondering how you got this little scar here."

"Oh . . . that is from when I was a girl. My brother and

I, we were riding on a bike and I was on the handlebars. And we went down this hill, it was called Highland Avenue—this was when we lived in Pennsylvania—and he lost control. The bike started weaving and I was so scared because I knew we were going to crash. And just as he really lost it and we were going down, he yelled, 'Ellie, you'll be all right!' Just like that. And because he had yelled that, he was right. I cut my chin but I didn't even cry. I always thought that was something, that he would try to yell something to me rather than worry about himself at a moment like that. But that was my brother."

Bosch dropped his hands from her face. He said, "I was also thinking that what happened between us was nice."

"I think so, too, Harry. Nice for a couple of nighthawks. Come back to bed now."

They went back in. Bosch first went into the bathroom and used his finger as a toothbrush and then crawled back under the sheet with her. The blue glow of a digital clock on the bedtable said 2:26 and Bosch closed his eyes.

When he opened them again the clock said 3:46 and there was an obnoxious chirping sound coming from somewhere in the room. He realized he was not in his own room. Then he remembered he was in Eleanor Wish's room. As he finally got oriented he saw her shadowy figure stooped next to the bed, her hands going through the pile of his clothes.

"Where is it?" she said. "I can't find it."

Bosch reached for his pants, traced his hands along the belt until he found the pager and turned it off without having to fumble with it. He had done it many times in the dark before.

"Jesus," she said. "That was rude."

Bosch swung his legs over the side of the bed, gathered the sheet around his waist and sat up. He yawned and then warned her that he was going to turn on the light. She said go ahead, and when the light came on it hit him like a diamond burst between his eyes. When his vision cleared, she was standing in front of him naked, looking down at the digital readout of the pager in his hand. Bosch finally looked down at the number but didn't recognize it. He wiped a hand across his face and rustled his hair. There was a telephone on the bedtable and he pulled it onto his lap. He dialed the number and then fumbled with his hands in his clothes for a cigarette, which he put in his mouth but didn't light.

Eleanor noticed her nakedness and walked over to a lounge chair to get her robe. After it was on she went into the bathroom and closed the door. Bosch heard water running. The other end of the line was picked up halfway through the first ring. Jerry Edgar didn't answer with a hello, just "Harry, where you at?"

"I'm not home. What is it?"

"This kid you were looking for, the one on the nine one one call, you found him, right?"

"Yeah, but we're looking for him again."

"Who's 'we'—you and the feebee woman?"

Eleanor came out of the bathroom and sat down on the edge of the bed next to him.

"Jerry, what are you calling me for?" Bosch asked. He was beginning to get a sinking feeling in his chest.

"What's the kid's name?"

Bosch was in a daze. It had been months since he had fallen so deeply asleep, only to be rousted out of it. He couldn't remember Sharkey's real name and he didn't want to ask Eleanor because Edgar might hear and then know they were together. Harry looked at Eleanor and when she began to speak, he touched his finger to her lips and shook his head.

"Is it Edward Niese?" Edgar spoke into the silence. "That the kid's name?"

The sinking feeling was gone. Bosch felt an invisible fist pressing up under his ribs and into the folds of his guts and heart.

"Right," he said. "That's the name."

"You gave him one of your business cards?"

"Right."

"Harry, you aren't looking for him anymore."

"Tell me about it."

"Come on out and see for yourself. I'm over at the bowl. Sharkey's in the pedestrian tunnel under Cahuenga. Park on the east side. You'll see the cars."

The Hollywood Bowl's east parking lot was supposed to be empty at 4:30 A.M. But as Bosch and Wish drove up Highland to the mouth of the Cahuenga Pass they saw that the north end of the lot was crowded with the usual grouping of official cars and vans that signal the violent, or at least unexpected, end of a life. There was yellow plastic crime scene tape strung in a square, boxing the entrance to the stairwell that went down to the pedestrian underpass. Bosch flashed his badge and gave his name to a uniform cop who was keeping the officers-on-the-scene list on a clipboard. He and Wish ducked under the tape and were met by the loud sound of an engine echoing from the mouth of the tunnel. Bosch knew by the sound that it was a generator making the juice for the crime scene lights. At the top step, before they began their descent, he turned to Eleanor and said, "You want to wait here? We don't both have to go."

"I'm a cop, for godsake," she said. "I've seen bodies before. You going to get protective of me now, Bosch? Tell you what. Want me to go down and you stay up here?"

Startled by her abrupt change in mood, Bosch didn't answer. He looked at her a moment longer, confused. He started down a few steps in front of her but stopped when he saw Edgar's large body come out of the tunnel and start up the steps. Edgar saw Bosch, and then Bosch saw his eyes go over his shoulder and take Eleanor Wish in.

"Hey, Harry," he said. "This your new partner? You must be getting along real fine already."

Bosch just stared at him. Eleanor was still three steps behind and probably hadn't heard the remark.

"Sorry, Harry," Edgar said just loud enough to be heard over the roar from the tunnel. "Out of line. Been a bad night. You should see who I got for a new partner, the useless fuck Ninety-eight Pounds stuck me with."

"I thought you were going to get—"

"Nope. Get this: Pounds put me with Porter from autos. The guy's a burned-out lush."

"I know. How'd you even get him out of bed for this?"

"He wasn't in bed. I had to track him down at the Parrot up in North Hollywood. It's one of them private bottle clubs. Porter gives me the number when we're first introduced as partners and tells me that's where he'll be most nights. Tells me he works a security detail there. But I called the off-duty assignments office at Parker Center to check it out and they got no record. I know the only thing he does there is booze. He must've been practically passed out when I called. The bartender said the pager on his belt went off but he didn't even hear it. Harry, I think the guy could blow a point two right now if we put a Breathalyzer on him."

Bosch nodded and frowned the required three seconds and then put Jerry Edgar's troubles aside. He felt Eleanor step down beside him and he introduced her to Edgar. They shook hands and smiled and Bosch said, "So, what have we got?"

"Well, we got these on the body," Edgar said, and he held up a clear plastic bag. There was a short stack of Polaroids in it. More nude shots of Sharkey. He hadn't wasted any time resupplying. Edgar turned the bag and there was Bosch's business card.

"It looks like the kid was a hustler down in Boytown," Edgar said, "but if you already pulled him in once you already know that. Anyway, I saw the card and figured he might be the kid from the nine one one call. If you want to come down and take a look, be my guest. We already processed the scene, so touch whatever you want. You can't hear yourself think in there, though. Somebody went through and knocked out every light in the tunnel. Haven't figured out whether that was the perp or the lights were knocked out before.

"Anyway, we had to set up our own. And our cables weren't long enough to put the generator up here. It's in there screaming like a five-horsepower baby."

He turned to head back into the tunnel but Bosch reached out and touched his shoulder.

"Jed, how'd you get the call on this?"

"Anonymous. It wasn't a nine one one line, so there's no tape or trace. Came in right to the Hollywood desk. Caller was a male, that's all the dipshit, one of those fat Explorer kids who took it, could tell us."

Edgar turned back into the subway. Bosch and Wish followed. It was a long hallway that curved to the right. The floor was dirty concrete, its walls were white stucco with a heavy overlay of graffiti. Nothing like a dose of urban reality as you are leaving the symphony at the bowl, Bosch thought. The tunnel was dark except for the bright splash of light that bathed the crime scene about halfway in. There Bosch could see a human form sprawled on its back. Sharkey. He could see men standing and working in the light. Bosch walked with the fingers of his right hand trailing along the stuccoed wall. It steadied him. There was an old, damp smell in the tunnel that was mixed with the new odor of gasoline and exhaust from the generator. Bosch felt beads of sweat start to form on his scalp and under his shirt. His breathing was fast and shallow. They passed the generator thirty feet in and in another thirty feet or so Sharkey was lying on the tunnel floor under the brutal light of the strobes.

The boy's head was propped against the tunnel wall at an unnatural angle. He seemed smaller and younger than Bosch remembered him. His eyes were half open and had the familiar glaze of the unseeing on them. He wore a black T-shirt that said Guns N Roses on it, and it was matted with his blood. The pockets of his faded jeans were pulled out and empty. At his side stood a can of spray paint in a plastic evidence bag. On the wall above his head a painted inscription read RIP Sharkey. The paint had been applied with an inexperienced hand and too much had been used. Black paint had run down the wall in thin lines, some of them into Sharkey's hair.

When Edgar yelled, "You want to see it?" above the din of the generator Bosch knew that he meant the wound. Because Sharkey's head was angled forward, the throat wound was not visible. Only the blood. Bosch shook his head no.

Bosch noticed the blood splatter on the wall and floor about three feet from the body. Porter the lush was comparing the shapes of the drops with those on splatter cards on a steel ring. A crime scene tech named Roberge was also photographing the spots. The blood on the floor was in round spots. The wall splatter drops were elliptical. You didn't need splatter cards to know the kid had been killed right here in the tunnel.

"The way it's looking," Porter said loudly to no one in particular, "somebody comes up behind him here, cuts him and pushes him down against the wall there."

"You only got it half right, Porter," Edgar said. "How's somebody come up behind somebody in a tunnel like this? He was with somebody and they did him. It was no sneak job, Porter."

Porter put the splatter cards in his pocket and said, "Sorry, partner."

He didn't say anything else. He was fat and broken down the way many cops get when they stay on longer than they should. Porter could still wear a size 34 belt, but above it a tremendous gut bloomed outward like an awning. He wore a tweed sport coat with a frayed elbow. His face was gaunt and as pallid as a flour tortilla, behind a drinker's nose that was large, misshapen and painfully red.

Bosch lit a cigarette and put the burnt match in his pocket. He crouched down like a baseball catcher next to the body and lifted the bag containing the paint can and hefted it. It was almost full, and that confirmed what he already knew, already feared. It was he who had killed Sharkey. In a way, at least. Bosch had tracked him down and made him valuable, or potentially valuable, to the case. Someone could not allow this. Bosch squatted there, elbows on knees, holding cigarette to mouth, smoking and studying the body, making sure he would not forget it.

Meadows had been part of this thing—the circle of connected events that had gotten him killed. But not Sharkey. He was street trash and his death here probably saved someone else's life down the line. But he did not deserve this. In this circle he was an innocent. And that meant things were out of control and there were new rules—for both sides. Bosch signaled with his hand to Sharkey's neck and a coroner's investigator pulled the body away from the wall. Bosch put one hand down on the ground to balance himself and stared for a long time at the ravaged neck and throat. He did not want to forget a single detail. Sharkey's head lolled back, exposing the gaping neck wound. Bosch's eyes never wavered.

When Bosch finally looked up from the body, he noticed that Eleanor was no longer in the tunnel. He stood up and signaled Edgar to come outside to talk. Harry didn't want to have to shout over the sound of the generator. When they got out of the tunnel, he saw that Eleanor was sitting alone on the top step. They walked up past her, and Harry put his hand on her shoulder as he went by. He felt it go rigid at his touch.

When he and his old partner were reasonably away from the noise, Harry said, "So what do the techs have?"

"Not a damned thing," Edgar said. "If it was a gang thing, it's one of the cleanest I've ever seen. Not a single print or partial. The spray can is clean. No weapon. No wits."

"Sharkey had a crew, used to stay at a motel near the Boulevard until today, but he wasn't into gangs," Bosch said. "It's in the files. He was a scammer. You know, with the Polaroids, rolling homosexuals, stuff like that."

"You're saying he's in the gang files but he isn't in a gang?"

"Right."

Edgar nodded and said, "He still could've been taken down by somebody who thought he was a gangbanger."

Wish walked over to them then but said nothing.

"You know this isn't a gang thing, Jed," Bosch said.

"I do?"

"Yeah, you do. If it was, there wouldn't be a full can of paint in there. No gangbanger's going to leave something like that behind. Also, whoever painted the wall in there didn't have the touch. The paint ran. Whoever did it, didn't know about spraying a wall."

"Come here a sec," Edgar said.

Bosch looked at Eleanor and nodded that it was okay.

He and Edgar walked away a few steps and stood near the crime scene tape.

"What did this kid tell you, and how come he was running around loose if he's part of the case?" he asked.

Bosch told him the basics of the story, that they didn't know if Sharkey was important to the case. But somebody apparently did or couldn't risk waiting to find out. As Bosch spoke he looked up over the hills and saw the first light of dawn outlining the tall palms at the top. Edgar took a step away and tilted his head up that way, too. But he wasn't looking at the sky. His eyes were closed. He eventually turned back to Bosch.

"Harry, you know what this weekend is?" he said. "It's Memorial Day weekend. It's the biggest three-day showing weekend of the year. Start of the summer season. Last year I sold four houses on this weekend, made almost as much as I made all year as a cop."

Bosch was confused by the sudden departure in the conversation. "What are you talking about?"

"What I'm talking about is . . . I'm not going to be busting my ass on this case. It isn't going to fuck up my weekend like the last one. So, what I'm saying is if you want it, I'll go to Pounds and tell him you and the FBI want to take it 'cause it goes with the one you are already working. Otherwise, I'm going to work it strictly as a nine-to-five."

"You tell Pounds whatever you want, Jed. It's not my call."

Bosch started back toward Eleanor, and Edgar said, "Just one thing. Who knew you had found the kid?"

Bosch stopped and looked at Eleanor. Without turning around, he said, "We took him off the street. We interviewed him over on Wilcox. The reports went to the bureau. What do you want me to say, Jed?"

"Nothing," Edgar said. "But, Harry, maybe you and the FBI there should have looked out for your witness a little better. Maybe saved me some time and that boy some life."

Bosch and Wish walked silently back to the car. Once inside Bosch said, "Who knew?"

"What do you mean?" she said.

"What he asked back there, who knew about Sharkey?" She thought for a moment. Then said, "On my end, Rourke gets the daily summary reports, and he got the memo on hypnosis. The summaries go to records and are copied to the senior special agent. The tape from the interview that you gave me is locked in my desk. Nobody's heard that. It hasn't been transcribed. So, I guess anyone could have seen the summaries. But don't even think about that, Harry. Nobody . . . It can't be."

"Well, they knew we found the kid and he might be important. What's that tell you? They've got to have somebody on the inside."

"Harry, that's speculation. It could have been a lot of things. Like you told him, we picked him up on the street. Anybody could have been watching. His own friends, that girl, anybody could have put out the word that we were looking for Sharkey."

Bosch thought about Lewis and Clarke. They must have seen them pick up Sharkey. What part were they playing? Nothing made sense.

"Sharkey was a tough little bastard," he said. "You think he just went walking with somebody into that tunnel? I think he didn't have a choice. And to do that, it maybe took somebody with a badge."

"Or maybe somebody with money. You know he'd go with somebody if there was money in it."

She didn't start the car and they sat in it thinking. Bosch finally said, "Sharkey was a message."

"What?"

"A message to us. See? They leave my card with him. They call it in on a no-trace line. And they do him in a tunnel. They want us to know they did it. They want us to know they've got somebody inside. They're laughing at us."

She started the car. "Where to?"

"The bureau."

"Harry, be careful with that stuff about an inside man. If you go trying to sell that and it's not true, you could give your enemies all they need to bury you."

Enemies, Bosch thought. Who are my enemies this time?

"I got that kid killed," he said. "The least I am going to do is find who did it."

Bosch looked through the cotton curtains in the waiting room, down at the veterans cemetery, while Eleanor Wish unlocked the door to the bureau offices. The ground fog had not burned off the field of stones yet, and from above it looked like a thousand ghosts rising from their boxes at once. Bosch could see the dark gash dug into the crest of the hill at the north side of the cemetery but still could not make out what it was. It looked almost like a mass grave, a long gouge into the hill, a huge wound. The exposed soil was covered with black plastic sheets.

"You want coffee?" Wish said from behind him.

"Of course," he said. He pulled himself away from the curtains and followed her in. The bureau was empty. They went into the office kitchen and he watched as she dumped a packet of ground coffee into a filter basket and turned the machine on. They stood there silently, watching the coffee slowly drip into a round glass pot on the heating pad. Bosch lit a cigarette and tried only to think about the coffee that was coming. She waved the smoke away with a hand but didn't tell him to put it out.

When the coffee was ready, Bosch took it black and it hit his system like a shot. He filled up a second cup and carried both into the squad room. He lit a cigarette off the butt of the first when he got to his temporary desk.

"My last one," he promised when he saw her looking.

Eleanor poured herself a cup of water from a bottle she took from her file drawer.

"You ever run out of that stuff?" he asked.

She ignored the question. "Harry, we can't blame ourselves for Sharkey. If we're to blame, then we might as well offer every person we talk to protection. Should we go up and grab his mother and put her in witness protection? What about the girl in the motel room that knew him? See, it gets crazy. Sharkey was Sharkey. You live by the street, you die by the street."

Bosch didn't say anything at first. Then he said, "Let me see the names."

Wish pulled out the files on the WestLand case. She rifled through them and pulled out a computer printout several pages long and folded accordion-style. She tossed it on the desk in front of him.

"That's the master there," she said. "Everybody who had a box. There are notes written after some of the names, but they probably are not germane. Most of that was if we thought they were scamming insurance or not."

Bosch started unfolding the printout and realized it was one long list and five shorter lists marked A through E. He asked what they were, and she came around the desk and looked over his shoulder. He smelled the apple in her hair.

"Okay, the long list is like I said, everybody who had a box. It's an all-inclusive list. Then we did five breakouts, A through E. The first—that's A—is a breakout on boxes rented within the three months prior to the burglary. Then B, we did a breakout on boxholders who reported no loss at all in the burglary. Then C is the list of dead ends; boxholders who were actually dead or we couldn't find because of changes in addresses or they had given phony information to rent them.

"Then the fourth and fifth breakouts are matching lists from the first three. D is anybody who rented a box in the previous three months and also reported no loss. E is any-body on the dead-end list who was also on the three-month list. Understand?"

He did. The FBI's thinking had been that the vault had to have been cased by the thieves before the break-in and that was most likely accomplished by simply going into the bank and renting a box. That way they had legitimate access; the guy who rented the box could go inside the vault anytime he wanted during business hours and have a look around. So the list including anybody who rented a box within three months of the robbery stood a good chance of also including the scout.

Second, it was likely that this scout would not want to draw attention to himself after the robbery, so he might report nothing stolen from his box. So that would put him on the D list. But if he made no report at all or had given untraceable information on his box rental card, then his name would be on the E list.

There were only seven names on the D list and five on the E list. One of the E names was circled. Frederic B. Isley of Park La Brea, the name of the man who had bought three Honda ATV's in Tustin. The other names had check marks next to them.

"Remember?" Eleanor said. "I said that name would come up again."

Harry nodded.

"Isley," she said. "We think he was the scout. Rented the box nine weeks before the burglary. The bank records show he made a total of four visits to the vault during the next seven weeks. But after the break-in, he never came back, whoever he was. Never filed a report. And when we tried to contact him we found the address was phony."

"Get a description?"

"Not one that would do us any good. Small, dark and maybe handsome was about as good as the vault clerks could do. We thought this guy was the scout even before we found out about the ATVs. When a boxholder wants to see his box, the clerk takes him in, unlocks the little door and then escorts him to one of the viewing rooms. When he's done, they both take the box back and the customer initials his box card. Kind of like at a library. So, when we looked at this guy's card we saw the initials—FBI. You're a man who doesn't like coincidences. Neither did we. We think somebody was having fun with us. Later, it was confirmed when we tracked the ATVs to Tustin."

Harry sipped his coffee.

"Not much good it did us," she said. "Never found him. In the debris of the vault after the burglary we were able to find his box. We printed it and the door. Nothing. We showed the vault clerks some mugs—Meadows was in there—and they couldn't make anybody."

"We could go back to them now with Franklin and Delgado, see if one of them was this Isley."

"Yeah. We will. I'll be right back."

She got up and left and Bosch went back to drinking coffee and studying the list. He read every name and address on the list, but nothing jogged his memory aside from the handful of names of celebrities, politicians and the like that had safe-deposit boxes. Bosch was going over the list a second time when Eleanor came back. She was carrying a piece of paper, which she slid onto his desk.

"I checked Rourke's office. He already sent most of the paperwork I turned in over to records. But the hypnosis memo was still in his in box, so he must not have seen it yet. I took it back. It's useless now and it might be better if he didn't see it."

Harry glanced at the memo and then folded the page and put it in his pocket.

"Frankly," she said, "I don't think any of the paper was out in the open long enough . . . I mean, I just don't see it. And Rourke . . . he's a technocrat, not a killer. Like they said about you at behavioral sciences, he wouldn't cross the line for money."

Bosch looked at her and found himself wanting to say something to please her, to get her back on his side. He could think of nothing and could not understand this new coldness in her manner.

"Forget it," he said, and then, looking down at the lists, he added, "How far did you people check out these people who reported no losses?"

She looked down at the printouts where Bosch had circled list B. There were nineteen names on the list.

"We ran each name for criminal records," she began. "We did a telephone interview and later a face-to-face. If an agent got weird vibes or somebody's story didn't play well, then another agent would come by unannounced to do a follow-up interview. Kind of get another opinion. I was not part of that. We had a second crew who handled most of the field interviews. If there is a particular name there that you are interested in, I could pull the interview summaries."

"What about the Vietnamese names on the lists? I count thirty-four boxholders with Vietnamese names, four are on the no-loss list, one on the dead-end list."

"What about the Vietnamese? There is also probably a breakout, if you look for it, on Chinese, Korean, whites, blacks and Latinos. These were equal opportunity bandits."

"Yeah, but you came up with a connection to Vietnam in Meadows. Now we have Franklin and Delgado, possibly involved. All three were MPs in Vietnam. We've got Charlie Company, which may or may not have a part in this. So, after Meadows became a suspect and you started pulling military records of tunnel rats, did you do any further checking with the Vietnamese on this list?"

"No—well, yes. On the foreign nationals we ran their names through INS to see how long they'd been here, whether they were legal. But that was about it." She was quiet a moment. "I can see what you are getting at. It's a flaw in the way we handled it. See, we didn't develop Meadows as a possible suspect until a few weeks after the robbery. By then most of these people had already been interviewed. After we started looking at Meadows, I don't think we went back to see if any of the names on the list fit in with him. You think one of the Vietnamese could have somehow been part of this?"

"I don't know what I'm thinking. Just looking for connections. Coincidences that aren't coincidences."

Bosch took a notebook out of his coat pocket and started making a list of the names, DOBs and addresses of the Vietnamese boxholders. He put the four who reported no loss and the name from the dead-end list at the top of his own list. He had just finished the list and closed the notebook when Rourke walked into the squad room, his hair still wet from his morning shower. He was carrying a coffee mug that said Boss on the side of it. He saw Bosch and Wish and then looked at his watch.

"Getting an early start?"

"Our witness, he turned up dead," Wish said, no expression on her face.

"Jesus. Where? They get somebody?"

Wish shook her head and looked at Bosch with a face that warned him not to start anything. Rourke looked at him also.

"Does it relate to this?" he said. "Any evidence of that?"

"We think so," Bosch said.

"Jesus!"

"You said that," Bosch said.

"Should we take the case, from LAPD, add it to the Meadows investigation?" He said this looking directly at Wish. Bosch was not part of the decision-making team here. She didn't answer, so Rourke added, "Should we have offered him protection?"

Bosch couldn't resist. "From who?"

A strand of wet hair dropped out of place and across Rourke's forehead. His face flushed deeply red.

"What the hell is that supposed to mean?"

"How'd you know LAPD had the case?"

"What?"

"You just asked if we should take the case from LAPD. How'd you know they had it? We didn't say."

"I just assumed. Bosch, I resent what that implies and I resent the hell out of you. Are you implying that I or someone—If you are saying there is a law enforcement leak on this case, then I will request an internal review today. But I'll tell you right now that if there was a leak it wasn't from the bureau."

"Then where the hell else could it have been? What happened to the reports we filed with you? Who saw them?"

Rourke shook his head.

"Harry, don't be ridiculous. I understand your feelings, but let's calm down and think for a minute. The witness was snatched off the street and interviewed at Hollywood Station, then dropped off at a public youth shelter.

"And, lastly, you're being followed around by your own department, Detective. I'm sorry, but even your own people apparently don't trust you."

Bosch's face grew dark. He felt betrayed in a sense. Rourke could only have known about the tail through Wish. She had made Lewis and Clarke. Why hadn't she said anything to him instead of Rourke? Bosch looked over at her but she was looking down at her desk. He looked back at Rourke, who was nodding his head as if it were on a spring.

"Yes, she made the tail on you the first day." Rourke looked around the empty squad room, obviously wishing he had a larger audience. He was moving his weight from one foot to the other now, like a boxer in his corner impatiently waiting for the next round to begin so he could deliver the knockout punch on a fading opponent. Wish continued to sit silently at her desk. And in that moment it seemed to Bosch to be a million years ago that they had held each other in her bed. Rourke said, "Maybe you should look at yourself and your own department before running around making reckless accusations."

Bosch said nothing. He just stood up and headed to the door.

"Harry, where are you going?" Eleanor called from her desk.

He turned around and looked at her a moment, then he kept walking.

•   •   •

Lewis and Clarke picked up Bosch's Caprice as soon as it came out of the federal garage. Clarke was driving. Lewis dutifully noted the time on the surveillance log.

He said, "He's got a bug up his ass, better move up on him some."

Bosch had turned west on Wilshire and was heading for the 405. Clarke increased his speed to stay with him in the morning rush hour traffic.

"I'd have a bug somewhere if I'd just lost my only witness," Clarke said. "If I'd gotten him killed."

"How you figure?"

"You saw it. He stuffed the kid in that shelter and went his merry way. I don't know what that kid saw or what he told them, but it was important enough for him to have to be eliminated. Bosch shoulda taken better care. Kept him under lock and key."

They went south on the 405. Bosch was ten cars ahead, now staying in the slow lane. The freeway was thick with a stinking, polluting mass of moving steel.

"I think he's going for the 10," Clarke said. "He's going into Santa Monica. Maybe back to her place, probably forgot his toothbrush. Or she's coming back to meet him for a nooner. You know what I say? I say we let him go and we go back to talk to Irving. I think we can build something on this witness thing. Maybe dereliction of duty. There is enough to get an administrative hearing. He'd at least get bounced out of homicide, and if Harry Bosch ain't allowed to be on the homicide table then he'll pick up and leave. One more notch on our barrel."

Lewis thought about his partner's idea. It wasn't bad. It could work. But he didn't want to pull off the surveillance without Irving's say-so.

"Keep with him," he said. "When he stops somewhere, I'll drop a quarter and see what Irving wants to do. When he buzzed me this morning about the kid, he seemed pretty stoked. Like things were getting good. So I don't want to pull off without his say-so."

"Whatever. Anyway, how'd Irving know about the kid getting snuffed so fast?"

"I don't know. Watch it here. He's taking the 10."

They followed the gray Caprice onto the Santa Monica Freeway. They were now going away from the working city, against the grain, and were in lighter traffic. But Bosch no longer was speeding. And he went past the Clover Field and Lincoln exits to Eleanor Wish's home, staying on the freeway until it curved through the tunnel and came out below the beach cliffs as the Pacific Coast Highway. He headed north along the coast, with the sun bright overhead and the Malibu mountains just opaque whispers ahead in the haze.

"Now what?" Clarke said.

"I don't know. Hang back some."

There wasn't much traffic on the PCH and they were having trouble keeping at least one car between them and Bosch's car at all times. Though Lewis still believed that most cops never bothered to check if they were being followed, today he was making an exception to that theory with Bosch. His witness had been murdered; he might instinctively think someone had been following him, or still was.

"Yeah, just hang back. We got all day and so does he." Bosch's pace held steady for the next four miles, until he turned into a parking lot next to Alice's and the Malibu pier. Lewis and Clarke cruised by. After a half mile Clarke made an illegal U-turn and headed back. When they pulled into the parking lot, Bosch's car was still there but they didn't see him.

"The restaurant again?" Clarke said. "He must love the place."

"It's not even open this early."

They both began looking around in all directions. There were four other cars at the end of the lot, and the racks on top of them said they belonged to the cluster of surfers rising and falling on the seas south of the pier. Finally, Lewis saw Bosch and pointed. He was halfway to the end of the pier, walking, with his head down and his hair blowing a hundred different ways. Lewis looked around for the camera and realized it was still in the trunk. He took a pair of binoculars out of the glove compartment and trained them on Bosch's diminishing figure. He watched until Bosch reached the end of the wooden planking and leaned his elbows on the railing.

"What's he doing?" Clarke asked. "Let me see."

"You're driving. I'm watching. He's not doing anything anyway. Just leaning there."

"He's got to be doing something."

"He's thinking. Okay? . . . There. He's lighting a cigarette. Happy? He's doing something. . . . Wait a minute."

"What?"

"Shit. We should've had the camera ready."

"What's this 'we' shit? That's your job today. I'm driving.

What's he doing?"

"He dropped something. Into the water."

Through the field glasses Lewis saw Bosch's body leaning limply on the railing. He was looking down into the water below. There was no one else on the pier as far as Lewis could see.

"What did he drop? Can you see?"

"How the fuck do I know what he dropped? I can't see the surface from here. Do you want for me to go out there and get one of the surfer boys to paddle over and see for us? I don't know what he dropped."

"Cool your jets. I was just asking. Now, can you remember the color of this object he dropped?"

"It looked white, like a ball. But it sort of floated."

"I thought you said you couldn't see the surface."

"I meant it floated down. I think it was a tissue or some kind of paper."

"What's he doing now?"

"Just standing there at the railing. He's looking down into the water."

"Crisis of conscience time. Maybe he'll jump and we can forget this whole damned thing."

Clarke giggled at his feeble joke. Lewis didn't.

"Yeah, right. I'm sure that's going to happen."

"Give me the glasses and go call in. See what Irving wants to do."

Lewis handed over the binoculars and got out. First, he went to the trunk, opened it and got out the Nikon. He attached a long lens and then took it around to the driver's window and handed it to Clarke.

"Get a picture of him out there, so we'll have something to show Irving."

Then Lewis trotted over to the restaurant to find a phone. He was back in less than three minutes. Bosch was still leaning on the rail at the end of the pier.

"Chief says under no circumstances are we to break off the tail," Lewis said. "He also said our reports sucked ass. He wants more detail, and more pictures. Did you get him?"

Clarke was too busy watching through the camera to answer. Lewis picked up the binoculars and looked. Bosch remained unmoving. Lewis couldn't figure it. What is he doing? Thinking? Why come all the way out here to think?

"Fucking Irving, that figures," Clarke suddenly said, dropping the camera into his lap to look at his partner.

"And yeah, I got a few pictures of him. Enough to make Irving happy. But he's not doing anything. Just leaning there."

"Not anymore," Lewis said, still looking through the binoculars. "Start her up. It's showtime."

Bosch walked off the pier after dropping the crumpled hypnotism memo into the water. Like a flower cast on a spoiled sea, it held its own on the surface for a few brief moments and then sank out of sight. His resolve to find Meadows's killer was now stronger: now he sought justice for Sharkey as well. As he made his way on the old planking of the pier he saw the Plymouth that had been following him pull out of the restaurant lot. It's them, he thought.

But no matter. He didn't care what they had seen, or thought they had seen. There were new rules now, and Bosch had plans for Lewis and Clarke.

He drove east on the 10 into downtown. He never bothered to check his mirror for the black car because he knew it would be there. He wanted it to be there.

When he got to Los Angeles Street, he parked in a no-parking zone in front of the U.S. Administration Building. On the third floor Bosch walked through one of the crowded waiting rooms of the Immigration and Naturalization Service. The place smelled like a jail—sweat, fear and desperation. A bored woman was sitting behind a sliding glass window working on the *Times* crossword. The window was closed. On the sill was a plastic paper-ticket dispenser like they use at a meat-market counter. After a few moments she looked up at Bosch. He was holding his badge up.

"Do you know a six-letter word for a man of constant sorrow and loneliness?" she asked after sliding the window open and then checking her nail for damage.

"Bosch."

"What?"

"Detective Harry Bosch. Buzz me in. I want to see Hector V."

"Have to check first," she said in a pouty way. She whispered something into the phone, then reached to Bosch's badge case and put her finger on the name on the ID card. Then she hung up.

"He says go on back." She buzzed the lock on the door next to the window. "He says you know the way."

Bosch shook Hector Villabona's hand in a cramped squad room much smaller than Bosch's own.

"I need a favor. I need some computer time."

"Let's do it."

That's what Bosch liked about Hector V. He never asked what or why before deciding. He was a let's-do-it type of guy. He didn't play bullshit games that Bosch had come to believe everybody in his profession played. Hector rolled his chair over to an IBM on a desk against the wall and entered his password. "You want to run names, right? How many?"

Bosch wasn't going to bullshit him, either. He showed him the list of thirty-four names. Hector whistled lowly and said, "Okay, we'll run them through, but these are Vietnamese. If their cases were not worked out of this office their files won't be here. I'll only have what's on the computer. Dates of entry, documentation, citizenship, whatever is on the computer. You know how it is, Harry."

Bosch did. But he also knew that Southern California was where most of the Vietnamese refugees made their homes after making the trip. Hector started typing in the names with two fingers, and twenty minutes later Bosch was looking at a printout from the computer.

"What are we looking for, Harry?" Hector said as he studied the list with him.

"I don't know. What do you see that is unusual?"

A few moments passed and Bosch thought Hector would say nothing was unusual. A dead end. But Bosch was wrong.

"Okay, on this one I think you will find he was connected."

The name was Ngo Van Binh. It meant nothing to Bosch other than it had come from the B list; Binh had reported nothing stolen from his safe-deposit box.

"Connected?"

"He had some kind of pull," Hector said. "Connected politically, I guess you would call it. See, his case number has the prefix GL. Those are files handled by our special cases bureau in D.C. Usually, SCB doesn't deal with people from the masses. Very political. Handles people like the shah and the Marcoses, Russian defectors if they are scientists or ballerinas. Stuff like that. Stuff I never see."

He nodded his head and put his finger on the printout.

"Okay, then we have the dates, they are too close. It happened too fast, which tells me this case was greased.

I don't know this guy from Adam, but I know this guy knew people. Look at the date of entry, May 4, 1975. That's just four days after the guy left Vietnam. You figure the first day is getting to Manila and the last day is getting to the States. That leaves only two days in between in Manila for him to get approval and get his ticket punched for the mainland. And at that time, I mean, man, they were coming in by the boatload to Manila. No way in two days unless it was greased. So what that means is this guy, this Binh, already had approval. He was connected. It's not that unusual, because a lot of people were. We got a lot of people out of there when the shit hit the fan. A lot of them were the elite. A lot of them just had money to pay to make them elite."

Bosch looked at the date Binh had left Vietnam. April 30, 1975. The same day Meadows left Vietnam for the last time. The day Saigon fell to the NVA.

"And this DOD?" Villabona said, pointing at another date. "Very short time to receive documentation. May 14. That's ten days after arrival this guy gets a visa. That's too fast for the average Joe. Or in this case, the average Ngo."

"So what do you think?"

"Hard to say. He could have been an operative. He could've just had enough money to get him on a helicopter. Lotta rumors still floating around from that time. People getting rich. Seats on military transports going for ten grand. No question visas going for more. Nothing ever confirmed."

"Can you pull the file on this guy?"

"Yeah. If I was in D.C."

Bosch just looked at him, and Hector finally said, "All

GLs are there, Harry. That's where the people that people are connected to are. Get it?"

Bosch didn't say anything.

"Don't get mad, Harry. I'll see what I can do. I'll make a couple calls. You going to be around later?"

Bosch gave him the FBI's number but didn't say it was the FBI. Then they shook hands again and Bosch left. In the first-floor lobby he watched through the smoked-glass doors, looking for Lewis and Clarke. When he finally saw the black Plymouth turn the corner as the two IAD detectives finished another circuit of the block, Bosch walked through the doors and down the steps to his car. In his peripheral vision he saw the IAD car slow and turn into the curb while they waited for him to get in his car and drive off.

Bosch did as they wanted. Because it was what he wanted.

Woodrow Wilson Drive winds counterclockwise around and up the side of the Hollywood Hills, the cracked, patchwork asphalt never wide enough at any point for two cars to pass without a cautious slowing. Going up, the homes on the left crawl vertically up the hillside. They are the old money, solid and secure. Spanish tile and stucco. To the right, the newer houses fearlessly swing their wood frame rooms out over the brown brush arroyos and daisies in the canyon. They are balanced on stilts and hope and cling as tenuously to the edge of the hill as their owners do to their positions at the studios down below. Bosch's home was fourth from the end on the right side.

As he drove around the final bend, the house came into sight. He looked at the dark wood, the shoebox design, seeking a sign that it had somehow changed—as if the exterior of the house could tell him if something was wrong with the interior. He checked the rearview then and caught the front end of the black Plymouth nosing around the curve. Bosch pulled into the carport next to his house and got out. He went inside without looking back at the tail car.

He had gone to the pier to think about what Rourke had said. And in doing so he thought about the hang-up call that was on his phone tape. Now, he went to the kitchen and played back his messages. First there was the hang-up call, which had come in Tuesday, and then a message from Jerry Edgar in the predawn hours today, when Edgar had called looking for Bosch to get him out to the Hollywood Bowl. Bosch rewound the tape and listened to the hang-up call again, silently chastising himself for not having picked up on its significance the first time he heard it. Someone had called, listened to his taped message and then hung up after the first message beep. The hang-up was on the tape. Most people, if they didn't want to leave a message, would simply hang up as soon as they heard Bosch's tape-recorded voice saying he wasn't in. Or, if they thought he was home, would have called out his name after the beep. But this caller had listened to the tape and then didn't hang up until after the beep. Why? Bosch had missed it at first, but now thought the call had been a transmitter test.

He went to the closet by the door and took out a pair of binoculars. He went to the living room window and looked through a crack in the curtain for the black Plymouth. It was a half-block farther up the hill. Lewis and Clarke had driven by the house, turned around and parked at the curb, facing downhill and ready to continue the tail if Bosch came out. Through the binoculars Bosch could see Lewis behind the wheel, watching the house. Clarke had his head back on the passenger seat and his eyes closed. Neither of them appeared to be wearing earphones. Still, Harry had to be sure. Without taking his eyes from the binoculars, he reached over to the front door and opened it a few inches and closed it. The men in the IAD car showed no reaction, no alert. Clarke's eyes remained closed. Lewis continued picking his teeth with a business card.

Bosch decided that if they had dropped a bug on him, it was transmitting to a remote. It was safer that way. Probably a sound-activated minireel hidden on the exterior of the house. They'd wait until he drove away and then one of them would jump out of the car and quickly collect the reel, replacing it with a fresh one. They could then catch up the tail on him before he got down the hill to the freeway. He walked away from the window and made a quick survey of the living room and kitchen. He studied the underside of tables and electric fixtures but he didn't find the bug and didn't expect to. The smart place, he knew, was the phone, which he was saving for last. It had a ready power source, and placement there would provide sound intake of the immediate interior of the house as well as any conversations that came in through the phone.

Bosch picked up the phone and with a small penknife that was attached to his key chain he popped the cover off the mouthpiece. There was nothing there that shouldn't be. Then he took the cover off the earpiece. It was there. Using the knife he carefully lifted out the speaker. Attached behind it by a small magnet was a small, flat, round transmitter about the size of a quarter. There were two wires attached to the device, which, he knew, was sound activated and called a T-9. One wire was wrapped around one of the phone's receiver wires, piggybacking power for the bug. The other wire went into the barrel of the handset. Bosch gingerly pulled it, and out came the backup energy source: a small, thin power pack containing a single AA battery. The bug ran off the phone's juice, but if the phone was disconnected from the wall, the battery could provide power for maybe another eight hours. Bosch disconnected the device from the phone and placed it on the table. It was now running off the battery. He just stared at it, thinking about what he was going to do. It was a standard police department wire. Pickup range, fifteen to twenty feet, designed to take in everything said in the room. The transmission range was minimal, maybe twenty-five yards at most, depending on how much metal was in the building.

Bosch went to the living room window again to look up the street. Lewis and Clarke still showed no sign of alert or that the bug had been discovered. Lewis was through picking his teeth.

Bosch turned on the stereo and put on a Wayne Shorter CD. He then went out a side door in the kitchen into the carport. He could not be seen from the IAD car. He found the tape recorder in the first place he looked; the junction box beneath the DWP electric meter on the back wall of the carport. The two-inch reels were turning to the sound of Shorter's saxophone. The Nagra recorder, like the T-9, was wired to the house current but had a battery backup. Bosch disconnected it and brought it inside, where he set it on the table next to its counterpart.

Shorter was finishing "502 Blues." Bosch sat in the watch chair, lit a cigarette and looked at the device as he tried to form a plan. He reached over, rewound the tape and pushed the play button. The first thing he heard was his own voice saying he wasn't there, then Jerry Edgar's message about the Hollywood Bowl. Then the next sounds were the door opening and closing twice, then Wayne Shorter's sax. They had changed reels at least once since the test call had been made. Then he realized that Eleanor Wish's visit had been taped. He thought about that and wondered if the bug had picked up what had been said on the back porch. Bosch's stories about himself and Meadows. He grew angry thinking about the intrusion, the delicate moment stolen by the two men in the black Plymouth.

He shaved, showered and dressed in a fresh set of clothes, a tan summer suit with pink oxford shirt and blue tie. Then he went to the living room and loaded the bug and recorder into the pockets of his jacket. He took another look through the curtains with the field glasses: still no movement in the Internal Affairs car. He went out the side door again and carefully climbed down the embankment to the base of the first stilt, an iron I beam. He gingerly made his way across the incline beneath his house. He noticed along the way that the dried brush was sprinkled with pieces of gold foil, the beer label he had picked at and dropped from the porch when he was with Eleanor.

Once he got to the other side of his property, he picked his way across the hill, going under the next three stilt houses. After the third, he scrambled up the hillside and looked around the front corner into the street. He was now behind the black Plymouth. He picked the burrs off the cuffs of his pants and then walked casually into the road.

• • •

Bosch came up unnoticed on the passenger-side door. The window was down and just before he flung the door open he thought he could hear snoring coming from the car.

Clarke's mouth was open and his eyes still shut when Bosch leaned in through the open door and grabbed both men by their silk ties. Bosch put his right foot on the doorsill for leverage and pulled both men toward him. Though there were two of them, the advantage belonged to Bosch. Clarke was disoriented and Lewis had little more idea what was happening. Pulling them by their ties meant that any struggle or resistance tightened the ties around their necks, cutting off their air. They came out almost willingly, tumbling like dogs on leashes and landing next to a palm tree planted three feet from the sidewalk. Their faces were red and sputtering. Their hands went to their necks, clawing at the knots of their ties as they fought to get air back into their pipes. Bosch's hands went to their belts and yanked away the handcuffs. As the two IAD detectives were gulping air through their reopened throats Bosch managed to cuff Lewis's left hand to Clarke's right. Then, on the other side of the tree, he got Lewis's right into the other set of cuffs. But Clarke realized what Bosch was doing and tried to stand up and pull away. Bosch grabbed his tie again and gave it a sharp yank down, Clarke's head came forward and his face rammed the palm tree. He was momentarily stunned and Bosch slapped the last cuff on his wrist. Both IAD cops were wallowing on the ground then, locked to each other with the palm tree in the middle of the circle of their arms. Bosch unholstered their weapons, then stepped back to catch his own breath. He threw their guns onto the front seat of their car.

"You're dead," Clarke finally managed to croak through his swollen throat.

They worked their way up into standing positions, the palm tree between them. They looked like two grown men caught playing ring-around-the-rosy.

"Assaulting a fellow officer, two counts," Lewis said. "Conduct unbecoming. We can get you for a half-dozen other things now, Bosch." He coughed violently, spittle hitting Clarke's suit coat. "Unhook us and maybe we can forget this."

"No way. We aren't forgetting a fucking thing," Clarke said to his partner. "He's going down like a flaming asshole."

Bosch took the listening device out of his pocket and held it out on his palm for them to see. "Who's going down?" he asked.

Lewis looked at the bug, recognizing what it was, and said, "We don't know anything about that."

"Course not," Bosch said. He took the recorder out of his other pocket and held that out, too. "Sound-sensitive Nagras, that's what you guys use on all your jobs, legal or not, isn't it? Found it in my phone. Same time I notice that you two dummies have been following me all over the city. Don't suppose you guys also dropped the bug on me so you could listen as well as watch?"

Neither Lewis nor Clarke answered and Bosch didn't expect them to. He noticed a small drop of blood poised at the edge of one of Clarke's nostrils. A car driving on Woodrow Wilson slowed and Bosch pulled his badge and held it up. The car kept going. The two IAD detectives did not call for help, which made Bosch begin to feel he was safe. This would be his play. The department had taken such bad publicity for illegally bugging officers, civil rights leaders, even movie stars in the past, that these two were not going to make an issue of this. Saving their own hides came before skinning Bosch.

"You got a warrant saying you can drop a bug on me?"

"Listen to me, Bosch," Lewis said. "I told you, we—"

"I didn't think so. Have to have evidence of a crime to get a warrant. Least that's what I always heard. But Internal Affairs doesn't usually bother with details like that. You know what your assault case looks like, Clarke? While you two are taking me to the Board of Rights and getting me fired for dragging you out of the car and getting grass stains on your shiny asses, I'm going to be taking you two, your boss Irving, IAD, the police chief and the whole fucking city to federal court on a Fourth Amendment case. Illegal search and seizure. I'll throw in the mayor, too, How's that?"

Clarke spit on the grass at Bosch's feet. A drop of blood from his nose fell onto his white shirt. He said, "You can't prove that came from us, 'cause it didn't."

"Bosch, what do you want?" Lewis blurted out, his rage turning his face a darker red than it had been when his tie had been tightened like a noose around his neck. Bosch started walking in a slow circle around them, so they had to constantly turn their heads or bend around the palm trunk to watch him.

"What do I want? Well, as much as I despise you two, I don't really want to have to drag your asses into court. Dragging them across the sidewalk was enough. What I want—"

"Bosch, you ought to get your fuckin' head examined," Clarke burst out.

"Shut up, Clarke," Lewis said.

"You shut up," Clarke said back.

"Matter of fact, I have had it examined," Bosch said. "And I still would rather have mine than yours. You'd need a proctologist to check yours out."

He said this as he circled close behind Clarke. Then he moved out a few steps and continued to make the rounds. "I'll tell you what, I'm willing to let bygones be bygones on this. All you have to do is answer a few questions and we're square on this little mix-up. I'll cut you loose. After all, we're all part of the family, right?"

"What questions, Bosch?" Lewis said. "What are you talking about?"

"When'd you start the tail?"

"Tuesday morning, we picked you up when you left the FBI," Lewis said.

"Don't tell him shit, man," Clarke said to his partner.

"He already knows."

Clarke looked at Lewis and shook his head like he couldn't believe what he was hearing.

"When'd you drop the bug in my phone?"

"Didn't," Lewis said.

"Bullshit. But never mind. You saw me interview the kid down in Boytown." It was a statement, not a question. Bosch wanted them to think he knew most of it and just needed the gaps filled in.

"Yeah," Lewis said. "That was our first day on it. So you made us. So fucking what?"

Harry saw Lewis pull his hand toward his coat pocket. He quickly moved in and got his hand in first. He pulled out a key ring that included a cuff key. He threw the keys into the car. Behind Lewis, he said, "Who'd you tell about it?"

"Tell?" Lewis said. "About the kid? Nobody. We didn't tell anybody, Bosch."

"You write up a daily surveillance log, don't you? You take pictures, don't you? I bet there's a camera in the backseat of that car. Unless you forgot and left it in the trunk."

"Course we do."

Bosch lit a cigarette and started walking again. "Where did it all go?"

It was a few moments before Lewis answered. Bosch saw him make eye contact with Clarke. "We turned in the first log and the film yesterday. Put it in the deputy chief's box. Like always. Don't even know if he looked at it yet. That's the only paper we've done so far. So, Bosch, take these cuffs off. This is embarrassing. People seein' us and all. We can still talk after."

Bosch walked up between them and blew smoke into the center of the huddle and told them the cuffs stayed on until the conversation was over. He then leaned close to Clarke's face and said, "Who else was copied?"

"With the surveillance report? Nobody was copied, Bosch," Lewis said. "That would violate department procedure."

Bosch laughed at that, shook his head. He knew they would not admit any illegality or violation of department policy. He started to walk away, back to his house.

"Wait a minute, wait a minute, Bosch," Lewis called out. "We copied the report to your lieutenant. All right? Come on back."

Bosch did and Lewis continued. "He wanted to be kept apprised. We had to do it. The DC, Irving, okayed it. We did what we were told."

"What did the report say about the kid?"

"Nothing. Just some kid is all. . . . Uh, 'Subject engaged juvenile in conversation. Juvenile was transported to Hollywood Station for formal interview,' something like that."

"Did you ID him in the report?"

"No name. We didn't even know his name. Honest, Bosch. We just watched you, that's all. Now uncuff us."

"What about Home Street Home? You watched me take him there. Was that in the report?"

"Yeah, on the log."

Bosch moved in close again. "Now here's the big question. If there is no complaint from the bureau anymore, why is IAD still on me? The FBI made the call to Pounds and withdrew the complaint. Then you guys act like you were called off but you weren't. Why?"

Lewis started to say something but Bosch cut him off. "I want Clarke to tell me. You're thinking too fast, Lewis."

Clarke didn't say a word.

"Clarke, the kid you saw me with ended up dead. Somebody did him because he talked to me. And the only people who knew he talked to me were you and your partner here. Something is going on here, and if I don't get the answers I need I'm just going to lay it all out, go public with it. You are going to find your own ass being investigated by Internal Affairs."

Clarke said his first two words in five minutes: "Fuck you."

Lewis jumped in then.

"Look, Bosch, I'll tell you. The FBI doesn't trust you. That's the thing. They said they brought you into the case, but they told us they weren't sure about you. They said you muscled onto the case and they were going to have to watch you, make sure you weren't pulling a scam. That's all. So we were told to drop back but stay on you. We did.

That's all, man. Now cut us loose. I can hardly breathe, and my wrists are starting to hurt with these cuffs. You really put them on tight."

Bosch turned to Clarke. "Where's your cuff key?"

"Right front pocket," he said. He was cool about it, refusing to look at Bosch's face. Bosch walked around behind him and reached both hands around his waist. He pulled a key ring out of Clarke's pocket and then whispered in his ear, "Clarke, you ever go in my home again and I'll kill you."

Then he yanked the detective's pants and boxer shorts down to his ankles and started walking away. He threw the key ring into the car.

"You bastard!" Clarke yelled. "I'll kill you first, Bosch."

As long as he kept the bug and the Nagra, Bosch was reasonably certain Lewis and Clarke would not seek departmental charges against him. They had more to lose than he. A lawsuit and public scandal would cut their careers off at the stairway to the sixth floor. Bosch got in his car and drove back to the Federal Building.

Too many people knew about Sharkey or had the opportunity to know, he realized as he tried to assess the situation. There was no clear-cut way of flushing out the inside man. Lewis and Clarke had seen the boy and passed the information on to Irving and Pounds and who knew who else. Rourke and the FBI records clerk knew about him as well. And those names didn't even include the people on the street who might have seen Sharkey with Bosch, or had heard that Bosch was looking for him. Bosch knew that he would have to wait for things to develop.

At the Federal Building, the red-haired receptionist behind the glass window on the FBI floor made him wait while she called back to Group 3. He checked the cemetery again through the gauze curtains and saw several people working in the trench cut in the hill. They were lining the earth wound with blocks of black stone that reflected sharp white light points in the sun. And Bosch at last believed he knew what it was they were doing. The door lock buzzed behind him and Bosch headed back. It was twelve-thirty and the heavy squad was out, except for Eleanor Wish. She sat at her desk eating an egg salad sandwich, the kind they sold in plastic triangle-shaped boxes at every government building cafeteria he'd ever been in. The plastic bottle of water and a paper cup were on the desk. They exchanged small hellos. Bosch felt that things had changed between them, but he didn't know how much.

"You been here since this morning?" he asked.

She said she hadn't. She told him that she had taken the mugs of Franklin and Delgado to the vault clerks at West-Land National and one of the women positively identified Franklin as Frederic B. Isley, the holder of a box in the vault. The scout.

"It's enough for a warrant, but Franklin isn't around," she said. "Rourke sent a couple crews to the addresses DMV had on both him and Delgado. Called back in a little while ago. Either they've moved on or never lived in the places in the first place. Looks like they're in the wind."

"So, what's next?"

"I don't know. Rourke's talking about closing shop on it until we catch them. You'll probably get to go back to your homicide table. When we catch one of them, we'll bring you down to work on him about the Meadows murder."

"Sharkey's murder, too. Don't forget that."

"That, too."

Bosch nodded. It was over. The bureau was going to close it down.

"By the way, you got a message," she said. "Someone called for you, said his name was Hector. That was all."

Bosch sat down at the desk next to hers and dialed Hector Villabona's direct line. He picked up after two rings.

"It's Bosch."

"Hey, what're you doing with the bureau?" he asked. "I called the number you gave and somebody said it was the FBI."

"Yeah, it's a long story. I'll tell you later. Did you come up with anything?"

"Not much, Harry, and I'm not going to, either. I can't get the file. This guy Binh, whoever he is, he has got some connections. Like we figured. His file is still classified. I called a guy I know out there and asked him to send it out. He called me back and said no can do."

"Why would it still be classified?"

"Who knows, Harry? That's why it's still classified. So people won't find this shit out."

"Well, thanks. It's not looking that important anymore."

"If you have a source at State, somebody with access, they might have better luck than me. I'm just the token beaner in the bean-counting department. But, listen, there is one thing this guy I know kind of let slip."

"What?"

"Well, see, I gave him Binh's name, you know, and when calls back he says, 'Sorry, Captain Binh's file is classified.' Just like that is how he said it. Captain, he called him. So this guy musta been a military guy. That's probably why they got him out of there and over here so fast. If he was military, they saved his ass for sure."

"Yeah," Bosch said, then he thanked Hector and hung up.

He turned to Eleanor and asked if she had any contacts in the State Department. She shook her head no. "Military intelligence, CIA, anything like that?" Bosch said. "Somebody with access to computer files."

She thought a moment and said, "Well, there is a guy on the State floor. I sort of know him from D.C. But what's going on, Harry?"

"Can you call him and tell him you need a favor?"

"He doesn't talk on the phone, not about business. We'll just have to go down there."

He stood up. Outside the office, while they waited for the elevator, Bosch told her about Binh, his rank, and the fact that he left Vietnam on the same day as Meadows. The elevator opened and they got on and she pushed seven. They were alone.

"You knew all along, that I was being tailed," Bosch said. "Internal Affairs."

"I saw them."

"But you knew before you saw them, didn't you?"

"Does it make a difference?"

"I think it does. Why didn't you tell me?"

She took a while. The elevator stopped.

"I don't know," she said. "I'm sorry. I didn't at first, and then when I wanted to tell you I couldn't. I thought it would spoil everything. I guess it did, anyway."

"Why didn't you at first, Eleanor? Because there was still a question about me?"

She looked into the stainless steel corner of the elevator.

"In the beginning, yes, we weren't sure about you. I won't lie about that."

"What about after the beginning?"

The door opened on the seventh floor. Eleanor moved through it, saying, "You're still here, aren't you?"

Bosch stepped out after her. He took hold of her arm and stopped her. They stood there as two men in almost matching gray suits charged through the open elevator door.

"Yes, I'm still here, but you didn't tell me about them."

"Harry, can we talk about this later?"

"The thing is, they saw us with Sharkey."

"Yes, I thought so."

"Well, why didn't you say anything when I was talking about the inside man, when I was asking about who you told about the kid?"

"I don't know."

Bosch looked down at his feet. He felt like the only man on the planet who didn't understand what was going on.

"I talked to them," he said. "They claim they just watched us with the kid. They never followed up to see what it was about. Said they didn't have his ID. Sharkey's name wasn't in their reports."

"And do you believe them?"

"Never have before. But I don't see them involved in this. It just doesn't fit. They're just after me and they'll do anything to get me. But not take out a witness. That's crazy."

"Maybe they're feeding information to someone who is involved and they just don't realize it."

Bosch thought about Irving and Pounds again.

"A possibility. The point is, there is an inside man. Somewhere. We know this. And it might be from my side. It might be yours. So we have to be very careful, about who we talk to and what we're doing."

After a moment he looked straight into her eyes and said, "Do you believe me?"

It took her a long time, but she finally nodded her head.

She said, "I can't think of any other way to explain what's happening."

Eleanor went up to a receptionist while Bosch hung back a bit. After a few minutes a young woman came out from a closed door and showed them down a couple of hallways and into a small office. No one was sitting behind the desk. They sat in two chairs facing the desk and waited.

"Who is this we're seeing?" Bosch whispered.

"I'll introduce you, and he can tell you what he wants you to know about him," she said.

Bosch was about to ask her what that meant when the door opened and a man strode in. He looked to be about fifty, with silvery hair that was carefully groomed and a strong build beneath the blue blazer. The man's gray eyes were as dull as day-old barbecue coals. He sat down and did not look at Bosch. He kept his eyes exclusively on Eleanor Wish.

"Ellie, good to see you again," he said. "How are you doing?"

She said she was doing fine, exchanged a few pleasantries and then got around to introducing Bosch. The man got up and reached across the desk to shake hands.

"Bob Ernst, assistant deputy, trade and development,

nice to meet you. So this is an official visit then, not just dropping by to see an old friend?"

"Yes, I'm sorry, Bob, but we are working on something and need some help."

"Whatever I can do, Ellie," Ernst said. He was annoying Bosch, and Bosch had only known him a minute.

"Bob, we need to background somebody whose name has come up on a case we are working," Wish said. "I think you are in a position that you could get that information for us without a great deal of inconvenience or time."

"That's our problem," Bosch added. "It's a homicide case. We don't have a lot of time to go through normal channels. To wait for things from Washington."

"Foreign national?"

"Vietnamese," Bosch said.

"Came here when?"

"May 4, 1975."

"Ah, right after the fall. I see. Tell me, what kind of homicide would the FBI and the LAPD be working on together that involves such ancient history, and history in another country as well?"

"Bob," Eleanor began, "I think—"

"No, don't answer that," Ernst yelped. "I think you are right. It would be best if we compartmentalized the information."

Ernst went through the motions of straightening his blotter and the knickknacks on his desk. Nothing was really out of order to begin with.

"How soon you need the information?" he finally said.

"Now," Eleanor said.

"We'll wait," Harry said.

"You realize, of course, I may not come up with anything, especially on short notice?"

"Of course," Eleanor said.

"Give me the name."

Ernst slid a piece of paper across his blotter. Eleanor wrote Binh's name on it and slid it back. Ernst looked at it a moment and got up without ever touching the paper.

"I'll see what I can do," he said and left the room.

Bosch looked at Eleanor.

" 'Ellie'?"

"Please, I don't allow anybody to call me that. That's why I don't take his calls and don't return them."

"You mean until now. You'll owe him now."

"If he finds something. And so will you."

"I guess I'll have to let him call me Ellie." She didn't smile.

"How'd you meet this guy, anyway?"

She didn't answer.

Bosch said, "He's probably listening to us right now."

He looked around the room, though obviously any listening devices would be hidden. He took out his cigarettes when he saw a black ashtray on the desk.

"Please, don't smoke," Eleanor said.

"Just a half."

"I met him once when we were both in Washington. I don't even remember what for now. He was assistant something-or-other with State back then, too. We had a couple of drinks. That's all. Sometime after that, he transferred out here. When he saw me in the elevator here and found out I was transferred, he started calling."

"CIA all the way, right? Or something close."

"More or less. I think. It doesn't matter if he gets what we need."

"More or less. I knew shitheads like him in the war. No matter how much he tells us today, there will be something more. Guys like that, information is their currency. They never give up everything. Like he said, they compartmentalize everything. They'll get you killed before they tell it all."

"Can we stop talking now?"

"Sure . . . Ellie."

Bosch passed the time smoking and looking at the empty walls. The guy didn't make much of an effort to make it look like a real office. No flag in the corner. Not even a picture of the president. Ernst was back in twenty minutes, and by then Bosch was on his second half-cigarette. As the assistant deputy for trade and development strode to his desk empty-handed, he said, "Detective, would you mind not smoking? I find it very bothersome in a closed room like this."

Bosch stubbed the butt out in the small black bowl on the corner of his desk.

"Sorry," he said. "I saw the ashtray. I thought—"

"It's not an ashtray, Detective," Ernst said in a somber tone. "That is a rice bowl, three centuries old. I brought it home with me after my stationing in Vietnam."

"You were working on trade and development then, too?"

"Excuse me, Bob, did you find anything?" Eleanor interjected. "On the name?"

It took Ernst a long moment to break his stare away from Bosch.

"I found very little, but what I did find may be useful. This man, Binh, is a former Saigon police officer. A captain. . . . Bosch, are you a veteran of the altercation?"

"You mean the war? Yes."

"Of course you are," Ernst said. "Then tell me, does this information mean anything to you?"

"Not a lot. I was in the bush most of my time. Didn't see much of Saigon except the Yankee bars and tattoo parlors. The guy was a police captain, should it mean something to me?"

"I suppose not. So let me tell you. As a captain, Binh ran the police department's vice unit."

Bosch thought about that and said, "Okay, he was probably as corrupt as everything else that went with that war."

"I don't suppose, coming from in the bush, you know much about the system, the way things worked in Saigon?" Ernst asked.

"Why don't you tell us about it? Sounds like that was your department. Mine was just trying to keep alive."

Ernst ignored the shot. He chose to ignore Bosch as well. He looked only at Eleanor as he spoke.

"It operated quite simply, really," he said. "If you dealt in substances, in flesh, gambling, anything on the black market, you were required to pay a local tariff, a tithe to the house, so to speak. That payment kept the local police away. It practically guaranteed your business would not be interrupted—within certain bounds. Your only worry then was the U.S. military police. Of course, they could be paid off as well, I suppose. There was always that rumor. Anyway, this system went on for years, from the very beginning until after the American withdrawal, until, I imagine, April 30, 1975, the day Saigon fell."

Eleanor nodded and waited for him to go on.

"The major American military involvement lasted longer than a decade, before that there was the French. We are talking many, many years of foreign intervention."

"Millions," Bosch said.

"What's that?"

"You are talking about millions of dollars in payoffs"

"Yes, absolutely. Tens of millions when added up over the years."

"And where does Captain Binh fit in?" Eleanor asked.

"You see," Ernst said, "our information at the time was that the corruption within the Saigon police department was orchestrated or controlled by a triad called the Devil's Three. You paid them or you did not do business. It was that simple.

"Coincidentally, or rather not coincidentally, the Saigon police had three captains whose domain corresponded, so to speak, quite nicely with the domain of the triad. One captain in charge of vice. One narcotics. One for patrol. Our information is that these three captains were, in fact, the triad."

"You keep saying 'Our information.' Is that trade and development's information? Where are you getting this?"

Ernst made a movement to straighten things on the top of his desk again and then stared coldly at Bosch. "Detective, you come to me for information. If you want to know where the source is, then you have made a mistake. You've come to the wrong person. You can believe what I tell you or not. It is of no consequence to me."

The two men locked eyes but said nothing else.

"What happened to them?" Eleanor asked. "The members of the triad."

Ernst pulled his eyes away from Bosch and said, "What happened is that after the United States pulled military forces in 1973 the triad's source of revenue was largely gone. But like any responsible business entity they saw it coming and looked to replace it. And our intelligence at the time was that they shifted their position considerably. In the early seventies they moved from the role of providing protection to narcotics operations in Saigon to actually becoming part of those operations. Through political and military contacts and, of course, police enforcement they solidified themselves as the brokers for all brown heroin that came out of the highlands and was moved to the United States."

"But it didn't last," Bosch said.

"Oh, no. Of course not. When Saigon fell in April 1975, they had to get out. They had made millions, an estimated fifteen to eighteen million dollars American each. It would mean nothing in the new Ho Chi Minh City and they wouldn't be alive to enjoy it anyway. The triad had to get out or they'd face the firing squads of the North Vietnamese Army. And they had to get out with their money. . . ."

"So, how'd they do it?" Bosch said.

"It was dirty money. Money that no Vietnamese police captain could or should have. I suppose they could have wired it to Zurich, but you have to remember you are dealing with the Vietnamese culture. Born of turmoil and distrust. War. These people did not even trust banks in their homeland. And besides it wasn't money anymore."

"What?" Eleanor said, puzzled.

"They had been converting all along. Do you know what eighteen million dollars looks like? Would probably fill a room. So they found a way to shrink it. At least, that's what we believe."

"Precious gems," Bosch said.

"Diamonds," Ernst said. "It is said eighteen million dollars' worth of the right diamonds would easily fit in two shoe boxes."

"And into a safe-deposit box," Bosch said.

"That could be, but, please, I don't want to know what I don't need to know."

"Binh was one of the captains," Bosch said. "Who were the other two?"

"I am told one of them was named Van Nguyen. And he is believed to be dead. He never left Vietnam. Killed by the other two, or maybe the North Vietnamese Army. But he never got out. That was confirmed by our agents in Ho Chi Minh after the fall. The other two did. They came here. And both had passes, arranged through connections and money, I suppose. I can't help you there. . . . There was Binh, who it seems you have found, and the other was Nguyen Tran. He came with Binh. Where they went and what they did here, I can't help you with. It's been fifteen years. Once they came across they were no longer our concern."

"Why would you allow them to come across?"

"Who says we did? You have to realize, Detective Bosch, that much of this information was put together after the fact."

Ernst stood up then. That was all the information he would decompartmentalize for today.

Bosch didn't want to go back up to the bureau. The information from Ernst was amphetamine in his blood. He wanted to walk. He wanted to talk, to storm. When they got in the elevator he pushed the button for the lobby and told Eleanor they were going outside. The bureau was like a fishbowl. He wanted a big room.

In any investigation, it had always seemed to Bosch, information would come slowly, like sand dropping steadily through the cinched middle of an hourglass. At some point, there was more information in the bottom of the glass. And then the sand in the top seemed to drop faster, until it was cascading through the hole. They were at that point with Meadows, the bank burglary, the whole thing. Things were coming together.

They went out through the front lobby and onto the green lawn where there were eight U.S. flags and a California state flag flapping lazily on poles posted in a semicircle. There were no protestors on this day. The air was warm and unseasonably humid.

"Do we have to walk out here?" Eleanor asked. "I would rather be upstairs, where we'd be near the phones. You could have a coffee."

"I want to smoke."

They walked north toward Wilshire Boulevard.

Bosch said, "It's 1975. Saigon is about to go down the sewer. Police Captain Binh pays people to get him and his share of diamonds out. Who he pays, we don't know. But we do know that he gets VIP treatment all the way. Most people took boats out, he flew. Four days from Saigon to the States. He is accompanied by an American civilian adviser to help smooth things. That's Meadows. He—"

"He may have been accompanied," she said. "You forgot the word 'may' there."

"We're not in court. I'm saying it the way I see it might've been, okay? Afterward, if you don't like it, you say it your way."

She raised her arms in a hands-off kind of way and Bosch continued.

"So, Meadows and Binh are together. Nineteen seventy-five. Meadows is working refugee security or something. See, he's getting out of there, too. He may or may not have known Binh from his old sideline, dealing heroin. The chances are he did. He was probably, in effect, working for Binh. Now, he may or may not have known what Binh was carrying with him to the States. Chances are he at least had an idea."

Bosch stopped to organize his thoughts and Eleanor reluctantly took over.

"Binh takes with him his cultural dislike or distrust for putting his money in the hands of bankers. He has an additional problem, too. His money is not kosher. It is undeclared, unknown and illegal for him to have. He can't declare it or make a normal deposit because this would be noticed and then have to be explained. So, he keeps this sizable fortune in the next best thing: a safe-deposit vault. Where are we going?"

Bosch didn't answer. He was too consumed by his thoughts. They were at Wilshire. When the walk sign flashed above the crosswalk they went with the flow of bodies. On the other side of the street they turned west; walking along the hedges that bordered the veterans cemetery. Bosch took over the story.

"Okay, so Binh's got his share in the safe-deposit box. He starts the great American dream as a refugee. Only he's a rich refugee. Meantime, Meadows comes back after the war, can't get into the groove of real life, can't beat his habit, and starts capering to feed it. But things aren't as easy as in Saigon. He gets caught, spends some time in stir. He gets out, goes back, gets out, then finally starts blocking some real time on federal raps on a couple of bank jobs."

There was an opening in the hedge and a brick walkway. Bosch followed it and they stood looking at the expanse of the cemetery, the rows of carved stones a weather-polished white against the sea of grass. The tall hedge buffered the sound from the street. It was suddenly very peaceful.

"It's like a park," Bosch said.

"It's a graveyard," she whispered. "Let's go."

"You don't have to whisper. Let's walk around. It's quiet."

Eleanor hesitated but then trailed him as he followed the bricks beneath an oak tree that shaded the graves of a grouping of World War I veterans. She caught up and continued the dialogue.

"So we have Meadows in TI. Somehow, he hears about this place Charlie Company. He gets the ear of the ex-soldier-slash-minister who operates the place, gets his backing and gets early release from TI. Now, at Charlie Company, he connects with two old war buddies. Or so we assume. Delgado and Franklin. Except there is only one day that all three of them are at Charlie Company at the same time. Just one day. Are you telling me they hatched this whole thing on that one day?"

"I don't know," Bosch said. "Could've been, but I doubt it. It might have been planned later, after they made that recontact at the farm. The important thing is that we have them together, or in close proximity, in Saigon, 1975. Now we have them together again at Charlie Company. After that, Meadows graduates, takes a few cover jobs until he finishes parole. Then he quits and disappears from view.

"Until?"

"Until the WestLand burglary. They go in, they hit the boxes until they find Binh's box. Or maybe they already knew which one was his. They must have followed him to plan the job and find out where he kept whatever was left of his share of the diamonds. We need to go back to the vault records and see if this Frederic B. Isley ever visited at the same time as Binh. I bet we find that he did. He saw which box was Binh's because he was in the vault with him at the same time.

"Then during the vault break-in, they hit his box and then all the others, taking everything as camouflage. The genius of it was that they knew Binh couldn't report what was taken from him because it did not exist, legally. They knew this. It was perfect. And what made it that way is them taking all the other stuff, to cover for the real target. The diamonds."

"The perfect crime," she said, "until Meadows pawned the bracelet with the jade dolphins on it. That gets him killed. Which brings us back to the question we had a few days ago. Why? And another thing that makes no sense: why, if he had helped loot the vault, was Meadows living in that dump? He was a rich man not acting like a rich man."

Bosch walked in silence for a while. It was the question he had been formulating an answer to since halfway through the meeting with Ernst. He thought about Meadows's eleven-month lease, paid in advance. If he were alive, he would be moving out next week. As they walked through the garden of white stone, it all seemed to fit together. There was no sand left in the top of the hourglass. He finally spoke.

"Because the perfect crime was only half over. By pawning the bracelet, he was giving it away too soon. So he had to go, and they had to get that bracelet back."

She stopped and looked at him. They were standing on the access road next to the World War II section. Bosch saw that the roots of another old oak had pushed some of the weathered stones out of alignment. They looked like teeth waiting for an orthodontist's hands.

"Explain that to me, what you just said," Eleanor said.

"They hit several of the boxes to cover that all they really wanted was what was in Binh's box. Okay?"

She nodded. They still weren't walking.

"Okay. So in order to keep that cover, what would be the thing to do? Get rid of the stuff from all the other boxes so it would never turn up again. And I don't mean fence it. I mean get rid of it, destroy it, sink it, bury it for good, somewhere it would never be found. Because the minute the first piece of jewelry or old coin or stock certificate turns up and the police find out about it, then they've got a lead and they'll come looking."

"So you think Meadows was killed because he pawned the bracelet?" she said.

"Not quite because of that. There is some other current moving through all of this. Why, if Meadows had a share of Binh's diamonds, would he even bother with a bracelet worth a few thousand bucks? Why would he live the way he lived? Doesn't make sense."

"You're losing me, Harry."

"I'm losing myself. But look at it this way for a minute. Say they—Meadows and the others—knew where both Binh and the other police captain, Nguyen Tran, were, and where each of them had stashed what was left of the diamonds they had brought over here. Say there were two banks and the diamonds were in two safe-deposit boxes. And say they were going to hit them both. So first they rip off Binh's bank. And now they are going for Tran's."

She nodded that she was following along. Bosch felt excitement building.

"Okay. So these things take time to plan, to put the

strategy together, to plan it for a time the bank is closed three days in a row because that's how much time they need to open enough boxes to make it look real. And then there is the time needed to dig the tunnel."

He'd forgotten to light a cigarette. He realized now and put one in his mouth, but started talking again before lighting it.

"You with me?"

She nodded. He lit the cigarette.

"Okay, then what would be the best thing to do after you have hit the first bank but before the second one is taken down? You lie low and you don't give a goddam hint away. You get rid of all the stuff taken as cover, all the stuff from the other boxes. You keep nothing. And you sit on the diamonds from Binh's box. You can't start to fence them, because it might draw attention to you and spoil the second hit. In fact, Binh probably had feelers out, looking for the diamonds. I mean, over the years, he was probably cashing them in piecemeal and was familiar with the gem-fencing network. So, they had to watch out for him, too."

"So Meadows broke the rules," she said. "He held something back. The bracelet. His partners found out and whacked him. Then they broke into the pawnshop and stole the bracelet back." She shook her head, admiring the plan. "The thing would still be perfect if he hadn't done that."

Bosch nodded. They stood there looking at each other and then around at the grounds of the cemetery. Bosch dropped his cigarette and stepped on it. At the same moment they looked up the hill and saw the black walls of the Vietnam Veterans Memorial.

"What's that doing there?" she asked.

"I don't know. It's a replica. Half size. Fake marble. I

think they move it around the country, in case somebody who wants to see it can't make it to D.C."

Eleanor's breath caught sharply and she turned to him. "Harry, this Monday is Memorial Day."

"I know. Banks closed two days, some three. We've got to find Tran."

She turned to head back to the bureau. He took a last look at the memorial. The long sheath of false marble with all the names carved into it was embedded in the side of the hill. A man in a gray uniform was sweeping the walkway in front of it. There was a pile of violet flowers from a jacaranda tree.

Harry and Eleanor were silent until they were out of the cemetery and walking back across Wilshire toward the Federal Building. She asked a question Bosch had been turning over in his mind and studying but had no good answer for.

"Why now? Why so long? It's been fifteen years."

"I don't know. Just might be the right time, that's all. People, things, unseen forces, sort of come together from time to time. That's what I believe. Who knows? Maybe Meadows forgot all about Binh and just saw him one day on the street and it all came to him. The perfect plan. Maybe it was someone else's plan or it really was hatched on that one day the three of them were together at Charlie Company. The whys you never really know. You just need the hows and the whos."

"You know, Harry, if they're out there, or I should say, under there, digging a new tunnel, then we have less than two days to find them. We have to put some crews underground and look for them." He thought that putting a crew in the city's tunnels looking for a possible entrance to a bandit tunnel was a long shot. She had told him there were more than 1,500 miles of tunnels under L.A. alone. They might not find the bandits' tunnel if they had a month. The key would be Tran. Find the last police captain, then find his bank. There you find the bandits. And the killers of Billy Meadows. And Sharkey.

He said, "Do you think Binh would give Tran to us?"

"He didn't report his fortune was taken from the vault, so he doesn't seem like the type that's going to tell us about Tran."

"Right. I think we should try finding him ourselves before we go to Binh. Let's make Binh the last resort."

"I'll start on the computer."

"Right."

The FBI computer and the computer networks it could access did not divulge the location of Nguyen Tran. Bosch and Wish found no mention of him in DMV, INS, IRS or Social Security files. There was nothing in the fictitious name filings in the Los Angeles County recorder's office, no mention of him in DWP records or the voter or property tax rolls. Bosch called Hector Villabona and confirmed that Tran entered the United States on the same day as Binh, but there was no further record. After three hours of staring at the amber letters on the computer screen, Eleanor turned it off.

"Nothing," she said. "He's using another name. But he hasn't legally changed it, at least in this county. Nobody has the guy."

They sat there dejected and quiet. Bosch took the last swallow of coffee from a Styrofoam cup. It was after five and the squad room was deserted. Rourke had gone home, after being informed of the latest developments and deciding not to send anyone into the tunnels.

"You know how many miles of underground flood-control tunnels there are in L.A.?" he had asked. "It's like a freeway system down there. These guys, if they are really down there, could be anywhere. We would be stumbling around in the dark. They'll have the advantage and one of us could get hurt."

Bosch and Wish knew he was right. They gave him no argument and set to work finding Tran. And they had failed.

"So now we go to Binh," Bosch said after finishing his coffee.

"You think he'll cooperate?" she said. "He'll know that if we want Tran, then we must know about their past. About the diamonds."

"I don't know what he'll do," he said. "I'll go see him tomorrow. You hungry?"

"We'll go see him tomorrow," she corrected and smiled. "And yes, I'm hungry. Let's get out of here."

They ate at a grill on Broadway in Santa Monica. Eleanor picked the place, and since it was near her apartment Bosch's spirits were high and he was relaxed. There was a trio playing in the corner on a wooden stage, but the place's brick walls made the sound harsh and mostly unnotable. Afterward, Harry and Eleanor sat in a comfortable silence while nursing espressos. There was a warmness between them that Bosch felt but couldn't explain to himself. He didn't know this woman who sat across from him. One look at those hard brown eyes told him that. He wanted to get behind them. They had made love, but he wanted to be in love. He wanted her.

Always seeming to know his thoughts, she asked, "Are you coming home with me tonight?"

• • •

Lewis and Clarke were on the second level of the parking garage across the street and down a half block from the Broadway Bar & Grill. Lewis was out of the car and crouched at the guardrail, watching through the camera. Its foot-long lens was steadied on a tripod and pointed at the front door of the restaurant, a hundred yards away. He was hoping the lights over the door, by the valet's stand, would be enough. He had high-speed film in the camera, but the blinking red dot in the viewfinder was telling him not to take the shot. There still wasn't enough light. He decided he would try anyway. He wanted a hand shot.

"You're not going to get it," Clarke said from behind him. "Not in this light."

"Let me do my work. If I don't get it, I don't get it. Who cares?"

"Irving."

"Well, fuck him. He tells us he wants more documentation. He'll get it. I'm only trying to do what the man says."

"We should try to go down there by that deli, get a closer—"

Clarke shut up and turned around at the sound of footsteps. Lewis kept his eye to the camera, waiting for the shot at the restaurant. The steps belonged to a man in a blue security uniform.

"Can I ask you what you guys are doing?" the guard asked.

Clarke badged him and said, "We're on the job."

The guard, a young black man, stepped closer to look at the badge and ID and raised his hand to hold it steady. Clarke jerked it up out of his reach.

"Don't touch it, bro. Nobody touches my badge."

"That says LAPD. You all check in with Santa Monica PD? They know you're out here?"

"Who the fuck cares? Just leave us alone."

Clarke turned around. When the guard didn't leave, he turned back and said, "Son, you need something?"

"This garage is my beat, Detective Clarke. I can be wherever I want to be."

"You can get the fuck outta here. I can—"

Clarke heard the camera shutter close and the sound of the automatic wind. He turned to Lewis, who stood up smiling.

"I got it—a hand shot," Lewis said as he stood up. "They're on the move, let's go."

Lewis collapsed the telescope legs of the tripod and quickly got in the passenger seat of the gray Caprice they had traded the black Plymouth for.

"See ya, bro," Clarke said to the guard. He got in behind the wheel.

The car backed out, forcing the security guard to jump out of the way. Clarke looked in the rearview mirror smiling as he drove toward the exit ramp. He saw the guard talking into a hand-held radio.

"Talk all you want, buddy boy," he said.

The IAD car pulled up to the exit booth. Clarke handed the parking stub and two dollars to the man in the booth. He took it but didn't lift the black-and-white-striped pipe that served as a gate.

"Benson said I have to hold you guys here," the man in the booth said.

"What? Who the fuck is Benson?" Clarke said.

"He's the security. He said hold it here a minute." Just then, both IAD officers saw Bosch and Wish drive by the garage, heading up to Fourth Street. They were going to lose them. Clarke held out his badge to the booth attendant.

"We're on the job. Open that goddam gate. Now!"

"He'll be along. I gotta do what he say. Else I'll lose my job."

"You open that gate or you're going to lose it, peckerwood," Clarke yelled.

He put his foot down and revved the engine to show be meant to drive through it.

"Why you think we got a pipe 'stead a flimsy piece a wood. You go ahead. That pipe'll take out your windshield, mister. You do what you want, but he's coming right along."

In the rearview, Clarke saw the security guard walking down the ramp. Clarke's face was becoming blotchy red with anger. He felt Lewis's hand on his arm.

"Cool it, partner," Lewis said. "They were holding hands when they came out of the restaurant. We won't lose them. They're only going to her place. I'll bet you a week's driving that we'll pick 'em up there."

Clarke shook his hand off and let out a long breath; that seemed to bring a more placid tone to his face. He said, "I don't care. I don't fucking like this shit one bit."

On Ocean Park Boulevard Bosch found a parking space across from Eleanor's building. He pulled in but made no move to get out of the car. He looked at her, still feeling the glow of a few minutes before but unsure where they were going with this. She seemed to know this, maybe even feel it herself. She put her hand on top of his and leaned over to kiss him. She whispered, "Come in with me."

He got out and came around to her side. She was already out and he closed the door. They rounded the front end of the car and then stood next to it, waiting for an approaching car to pass by. The car's high beams were on and Bosch turned away and looked at Eleanor. So it was she who first noticed the high beams drift toward them.

"Harry?"

"What?"

"Harry!"

Then Bosch turned back to the approaching car and saw the lights—actually four beams from two sets of square side-by-side headlights—bearing down on them. In the few seconds that were left Bosch clearly came to the conclusion that the car was not drifting their way but rather driving at them. There was no time, yet time seemed to go into suspension. In what seemed to him to be slow motion, Bosch turned to his right, to Eleanor. But she needed no help. In unison, they leapt onto the hood of Bosch's car. He was rolling over her and they were both tumbling toward the sidewalk when his car lurched violently and there was a high-pitched keening sound of tearing metal. Bosch saw a shower of blue sparks pass in his peripheral vision. Then he landed on top of Eleanor on the thin strip of sod that was between the curb and the sidewalk. They were safe, Bosch could sense. Scared, but safe for the moment.

He came up, gun out and steadied by both hands. The car that had come after them was not stopping. It was already fifty yards east, heading away and picking up speed. Bosch fired one round that he thought ricocheted off the rear window, the bullet too weak at that distance to penetrate the glass. He heard Eleanor's gun fire twice at his side, but saw no damage to the hit-and-run car.

Without a word they both piled into Bosch's car through the passenger door. Bosch held his breath while he turned the key, but the engine started and the car squealed away from the curb. Bosch rocked the steering wheel from side to side as he picked up speed. The suspension felt a little loose. He had no idea what the extent of the damage was. When he tried to check the side-view mirror he saw it was gone. When he turned on the lights, only the passenger-side beam worked.

The hit-and-run car was at least five blocks ahead, near the crest where Ocean Park Boulevard rises and then drops from sight. The lights on the speeding car went out just as it dropped over the hill out of sight. He was heading for Bundy Drive, Bosch thought. From there a short jog to the 10. And from there he would be gone and they'd never catch him. Bosch grabbed the radio and called in an Officer Needs Assistance. But he could not provide a description of the car, only the direction of the chase.

"He's going for the freeway, Harry," Eleanor yelled. "Are you okay?"

"Yeah. Are you? Did you get a make?"

"I'm fine. Scared is all. No make. American, I think. Uh, square headlights. No color, just dark. I didn't see the color. We won't catch him if he makes the freeway."

They were heading east on Ocean Park, parallel to the 10, which was about eight blocks to the north. They approached the top of the crest, and Bosch cut off the one working headlight. As they came over, he saw the unlit form of the hit-and-run car passing through the lighted intersection at Lincoln. Yeah, he was going for Bundy. At Lincoln, Bosch took a left and floored the gas pedal. He put the lights back on. And as the car's speed increased there was a thumping sound. The front left tire and alignment were damaged.

"Where are you going?" Eleanor shouted.

"I'm going for the freeway first."

Bosch had no sooner said that than the freeway entrance signs came up and the car made a wide, arcing right turn onto the ramp. The tire held up. They sped down the ramp into the traffic.

"How'll we know?" Eleanor shouted. The noise from the tire was very loud now, almost a continual throbbing.

"I don't know. Look for the square lights."

In one minute they were coming up on the Bundy entrance, but Bosch had no idea whether they had beaten the other car or if it was already well ahead of them. A car was coming up the ramp and into the merging lane. The car was white and foreign.

"I don't think so," Eleanor called.

Bosch gunned it to the floor again and moved ahead. His heart was pounding almost as fast as the tire, half with the excitement of the chase, half with the excitement of still being alive and not broken on the street in front of Eleanor's apartment. He was gripping the steering wheel at the ten and two o'clock positions, urging the car on as if he held the reins of a galloping horse. They were moving through sparse traffic at ninety miles an hour, both of them looking at the front ends of the cars they passed, searching for the four square lights or a damaged right side.

A half-minute later, Bosch's knuckles as white as bones wrapped around the wheel, they came upon a maroon Ford going at least seventy in the slow lane. Bosch swung out from behind and passed alongside. Eleanor had her gun in her hands but was holding it below the window so it could not be seen from outside the car. The white male driver didn't even look over or register notice. As they pulled ahead, Eleanor shouted, "Square lights, side by side."

"Is it the car?" Bosch called back excitedly.

"I can't—I don't know. Can't see the right side for damage. It could be. The guy isn't showing anything."

They were three-quarters of a car length ahead now.

Bosch grabbed the portable pull-over light off the transmission hump on the floor and swung it out the window onto the roof. He switched on the revolving blue light and slowly began to angle the Ford onto the shoulder. Eleanor put her hand out the window and signaled the car over. The driver began to comply. Bosch braked sharply and let the other car shoot by onto the shoulder, then Bosch swung his car onto the shoulder behind it. When both had stopped alongside a sound barrier wall Bosch realized he had a big problem. He put on the high beams, but still only the passenger-side headlight responded. The car in front was too close to the wall for Bosch and Wish to see if the right side was damaged. Meantime, the driver sat in his car, mostly shrouded in darkness.

"Shit," Bosch said. "Okay. Don't come up till I say it's clear, okay?"

"Got it," she said.

Bosch had to throw his weight hard against the door to open it. He came out of the car, gun in one hand and flashlight in the other. He held the light out away from his body and trained its beam on the driver of the car ahead.

The roar of passing traffic in his ears, Bosch started to shout, but a diesel horn drowned him out and a blast of wind from the passing semi shoved him forward. Bosch tried again, shouting for the driver to stick both hands out the side window where Bosch could see them. Nothing.

Bosch shouted the order again. After a long moment, with Bosch poised off the left rear fender of the maroon car, the driver finally complied. Bosch ran the flash beam through the back window and saw no other occupants. He ran up and put the light on the driver and ordered him to step out slowly.

"What is this?" the man protested. He was small, with pale skin, reddish hair and a transparent mustache. He opened the car door and stepped out with his hands up. He was wearing a white button-down shirt and beige pants held up by suspenders. He looked out into the passing field of cars, almost as if beckoning for a witness to this commuter's nightmare.

"Can I see a badge?" he stammered. Bosch rushed forward, spun him around and slammed his body into the side of his car, his head and shoulders over its roof. With one hand on the back of the man's neck, holding him down, and the other holding the gun to his ear, Bosch shouted to Eleanor that it was clear.

"Check the front side."

The man beneath Bosch let out a moaning sound, like a scared animal, and Bosch could feel him shaking. His neck felt clammy. Bosch never took his eyes off him to see where Eleanor was. Suddenly her voice was right behind him.

"Let him go," she said. "It's not him. There's no damage. We've got the wrong car."

Part VI
Friday, May 25

They were interviewed by the Santa Monica police, the California Highway Patrol, LAPD and the FBI. A DUI unit had been called to give Bosch a sobriety test. He passed. And by 2 A.M. he sat in an interview room at the West Los Angeles bureau, bone-tired and wondering if the Coast Guard or IRS would be next. He and Eleanor had been separated and he hadn't seen her since they had arrived three hours earlier. It bothered him that he could not be with her to protect her from the interrogators. Lieutenant Harvey "Ninety-eight" Pounds came into the room then and told Bosch they were finished for the night. Bosch could tell that Ninety-eight was angry, and it wasn't just because he had been rousted from home.

"What kind of cop doesn't get the make of the car that tries to run him down?" he asked.

Bosch was used to the second-guessing tone to the questions. It had been that way all night.

"Like I told every one of those guys before you, I was a little busy at the time. I was trying to save my ass."

"And this guy you pull over," Pounds cut in. "Jesus,

Bosch, you rough him up on the side of the freeway. Every asshole with a car phone is dialing nine one one reporting kidnap, murder, who knows what else. Couldn't you have tried to get a look at the right side of his car before you pulled him over?"

"It was impossible. All of this is covered in the report we typed up, Lieutenant. I've gone over it, seems like ten times already."

Pounds acted as though he didn't hear. "And he's a lawyer no less."

"So what?" Bosch said, now losing his patience. "We apologized. It was a mistake. The car looked the same. And if he is going to sue anybody it will be the FBI. They've got deeper pockets. So don't worry about it."

"No, he'll sue us both. He's already talking about it, fer crissake. And this is not the time to try to be funny, Bosch."

"It's also not the time to be worried about what we did or didn't do right. None of the suits that have come in here to interview me have seemed to care that somebody might be trying to kill us. They just want to know how far away I was when I fired and whether I endangered bystanders and why I pulled that car over without probable cause. Well, fuck it, man. Somebody is out to kill my partner and me. Excuse me if I'm not feeling particularly sorry for the lawyer who got his suspenders twisted."

Pounds was ready for that argument.

"Bosch, for all we have evidence of, it could have just been a drunk. And what do you mean 'partner'? You are on a day-to-day loan to this investigation. And after tonight, I think the loan is going to be withdrawn. You've spent five solid days on this case, and from what I understand from Rourke, you've got nothing."

"It was no drunk, Pounds. We were a target. And I don't care what Rourke says we have, I'm going to clear this one. And if you'd quit undermining the effort, believe in your own people for once and maybe get those Internal Affairs assholes off me, you might be in line for a piece of the honors when it happens."

Pounds's eyebrows arched like roller coasters.

"Yeah, I know about Lewis said Clarke," Bosch said. "And I know their paper was being copied to you. I guess they didn't tell you about the little talk we had? I caught 'em snoozing outside my house."

It was clear from his expression that Pounds had not heard. Lewis and Clarke were staying low and Bosch would not get jammed up over what he had done to them. He began to wonder where the two IAD detectives had been when he and Eleanor had almost been run down.

Meanwhile, Pounds remained silent for a long time. He was a fish swimming around the bait Bosch had cast, seeming to know there was a hook in it but thinking there might be a way to get the bait without the hook. Finally he told Bosch to give him a rundown on the week's investigation. He was on the hook now. Bosch ran the case down for him, and though Pounds never spoke once during the next twenty minutes Bosch could tell by his roller-coasting eyebrows whenever he heard something that Rourke had neglected to bring up.

When the story was finished, there was no more talk from Pounds of Bosch's being withdrawn from the case. Nevertheless, Bosch felt very tired of the whole thing. He wanted to sleep, but Pounds still had questions.

"If the FBI isn't putting people into the tunnels, should we?" he asked.

Bosch could see he was thinking in terms of being in

on the bust, if there was one. If he put LAPD people into the drainage tunnels, the FBI wouldn't be able to crowd the department out when the credit for the bust came. Pounds would receive a slap on the back from the chief if he could defend against such a maneuver.

But Bosch had come to believe that Rourke's reasoning was sound and correct. A tunnel crew would stand a good chance of stumbling into the thieves and maybe getting killed.

"No," Bosch told Pounds. "Let's first see if we can get a fix on Tran and where he keeps his stash. For all we know, it might not even be a bank."

Pounds stood up, having heard enough. He said Bosch was free to go. As the lieutenant headed to the interview room door he said, "Bosch, I don't think you'll have any problems with this incident tonight. It sounds to me like you did what you could. The lawyer got his feathers ruffled but he'll settle down. Or just settle."

Bosch didn't say anything or smile at his meager joke.

"One thing," Pounds continued. "The fact that this happened in front of Agent Wish's home is a bit troubling because it has the appearance of impropriety. Just a hint, no? You were just walking her to the door, weren't you?"

"I don't really care how it appeared, Lieutenant," Bosch answered. "I was off duty."

Pounds looked at Bosch a moment, shook his head as if Bosch had ignored his outstretched hand, and then went through the door of the small room.

Bosch found Eleanor sitting by herself in an interview room next to his. Her eyes were closed and she had her head propped on her hands, her elbows up on the scarred wooden table. Her eyes opened as he walked in. She smiled and he immediately felt healed of fatigue, frustration and anger. It was a smile a child gives another when they've gotten away with something on the adults.

"All done?" she said.

"Yeah. You?"

"Been done more than an hour. You are the one they wanted to grill."

"As usual. Rourke has left?"

"Yeah, he split. Said he wants me to check in with him every other hour tomorrow. After what happened tonight, he thinks he hasn't kept a tight enough rein on this."

"Or you."

"Yeah. It looks like there is some of that, too. He wanted to know what we were doing at my place. I told him you were just walking me to my door."

Bosch sat down wearily at the other side of the table and dug a finger into a cigarette pack in search of the last one. He put it in his mouth but didn't light it.

"Besides being titillated or jealous of what we might have been doing, who does Rourke think tried to take us out?" he asked. "A drunk driver, like my people seem to think?"

"He did mention the drunk driver theory. He also asked whether I have a jealous ex-boyfriend. Other than that, there doesn't seem to be a great amount of concern that it might have something to do with our case."

"I hadn't thought of the ex-boyfriend angle. What did you tell him?"

"You're as conniving as he is," she said, flashing her brilliant smile. "I told him it wasn't any of his business."

"Good going. Is it mine?"

"The answer is no." She let him hang over the cliff a few seconds, then added, "That is, no jealous ex-boyfriends. So, can we leave now and get to where we were"—she looked at her watch—"about four hours ago?"

Bosch was awake in Eleanor Wish's bed long before dawn light crept around the curtain drawn across the sliding glass door. Unable to defeat insomnia, he finally got up and took a shower in the downstairs bathroom. After, he looked through her kitchen cabinets and refrigerator and began to put together a breakfast of coffee, eggs and cinnamon raisin bagels. He couldn't find any bacon.

When he heard the shower upstairs go off, he carried a glass of orange juice up and found her in front of the bathroom mirror. She was naked and braiding her hair, which she'd divided into three thick hanks. He was entranced by her and watched as she expertly maneuvered her hair into a French braid. She then accepted the juice and a long kiss from Bosch. She put on her short robe and they went downstairs to eat.

After, Harry opened the kitchen door and stood just outside it while he smoked a cigarette.

"You know," he said, "I'm just happy nothing happened."

"You mean last night on the street?"

"Yeah. To you. I don't know how I'd've handled it. I know we just met and all, but . . . uh, I care. You know?"

"Me too."

Bosch had taken a shower, but his clothes were as fresh as the ashtray in a used car. After a while he said he had to leave, to go by his house and change. Eleanor said she would go into the bureau and check for fallout from last night's activities and get whatever was on file about Binh. They agreed to meet at Hollywood Station, on Wilcox, because it was closest to Binh's business, and

Bosch needed to turn in his damaged car, anyway. She walked him to the door and they kissed as if she were seeing him off to a day at the office at the accounting firm.

When Bosch got to his house, he found no messages on the phone machine and no sign that the place had been entered. He shaved and changed clothes and then headed down the hill through Nichols Canyon and then over to Wilcox. He was at his desk, updating the Investigating Officer's Chronological Report forms, when Eleanor came in at ten. The squad room was full and most of the detectives who were male stopped what they were doing to check her out. She had an uncomfortable smile on her face when she sat down in the steel chair next to the homicide table.

"Anything wrong?"

"I just think I would rather walk through Biscailuz," she said, referring to the sheriff's jail downtown.

"Oh. Yeah, these guys can leer better than most flashers. You want a glass of water?"

"No. I'm fine. Ready?"

"Let's do it."

They took Bosch's new car, which was actually at least three years old and had seventy-seven thousand miles on it. The station fleet manager, a permanent desk assignee since he'd had four fingers blown off by a pipe bomb he stupidly picked up one Halloween, said it was the best he could do. Budget restraints had halted the replacement of cars, though repairing the old ones actually cost the department more. At least, Bosch learned after starting the car, the air conditioner worked reasonably well. There was a light Santa Ana condition kicking up and the forecast was for an unseasonably warm holiday weekend.

Eleanor's research on Binh showed he had an office and business on Vermont near Wilshire. There were more Korean-run shops in the area than Vietnamese, but they coexisted. As near as Wish had been able to find out, Binh controlled a number of businesses that imported cheap clothing and electronic and video merchandise from the Orient and then moved it through Southern California and Mexico. Many of the items turistas thought they were getting on the cheap in Mexico and then bringing back to the States had already been here. It all seemed successful on paper, though it was small-time. Still, it was enough to make Bosch question if Binh even needed the diamonds. Or ever had any.

Binh owned the building his office and discount video equipment store was based in. It was a 1930s auto showroom that had been converted years before Binh had ever seen it. Unreinforced concrete block fronted with wide picture windows and guaranteed to come down in a decent shaker. But for someone who had made it out of Vietnam the way Binh had, earthquakes were probably viewed as a minor inconvenience, not a risk.

After they found an empty parking space across the street from Ben's Electronics, Bosch told Eleanor he wanted her to handle the questioning, at least at first. Bosch said he figured that Binh might be more inclined to talk to the feds than to the locals. They decided on a plan to small-talk him and then ask about Tran. Bosch didn't tell her that he also had a second plan in mind.

"Doesn't exactly look like the kind of place run by a guy with a box full of diamonds in a bank vault," Bosch said as they got out of the car.

"That is *had* in the bank," she said. "And remember, he couldn't flaunt that stuff. He had to be like every other

Joe Immigrant. The appearance of living day to day. The diamonds, if there were any, were the collateral for this place, for his American success story. But it had to look like he made it from scratch."

"Wait a second," Bosch said as they got to the other side of the street. He told Eleanor he had forgotten to ask Jerry Edgar to fill in on a court appearance for him that afternoon. He pointed to a pay phone at a service station next to Binh's building and trotted over. Eleanor stayed behind, looking in the windows of the store.

Bosch called Edgar but didn't say anything about a court appearance.

"Jed, I need a favor. You won't even have to get up."

Edgar hesitated, as Bosch thought he would.

"What do you need?"

"You aren't supposed to say it like that. You're supposed to say, 'Sure, Harry, what do you need?' "

"Come on, Harry, we both know we're under the glass. We've got to be careful. Tell me what you need. I'll tell you if I can do it."

"All I want you to do is buzz me in ten minutes. I need to get out of a meeting. Just buzz me, and when I call in, just put the phone down for a couple minutes. And if I don't call in, buzz me again in five minutes. That's it."

"That's all you need? Just the buzz?"

"Right. Ten minutes from now."

"Okay, Harry," Edgar said, relief in his voice. "Hey, I heard about your thing last night. That was close. And word around here is that it wasn't no drunk driver. You watch your ass."

"Always. What's going on with Sharkey?"

"Nothing. I ran down his crew like you told me. Two of 'em told me they were with him that night. I think they were rolling faggots. They said they lost sight of him after he got in a car. That was a couple hours before the desk got the call that he was in the tunnel up at the bowl. I figure whoever was in that car did him."

"Description?"

"The car? Not very good. Dark color, American sedan. Something new. That's about it."

"What kind of headlights?"

"Well, I showed 'em the car book and they picked different taillights. One guy's got round, the other says rectangle. But on the headlights. They both said they—"

"Square, side-by-side squares."

"Right. Hey, Harry, you thinking this is the car that came down on you and the FBI woman? Jesus! We ought to get together on this."

"Later. Maybe later. Meantime, buzz me in ten minutes."

"Ten minutes, right."

Bosch hung up and went back to Eleanor, who was looking through the plate-glass window at the ghetto blasters on display. They entered the store, shook off two salesmen, walked around a stack of boxed camcorders on sale for $500 each and told a woman standing at a cash register station in the back that they were there to see Binh. The woman stared blankly at them until Eleanor showed her badge and federal ID card.

"You wait here," the woman said and then disappeared through a door located behind the cash counter. There was a small mirrored window in the door that reminded Bosch of the interview room back at Wilcox. He looked at his watch. He had eight minutes.

• • •

The man who emerged from the door behind the cash register looked to be about sixty years old. He had white hair. He was short but Bosch could tell he had once been physically powerful for his size. Built wide and low to the ground, he now was softened by an easier life than he had had in his native land. He wore silver-framed glasses with a pink tint and an open-collar shirt and golf slacks. His breast pocket sagged with the weight of almost a dozen pens and a clip-on pocket flashlight. Ngo Van Binh was low key all the way.

"Mr. Binh? My name is Eleanor Wish. I am from the FBI. This is Detective Bosch, LAPD. We'd like to ask you a few questions."

"Yes," he said, the stern expression on his face unchanging.

"It's about the break-in at the bank where you had a safe-deposit box."

"I reported no loss, my deposit box had sentimental occupants only."

Diamonds ranked fairly high up there on the sentimental range, Bosch thought. "Mr. Binh, can we go back to your office and talk privately?" he said instead.

"Yes, but I suffered no loss. You look. It is in the reports."

Eleanor held her hand out, urging Binh to lead the way. They followed him through the door with the mirror window and into a warehouselike storage room. There were hundreds of boxes of electronic appliances on steel shelves going to the ceiling. They passed through into a smaller room that was a repair or assembly shop. There was a woman sitting at a tool bench with a bowl of soup held to her mouth. She did not look up as they passed. There were two doors at the back of the shop, and the procession went through one into Binh's office. It was here that Binh shed his peasant trappings. The office was large and plush, with a desk and two chairs to the right and a dark leather L-shaped couch to the left. The couch was at the edge of an Oriental rug that featured a three-headed dragon poised to strike. The couch faced two walls of shelves filled by books and stereo and video equipment, much finer than what Bosch had seen out front. We should have braced him at his home, Bosch thought. Seen how he lived, not how he worked.

Bosch quickly scanned the room and saw a white telephone on the desk. It would be perfect. It was an antique, the kind where the handset was cradled above a rotary dial. Binh moved toward his desk but Bosch quickly spoke up.

"Mr. Binh? Would it be okay if we sat over here on the couch? We'd like to keep this as informal as possible. We sit at desks all day, to tell you the truth."

Binh shrugged his shoulders as though it made no difference to him, that they were inconveniencing him no matter where they sat. It was a distinctly American gesture, and Bosch believed his seeming difficulty with English was a front used to better insulate him. Binh sat down on one side of the L-shaped couch and Eleanor and Bosch took the other.

"Nice office," Bosch said and looked around. He saw no other phone in the room.

Binh nodded. He offered no tea or coffee, no small talk. He just said, "What do you want, please?"

Bosch looked at Eleanor.

She said, "Mr. Binh, we are just retracing our steps. You reported no financial loss in the vault break-in. We—"

"That is right. No loss."

"That is correct. What did you keep in the box?"

"Nothing."

"Nothing?"

"Papers and such, no value. I told this to everyone already."

"Yes, we know. We are sorry to bother you again. But the case remains open and we have to go back and see if we missed anything. Could you tell me in specific detail what papers you lost? It might help us, if we make a recovery of property and can identify who it belongs to."

Eleanor took a small notebook and pen out of her purse. Binh looked at his two visitors as if he could not possibly see how his information could help. Bosch said, "You'd be surprised sometimes what little things can—"

His pager tone sounded and Bosch pulled the device off his belt and looked at the number display. He stood up and looked around, as if he was just noticing the room for the first time. He wondered if he was overdoing it.

"Mr. Binh, can I use your phone? It'll be local."

Binh nodded, and Bosch walked to the front of the desk, leaned over and picked up the handset. He made a show of checking the pager number again, then dialed Edgar's number. He remained standing with his back to Eleanor and Binh. He looked up at the wall, as if studying the silk tapestry that hung there. He heard Binh begin to describe to Eleanor the immigration and citizenship papers that had been taken from his safe-deposit box. Bosch put the pager in his coat pocket and came out with the small pocketknife, the T-9 phone bug and the small battery he had disconnected from his own phone.

"This is Bosch, who paged me?" he said into the phone when Edgar picked up. After Edgar put the phone down, he said, "I'll hold a few minutes, but tell him I'm in the middle of an interview. What's so important?"

With his back still to the couch and Binh still talking, Bosch turned slightly to the right and cocked his head as if he were holding the phone to his left ear, where Binh could not see it. Bosch brought the handset down to stomach level, used the knife to pop off the earpiece cover—clearing his throat as be did this—and then pulled out the audio receiver. With one hand he connected the bug to its battery—he had practiced doing it earlier while waiting for the new car in the fleet yard at Wilcox. Then he used his fingers to shove the bug and battery into the barrel of the handset. He put the receiver back in and snapped on the cover, coughing loudly to camouflage any sound.

"Okay," Bosch said into the phone. "Well, tell him I'll call back when I am through here. Thanks, man."

He put the phone back on the desk while returning the knife to his pocket. He went back to the couch, where Eleanor was writing in a notebook. When she was finished she looked at Bosch and Bosch knew without any sign that now the interview would shift into a new direction.

"Mr. Binh," she said. "Are you sure that is all you had in the box?"

"Yes, sure, why do you ask me so much?"

"Mr. Binh, we know who you are and the circumstances of your coming to this country. We know you were a police officer."

"Yes, so? What's it mean?"

"We also know other things—"

"We know," Bosch cut in, "you were very highly paid

as a police officer in Saigon, Mr. Binh. We know that for some of your work you were paid in diamonds."

"What does this mean, what he says?" Binh said, looking at Eleanor and gesturing with his hand to Bosch. He was lapsing into the defense of language barrier. He seemed to know less English as the interview went on.

"It means what he says," she answered. "We know about the diamonds you brought here from Vietnam, Captain Binh. We know you kept them in the safe-deposit box. We believe the diamonds were the motivation for the vault break-in."

The news didn't shake him, he may have already considered as much. He did not move. He said, "This not true."

"Mr. Binh, we've got your package," Bosch said. "We know all about you. We know what you were in Saigon, what you did. We know what you took with you when you came here. I don't know what you are into now—it all looks legit, but we don't really care. What we do care about is who ripped off that bank. And they ripped it off because of you. They took the collateral for all this and everything else you've got. Now, I don't think we are telling you something that you probably haven't figured out or thought about on your own. In fact, you might have even thought your old partner Nguyen Tran was behind it because he knew what you had and maybe where it was. Not a bad guess, but we don't think so. In fact, we think he is next on the list."

Not a crack formed on the stone that was Binh's face.

"Mr. Binh, we want to talk to Tran," Bosch said. "Where is he?"

Binh looked down through the coffee table in front of him to the three-headed dragon on the rug beneath it. He put his hands together on his lap, shook his head and said, "Who is this Tran?"

Eleanor glared at Bosch and tried to salvage what rapport she had had with the man before he butted in.

"Captain Binh, we're not interested in taking any action against you. We simply want to stop another vault break-in before it happens. Can you help us, please?"

Binh didn't answer. He looked down at his hands.

"Look, Binh, I don't know what you've got going on this," Bosch said. "You might have people out there trying to find the same people we are, I don't know. But I'm telling you right now, you are out of it. So tell us where Tran is."

"I don't know this man."

"We are your only hope. We have to get to Tran. The people that ripped you off, they are in the tunnels again. Right now. If we don't get to Tran this weekend, there won't be anything left for you or him."

Binh remained a stone, as Bosch expected. Eleanor stood up.

"Think about it, Mr. Binh," she said.

"We're running out of time, and so is your old partner," Bosch said as they headed for the door.

After walking through the showroom door Bosch looked both ways for traffic and ran across Vermont to the car. Eleanor walked it, anger making her strides stiff and jerky. Bosch got in and reached to the floor behind the front seat for the Nagra. He turned it on and set the recording speed at its fastest level. He didn't think the wait would be long. He hoped all the electronic equipment in the store would not skew the reception. Eleanor got in the passenger side and started to complain.

"That was magnificent," she said. "We'll never get anything out of that guy now. He's just going to call up Tran and—what the hell is that?"

"Something I picked up from the shooflies. They dropped a bug in my phone. Oldest trick in the IAD book."

"And you just put it in . . ." She pointed across the street and Bosch nodded.

"Bosch, do you realize what could happen to us, what this means? I'm going back in there and getting—"

She opened the car door but he reached across and pulled it closed.

"You don't want to do that. This is our only way to get to Tran. Binh wasn't going to tell us, no matter how we handled the interview, and deep down behind those angry eyes you know it. So it's this or nothing. Binh warns Tran and we never know where he is, or we use this to maybe find him. Maybe. We'll probably know soon enough"

Eleanor looked straight forward and shook her head.

"Bosch, this could mean our jobs. How could you do this without consulting me?"

"For that reason. It could mean *my* job. You didn't know."

"I'd never prove it. The whole thing looks like a setup. I keep him occupied while you do your little charade on the phone."

"It was a setup, only you didn't know. Besides, Binh and Tran are not the targets of our investigation. We are not gathering evidence against them, just from them. This will never go in a report. And if he finds the bug, he can't prove I put it there. There was no register number. I looked. The suits weren't stupid enough to make it traceable. We're clear. You're clear. Don't worry."

"Harry, that is hardly reassur—"

The red light on the Nagra flicked on. Someone was using Binh's phone. Bosch checked to make sure the tape was rolling.

"Eleanor, you make the call," Bosch said, holding the recorder up on the palm of his hand. "Turn it off if you want. Your choice."

She turned and looked at the recorder, then at Bosch. Just then the dialing stopped and it was silent in the car. A phone began to ring at the other end of Binh's call. She turned away. Someone answered the phone. A few words were exchanged in Vietnamese and then more silence.

Then a new voice was on the line and a conversation began, also in Vietnamese. Bosch could tell one of the voices belonged to Binh. The other sounded like a man about Binh's age. It was Binh and Tran, together again. Eleanor shook her head and forced a short laugh.

"Brilliant, Harry, now who do we get to translate? We aren't letting anyone else know about this. We can't risk it."

"I don't want to translate it." He turned the receiver off and rewound the tape. "Get out your little pad and pen."

Bosch adjusted the recorder to its slowest speed and hit the play button. When the dialing started, it was slow enough that Bosch could count the clicks. Bosch called the numbers out to Eleanor, who wrote them down. They had the number Binh had dialed.

The phone number was a 714 area code. Orange County. Bosch switched the receiver on; the telephone conversation between Binh and the unknown man was continuing. He turned it off and picked up the radio microphone. He gave a dispatcher the phone number and asked for the name and address that went with it. It would take a few minutes while someone looked it up in a reverse directory. Meantime, Bosch started the car and headed south toward Interstate 10. He had already connected with the 5 and was heading into Orange County when the dispatcher got back to him.

The phone number belonged to a business called the Tan Phu Pagoda in Westminster. Bosch looked over at Eleanor, who looked away.

"Little Saigon," he said.

Bosch and Wish got to the Tan Phu Pagoda from Binh's business in an hour. The pagoda was a shopping plaza on Bolsa Avenue where no sign was printed in English. The building was off-white stucco with glass fronts on the half-dozen shops that lined the parking lot. Each was a small establishment that sold mostly unneeded junk like electronic equipment or T-shirts. There were competing Vietnamese restaurants on either end. Next to one of the restaurants was a glass door that led to an office or business without a front display window. Though neither Bosch nor Wish could decipher the words on the door, they immediately figured it was the entrance to the shopping center office.

"We need to get in there and confirm that's Tran's place, see if he's there and if there are other exits," Bosch said.

"We don't even know what he looks like," Wish reminded him.

He thought a moment. If Tran wasn't using his real name, it would tip him off to go in asking for him.

"I've got an idea," Wish said. "Find a pay phone. Then I'll go in the office. You dial the number you got off the tape and when I'm in there I'll see if it rings. If I hear a

phone we have the right place. I'll also try to scope out
Tran and the exits."

"Phones might be ringing in there every ten seconds,"
Bosch said. "It might be a boiler room or a sweatshop.
How will you know it's me?"

She was silent a moment.

"Chances are they don't speak English, or at least not
well," she said. "So you ask whoever answers to speak
English or get someone who can. When you get someone
who understands, say something that will get a reaction
I'll be able to see."

"You mean if the phone rings in a place where you will
see."

She shrugged, her eyes showing him she was tired of
his shooting down every suggestion she made. "Look, it's
the only thing we can do. Come on, there's a phone, we
don't have a lot of time."

He drove out of the parking lot and a quarter block
down to a pay phone out front of a liquor store. Wish
walked back to the Tan Phu Pagoda and Bosch watched
until she reached the door of the office. He dropped a
quarter in the phone and dialed the number he had written on his pad in front of Binh's. The line was busy. He
looked back at the office door. Wish was gone from view.
He dropped the quarter and dialed again. Busy. He did it
in quick succession two more times before he got a ring.
He was thinking that he had probably dialed the wrong
number, when the call was answered.

"Tan Phu," a male voice said. Young, Asian, probably
early twenties, Bosch thought. Not Tran.

"Tan Phu?" Bosch asked.

"Yes, please."

Bosch could not think of what to do. He whistled into

the phone. The comeback was a staccato verbal attack of which Bosch could not understand a single word or sound. Then the phone at the other end was slammed down. Bosch walked back to the car and drove back toward the shopping plaza and into the narrow parking lot. He was cruising through it slowly when Wish appeared at the glass door with a man. An Asian. Like Binh, he had gray hair and had the aura; unspoken power, unflexed muscle. He held the door open for Eleanor and nodded to her as she said thanks. He watched her walk off and then disappeared inside again.

"Harry," she said as she got in the car, "what did you say to the guy on the phone?"

"Not a word. So it was that office?"

"Yeah. I think that was our Mr. Tran who held the door for me. Nice guy."

"So what did you do to become such great pals?"

"I told him I was a real estate lady. When I went in I asked to see the boss. Then Mr. Gray Hair came out of a back office. He said his name was Jimmie Bok. I said I represented Japanese investors and asked if he was interested in taking an offer on the shopping center. He said no. He said, in very fine English, 'I buy, I don't sell.' Then he escorted me out. But I think that was Tran. Something about him."

"Yeah, I saw it," Bosch said. Then he picked up the radio and asked dispatch to run the name Jimmie Bok on the NCIC and DMV computers.

Eleanor described the inside of the office. A central reception area, a hallway running behind it with four doors, including one at the rear that looked like an exit, judging by the double lock. No women. At least four men other than Bok. Two of them looked like hired muscle. They stood up from the reception room couch when Bok walked out of the middle door in the hallway.

Bosch drove out of the lot and around the block. He cut up the alley that ran behind the shopping plaza. He stopped when he had driven far enough to see a gold stretch Mercedes parked next to a rear door to the complex. There was a double lock on the door.

"That's got to be his wheels," Wish said.

They decided they would watch the car. Bosch drove on by it to the end of the alley and parked behind a Dumpster. Then he realized it was full of garbage from the restaurant. He backed out and drove out of the alley completely. He parked on the side street so that by looking out the passenger side of the car, they both could see the rear end of the Mercedes. Bosch could also look at Eleanor at the same time.

"So, I guess we wait," she said.

"Guess so. No way of telling whether he'll do anything after Binh's warning. Maybe he did something after Binh got ripped off last year and we're just spinning our wheels."

Bosch got a radio callback from the dispatcher; Jimmie Bok had a clean driving record. He lived in Beverly Hills and he had no criminal record. Nothing else.

"I'm going back to the phone," Eleanor announced. Bosch looked at her. "I have to check in. I'll tell Rourke we're set up on this guy and see if he can't shake someone loose to maybe call some banks and run his name. To see if he is a customer. I'd also like to run him on the property computer. He said, 'I buy, I don't sell.' I'd like to know what he buys."

"Fire a shot if you need me," Bosch said, and she smiled as she opened the door.

"You want something to eat?" she asked. "I'm thinking about getting takeout for lunch from one of those restaurants up front."

"Just coffee," he said. He hadn't eaten Vietnamese food in twenty years. He watched her walk around to the front of the center.

About ten minutes after she was gone, as Bosch watched the Mercedes, he saw a car pass by the other end of the alley. He immediately made it as a police sedan. A white Ford LTD without wheel covers, just the cheap hubcaps that revealed the matching white wheels. It had been too far away for him to see who was in it. He alternately looked at the Mercedes and then at the rearview mirror to see if the LTD was coming around the block. But in five minutes, he never saw it.

Wish was back ten minutes after that. She was carrying a grease-stained brown bag from which she pulled one coffee and two goldfish cartons. Steamed rice and crab boh, she said. He passed on her offer and rolled his window down. He sipped the coffee she handed to him and grimaced.

"Tastes like it was made in Saigon and shipped over," he said. "Did you get Rourke?"

"Yeah. He's going to get somebody to check Bok out and page me if they come up with anything. He wants to know, on a radio patch-through, the minute the Mercedes starts moving."

Two hours passed easily as they small-talked and watched the gold Mercedes. Eventually Bosch announced that he was going to break camp and drive around the block just to change the pace. What he didn't say was that he was bored and his butt was falling asleep and that he wanted to look for the white LTD.

"Do you think maybe we should call to see if he's still there, and then hang up if he gets on?" she said.

"If Binh gave him the warning, a call like that might shake him up, make him think something is going on, make him more cautious."

He drove the car up to the corner and along the front of the shopping plaza. Nothing unusual caught his eye. He went around the block and parked in the same spot again. He had not seen the LTD.

As soon as they were back in position, Wish's pager sounded and she got out to go to the phone again. Bosch concentrated on the gold Mercedes and forgot about the LTD for the time being. But after Eleanor was gone twenty minutes he began to get nervous. It was after 3 P.M. and Bok/Tran had not left as they expected he would. Something didn't seem right. But what? Bosch looked up at the front corner of the shopping center, studying it and waiting for Eleanor to make the turn around the stucco siding. He heard a sound, like a muffled impact. Two or three of them. Shots? He thought of Eleanor, and his heart was pushed by a fist up into his throat. Or had the sound been car doors closing? He looked at the Mercedes but could only see the trunk and taillights. He saw no one around the car. Back at the front corner; no Eleanor. Then back at the Mercedes, and he saw the brake lights go on. Bok was leaving. Bosch started the car and drove up to the corner, his rear tires spitting gravel as he gunned it forward. At the corner he saw Eleanor walking along the sidewalk toward him. He honked the horn and signaled for her to hurry. Eleanor trotted to the car and was just getting in when the Mercedes appeared in Bosch's rearview mirror and turned out of the alley toward them.

."Get down," he said and pulled Eleanor down on the seat.

The Mercedes floated by and turned onto Bolsa. He released his grip on her neck. "What the hell do you think you're doing?" she demanded as she came up.

Bosch pointed at the Mercedes, which was heading away. "They were coming by. You would've been made because you went in the office today. What took you so long?"

"They had to track down Rourke. He wasn't in his office."

Harry pulled out and started following the Mercedes from a distance of about two blocks. After a long moment composing herself, Eleanor said, "Is he by himself?"

"I don't know. I didn't see him get in. I was looking up at the corner for you. I think I heard more than one car door close. I'm sure I did."

"But you don't know if Tran was one of them who got in?"

"Right. Don't know. But it's getting late. I figure it's gotta be him."

Bosch realized then that he might have fallen for the oldest ruse in the surveillance book. Bok, or Tran, or whoever he was, could have simply sent one of his minions in the hundred-thousand-dollar car to draw away the tail.

"What do you think, go back?" he said.

Wish didn't answer until he looked over at her. "No," she said. "Go with what we got. Don't second-guess yourself. You're right about the time. A lot of banks close at five before a holiday weekend. He had to get going. He was warned by Binh. I think it's him."

Bosch felt better. The Mercedes turned west and then

north again on the Golden State Freeway toward Los Angeles. The traffic crept slowly into downtown, and then the gold car went west on the Santa Monica Freeway, exiting on Robertson at twenty minutes before five. They were heading into Beverly Hills. Wilshire Boulevard was lined with banks from downtown to the ocean. As the Mercedes turned west, Bosch felt they had to be close. Tran would keep his treasure at a bank near his home, he thought. The gamble had been right. He relaxed a bit and finally got around to asking Eleanor what Rourke had said when she called in.

"He confirmed through the Orange County clerk's office that Jimmie Bok is Nguyen Tran. They had a fictitious name filing. He changed his name nine years ago. We should've checked Orange County. I forgot about Little Saigon.

"Also," she said, "if this guy Tran had diamonds, he might have used them all up already. Property recs show he owns two more shopping centers like that one back there. In Monterey Park and Diamond Bar."

Bosch told himself it was still possible. The diamonds could be the collateral for the real estate empire. Just like with Binh. He kept his eyes on the Mercedes, only a block ahead now because rush hour was in full force and he didn't want to get cut off. He watched the black windows of the car move along the rich street, and he told himself it was heading to the diamonds.

"And I saved the best for last," Wish announced then. "Mr. Bok, also known as Mr. Tran, controls his many holdings through a corporation. The title of said corporation, according to the records check by Special Agent Rourke, is none other than Diamond Holdings, Incorporated."

They passed Rodeo Drive and were in the heart of the commercial district. The buildings lining Wilshire took on more stateliness, as if they knew they had more money and class in them. Traffic slowed to a crawl in some areas, and Bosch got as close as two car lengths behind the Mercedes, not wanting to lose the car on a missed light. They were almost to Santa Monica Boulevard and Bosch was beginning to figure they were headed to Century City. Bosch looked at his watch. It was four-fifty. "If this guy is going to a bank in Century City, I don't think he's going to make it."

Just then the Mercedes made a right turn into a parking garage. Bosch slowed to the curb and without saying a word Wish jumped out and walked into the garage. Bosch took the next right and went around the block. Cars were pouring out of office parking lots and garages, cutting in front of him again and again. When he finally got around, Eleanor was standing at the curb at the same spot where she had jumped out. He pulled up and she leaned into the window.

"Park it," she said, and she pointed across the street and down half a block. There was a rounded structure that was built out to the street from the first floor of a highrise office building. The walls of the semicircle were glass. And inside this huge glass room Bosch saw the polished steel door of a vault. A sign outside the building said Beverly Hills Safe & Lock. He looked at Eleanor and she was smiling.

"Was Tran in the car?" he asked.

"Of course. You don't make mistakes like that."

He smiled back. Then he saw a space open up at a meter just ahead. He drove up and parked.

• • •

"Since we started thinking there would be a second vault hit, my whole orientation was banks," Eleanor Wish said. "You know, Harry? Maybe a savings and loan. But I drive by this place a couple times a week. At least. I never considered it."

They had walked down Wilshire and were standing across the street from Beverly Hills Safe & Lock. She was actually standing behind him and peeking at the place over his shoulder. Tran, or Bok as he was now known, had seen her earlier, and they couldn't risk his spotting her here. The sidewalk was clogged with office types that were pouring through the revolving glass doors of the buildings, heading to parking garages and trying to get even a five-minute jump on the traffic, on the holiday weekend.

"It fits though," Bosch said. "He comes here, doesn't trust banks, like your friend at State was talking about. So he finds a vault without a bank. Here it is. But even better. As long as you have the money to pay, these places don't need to know who you are. No federal banking regulations because it isn't a bank. You can rent a box and only identify yourself with a letter or a number code."

Beverly Hills Safe & Lock had all the appearances of a bank but was far from it. There were no savings or checking accounts. No loan department, no tellers. What it offered was what it showed in the front window. Its polished steel vault. It was a business that protected valuables, not money. In a town like Beverly Hills, this was a precious commodity. The rich and famous kept their jewels here. Their furs. Their prenuptial agreements.

And it all sat out there in the open. Behind glass. The business was the bottom floor of the fourteen-story J. C. Stock Building, a structure unnotable save for the glass vault room that protruded in a half circle from the first-floor facade. The entrance to Beverly Hills Safe & Lock was on the side of the building at Rincon Street, where Mexicans in short yellow jackets stood ready to valet a client's car.

After Bosch had dropped Eleanor off and gone around the block, she had watched Tran and two bodyguards get out of the gold Mercedes and walk to the safe and lock. If they thought they might be followed, they hadn't shown it. They never looked behind them. One of the bodyguards carried a steel briefcase.

Eleanor said, "I think I made at least one of the bodyguards as carrying. The other's coat was too baggy. Is that, him? Yeah, there he is."

Tran was being escorted by a man in a dark-blue banker's suit into the vault room. A bodyguard trailed behind with the steel briefcase. Bosch saw the heavy man's eyes sweep the sidewalk outside until Tran and Banker's Suit disappeared through the vault's open door. The man with the briefcase waited. Bosch and Wish also waited, and watched. It was about three minutes before Tran came out, followed by the suit, who carried a metal safe-deposit box about the size of a woman's shoe box. The bodyguard took up the rear, and the three men walked out of the glass room, out of sight.

"Nice, personal service," Wish said. "Beverly Hills all the way. He's probably taking it into a private sitting room to make the transfer."

"Think you can get ahold of Rourke and get a crew over here to follow Tran when he leaves?" Bosch asked. "Use a landline. We have to stay off the air in case the people underground have someone up top listening to our frequencies."

"I take it we're staying here with the vault?" she asked, and Bosch nodded. She thought a moment and said, "I'll make the call. He'll be glad to know we found the place. We'll be able to put the tunnel crew down."

She looked about, saw a pay phone next to a bus stop on the next corner and made a move to walk that way. Bosch held her arm.

"I'm going to go inside, see what's up. Remember, they know you, so stay out of sight until they're gone."

"What if they split before reinforcements come?"

"I'm staying with that vault. I don't care about Tran. You want the keys? You can take the car and tail him."

"No, I'll stay with the vault. With you."

She turned and headed toward the phone. Bosch crossed Wilshire and went in the safe and lock, passing an armed security guard who had been walking toward the door with a key ring in his hand.

"Closing up, sir," said the guard, who had the swagger and gruffness of an ex-cop.

"I'll only be a minute," Bosch said without stopping.

Banker's Suit, who had led Tran into the vault, was one of three young, fair-haired men sitting at antique desks on the plush gray carpet in the reception area. He glanced up from some papers on his desk, sized up Bosch's appearance and said to the younger of the other two, "Mr. Grant, would you like to help this gentleman."

Though his unspoken answer was no, the one called Grant stood up, came around his desk and with the best phony smile in his arsenal approached Bosch.

"Yes, sir?" the man said. "Thinking of opening a vault account with us?"

Bosch was about to ask a question when the man stuck out his hand and said, "James Grant, ask me anything.

Though we are running a little short of time. We are closing for the weekend in a few minutes."

Grant drew up his coat sleeve to check his watch to confirm closing time.

"Harvey Pounds," Bosch said, taking his hand. "How did you know I don't already have a vault account?"

"Security, Mr. Pounds. We sell security. I know every vault client on sight. So do Mr. Avery and Mr. Bernard." He turned slightly and nodded at Banker's Suit and the other salesman, who solemnly nodded back.

"Not open weekends?" Bosch asked, trying to sound disappointed.

Grant smiled. "No, sir. We find our clients are the type of people who have well-planned schedules, well-planned lives. They reserve the weekend for pleasures, not errands like these others you see. Scurrying to the banks, the ATMs. Our clients are a measure above that, Mr. Pounds. And so are we. You can appreciate that."

There was a sneer in his voice when he said this. But Grant was right. The place was as slick as a corporate law office, with the same hours and the same self-important front men.

Bosch took an expansive look around. In an alcove to the right where there was a row of eight doors he saw Tran's two bodyguards standing on each side of the third door. Bosch nodded at Grant and smiled.

"Well, I see you have guards all over the place. That's the kind of security I'm looking for, Mr. Grant."

"I beg your pardon, Mr. Pounds, those men are merely waiting for a client who is in one of the private offices. But I assure you our security provision can't be compromised. Are you looking for a vault with us, sir?"

The man had more creepy charm than an evangelist. Bosch disliked him and his attitude.

"Security, Mr. Grant, I am looking for security. I want to lease a vault but I need to be assured of the security, from both outside and inside problems, if you know what I mean."

"Of course, Mr. Pounds, but do you have any idea of the cost of our service, the security we provide?"

"Don't know and don't care, Mr. Grant. See, the money is not the object. The peace of mind is. Agreed? Last week my next-door neighbor, I'm talking about just three doors down from the former president, had a burglary. The alarm was no obstacle to them. They took very valuable things. I don't want to wait for that to happen to me. No place is safe these days."

"Truly a shame, Mr. Pounds," Grant said, an unbridled note of excitement in his voice. "I didn't realize it was getting that way in Bel Air. But I couldn't agree more with your plan of action. Have a seat at my desk and we can talk. Would you like coffee, perhaps some brandy? It is near the cocktail hour, of course. Just one of the little services we provide that a banking institution cannot."

Grant laughed then, silently, with his head nodding up and down. Bosch declined the offer and the salesman sat down, pulling his chair in behind him. "Now, let me tell you the basics of how we work. We are completely non-regulated by any government agency. I think your neighbor would be happy about that."

He winked at Bosch, who said, "Neighbor?"

"The former president, of course." Bosch nodded and Grant proceeded. "We provide a long list of security services, both here and for your home, even an armed security escort if needed. We are the complete security consultant. We—"

"What about the safe-deposit vault?" Bosch cut in. He knew Tran would be coming out of the private office at any moment. He wanted to be in the vault by then.

"Yes, of course, the vault. As you saw, it is on display to the world. The glass circle, as we call it, is perhaps our most brilliant security ploy. Who would attempt to breach it? It is on display twenty-four hours a day. Right on Wilshire Boulevard. Genius?"

Grant's smile was wide with triumph. He nodded slightly in an effort to prompt agreement from his audience.

"What about from underneath?" Bosch asked, and the man's mouth dropped back into a straight line.

"Mr. Pounds, you can't expect me to outline our structural security measures, but rest assured the vault is impregnable. Between you, me and the lamppost, you won't find a bank vault in this town with as much concrete and steel in the floor, in the walls, in the ceiling of that vault. And the electrical? You couldn't—if you excuse the expression—break wind in the circle room without setting off the sound, motion and heat sensors."

"May I see it?"

"The vault?"

"Of course."

"Of course."

Grant adjusted his jacket and ushered Bosch toward the vault. A glass wall and a mantrap separated the semicircular vault room from the rest of Beverly Hills Safe & Lock. Grant waved his hand at the glass and said, "Double-plated tempered glass. Vibration alarm tape between the sheets of glass to make tampering impossible.

You'll find this on the exterior windows as well. Basically, the vault room is sealed in two plys of three-quarter-inch glass."

Using his hand again like a model pointing out prizes on a game show, Grant indicated a boxlike device beside the door to the mantrap. It was about the size of an office water fountain, and a circle of white plastic was inlaid on top. On the circle was the black outline of a hand, its fingers splayed.

"To get in the vault room, your hand must be on file. The bone structure. Let me show you."

He placed his right hand on the black silhouette. The device began to hum and the white plastic inlay was lit from inside the machine. A bar of light swept below the plastic and Grant's hand, as if it were a Xerox machine.

"X-ray," Grant said. "More positive than fingerprints, and the computer can process it in six seconds."

In six seconds the machine emitted a short beep and the electronic lock on the first door of the trap snapped open. "You see, your hand becomes your signature here, Mr. Pounds. No need for names. You give your box a code and you put the bone structure of your hand on file with us. Six seconds of your time is all we need."

Behind him Bosch heard a voice he recognized as belonging to Banker's Suit, the one called Avery. "Ah, Mr. Long, are we finished?"

Bosch glanced around to see Tran emerging from the alcove. Now he was the one who carried the briefcase. And one of the bodyguards carried the safe-deposit box. The other big man looked right at Bosch. Bosch turned back to Grant and said, "Can we go in?"

He followed Grant into the mantrap. The door closed behind them. They were in a glass-and-white-steel room about twice the size of a telephone booth. There was a second door at the end. Behind it stood another uniformed guard.

"This is just a detail we borrowed from the L.A. County Jail," Grant said. "This door in front of us cannot open unless the one behind us is closed and locked. Maury, our armed guard, makes a final visual check and opens the last door. You see, we have the human and electronic touch here, Mr. Pounds." He nodded to Maury, who unlocked and opened the last door of the trap. Bosch and Grant walked out into the vault room. Bosch didn't bother to mention that he had just successfully circumvented the elaborate security obstacles by playing on Grant's greed and pitching a story with a Bel Air address.

"And now into the vault," Grant said, holding his hand out like a congenial host.

The vault was larger than Bosch had envisioned. It was not wide but it extended far back into the J. C. Stock Building. There were safe-deposit boxes along both side walls and in a steel structure running down the center of the vault. The two began walking down the aisle to the left as Grant explained that the center boxes were for larger storage needs. Bosch could see that the doors were much larger than those on the side walls. Some were big enough to walk through. Grant saw Bosch staring at these and smiled.

"Furs," he said. "Minks. We do very good business storing expensive furs, gowns, what have you. The ladies of Beverly Hills keep them here in the off season. Tremendous insurance savings, not to mention the peace of mind."

Bosch tuned out the sales pitch and watched as Tran walked into the vault, trailed by Avery. Tran still had the briefcase, and Bosch noticed a thin band of polished steel on his wrist. He was handcuffed to the briefcase. Bosch's adrenaline kicked in at a higher notch. Avery stepped up to an open box door marked 237 and slid the deposit box in. He closed the door and used a key in one of the two locks on the door. Tran stepped up and put his own key in the other lock and turned it. He then nodded to Avery and both men walked out, Tran never having looked at Bosch.

Once Tran was gone, Bosch announced that he had seen enough of the vault and headed out also. He walked to the double-plated glass and looked out on Wilshire Boulevard and watched Tran, flanked by the two massive guards, making his way to the parking garage where the Mercedes was parked. No one followed them. Bosch looked around but didn't see Eleanor.

"Is something wrong, Mr. Pounds?" Grant said from behind him.

"Yes," Bosch said. He reached into his coat pocket and brought out his badge wallet. He held it up over his shoulder so Grant could see it from behind. "You better get me the manager of this place. And don't call me Mr. Pounds anymore."

Lewis stood at a pay phone in front of a twenty-four-hour diner called Darling's. He was around the corner and about a block from Beverly Hills Safe & Lock. It had been more than a minute since Officer Mary Grosso had answered the call and said she would get Deputy Chief Irving on the line. Lewis was thinking that if the man wanted hourly updates—by landline, no less—then the least he could do was take the damn call promptly. He switched the phone to his other ear and dug in his coat pocket for something to pick his teeth with. His wrist was sore where it chafed against the pocket. But thinking about being handcuffed by Bosch only made him angry, so he tried to concentrate on the investigation. He had no idea what was going on, what Bosch and the FBI woman were up to. But Irving was convinced there was a caper on, and so was Clarke. If so, Lewis promised himself at the pay phone, he would be the one who would squeeze the cuffs on Bosch's wrists.

An old tramp with scary eyes and white hair shuffled up to the pay phone next to tbe one Lewis was at and checked the change slot. It was empty. He reached a finger toward the slot of the phone Lewis was using, but the IAD detective batted it away.

"Anything there, it's mine, pop," Lewis said.

Undeterred, the tramp said, "You got a quarter so I can get something to eat?"

"Fuck off," Lewis said.

"What?" a voice said.

"What?" Lewis said, and then realized the voice had come from the phone. It was Irving. "Oh, not you, sir. I didn't realize you were—uh, I was talking, uh, I'm having a problem here with someone. I—"

"You speak like that with a citizen?"

Lewis reached a hand into his pants pocket and pulled out a dollar bill. He handed it to the white-haired man and shooed him away.

"Detective Lewis, are you there?"

"Yes, Chief. Sorry. I've taken care of the situation now. I wanted to report. There has been an important development."

He hoped this last would draw Irving's attention away from the earlier indiscretion.

Irving said, "Tell me what you have. Do you still have Bosch in sight?"

Lewis exhaled sharply, relieved.

"Yes," he said, "Detective Clarke is continuing surveillance while I make this report."

"All right, then give it to me. It is Friday evening, Detective, I would like to get home at a reasonable hour."

Lewis spent the next fifteen minutes updating Irving on Bosch's tail of the gold Mercedes from Orange County to the Beverly Hills Safe & Lock. He said the tail was terminated at the safe and lock, which appeared to have been the intended destination.

"What are they doing now, Bosch and the bureau woman?"

"They are still in there. It looks like they are interviewing the manager. Something's going on. It was like they didn't know where they were going but once they got to this place, they knew this was it."

"Was what?"

"That's it. I don't know. Whatever it is they are up to. I think the guy they followed made a deposit. There is a vault, a large vault in the front window of the place."

"Yes, I know where you are talking about."

Irving did not speak for a long period, and Lewis, his report completed, knew better than to interrupt. He started daydreaming about cuffing Bosch's hands behind his back and walking him past a battery of television cameras. He heard Irving clear his throat.

"I don't know their plan," the deputy chief said. "But I want you to stay with them. If they don't go home tonight, neither do you. Understood?"

"Yes, sir."

"If they allowed the Mercedes Benz to go on, then it

must be the vault they wanted to find. They will place the vault under surveillance. And you, in turn, will continue to keep them under surveillance."

"Yes, Chief," Lewis said, though he was still lost.

Irving spent the next ten minutes giving his detective instructions and his theory of what was happening with Beverly Hills Safe & Lock. Lewis pulled out a pad and pen and took some quick notes. At the end of the one-sided dialogue, Irving entrusted Lewis with his home telephone number and said, "Don't move in without my prior approval. You can call me at the number at any time, day or night. Understood?"

"Yes, sir," Lewis said urgently.

Irving hung up without saying another word.

Bosch waited in the reception area without telling Grant or the other salesmen what was going on until Wish arrived. They stood behind their fancy desks with their mouths open. When Eleanor came to the door it was locked. She knocked and held up her badge. The guard let her in and she walked into the reception area.

As the salesman named Avery opened his mouth to say something, Bosch said, "This is FBI Agent Eleanor Wish. She is with me. We are going to step into one of your client offices for a private conversation. Just take a minute. If there is a head man here, we'd like to speak to him as soon as we come out."

Grant, still flustered, just pointed to the second door in the alcove. Bosch went in the third door and Wish followed. He closed the door on all three of the salesmen's eyes and locked it.

"So, what have we got? I don't know what to tell them," he whispered as he looked around the desk and two chairs in the room for a scrap of paper or anything else Tran might have mistakenly left behind. There was nothing. He opened the drawers of the mahogany desk. There were pens and pencils and envelopes and a stack of bond paper. Nothing else. There was a fax machine on a table against the wall opposite the door but it was not turned on.

"We watch and wait," she said, speaking very quickly. "Rourke says he is putting together a tunnel crew. They'll go in and have a look around. They're going to get with DWP first to see exactly what's down there. They should be able to figure what the best spot for a tunnel would be and then they'll go from there. Harry, you really think this is it?"

He nodded. He wanted to smile but didn't. Her excitement was contagious.

"Did he get a tail on Tran in time?" he asked. "By the way, here they know him as Mr. Long."

There was a knocking on the door and someone's voice saying, "Excuse me. Excuse me." Bosch and Wish ignored it.

"Tran, Bok, now Long," Wish said. "I don't know about the tail. Rourke said he was going to try. I gave him the plate and told him where the Mercedes was parked. Guess we'll find out later. He said he'd also send over a crew to work the surveillance with us. We are going to have a surveillance meeting in the garage across the street at eight o'clock. What did they say here?"

"I haven't told them what's going on yet."

There was another knock, this one louder.

"Well, then, let's go see the head man."

The owner and chief operating officer of Beverly Hills Safe & Lock turned out to be Avery's father, Martin B.

Avery III. He was of the same stock as many of his customers and wanted everybody to know it. He had a private office at the rear of the alcove. Behind his desk was a collection of framed photographs attesting to the fact that he was not just another chiseler feeding off the rich. He was one of them. There was Avery III with a couple of presidents, a movie mogul or two, and English royalty. One photo was of Avery and the Prince of Wales in full polo regalia, though Avery appeared too thick around the middle and loose in the jowls to be much of a horseman.

Bosch and Wish summarized the situation for him and he was immediately skeptical. He said his vault was impregnable. They told him to save the sales pitch and asked to see design and operation plans for the vault. Avery III flipped his $60 blotter over, and there was the vault schematic taped to the back. It was clear that Avery III and his blow-cut salesmen were overselling the vault. Starting from its outermost skin and going inward, it was one-inch steel plating followed by a foot of rebarred concrete followed by another inch of steel. The vault was thicker on the bottom and top, where there was another two-foot layer of concrete. As with all vaults, the most impressive thing was the thick steel door, but that was for show. Just like the hand X-ray and the mantrap. Only a show. Bosch knew that if the tunnel bandits were really down below, they would have little trouble coming up for air.

Avery III said that there had been a vault alarm on each of the past two nights, including two alarms on Thursday night. Each time he was called at home by the Beverly Hills police. He in turn called his son, Avery IV, and dispatched him to meet the officers. The officers and the heir then entered the business and reset the alarm after finding nothing amiss.

"We had no idea that there might be someone in the sewers below us," Avery III said. He said it like the word sewers was wholly beneath his usage. "Hard to believe, hard to believe."

Bosch asked more detailed questions about the vault's operation and security devices. Not realizing its significance, Avery III mentioned matter-of-factly that unlike conventional bank vaults his vault had a time-lock override. He had a code he could enter into the computer lock which would purge the time-lock coordinates. He was able to open the vault door anytime.

"We must accede to our client's needs," he explained. "If a Beverly Hills lady should call on a Sunday because she needs her tiara for the charity ball, I want to be able to get that tiara for her. You see, it is the service we sell."

"Do all your clients know about that weekend service?" Wish asked.

"Of course not," Avery III said. "Only a select few. You see, we charge a hefty fee. We must bring in a security guard to do it."

"How long does it take to do the override and swing the door open?" Bosch asked.

"Not long. I tap in the override code on the keypad next to the vault door and it is done in a matter of seconds. You then set the vault unlock code in, then turn the wheel and the door opens under its own weight. Thirty seconds, perhaps a minute, perhaps less."

Not fast enough, Bosch thought. Tran's box was located near the front of the vault. That's where the bandits would be working. They would see and probably hear the vault door being opened. No element of surprise.

An hour later, Bosch and Wish were back in his car. They had moved to the second level of the parking garage across Wilshire and east a half block from Beverly Hills Safe & Lock. From there they had an open view of the vault room. After they had left Avery III and taken the surveillance position, they had watched as Avery IV and Grant swung the huge stainless steel vault door closed. They turned the wheel and typed on the computer keypad, locking it. Then the lights inside the business went out, all except those in the glass vault room. Those always stayed on to display the very symbol of the security they offered.

"You think they'll come through tonight?" Wish asked.

"Hard to say. Without Meadows, they're down a man. They might be behind schedule."

They had told Avery III to go home and be ready for a call out. The owner had agreed but remained skeptical of the whole scenario Bosch and Wish had spun for him.

"We are going to have to get them from underground," Bosch said, his hands holding the steering wheel as if he were driving. "We'd never get that door open fast enough."

Bosch idly looked to his left, up Wilshire. He saw a white LTD with police wheels parked at the curb a block away. It was parked next to a fire hydrant and there were two figures in it. He still had company.

Bosch and Wish stood next to his car, which was parked on the second level of the garage facing the retainer wall at the south end. The garage had been virtually empty for more than an hour, but the drab concrete enclosure smelled of exhaust fumes and burning brakes. Bosch was sure the brakes smell was from his car. The stop-and-go tail from Little Saigon had taken its toll on the replacement car. From their position they could look across Wilshire and west a half block to the vault showroom of Beverly Hills Safe & Lock. Farther down Wilshire the sky was pink and the setting sun a deep orange. Evening lights were coming on in the city and traffic was thinning out. Bosch looked east up Wilshire and could see the white LTD parked at the curb, its occupants shadows behind the tinted windshield.

At eight o'clock a procession of three cars, the last a Beverly Hills patrol car, came up the ramp and cut across the empty parking spaces to where Bosch and Wish stood at the wall.

"Well, if our perps have their lookout in any of these high rises and they saw this little parade, you can bet he is pulling them out now," Bosch said.

Rourke and four other men got out of the two unmarked cars. Bosch could tell by the suits that three of them were agents. The fourth man's suit was a little too worn, its pockets baggy like Bosch's. He carried a cardboard tube. Harry figured him for the DWP supe Wish had said was coming. Three Beverly Hills uniforms, one with captain's bars on his collar, got out of the patrol car. The captain was also carrying a rolled tube of paper.

Everybody converged at Bosch's car and used its hood as the meeting table. Rourke made some quick introductions. The three from BHPD were there because the operation was in their jurisdiction. Interdepartmental courtesy, Rourke said. They were also on hand because Beverly Hills Safe & Lock had filed a design plan with the local police department's commercial security division. They would only observe the meeting, Rourke said, and be called on later if their department was needed for backup. Two of the FBI agents, Hanlon and Houck, would work the overnight surveillance with Bosch and Wish. Rourke wanted a view of Beverly Hills Safe & Lock from at least two angles. The third agent was the FBI's SWAT coordinator. And the last man was Ed Gearson, a DWP underground facilities supervisor.

"Okay, let's set the battle plans," Rourke announced at the end of the introductions. He took the cardboard tube from Gearson without asking and slid out a rolled blueprint. "This is a DWP schematic print for this area. It has all the utility lines, the tunnels and culverts. It tells us exactly what is down there."

He unfurled the grayish map with smeared blue lines on it across the hood. The three Beverly Hills cops anchored the other end with their hands. It was getting dark in the garage and the SWAT man, an agent named Heller, held a penlight with a surprisingly wide and bright beam over the drawing. Rourke took a pen out of his shirt pocket, pulled on it until it telescoped into a pointer.

"Okay, we are . . . right . . ." Before he could find the spot Gearson reached his arm into the light and put a finger on the map. Rourke brought his pen point over to the spot. "Yes, right here," he said and gave Gearson a don't-fuck-with-me look. The DWP man's shoulders seemed to stoop a little more in his threadbare jacket.

Everyone around the car leaned in closer over the hood to study the location. "Beverly Hills Safe & Lock is here," Rourke said. "The actual vault is here. Can we see your blueprint, Captain Orozco?"

Orozco, who was built like an inverted pyramid, broad shoulders over thin hips, unrolled his drawing across the top of the DWP print. It was a copy of the drawing Avery III had shown Bosch and Wish earlier.

"Three thousand square feet of vault space," said Orozco, indicating the vault area with his hand. "Small private boxes along the sides and free-standing closets down the middle. If they are under there, they could come up through the floor anywhere along these two aisles. So we are talking about a range of about sixty feet in which they could come through the floor."

"Now, Captain," Rourke said, "if you pick that up and we look back at the DWP chart, we can place that break-through zone right here." With a Day-Glo yellow under-liner he outlined the floor of the vault on the utility map. "Using that as a guide, we can see the subterranean structures that offer the closest proximity. What do you think, Mr. Gearson?"

Gearson leaned over the car hood another few inches and studied the utility map. Bosch also leaned in. He saw thick lines he assumed indicated major east-west drainage lines. The kind the tunnelers would seek. He noticed that they corresponded to major surface streets: Wilshire, Olympic, Pico. Gearson pointed out the Wilshire line, saying it ran thirty feet below ground and was large enough to drive a truck through. With his finger, the DWP man traced the Wilshire line east ten blocks to Robertson, a major north-south stormwater line. From that intersection, he said, it was just a mile south to an open drainage culvert that ran alongside the Santa Monica Freeway. The opening at the culvert was as big as a garage door and blocked only by a gate with a padlock on it.

"I'd say that's where they could've come in," Gearson said. "Like following surface streets. You take the

Robertson line up to Wilshire. Take a left and you're practically here by your yellow line. The vault. But I don't think they'd dig a tunnel off the Wilshire line."

"No?" Rourke said. "How so?"

"Too busy is how so," Gearson said, sensing he was the man with the answers as nine faces peered at him from around the car hood. "We got DWP people underground all the time in these main lines. Checking for cracks, blockages, problems of any sort. And Wilshire's the main drag down there, east and west. Just like up top. If somebody knocked a hole in the wall it'd get noticed. See?"

"What if they were able to conceal the hole?"

"You're talking about like they did a year or so ago in that burglary downtown. Yeah, that might work again, maybe somewhere else, but there is a good chance on the Wilshire line that it'd be seen. We look for that sort of thing now. And, like I said, there's a lot of traffic on the Wilshire line."

There was silence as they took time to consider this. The engines of the cars ticked away the heat.

"Then where would they dig, Mr. Gearson, to get into this vault?" Rourke finally said.

"We got all manner of linkups down there. Don't think us guys don't think of this from time to time when we're working down there. You know, the perfect crime and all that. I've hashed stuff like this around, especially when I read about that last one in the papers. I think if you are saying that's the vault they want to get into, then they'd still do just like I said: come up Robertson and then over on the Wilshire line. But then I think they'd move down one of the service tunnels to sort of stay out of sight. The service tunnels are three to five feet wide. They're round.

Plenty of room to work and move equipment. They hook up the main artery lines to the street storm drains and the utility systems in the buildings along here."

He put his hand back into the light and traced the smaller lines he was talking about on the DWP map.

"If they did this right," he said, "what they did was get in the gate down by the freeway and drive their equipment and all up to Wilshire and then over to your target area. They unload their stuff, hide it in one of these service tunnels, as we call 'em, and then take their vehicle back out. They hike back in on foot and set to work in the service tunnel. Hell, they could be working in there five, six weeks before we might have occasion to go up that particular line."

Bosch still thought it sounded too simple.

"What about these other storm lines?" he asked, indicating Olympic and Pico on the map. There was a cross-hatch pattern of the smaller service tunnels running from these lines north toward the vault. "What about using one of these and coming up behind the vault?"

Gearson scratched his bottom lip with a finger and said, "That's fine. There's that too. But the thing is, these lines aren't going to get you as close to the vault as these Wilshire offshoots. See what I mean? Why would they dig a hundred-yard tunnel when they could dig a hundred-footer here?"

Gearson liked holding court, the idea of knowing more than the silk suits and uniforms around him. Having finished his speech, he rocked back on his heels, a satisfied look on his face. Bosch knew the man was probably correct on every detail.

"What about earth displacement?" Bosch asked him.

"These guys are digging a tunnel through dirt and rock, concrete. Where do they get rid of it? How?"

"Bosch, Mr. Gearson is not a detective," Rourke said. "I doubt that he knows every nuance of—"

"Easy," Gearson said. "The floors of the main lines like Wilshire and Robertson are graded three degrees to center. There is always water running down the center, even most days during a drought. It might not be raining up top but water flows, you know. You'd be surprised how much. Either it's runoff from the reservoirs or commercial use or both. Your fire department gets a call, where you think the water goes when they are done puttin' the fire out? So what I am saying is, if they had enough water they could use it to move the displaced earth or whatever you want to call it."

"It's got to be tons." Hanlon spoke for the first time.

"But it's not several tons at once. You said they took days to dig this. You spread it out over days and the runoff could handle it. Now, if they are in one of the service tunnels they'd have to figure a way to get water through there, down to your main line. I'd check your fire hydrants in the area. You got one leaking or had a report of somebody opening one up, that'd be your boys."

One of the uniforms leaned to Orozco's ear and said something. Orozco leaned over the hood and raised his finger above the map. Then he poked it down on a blue line. "We had a hydrant vandalized here two nights ago."

"Somebody opened it up," the uniform who had whispered to the captain said, "and used a bolt cutter to cut the chain that holds the cap. They took the cap with them, and it took the fire department an hour to get out here with a replacement."

"That would be a lot of water," Gearson said. "That

would have taken care of some of your earth displacement."

He looked at Bosch and smiled. And Bosch smiled back. He liked when pieces of the puzzle began to fit.

"Before that, let's see, Saturday night it was, we had an arson," Orozco said. "A little boutique in behind the Stock Building off Rincon."

Gearson looked at the spot Orozco pointed to on the blueprint as being the location of the boutique. He put his own finger on the fire hydrant location. "The water from both of those things would have gone into three street catches, here, here and here," he said, moving his hand deftly over the gray paper. "These two drain to this line. The other drains here."

The investigators looked at the two drainage lines. One ran parallel to Wilshire, behind the J. C. Stock Building. The other ran perpendicular to Wilshire, a straight offshoot, and next to the building.

"Either one and we're still looking at, what, a hundred-foot tunnel?" Wish said.

"At least," Gearson said. "If they had a straight shot. They might've hit ground utilities or hard rock and had to divert some. Doubt any tunnel down there could be a straight shot."

The SWAT expert tugged Rourke's cuff and the two walked away from the crowd for a whispered conversation. Bosch looked at Wish and softly said, "They're not going to go in."

"What do you mean?"

"This isn't Vietnam. Nobody has to go down there. If Franklin and Delgado and anybody else are down there in one of these lines, there's no way to go in safely and unannounced. They hold all the advantages. They'd know we're coming."

She studied his face but didn't say anything.

"It would be the wrong move," Bosch said. "We know they're armed and probably have trips set up. We know they're killers."

Rourke came back to the gathering around the car hood and asked Gearson to wait in one of the bureau cars while he finished up with the investigators. The DWP man walked to the car with his head down, disappointed he was no longer part of the plan.

"We're not going in after them," Rourke said after Gearson shut the car door. "Too dangerous. They have weapons, explosives. We have no element of surprise. It adds up to heavy casualties for us. . . . So, we trap them. We let things take their course and then we will be there waiting, safely, when they come out. Then we'll have surprise on our side.

"Tonight SWAT will make a recon run through the Wilshire line—we'll get some DWP uniforms from Gearson—and look for their entry point. Then we'll set up and wait in whatever's the best location. Whatever's safest from our standpoint."

There was a beat of silence, punctuated by a horn from the street, before Orozco protested.

"Wait a minute, wait a minute." He waited until every face was on his. Except Rourke's. He didn't look at Orozco at all.

"We can't be talking about sitting out here with our thumbs up our asses and letting these people blast their way into that vault," Orozco said. "To let them go in and pry open a couple hundred boxes and then just back out.

My obligation is to protect the property of the citizens of Beverly Hills, who probably happen to constitute ninety percent of that business's customers. I'm not going along with this."

Rourke collapsed his pen pointer, put it in the inside pocket of his coat and then spoke. He still did not look at Orozco.

"Orozco, your exception can be noted for the record, but we're not asking you to go along with this," Rourke said. Bosch noticed that along with failing to address Orozco by his rank, Rourke had dropped all pretense of courtesy.

"This is a federal operation," Rourke continued. "You are here as a professional courtesy. Besides, if my thinking is correct, they will open one deposit box only. When they find it empty they will cancel the operation and leave the vault."

Orozco was lost. His face showed it. Bosch could see he obviously had not been given many details of the investigation. He felt sorry for him, hung out to dry by Rourke.

"There are things we can't discuss at this point," Rourke said. "But we believe their target is only one box. We have reason to believe it is now empty. When the perps break into the vault and open that particular box and find it is empty, we believe they will back out in a hurry. Our job now is to be ready for that."

Bosch wondered about Rourke's supposition. Would the thieves back out? Or would they think they had the wrong box and keep drilling, looking for Tran's diamonds? Or would they loot the other boxes in hope of stealing property valuable enough to make the tunnel caper worth it? Bosch didn't know. He certainly wasn't as sure as Rourke, but then he knew the FBI agent might just be posturing to get Orozco out of the way.

"What if they don't back out?" Bosch asked. "What if they keep drilling?"

"Then we all have a long weekend ahead of us," Rourke said, "because we are going to wait them out."

"Either way, you're going to put that place out of business," Orozco said, pointing in the direction of the Stock Building. "Once it is known that somebody blew a hole through the vault they've got sitting out there in the big window, there will be no public confidence. Nobody will put their property in there."

Rourke just stared at him. The captain's plea was falling on deaf ears.

"If you can catch them after they break in, why not before?" Orozco said. "Why don't we open up that place, run a siren, make some noise, even sit a patrol car out front? Do something to let 'em know we are here and we know about them. That'll scare 'em out before they break in. We catch them, we save the business. We don't, we still save the business and we get them another day."

"Captain," Rourke said, the false congeniality back, "if you let them know we are here, you take away our one advantage—surprise—and invite a firefight in the tunnels and perhaps up on the street in which they will not care who is hurt, who is killed. That's including themselves and perhaps innocent bystanders. Then, how do we explain to the public and even ourselves that we did it this way because we wanted to try to save a business?"

Rourke waited a beat to let his words sink in, then said, "You see, Captain, I am not going to hedge on safety on this operation. I can't. These men that are down there, they don't scare. They kill. Two people that we know about, including a witness. And that's only this week. No way are we going to let them get away. No fucking way."

Orozco leaned across the hood and rolled his blueprint up. As he snapped a rubber band around it, he said, "Gentlemen, don't fuck up. If you do, my department and I will not hold back our criticism or the details of what was discussed at this meeting. Good night."

He turned and walked back to the patrol car. The two uniforms followed without being told to. Everybody else just watched. When the patrol car drove down the ramp, Rourke said, "Well, you heard the man. We can't fuck this up. Anybody else want to suggest something?"

"What about putting people in the vault now and waiting for them to come up?" Bosch said. He hadn't really considered it but threw it out as it came to him.

"No," the SWAT man said. "You put people in the vault and they are in a corner. No options. No way out. I wouldn't even ask my men for volunteers."

"They could be injured by the blast," Rourke added. "No telling where or when the perps will come up."

Bosch nodded. They were right.

"Can we open the vault and go in, once we know they have come up?" one of the agents said. Bosch couldn't remember now whether he was Hanlon or Houck.

"Yes, there's a way to take the door off the time lock," Wish said. "We'd need to get Avery, the owner, back out here."

"From what Avery said, it looks like that would take too long," Bosch said. "Too slow. Avery can take it off time lock and open it, but it's a two-ton door that swings open on its own weight. At best, it would take a half minute to get it open. Maybe less, but they'd still have the drop on us, the people inside. Same risk as coming at them through the tunnels."

"What about a flash bang?" one of the agents said. "We open the vault door just a bit and throw in a flash grenade. Then we go in and take them."

Rourke and the SWAT man shook their heads in unison.

"For two reasons," the SWAT man said. "If they wire the tunnel as we assume they will, the flash could detonate the charges. We could see Wilshire Boulevard out there drop thirty feet, and we don't want that. Think of the paperwork."

When no one smiled, he continued. "Secondly, that's a glass room we are talking about. Our position in there would be very vulnerable. If they have a lookout, we're dead. We think they go with radio silence when they've got the explosives out. But what if they don't and this lookout lets them know we're out there. They might be ready to toss something out at us while we're tossing something in."

Rourke added his own thoughts. "Never mind the lookout. We put a SWAT team in that glass room and they can watch it on TV. We'll have every station in L.A. with a camera out on the sidewalk and traffic backed up to Santa Monica. It'd be a circus. So forget that. SWAT will get with Gearson, do the recon and get the exits down by the freeway covered. We wait for them underneath and we take 'em on our terms. That's it."

The SWAT man nodded and Rourke continued. "Starting tonight we'll have twenty-four-hour surveillance topside on the vault. I want Wish, Bosch, on the vault side of the building. Hanlon, Houck, on Rincon Street so you can see the door. If it looks or sounds like it is going down, I want to be alerted and I will alert SWAT to stand by. Use landlines if possible. We don't know if they are monitoring our freeks. You people on the surveillance will have to work out a code to use on the radio. Everybody got that?"

"What if there is an alarm?" Bosch asked. "There have been three so far this week."

Rourke thought a moment and said, "Handle it routinely. Meet the callout manager, Avery or whoever, at the door and reset the alarm and send him on his way. I'll get back to Orozco and tell him to send his patrols on the alarms but we'll handle things."

"Avery will get the callouts," Wish said. "He already knows what we think is going to happen here. What if he wants to open the vault, take a look around?"

"Don't let him. It's that simple. It's his vault but his life would be endangered. We can prevent it."

Rourke looked around at the faces. There were no more questions.

"Then that's it. I want people in position in ninety minutes. That gives you all-nighters time to eat, piss and get coffee. Wish, give me status reports, landline, at midnight and oh six hundred. Got it?"

"Got it."

Rourke and the SWAT man got in the car where Gearson was waiting and drove down the ramp. Bosch, Wish, Hanlon, and Houck then worked out a radio code to use. They decided to switch the streets in the surveillance area with the names of streets downtown. The idea was if anyone was listening to the simplex 5 public safety frequency, they would think they were hearing reports on a surveillance at Broadway and First Street in downtown instead of Wilshire and Rincon in Beverly Hills. They also decided to refer to the vault room as a pawnshop while on the radio. That done, the two sets of investigators split up and agreed to check in at the start of the surveillance. As Hanlon and Houck's car headed toward the ramp, Bosch, alone with Wish for the first time since the plans were set, asked what she thought.

"I don't know. I don't like the idea of letting them go into the vault and then run around loose down there after. I wonder if the SWAT team can really cover everything."

"I guess we'll find out."

A car came up the ramp and drove toward them. The lights blinded Bosch, and for a moment he thought of the car that had come at them the night before. But then the car swerved and came to a stop. It was Hanlon and Houck. The passenger window was rolled down and Houck held a thick manila envelope out the window.

"Mail call, Harry," the agent said. "Forgot we were supposed to give this to you. Somebody from your office dropped it by the bureau today, said you were waiting for it but hadn't been by Wilcox to get it."

Bosch took the envelope and held it out away from his body. Houck noticed the discomfort on his face.

"The guy's name was Edgar, a black guy, said you used to be partners," Houck said. "Said it had been sitting in your mailbox two days and he thought it might be important. Said he was showing somebody a house out in Westwood and decided to drop it by while he was in the area. That sound legit to you?"

Bosch nodded and the two agents drove away again. The heavy envelope was sealed but the return address was the U.S. Armed Services Records Archive in St. Louis. He tore off the end of the envelope and looked inside. There was a thick file of papers.

"What is it?" Wish asked.

"It's Meadows's package. I forgot I ordered it. Did it Monday, before I knew you guys were on the case. Anyway, I've already seen this stuff."

He tossed the envelope through the open window of the car onto the backseat.

"Hungry?" she asked him.

"I want some coffee at least."

"I know a place."

Bosch was sipping steaming black coffee from a plastic cup he had taken from the restaurant, an Italian place on Pico behind Century City. He was in the car, back in place on the second floor of the parking garage across Wilshire from the vault. Wish opened the door and got in after making her midnight check-in call to Rourke.

"They found the Jeep."

"Where?"

"Rourke says SWAT did the reconnaissance ride through the Wilshire storm sewer but found no sign of intruders or a tunnel entry. Looks like Gearson was right. They're tucked in one of the smaller tributary lines. Anyway, the SWAT guys then went down to the drainage wash by the freeway to set the trap. They were deploying at three exit positions from the tunnels when they came across the Jeep. Rourke said there's a car pool parking lot down by the freeway. There's a beige Jeep parked with a covered trailer attached. It's theirs. The three blue ATVs are in the trailer."

"Is he getting a warrant?"

"Yeah, he's got somebody trying to find a judge now. So they'll have it. But they aren't going to go near it until they take down the operation. In case their plan is for someone to come out and get the ATVs. Or somebody already outside is going to show up and drive 'em in.

Bosch nodded and sipped. It was the smart way to go. He remembered he had a cigarette going in the ashtray and tossed it out the open window.

As if guessing what he would be thinking, she said, "Rourke said that from what they could see there was no blanket in the back of the Jeep. But if it's the Jeep Meadows's body was carried to the reservoir in, there still should be fiber evidence."

"What about the seal that Sharkey saw on the door?"

"Rourke said there was no seal. But there could have been one and they just took it off when they were leaving the Jeep out there."

"Yeah," Bosch said. After a few moments of thought, he said, "Does it bother you how everything is just coming together so well?"

"Should it?"

Bosch shrugged his shoulders. He looked up Wilshire. The curb in front of the fireplug was empty. Since they had come back from dinner Bosch hadn't seen the white LTD, which he'd been sure was an IAD car. He didn't know if Lewis and Clarke were around or had called it a night.

"Harry, good detective work pays off with cases that come together," Eleanor told him. "I mean, we aren't out of the dark on this by a long shot. But I think we finally have a measure of control. Damned sight better than we were three days ago. So why the worry when a few things finally start coming together?"

"Three days ago Sharkey was still alive."

"Well, while you're taking the blame for that, why don't you add everybody else who has ever made a choice and gotten themselves killed. You can't change those things, Harry. And you're not supposed to be a martyr."

"What do you mean, choice? Sharkey didn't make any choice."

"Yes, he did. When he chose the streets, he knew he might die on the streets."

"You don't believe that. He was a kid."

"I believe that shit happens. I believe that the best you can do in this job is come out even. Some people win and some lose. Hopefully, half the time it is the good guys who win. That's us, Harry."

Bosch drank his cup dry and they sat in silence for a while after that. They had a clear view of the vault sitting at the center of the glass room like a throne. Out there in the open, polished and shiny under the bright ceiling lights, it said "Take me" to the world, he thought. And somebody would. We're going to let them.

Wish picked up the radio handset, keyed the transmit button twice and said, "Broadway One to First, do you guys copy?"

"We copy, Broadway. Anything?" It was Houck's voice on the comeback. There was a lot of static, as the radio waves ricochetted off the tall buildings in the area.

"Only checking. What's your position?"

"We are due south of the front door of the pawnshop. A clear view of nothing going on."

"We're east. Can see the—" She clicked off the mike and looked at Bosch. "We forgot a code for the vault. Got any ideas?"

Bosch shook his head no, but then said, "Saxophone. I've seen saxophones hanging in pawnshop windows. Musical instruments, lots of them."

She clicked the mike open again. "Sorry, First Street, had technical difficulty. We are east of the pawnshop, have the piano in the window in sight. No activity inside."

"Stay awake."

"That's a K. Broadway out."

Bosch smiled and shook his head.

"What?" she said. "What?"

"I've seen lots of musical instruments in pawnshops, but I don't know about a piano. Who is going to take a piano to a pawnshop? You'd need a truck. We've blown our cover now." He picked up the radio mike, but without clicking the transmit button, and said, "Uh, First Street, check that. It's not a piano in the window. That's an accordion. Our mistake."

She slugged him on the shoulder and told him to never mind the piano. They settled into an easy silence. Surveillance jobs were the bane of most detectives' existence. But in his fifteen years on the job Bosch had never minded a single stakeout. In fact, many times he enjoyed them when he was with good company. He defined good company not by the conversation but by the lack of it. When there was no need to talk to feel comfortable, that was the right company. Bosch thought about the case and watched the traffic pass by the vault. He recapped the events as they had occurred, in order, from start to present. Revisiting scenes, listening to the dialogue over again. He found that often this reaccounting helped him make the next choice or step. What he mulled over now, poking at it like a loose tooth with his tongue, was the hit-and-run. The car that had come at them the night before. Why? What did they know at that point that made them so dangerous? It seemed to be a foolish move to kill a cop and a federal agent. Why was it undertaken? His mind then drifted to the night they had spent together after all the questions were asked by all the supervisors. Eleanor was spooked. More so than he. As he had held her in her bed, he felt as though be were calming a frightened animal. Holding and caressing her as she breathed into his neck. They had not made love. Just held each other. It had somehow seemed more intimate.

"Are you thinking about last night?" she asked then.

"How did you know?"

"A guess. Any ideas?"

"Well, I think it was nice. I think we—"

"I'm talking about who tried to kill us last night."

"Oh. No, no ideas. I was thinking about the after."

"Oh. . . . You know, I didn't thank you, Harry, for being with me like that, not expecting anything."

"I should thank you."

"You're sweet."

They drifted into their own thoughts again. Leaning against the door with his head against the side window, Bosch rarely took his eyes off the vault. Traffic on Wilshire was light but steady. People heading to or from the clubs over on Santa Monica Boulevard or around Rodeo Drive.

There was probably a premiere at nearby Academy Hall. It seemed to Bosch that every limousine in L.A. was working Wilshire this night. Stretch cars of all makes and colors cruised by, one by one. They moved so smoothly they seemed to float. They were beautiful, and intriguing with their black windows. Like exotic women in sunglasses. A car built just for this city, Bosch thought.

"Has Meadows been buried?"

The question surprised him. He wondered what tumble

of thought led to it. "No," he answered. "Monday, over at the veterans cemetery."

"A Memorial Day funeral, sounds kind of fitting. So his life of crime did not disqualify him from being placed in such sacred ground?"

"No. He did his time over there in Vietnam. They've saved a space for him. There's probably one there for me, too. Why did you ask?"

"I don't know. Just thinking is all. Will you go?"

"If I'm not sitting here watching this vault."

"That will be nice of you. I know he meant something to you. At one point in your life."

He let it drop, but then she said, "Harry, tell me about the black echo. What you said the other day. What did you mean?"

For the first time he looked away from the vault and at Eleanor. Her face was in darkness, but headlights from a passing car lit the interior of the car for a moment and he could see her eyes on his. He looked back at the vault.

"There isn't anything really to tell. It's just what we called one of the intangibles."

"Intangibles?"

"There was no name for it, so we made up a name. It was the darkness, the damp emptiness you'd feel when you were down there alone in those tunnels. It was like you were in a place where you felt dead and buried in the dark. But you were alive. And you were scared. Your own breath kind of echoed in the darkness, loud enough to give you away. Or so you thought. I don't know. It's hard to explain. Just . . . the black echo."

She let some time slide between them before she said, "I think your going to the funeral is nice."

"Is something wrong?"

"What do you mean?"

"What I said. The way you're talking. You haven't seemed right since last night. Like something—I don't know, forget it."

"I don't know, either, Harry. You know, after the adrenaline wore off, I guess I kind of just got scared. Made me start thinking about things."

Bosch nodded his head but didn't say anything. His mind drifted and he remembered a time in the Triangle when a company that had taken heavy casualties from sniper fire stumbled onto the entrance to a tunnel complex. Bosch, Meadows and a couple of other rats named Jarvis and Hanrahan were dropped at a nearby LZ and escorted to the hole. The first thing they did was drop a Couple of LZ flares, a blue one and a red one, into the hole and blow the smoke in with a Mighty Mite fan, to find the other entrances in the jungle. Pretty soon ribbons of smoke started curling out of the ground at a couple dozen spots for two hundred yards in all directions. The smoke was coming up through the spider holes the snipers used as firing positions or to move in and out of the tunnels. There were so many of them, the jungle was turning purple from the smoke. Meadows was stoned. He popped a cassette into the portable tape player he always carried and started blasting Hendrix's "Purple Haze" into the tunnel. It was one of Bosch's most vivid memories, aside from his dreams, of the war.

He never liked rock and roll after that. The jolting energy of the music reminded him too much of the war.

"Did you ever go see the memorial?" Eleanor asked.

She didn't have to say which one. There was only the one, in Washington. But then he remembered the long black replica he had watched them installing at the cemetery by the Federal Building.

"No," he said after a while. "I've never seen it."

After the air in the jungle cleared and the Hendrix tape was done, the four of them had gone into the tunnel while the rest of the company sat on backpacks and chowed and waited. An hour later, only Bosch and Meadows had come back. Meadows carried with him three NVA scalps. He held them up for the troops above ground and yelled, "You're looking at the baddest blood brother in the black echo." And so came the name. Later, they found Jarvis and Hanrahan in the tunnels. They had fallen into punji traps. They were dead.

Eleanor said, "I visited it when I was living in D.C. I couldn't make myself go to the dedication in eighty-two. But a lot of years later I finally got the courage. I wanted to see my brother's name. I thought maybe it would help me sort things out, you know, about what happened with him."

"And did it?"

"No. Made it worse. It made me angry. It left me with this need for justice, if that makes sense. I wanted justice for my brother."

The silence filled the car again and Bosch poured more coffee into his cup. He was beginning to feel the onset of caffeine jitters but couldn't stop. He was addicted. He watched a couple of drunks who were stumbling down the street stop in front of the window before the vault. One of the men threw his hands up as if trying to gain a measure of the vault's huge door. After a while they moved on. He thought of the rage Eleanor must have felt because of her brother. The helplessness. He thought of his own rage. He knew the same feelings, maybe not to the same degree but from a different perspective. Anybody who was touched by the war knew some part of those feelings. He had never worked it out completely and wasn't sure he wanted to. The anger and sadness gave him something that was better than complete emptiness. Is that what Meadows felt? He wondered. The emptiness. Is that what bounced him from job to job and needle to needle until he was finally and fatally used up on this last mission? Bosch decided that he would go to Meadows's funeral, that he owed him that much.

"You know what you were telling me the other day about that guy, the Dollmaker killer?" Eleanor asked.

"What about it?"

"IAD, they tried to make a case that you executed him?"

"Yes, I told you. They tried. But it wasn't there. All they got me on was suspension for procedure violations."

"Well, I just wanted to say that even if they were right, they were wrong. That would have been justice in my book. You knew what would happen with a guy like that. Look at the Night Stalker. He'll never get the gas. Or it'll take twenty years."

Bosch felt uncomfortable. He had only thought of his motives and actions in the Dollmaker case when alone. He never spoke aloud about it. He didn't know where she was going with this.

She said, "I know if it was true you could never admit it, but I think you either consciously or subconsciously made a decision. You went for justice for all those women, his victims. Maybe even for your mother."

Shocked, Bosch turned to her and was about to ask how she knew about his mother and how she had come to think of her relation to the Dollmaker. Then he remembered the files again. It was probably in there somewhere. When he had applied to the department, he had to say on the forms if he or any close relatives had ever been the victim of a crime. He had been orphaned at eleven, he wrote, when his mother was found strangled in an alley off Hollywood Boulevard. He didn't need to write what she did for a living. The location and crime said enough.

When he recovered his cool, Bosch asked Eleanor what her point was.

"No point," she said. "I just . . . respect that. If it were me, I would have liked to have done the same thing, I think. I hope I would have been brave enough."

He looked over at her, the darkness shielding both their faces. It was late now and no car lights drifted by to show them to each other.

"You go ahead and take the first shift sleeping," he said. "I drank too much coffee."

She didn't answer. He offered to get out a blanket he had put in the trunk, but she declined.

"Did you ever hear what J. Edgar Hoover said about justice?" she asked.

"He probably said a lot, but I don't recall any of it off-hand."

"He said that justice is incidental to law and order. I think he was right."

She said nothing else and after a while he could hear her breathing turn deeper and longer. When the rare car drove by he would look over at her face as the light washed across it. She slept like a child, with her head leaning against her hands. Bosch cracked the window and lit a cigarette. He smoked and wondered if he could or would fall in love with her, and she with him. He was thrilled and disquieted by the thought, all at the same time.

Part VII
Saturday, May 26

G ray dawn came up over the street and filled the car with weak light. The morning also brought with it a gentle drizzle that wet the street and put a smear of condensation on the lower half of the windows of Beverly Hills Safe & Lock. It was the first rain of any kind in months that Bosch could remember. Wish slept and he watched the vault: overhead lights still glowed on the chrome-and-brushed-steel finish. It was past six o'clock, but Bosch had forgotten the check-in call to Rourke and let Eleanor sleep. In fact, during the night he had never wakened her so that he could take a turn sleeping. He just never got tired. Houck checked in on the radio at three-thirty to make sure someone was awake. After that there were no disturbances and no activity in the vault room. For the rest of the night Bosch thought alternately of Eleanor Wish and the vault he watched.

He reached for the cup on the dashboard and checked for even a cold gulp of coffee, but it was empty. He dropped the empty over the seat to the floor. As he did this, he noticed the package from St. Louis on the backseat. He reached back and grabbed the manila envelope. He pulled out the thick sheaf of papers and idly looked through them while glancing up at the vault every few seconds.

Most of Meadows's military records he had already seen. But he quickly noticed that there were several that had not been in the FBI jacket Wish had given him. This was a more complete record. There was a photostat of his draft report notice and medical exam. There were also medical records from Saigon. He had been treated twice for syphilis, once for acute stress reaction.

Paging through the package, he stopped when his eyes fell on a copy of a two-page letter from a Louisiana congressman named Noone. Curious, Bosch began to read. It was dated 1973 and was addressed to Meadows at the embassy in Saigon. The letter, bearing the official congressional seal, thanked Meadows for his hospitality and help during the congressman's recent fact-finding visit. Noone noted that it had been a pleasant surprise to find a fellow New Iberian in the strange country. Bosch wondered how much of a coincidence it had been. Meadows had probably been assigned to security for the congressman so they would hit it off and the legislator would go back to Washington with a high opinion of personnel and morale in Southeast Asia. There are no coincidences.

The second page of the letter congratulated Meadows on a fine career and referred to the good reports Noone had received from Meadows's commanding officer. Bosch read on. Meadows's involvement in stopping an illegal entry into the embassy hotel during the congressman's stay was mentioned; a Lieutenant Rourke had furnished details of Meadows's heroics to the congressman's staff. Bosch felt a trembling below his heart, as if the blood was draining from it. The letter finished with some small talk about the home parish. There was the large, flowing signature of the congressman and a typed notation in the bottom left margin:

cc: U.S. Army, Records Division, Washington, D.C. Lt. John H. Rourke, U.S. Embassy, Saigon, V.N. The Daily Iberian; attention news editor

Bosch stared at the second page for a long time without moving or breathing. He actually thought he felt the beginning sensation of nausea and wiped his hand across his forehead. He tried to think if he had ever heard Rourke's middle name or initial. He couldn't remember. But it didn't matter. There was no doubt. No coincidences.

Eleanor's pager sounded, startling them both like a shot. She sat forward and began fumbling with her purse until she found the pager and shut off the noise.

"Oh, God, what time is it?" she said, still disoriented.

He said it was six-twenty and only then remembered that they were supposed to have checked in with Rourke on a landline twenty minutes earlier. He slid the letter back into the stack of papers and put them back in the envelope. He threw it back on the backseat.

"I've got to call in," Wish said.

"Hey, take a couple of minutes to wake up," Bosch replied quickly. "I'll call in. I've got to find a restroom anyway, and I'll get some coffee and water."

He opened the door and stepped out before she could protest the plan. She said, "Harry, why did you let me sleep?"

"I don't know. What's his number?"

"I should call him."

"Let me. Give me the number."

She gave it to him and Bosch walked around the corner and a short distance to the twenty-four-hour diner called Darling's. He was in a daze the whole way, ignoring the panhandlers who had come out with the sun, trying to fathom that it was Rourke who was the inside man. What was he doing? There was a part of this that was missing and Bosch couldn't figure it. If Rourke was the insider, then why would he allow them to set up surveillance on the vault? Did he want his people caught? He saw the pay phones out front of the restaurant.

"You're late," Rourke said after picking up on half a ring.

"We forgot."

"Bosch? Where's Wish? She's supposed to make the call."

"Don't worry about it, Rourke. She's watching the vault like she's supposed to. What are you doing?"

"I've been waiting to hear from you people before I headed in. Did you two fall asleep or what? What is happening there?"

"Nothing is happening. But you already know that, don't you?"

There was a silence during which an old panhandler walked up to the booth and asked Bosch for money. Bosch put his hand on the man's chest and firmly pushed him away.

"You still there, Rourke?" he said into the phone.

"What was that supposed to mean? How do I know what's going on there when you people don't call in like you're supposed to? And you with the veiled references all the time. Bosch, I don't get you."

"Let me ask you something. Did you really put people down at the tunnel exits, or was that blueprint and your pointer and the SWAT guy all for show?"

"Put Wish on the line. I don't know what you're saying."

"Sorry, she can't come to the phone at the moment."

"Bosch, I'm calling you in. Something is wrong. You've been out all night on this. I think you should—no, I'll get a couple of fresh people out there. I'm going to have to call your lieutenant and—"

"You knew Meadows."

"What?"

"What I said. You knew him. I have his file, man. His *complete* file. Not the edited version you gave Wish to give me. You were his CO at the embassy in Saigon. I know."

More silence. Then, "I was CO to a lot of people, Bosch. I didn't know them all."

Bosch shook his head.

"That's weak, Lieutenant Rourke. Really weak. That was worse than just admitting it. I tell you what, I'll see you around."

Bosch hung up the phone and went into Darling's, where he ordered two coffees and two mineral waters. He stood by the cash register, waiting for the girl to put the order together, and looking out the window. He was thinking only of Rourke.

The girl came up to the cash register with the order in a cardboard carry-out box. He paid and tipped her and went back out to the pay phone.

Bosch called Rourke's number again with no plan

other than to see if he was on the phone or had left. He hung up after ten rings. Then he called the LAPD dispatch center and told an operator to call FBI dispatch and ask if they had a SWAT callout working in the Wilshire area in or near Beverly Hills and if they needed any help. While he waited he tried to put his mind inside Rourke's caper. He opened up one of the coffees and sipped it.

The dispatcher came back on the line with a confirmation that FBI did have a SWAT surveillance in the Wilshire district. No backup was requested. Bosch thanked her and hung up. Now he thought he knew what Rourke was doing. It had to be that there were no men about to break into the vault. The setup on the vault was just that, a setup. The vault was a decoy. Bosch thought about how he had let Tran go his way after following him to the vault. What he had done was flush the second captain out, with his diamonds, so Rourke could have at him. Bosch had simply played into his hands.

When Bosch got back to the car he saw that Eleanor was looking through Meadows's files. She hadn't gotten to the congressman's letter yet.

"Where have you been?" she said good-naturedly.

"Rourke had a lot of questions." He took the Meadows file out of her hands and said, "There is something I want you to see here. Where did you get the file on Meadows that you showed me?"

"I don't know. Rourke got it. Why?"

He found the letter and handed it to her without saying anything.

"What is this? Nineteen seventy-three?"

"Read it. This is Meadows's file, the one I had copied and sent from St. Louis. There is no letter like this one in the file Rourke gave you to give me. He sanitized it. Read, you'll see why."

He glanced over at the vault door. Nothing was happening and he didn't expect anything to be. Then he watched her as she read. She raised an eyebrow as she scanned both pages, not seeing the name.

"Yes, so he was some kind of a hero, it says. I don't—" Her eyes widened as she got to the bottom. "Copied to Lieutenant John Rourke."

"Uh huh. You also missed the first reference."

He pointed to the sentence that named Rourke as Meadows's CO.

"The inside man. What do you think we should do?"

"I don't know. Are you sure? This doesn't prove anything."

"If it was a coincidence, he should have said he knew the guy, cleared it up. Like me. I came in. He didn't because he didn't want the connection known. I called him on it when we were on the phone. He lied. He didn't know we had this."

"Now he knows you know?"

"Yeah. I don't know what he thinks I know. I hung up on him. The question is, what do we do about it? We're probably spinning our wheels here. The whole thing's a charade. Nobody's going into that vault. They probably took Tran down after he checked his diamonds out and left. We led him right to slaughter."

Then he realized that maybe the white LTD belonged to the robbers, not Lewis and Clarke. They had followed Bosch and Wish to Tran.

"Wait a minute," Eleanor said. "I don't know. What about the alarms all week? The fire hydrant and the arson? It has to be happening like we thought."

"I don't know. Nothing is making sense right now. Maybe Rourke is leading his people into a trap. Or a slaughter."

They both stared ahead at the vault. The rain had slacked off, the sun was completely up now and it set the steel door aglow. Eleanor finally spoke.

"I think we have to get some help. We have Hanlon and Houck sitting on the other side of the bank, and SWAT, unless that was part of Rourke's charade."

Bosch told her he had checked on the SWAT surveillance and learned that it actually was in place.

"Then what is Rourke doing?" she said.

"Pushing all the buttons."

They kicked it around for a few minutes and decided to call Orozco at Beverly Hills police. First, Eleanor checked in with Hanlon and Houck. Bosch wanted to keep them in place.

"You guys awake over there?" she said into the Motorola.

"That's a ten-four, barely. I feel like that guy stuck in his car in the overpass after the earthquake up in Oakland. What's up, anything?"

"No, just checking. How's the front door?"

"Not a knock all night."

She signed off and there was a moment of silence before Bosch turned to get out of the car, to call Orozco. He stopped and looked back at her.

"You know, he died," he said.

"Who died?"

"The guy that was in that overpass."

Just then there was a thump that slightly shook the car. Not as much a sound as a vibration, an impact, not unlike the first jolt of an earthquake. There was no following vibration. But after one or two seconds an alarm sounded. The ringing came loud and clear from the Beverly Hills Safe & Lock Company. Bosch sat bolt upright, staring into the vault room. There was no visible sign of intrusion. Almost immediately, the radio crackled with Hanlon's voice.

"We've got a bell. What's our plan of action?"

Neither Bosch nor Wish answered the radio call at first. They just sat staring at the vault, dumbfounded. Rourke had let his people walk right into a trap. Or so it seemed.

"Son of a bitch," Bosch said. "They're in."

Bosch said, "Tell Hanlon and Houck to stay cool until we get orders."

"And who is going to give the orders?" Eleanor asked.

Bosch didn't answer. He was thinking of what was going on in the vault. Why would Rourke lead his people into a setup?

"He must not have been able to warn them, tell them that the diamonds aren't there and that we're up here," he said. "I mean, twenty-four hours ago we didn't know about this place or what was going on. Maybe by the time we got on to it, it was too late. They were too far in."

"So they are just proceeding as planned," Eleanor said.

"They'll pop Tran's box first, if they've done their homework and know which one it is. They'll find it empty, and then what do they do? Split, or open more boxes until they get enough stuff to make the whole thing worth their while?"

"I think they split," she answered. "I think when they open Tran's box and find no diamonds, they figure something is going down and get the hell out of there."

"Then we won't have much time. My guess is they will get stuff ready in the vault but they won't actually drill the box until after we've reset the alarm and cleared the scene. We can delay the resetting a bit, but too long and they might get suspicious and clear out, looking and ready for our people in the tunnels."

He got out of the car and looked back at Eleanor.

"Get on the radio. Tell those guys to stay put, then get a message to your SWAT people. Tell them we think we've got people in the vault."

"They'll want to know why Rourke isn't telling them."

"Think of something. Tell them you don't know where Rourke is."

"Where are you going?"

"To meet the patrol callout for the alarm. I'll have them call Orozco out here."

He slammed the door shut and walked down the garage ramp. Eleanor made the radio calls.

As Bosch approached Beverly Hills Safe & Lock he took his badge wallet out, folded it backward and hooked it in the breast pocket of his coat. He turned the corner around the glass vault room and jogged to the front steps just as a Beverly Hills patrol car pulled up, lights flashing but no siren. Two patrolmen got out, sliding their sticks out of the PVC pipe holders on the doors and then into the rings on their belts. Bosch introduced himself, told them what he was doing and asked them to get a message through to Captain Orozco as soon as possible. One of the cops said the manager, a guy named Avery, was being called out to reset the alarm while the cops checked the place out. All routine. They said they were getting to know the guy, it was the third alarm they had been called to here this week. They also said they already had orders to report any calls to this address to Orozco at his home, no matter the hour.

"You mean these callouts, they weren't false alarms?" said the one named Onaga.

"We aren't sure," Bosch said. "But we want to handle this like it is a false alarm. The manager gets called out and together you reset the alarm and everybody goes on their way. Okay? Just nice and relaxed. Nothing unusual."

"Good enough," said the other cop. The copper plate over his pocket said Johnstone. Holding his nightstick in place on his belt, he trotted back to their cruiser to make the call to Orozco.

"Here's our Mr. Avery now," Onaga said.

A white Cadillac floated to a stop at the curb behind the Beverly Hills car. Avery III, who was wearing a pink sport shirt and madras slacks, got out and walked up. He recognized Bosch and greeted him by name.

"Has there been a break-in?"

"Mr. Avery, we think something might be going on here, we don't know. We need time to check it out. What we want for you to do is open up the office, take a walk around like you usually do, like you did when the alarms went off earlier this week. Then reset the alarm and lock up again."

"That's it? What if—"

"Mr. Avery, what we want you to do is get in your car and drive away like you usually do, like you're going home. But I want you to go around the corner to Darling's. Go in and have a coffee. I'll either come by to tell you what is happening or send for you. I want you to relax. We can handle whatever comes up here. We have other people checking it out, but for the sake of appearances; we want to make it seem that we are passing this off as another false alarm."

"I see," Avery said, digging a key ring from his pocket. He walked to the front door and opened it. "And by the way, that is not the vault alarm that is ringing. It is the exterior alarm, set off by vibrations on the windows of the vault room. I can tell. It's a different tone, you see."

Bosch figured the tunnelers had disabled the vault alarm system, not realizing the exterior alarm was a separate system.

Onaga and Avery went in, with Bosch trailing behind. As Harry stood in the entryway looking for smoke and not seeing any, sniffing for cordite but not smelling any, Johnstone came in. Bosch put his hands to his lips to warn the officer against yelling above the sound of the alarm. Johnstone nodded, cupped his hand to Bosch's ear and told him that Orozco would be there in twenty minutes tops. He lived up in the Valley. Bosch nodded and hoped it would be soon enough.

The alarm shut off and Avery and Onaga came out of Avery's office into the lobby, where Johnstone and Bosch waited. Onaga looked at Bosch and shook his head, indicating nothing amiss.

"Do you usually check the vault room?" Bosch asked.

"We just look around," Avery said. He proceeded to the X-ray machine, switched it on and explained it took fifty seconds to warm up. They passed the time without talking. Finally, Avery put his hand on the reader. It read it and approved the bone structure and the lock on the first door of the mantrap snapped open.

"Since I don't have my man inside the vault room, I have to override the lock on the second door," Avery said.

"Gentlemen, if you don't mind not looking once we are in."

The four of them moved into the tiny mantrap and Avery pushed a set of numbers on the combination lock on the second door. It snapped open and they moved into the vault room. There was nothing to see but steel and glass. Bosch stood near the vault door and listened but heard nothing. He walked to the glass wall and looked up Wilshire. He could see that Eleanor was back in the car on the second floor of the garage. He turned his attention to Avery, who walked up to his side as if to look out the window himself but instead huddled into a conspiratorial posture.

"Remember, I can open the vault," he said in a low whisper.

Bosch looked at him and shook his head, then said, "No. I don't want to do that. Too dangerous. Let's get out of here."

Avery had a perplexed look on his face, but Bosch walked away. Five minutes later Beverly Hills Safe & Lock was cleared and locked down. The two cops went back out on patrol and Avery left. Bosch walked back to the garage. The street was busier now, and the noise of the day had begun. The garage was filling with cars and the stink of exhaust. Inside the car, Wish told him that Hanlon, Houck, and SWAT were in holding positions. He told her Orozco was on the way.

Bosch wondered how long it would take before the men in the tunnel believed it was safe to start drilling. Orozco was still ten minutes away. It was a long time.

"So what do we do when he gets here?" she said.

"His town, his call," he said. "We just lay it out for him and do whatever he wants to do. We tell him we have one fucked-up operation going here and we don't know who to trust. Not the guy in charge of it, at least."

They sat in silence for a minute or two after that. Bosch smoked a cigarette and Eleanor didn't say anything about it. She seemed lost in her own thoughts, a puzzled look on her face. They both nervously checked their watches every thirty seconds or so.

Lewis waited until the white Cadillac he tailed had turned north off Wilshire. As soon as the car was out of sight of Beverly Hills Safe & Lock, Lewis picked the blue emergency light up off the floor and put it on the dashboard. He flicked it on, but the driver of the Cadillac was already pulling to the side of the road in front of Darling's. Lewis got out of his car and walked up to the Caddy; he was met halfway by Avery.

"What is going on, officer?" Avery said.

"Detective," Lewis said and he opened his badge wallet. "Internal Affairs, LAPD. I need to ask you a few questions, sir. We are conducting an investigation of the man, Detective Harry Bosch, who you were just speaking with at Beverly Hills Safe & Lock."

"What do you mean 'we'?"

"I left my partner on Wilshire so he can keep an eye on your business. But what I would like is for you to step into my car so we can talk for a few minutes. Something is going on and I need to know what."

"That Detective Bosch—hey, how do I know you are for real?"

"How do you know he is? The thing is, we have had Detective Bosch under surveillance for a week, sir, and we know he is engaged in activities that could be, if not illegal, embarrassing to the department. We aren't sure what at this juncture. That's why we need you, sir. Would you step into the car, please?"

Avery took two tentative steps toward the IAD car and then seemed to decide, What the heck. He moved quickly to the passenger side and got in. Avery identified himself as the owner of Beverly Hills Safe & Lock and briefly told Lewis what had been said during his two encounters with Bosch and Wish. Lewis listened without commenting, then opened the car door. "Wait here, please. I'll be right back."

Lewis walked briskly up to Wilshire; he stood on the corner a few moments apparently looking for someone, then made an elaborate show of checking his watch. He came back to the car and slid in behind the wheel. On Wilshire, Clarke was waiting in the alcove of a store entrance and watching the vault. He caught sight of Lewis's signal and strolled casually to the car.

As Clarke climbed into the backseat, Lewis said, "Mr. Avery here says that Bosch told him to go to Darling's and wait, said there may be people in the vault. Come up from underground."

"Did Bosch say what he would be doing?" Clarke asked.

"Not a word," Avery said.

Everyone was silent, thinking. Lewis couldn't figure it. If Bosch was dirty, what was he doing? He thought some more on this and realized that if Bosch was involved in ripping off the vault, he was in a perfect situation by being the man calling the shots on the outside. He could confuse the coverage on the burglary. He could send all the manpower to the wrong place while his people in the vault went safely the opposite way.

"He's got everybody by the short hairs," Lewis said, more to himself than to the other two men in the car.

"Who, Bosch?" Clarke asked.

"He is running the caper. Nothing we can do but watch. We can't get in that vault. We can't go underground without knowing where we are going. He's already got the bureau's SWAT team tied up down by the freeway. They're waiting for burglars that aren't coming, goddammit."

"Wait a minute, wait a minute," Avery said. "The vault. You can get in it."

Lewis turned fully around in his seat to look at Avery. The vault owner told them that federal banking regulations didn't apply to Beverly Hills Safe & Lock because it wasn't a bank, and how he had the computer code that would open the vault.

"Did you tell this to Bosch?" Lewis asked.

"Yesterday and today."

"Did he already know?"

"No. He seemed surprised. He asked detailed questions on how long it would take to open the vault, what I had to do, things like that. Then today, when we had the alarm, I asked him if we should open it. He said no. Just said to get out of there."

"Damn," Lewis said excitedly. "I better call Irving."

He leapt from the car and trotted to the pay phones in front of Darling's. He dialed Irving at home and got no answer. He dialed the office and only got the duty officer. He had the officer page Irving with the pay phone number. He then waited for five minutes, pacing in front of the phone and worrying about the time going by. The phone never rang. He used the one next to it to call the duty officer back to make sure Irving had been paged. He had. Lewis decided he couldn't wait. He would have to make this call himself and it would be he who would become the hero. He left the bank of phones and went back to the car.

"What'd he say?" Clarke asked.

"We go in," Lewis said. He started the car.

The police radio keyed twice and then Hanlon's voice came on.

"Hey, Broadway, we have visitors over here on First."

Bosch grabbed up the radio.

"What have you got, First? Nothing showing on Broadway."

"We've got three white males going in on our side. Using a key. Looks like one is the man that was here earlier with you. Old guy. Plaid pants."

Avery. Bosch held the microphone up to his mouth and hesitated, not sure what to say. "Now what?" he said to Eleanor. Like Bosch, she was staring down the street at the vault room, but there was no sign of the visitors. She said nothing.

"Uh, First," Bosch said into the mike. "Did you see any vehicle?"

"None seen," Hanlon's voice came back. "They just walked out of the alley on our side. Must have parked there. Want us to take a look?"

"No, hold there a minute."

"They are now inside, no longer in visual contact. Advise, please."

He turned to Wish and raised his eyebrows. Who could it be?

"Ask for descriptions of the two with Avery," she said. He did.

"White males," Hanlon began. "Number one and two in suits, worn and wrinkled. White shirts. Both early thirties. One with red hair, stocky build, five-eight, one-eighty. The other, dark-brown hair, thinner. I don't know, I'd say these guys were cops."

"Heckle and Jeckle?" Eleanor said.

"Lewis and Clarke. It's gotta be them."

"What are they doing in there?"

Bosch didn't know. Wish took the radio from him.

"First?"

The radio clicked.

"Reason to believe the two subjects in suits are Los Angeles police officers. Stand by."

"There they are," Bosch said, as three figures moved into the glare in the vault room. He opened the glove compartment and grabbed a pair of binoculars.

"What are they doing?" Wish asked as he focused.

"Avery is at the keypad next to the vault. I think he is opening the damned thing."

Through the binoculars, Bosch saw Avery step away from the computer board and move to the chrome wheel on the vault door. He saw Lewis turn slightly and glance up the street in the direction of the parking garage. Was there a slight trace of a smile there? Bosch thought he saw it. Then through the binoculars he saw Lewis draw his weapon from an underarm holster. Clarke did likewise and Avery started turning the wheel, the captain steering the Titanic.

"Those dumb assholes, they are opening it!"

Bosch leapt out of the car and started running down the ramp. He unholstered his gun and held it up as he ran. He glanced along Wilshire and saw an opening in the sporadic traffic. He bounded across the street, Wish just a short distance behind him.

Bosch was still twenty-five yards away and knew he would be too late. Avery had stopped turning the vault wheel, and Bosch could see him pull back with all his weight. The door began slowly to move open. Bosch heard Eleanor's voice behind him.

"No!" she yelled. "Avery, no!"

But Bosch knew the double glass made the vault room silent. Avery couldn't hear her, and Lewis and Clarke wouldn't have stopped what they were doing even if they could hear.

What happened was like a movie to Bosch. An old movie on a TV set with the sound turned down. The slowly opening vault door, with its widening band of blackness inside, gave the picture an ethereal, almost underwater quality, a slow-motion inevitability. Bosch felt as if he were on a moving sidewalk going the wrong way, running but getting no closer. He kept his eyes on the vault door. The black margin opening wider. Then Lewis's body moved into Bosch's line of sight and toward the opening vault. Almost immediately, propelled by some unseen force, Lewis jerked backward. His hands flew up and his gun hit the ceiling and then fell soundlessly to the floor. As he backpedaled from the vault, his back and head ripped open and blood and brain spattered the glass wall behind him. As Lewis was hurled away from the vault door, Bosch could see the muzzle flash from the darkness inside. And then spiderwebs of cracks crazed the double glass as bullets struck silently. Lewis backstepped into a panel of the weakened glass and crashed through onto the sidewalk three feet below.

The vault was half open now and the shooter had freer

range. The barrage of machine-gun fire turned toward Clarke, who stood unprotected, his mouth open in shock. Bosch could hear the shots now. He saw Clarke attempt to jump away from the line of fire. But it wasn't worth the effort. He, too, was thrown backward by the force of bullets impacting. His body slammed into Avery and both men fell to the polished marble floor in a heap.

The gunfire from the vault ended.

Bosch jumped through the opening where the wall of glass had been and slid on his chest across the marble and glass dust. In the same instant he looked into the vault and saw the blur of a man dropping through the floor. The movement made a swirl in the concrete dust and smoke that hung inside the vault. Like a magician, the man just disappeared in the mist. Then, from the darkness farther inside, a second man moved into the view framed by the doorway. He sidestepped to the hole, swinging an M-16 assault rifle in a covering, side-to-side sweep. Bosch recognized him as Art Franklin, one of the Charlie Company graduates.

When the black hole of the M-16 came his way, Bosch leveled his gun with both hands, wrists on the cold floor, and fired. Franklin fired at the same time. His shots went high, and Bosch heard more glass shattering behind him. Bosch fired two more rounds into the vault. He heard one ping off the steel door. The other caught Franklin in the upper right chest, knocking him to the floor on his back. But in one quick motion, the injured man rolled and went headfirst through the floor. Bosch kept his gun on the doorway to the vault, waiting for anybody else. But there was nothing, only the sound of Clarke and Avery, gagging and moaning on the floor to his left. Bosch stood up but kept the gun trained on the vault. Eleanor climbed into the room then, her Beretta in hand. In marksman crouches, Bosch and Wish approached the vault from either side of the door. There was a light control next to the computer keypad on the steel wall, right of the door. Bosch hit the switch and the interior vault was flooded with light. He nodded to her and Wish went in first. Then he followed. It was empty.

Bosch came out and quickly went to Clarke and Avery, who were still tangled on the floor. Avery was saying, "Dear God, Dear God." Clarke had both hands clamped to his own throat and was gasping for air, his face turning so red that for one bizarre moment it looked to Bosch as if he were strangling himself. He was lying across Avery's midsection and his blood was over both of them.

"Eleanor," Bosch shouted. "Get backup and ambulances. Tell SWAT that they're coming. At least two. Automatic weapons."

He pulled Clarke off Avery and by grabbing the shoulders of his jacket, dragged him out of the line of fire from the vault. The IAD detective had taken a round in the lower neck. Blood was seeping from between his fingers and there were small blood-tinted bubbles at the corners of his mouth. He had blood in his chest cavity. He was shaking and going into shock. He was dying. Harry turned back to Avery, who had blood on his chest and neck and a brownish-yellow piece of wet sponge on his cheek. A piece of Lewis's brain.

"Avery, you hit?"

"Yes, uh . . . uh, uh, I think . . . I don't know," he managed in a strangled voice.

Bosch knelt next to him and quickly scanned his body and bloody clothes. He wasn't hit and Harry told him so. Bosch went back to where the double-glazed window had been and looked down at Lewis on his back on the sidewalk. He was dead. The bullets, having caught him in a rising arc, had stitched their way up his body. There were entry wounds on his right hip, stomach, left chest, and left of center of his forehead. He had been dead before he hit the glass. His eyes were open, staring at nothing.

Wish came in from the lobby then.

"Backup on the way," she said.

Her face was red and she was breathing almost as hard as Avery. She seemed barely in control of the movement of her eyes, which flitted about the room.

"When backup gets here," Bosch said, "tell them if they go into the tunnels that there is an officer friendly down there. I want you to tell your SWAT people that, too."

"What are you talking about?"

"I'm going down. I hit one, I don't know how bad. It was Franklin. Another went down ahead of him, Delgado. But I want the good guys to know I'm down there. Tell 'em I'm in a suit. The two I chased down there were in black fatigues."

He opened his gun and took out the three spent cartridges and reloaded with bullets from his pocket. A siren was sounding in the distance. He heard a sharp pounding and looked through the glass wall and the lobby to see Hanlon pounding the heel of his gun on the glass front door. From that angle the FBI agent could not see that the glass wall of the vault room had been shattered. Bosch motioned him to come around.

"Wait a minute," Wish said. "You can't do this. Harry, they have automatic weapons. Wait till the backup is here and we come up with a plan."

He moved to the vault door, saying, "They already

have a head start. I gotta go. Make sure you tell them I'm down there."

He stepped past her into the vault, hitting the light switch as he went. He looked over the edge of the blast hole. The drop was about eight feet. There were chunks of broken concrete and rebar at the bottom. He could see blood in the rubble, and a flashlight.

There was too much light. If they were waiting down there for him he would be a sitting duck. He backed out and around behind the vault door. He put his shoulder against it and slowly began to push the huge slab of steel closed.

Bosch could hear several sirens approaching now. Looking out into the street he saw an ambulance and two police cars coming down Wilshire. The unmarked car with Houck in it screeched to a halt in front and he came out with handgun drawn. The door was halfway closed and finally moving under its own force. Bosch slipped around it and back into the vault. He stood there over the blast hole as the door slowly closed and the light dimmed. He realized he had poised at such a moment many times before. It was always at the edge, at the entrance, that the moment was most thrilling and frightening to him. He would be at his most vulnerable at the moment he dropped into the hole. If Franklin or Delgado was down there waiting for him, they had him.

"Harry," he heard Wish call to him, though he couldn't understand how her voice made it through the now paper thin opening. "Harry, be careful. There may be more than two."

Her voice echoed in the steel room. He looked down into the hole and got his bearings. When he heard the vault door click shut and there was only blackness, he jumped.

As he came down in the rubble Bosch crouched and fired a shot from his Smith & Wesson into the blackness and then hurled himself flat against the bottom of the tunnel. It was a war trick. Shoot before they shoot you. But nobody was waiting for him. There was no return fire. No sound, except the faraway sound of running footsteps on the marble floor above and outside the vault. He realized he should have warned Eleanor, told her the first shot would be his.

He held his lighter out away from his body and snapped it on. Another war trick. Then he picked up the flashlight, turned it on and looked around. He saw that he had fired his shot into a dead end. The tunnel the thieves had dug to the vault went the other way. West, not east as they had thought when they looked over the blueprints the night before. That meant they had not come from the storm line Gearson had guessed they would. Not from Wilshire, but maybe Olympic or Pico to the south, or Santa Monica to the north. Bosch realized that the DWP man and all the rest of the agents and cops had been skillfully led astray by Rourke. Nothing would be as they had planned or thought. Harry was on his own. He focused the beam down the tunnel's black throat. It sloped down and then up, giving him only about thirty feet of visibility. The tunnel went west. The SWAT team was waiting to the south and east. They were waiting for nobody.

Holding the flashlight off to the right, away from his body, he began to crawl down the passageway. The tunnel was no taller than three and a half feet, top to bottom, and maybe three feet wide. He moved slowly, holding his gun in the same hand he used to crawl with. There was the smell of cordite in the air, and bluish smoke hung in the beam of the flashlight. Purple Haze, Bosch thought. He felt himself perspiring freely, from the heat and the fear. Every ten feet he stopped to wipe sweat out of his eyes with the sleeve of his jacket. He didn't take the jacket off because he didn't want to differ from the description given to the people who would follow him in. He didn't want to be killed by friendly fire.

The tunnel alternately curved left and then right for fifty yards, causing Bosch to become confused about his direction. At one point it dipped below a utility pipeline. And at times he could hear the rumble of traffic, making the tunnel sound like it was breathing. Every thirty feet burned a candle placed in a notch dug into the tunnel wall. In the sandy, chunky rubble at the bottom of the tunnel he looked for trip-wires but found a trail of blood.

After a few minutes of slow travel, he turned the flashlight off and sank back on his calves to rest and try to control the sound of his breathing. But he could not seem to get enough air into his lungs. He closed his eyes for a few moments, and when he opened them he realized there was a pale light coming from the curve ahead. The light was too steady to be from a candle. He started moving slowly, keeping the flashlight off. When he made his way around the bend, the tunnel widened. It was a room. Tall enough to stand in and wide enough to live in, he thought, during the dig.

The light came from a kerosene lantern sitting on top of an Igloo cooler in the corner of the underground room. There were also two bedrolls and a portable Coleman gas stove. There was a portable chemical toilet. He saw two gas masks and also two backpacks with food and equipment in them. And there were plastic bags full of trash. It was the camp room, like the one Eleanor had assumed was used during the dig into the WestLand vault. Bosch looked at all the equipment and thought of Eleanor's warning about there possibly being more than two. But she had been wrong. Just two of everything.

The tunnel continued on the other side of the camp room, where there was another three-foot-wide hole. Bosch turned the lantern flame off so he wouldn't be backlit and crawled into the passageway. There were no candles in the walls here. He used the flashlight intermittently, turning it on to get his bearings and then crawling a short distance in the dark. Occasionally, he stopped, held his breath and listened. But the sound of traffic seemed farther away. And he heard nothing else. About fifty feet past the camp room the tunnel reached a dead end, but Bosch saw a circular outline on the floor. It was a plywood circle covered with a layer of dirt. Twenty years earlier he would have called it a rathole. He backed away, crouched down and studied the circle. He saw no indication it was a trap. In fact, he did not expect one. If the tunnelers had rigged the opening, it would have been to guard against entry, not exit. The explosives would be on this side of the circle. Nevertheless, he took his keychain knife out and carefully ran its edge around the circle, then lifted it up a half inch. He pointed the light into the crack and saw no wires or attachments to the underside of the plywood. He then flipped it up. There were no shots. He crawled to the edge of the hole and saw another tunnel below. He dropped his arm and the flashlight through the hole and flicked on the beam. He swept it around and braced for the inevitable gunfire. Again, none came. He saw that the lower passageway was perfectly round. It was smooth concrete with black algae and a trickle of water at the bottom of its curve. It was a stormwater drainage culvert.

He dropped through the hole and immediately lost his footing on the slime and slipped onto his back. He propped himself up and with the flashlight began looking for a trail in the black slime. There was no blood, but in the algae there were scrape marks that could have been made with shoes digging for purchase. The trickle of water moved in the same direction as the scrape marks. Bosch went that way.

By now, he had lost his sense of direction, but he believed that he was heading north. He turned off the beam and moved slowly for twenty feet before flicking it on again. When he did so, he saw that the trail was confirmed. A smeared handprint of blood was at about three o'clock on the curved wall of the pipe. Two feet farther and at five o'clock there was another. Franklin was losing blood and strength quickly, he guessed. He had stopped here to check the wound. He would not be too much farther ahead.

Slowly, trying to lower the noise of his breathing, Bosch moved forward. The pipe smelled like a wet towel and the air was damp enough to put a film on his skin. The sound of traffic rumbled from somewhere nearby. There was the sound of sirens. He felt the pipe was on a gradual downward slope that kept the trickle of water moving. He was going deeper underground. There were cuts on his knees that bled and stung as he slipped and scraped along the bottom.

After maybe a hundred feet Bosch stopped and put on the beam, still holding it out to the side of his body and ready with the gun in his other hand. There was more blood on the curving wall ahead. When he switched off the flashlight, he noticed that the darkness changed farther ahead. There was light with a gray-dawn quality to it. He could tell that the pipeline ended, or rather, connected with a passageway where there was dim light. He realized then that he could hear water. A lot of water compared to what was running between his knees. It sounded like there was a river channel up ahead.

He moved slowly and quietly to the edge of the dim light. The pipeline he crouched in was a porthole on the side of a long hallway. He was in the tributary. Across the floor of the huge hallway, silvery black water moved. It was an underground canal. Looking at it, Bosch could not tell if the water was three inches or three feet deep.

Squatting at the edge, he first listened for sounds other than lapping water. Hearing nothing, he slowly extended his upper body forward to look down the hallway. The water was flowing to his left. He first looked that way and could see the dim outline of the concrete passageway curving gradually to the right. There was shadowy light filtering down at intervals from holes in the ceiling. He guessed that this light came from drain holes drilled in manholes thirty feet above. This was a main line, as Ed Gearson would say. Which one it was Bosch didn't know and no longer cared. There was no blueprint for him to follow, to tell him what to do.

He turned to look upstream and immediately pulled his head back into his pipe like a turtle. There was a dark form against the inside wall of the passage. And Bosch had seen two orange eyes glowing in the darkness, looking right at him.

Bosch didn't move and barely breathed for a whole minute. Stinging sweat dripped into his eyes. He closed

them but heard nothing but the sound of the black water.
Then slowly he moved back to the edge until he could see
the dark form again. It hadn't moved. Two eyes, like the
alien eyes of someone who looks into the flash in a snapshot, stared back at Bosch. He edged the flashlight
around the corner and hit the switch. In the beam he saw
Franklin slumped against the wall; his M-16 was
strapped around his chest, but his hands had fallen away
from it into the water. The end of the barrel dipped to the
water also. Franklin wore a mask that Bosch took a few
seconds to realize was not a mask. He wore NVGs—
night-vision goggles.

"Franklin, it's over," Bosch called. "I'm police. Give it
up."

There was no reply and Bosch didn't expect one. He
glanced up and down the main line one more time and
then jumped down into the water. The water just covered
his ankles. He kept his gun and the light on the still figure but didn't believe he would need the weapon.
Franklin was dead. Bosch saw that blood still seeped
from a chest wound and down the front of his black T-
shirt. Then it mixed into the water and was carried away.
Bosch checked the man's neck for a pulse and found
none. He holstered his gun and lifted the M-16 over the
dead man's head. Then he pulled the night goggles off the
corpse and put them on.

He looked one way down the long hallway and then
the other. It was like looking at an old black-and-white
TV. But the whites and grays had an amber tint. It would
take some getting used to, but he could see his way better with the goggles and he kept them on.

Next he checked the supply pockets on the thighs of
Franklin's black fatigue pants. He found a sopping wet

package of cigarettes and matches. There was an extra clip of bullets, which Bosch put in his jacket pocket, and a folded piece of wet paper on which blue ink was bleeding through and blurring. He carefully unfolded it and could tell that it had been a hand-drawn map. No names identifying anything. Just smeared blue lines. There was a square box near the center, which Bosch took to represent the vault. The blue lines were the drainage tunnels. He turned the map around in his hand, but the pattern did not seem familiar. A line running along the front of the box was the heaviest drawn. He figured that might be Wilshire or Olympic. Lines that intersected this were the cross streets, Robertson, Doheny, Rexford and others. There was a crosshatching of more lines continuing to the side of the page. Then a circle with an X through it. The exit point.

Bosch decided the map was useless, for he didn't know where he was or what direction he had taken. He dropped it into the water and watched it float off. In that moment he decided that he would follow the current. As good a choice as any.

Bosch splashed through the water, moving with the current, in a direction he thought was west. The black water curled against the wall in orange-tinted eddies. The water was above his ankles and filled his shoes, making his steps plodding and unsteady.

He thought about how Rourke had played it so well. It didn't matter if the Jeep and the ATVs had been found down by the freeway. That was all a decoy, a setup. Rourke and his bandits had shown the obvious, then done the opposite. Rourke had talked everybody into believing it while setting the battle plans the night before. The

SWAT team was waiting down there with a reception no one would attend.

He looked for signs of a trail in the passageway but found nothing. The water took all chance of that away with it. There were painted markings on the walls, even gang graffiti, but each scribble could have been there for years. He looked at it all but recognized none as a signal or direction. This time, Hansel and Gretel didn't leave a trail.

The traffic sounds grew louder now, and there was more light. Bosch flipped up the NVGs and saw shadowy cones of bluish light filtering down every hundred feet or so from manholes and drains. After a while he came to an underground intersection, and as the water from his line collided and splashed with water moving in the other channel, Bosch crept along the side wall and slowly looked around the corner. He saw and heard no one. He had no clue as to which way to go. Delgado could have gone in any of three different directions. Bosch decided to follow the new passageway to the right because it would take him, he believed, farther away from the SWAT setup.

He had taken no more than three steps into the new tunnel when he heard a loud whisper from ahead.

"Artie, you going to make it? Come on, hurry. Artie!" Bosch froze. It came from about twenty yards dead ahead. But he couldn't see anyone. He knew that it had been the NVGs he wore—the orange eyes—that had prevented him from walking into an ambush. But the cover wouldn't last long. If he got much closer, Delgado would know that he wasn't Franklin.

"Artie!" the voice called hoarsely again. "Come on!"

"Coming," Bosch whispered. He took one step forward and felt instinctively that it hadn't worked. Delgado would know. He dove forward, bringing the M-16 up as he went down.

Bosch saw a whirl of movement ahead and to the left, then saw a muzzle flash. The sound of gunfire was deafening in the concrete tunnel. Bosch returned fire and kept his finger tight on the trigger until he heard the injector go dry of bullets. His ears were ringing, but he could tell that Delgado, or whoever was up there, had stopped also. Bosch heard him snap a new clip into his weapon, then running footsteps on a dry floor. Delgado was moving away, in another passageway ahead. Harry jumped up and followed, pulling the empty clip out of his borrowed gun and replacing it with the backup as he went.

In twenty-five yards he came to a tributary pipeline. It was about five feet in diameter and Bosch had to take a step up to move into it. There was black algae rimming the bottom but no running water. Lying in the scum was the empty clip from an M-16.

Bosch had the right tunnel, but he no longer heard Delgado's footsteps. He began moving in the pipe quickly. There was a slight incline and in about thirty seconds he reached a lighted junction room thirty feet below a grated drain. On the other side of this room the pipeline continued. Bosch had no choice but to follow, this time with the pipe running on a gradual decline. He went another fifty yards before he could see that the line he was in emptied into a larger passage—a main line. He could hear water running up ahead.

Bosch realized too late that he was moving too fast to stop. As he lost his footing and slid on the algae toward the opening, it became clear to him that he had followed Delgado into a trap. Bosch dug his heels into the black slime in a worthless effort to stop himself. Instead, he went feet first, arms flailing for balance, into the new passageway.

It seemed odd to him, but he felt the bullet tear into his right shoulder before he heard the gunfire. It felt as though a hook on a rope had swung down from above, embedded in his right shoulder and then yanked him backward off his feet and down.

He let go of the gun and fell what seemed to him to be a hundred feet. But, of course, it wasn't. The floor of the passageway with its two inches of water came up like a wall of water and hit him in the back of the head. The goggles flew off and he watched, idly and detached, as sparks arced above him and bullets bit into the wall and ricocheted away.

When he came to it felt like he had been out for hours, but he quickly realized it was only a few seconds. The sound of the gunfire still echoed down the tunnel. He smelled cordite. He heard running steps again. Running away, he thought. He hoped.

Bosch rolled in the darkness and water and spread his hands out to find the M-16 and the goggles. He gave up after a while and tried to draw his own gun. The holster was empty. He sat up and pushed himself against the wall. He realized his right hand was numb. The bullet had hit him in the ball of the shoulder, and his arm hummed with dull pain from the point of impact down to the dead hand. He could feel blood running under his shirt and down his chest and arm. It was a warm counterpoint to the cool water swirling around his legs and balls.

He became aware that he was gasping for air and tried to regulate his intake. He was going into shock and he knew it. There was nothing he could do.

The sound of the steps, the running away, stopped then. Bosch held his breath and listened. Why had he stopped? He was home free. Bosch scissored his legs along the floor of the tunnel, still looking for one of the weapons. There was nothing there, and it was too dark to see where they had fallen. The flashlight was gone as well.

There was a voice then, too far away and too muffled to be distinguished or understood, but someone was talking. And then there was a second voice. Two men. Bosch tried to make out what was said but couldn't. The second voice suddenly grew shrill, then there was a shot, and then another. Too much time had elapsed between shots, Bosch thought. That wasn't the M-16.

As he thought about the significance of this, he heard the sound of steps in water again. After a while, he could tell the steps were coming through the darkness toward him.

There was nothing hurried about the steps that came through the water toward Bosch. Slow, even, methodical, like a bride coming down the aisle. Bosch sat slumped against the wall and again swished his legs along the watery, slimy floor in hopes of locating one of the weapons.

They were gone. He was weak and tired, defenseless. The humming pain in his arm had moved up a notch to a throb. His right hand was still useless, and he was pressing his left against the torn flesh of his shoulder. He was shaking badly now, his body in shock, and he knew he would soon pass into unconsciousness and not wake up.

Now Bosch could see the beam of a small light moving toward him in the tunnel. He stared fixedly at it with his mouth dropped open. Some of his muscle controls were already shutting down. In a few moments the slosh-ing steps stopped in front of him and the light hung there above his face like a sun. It was just a penlight but it was still too bright; he couldn't see behind it. Just the same, he knew whose face would be back there, whose hand held the light and what was in the other.

"Tell me," he said in a hoarse whisper. He hadn't real-ized how parched his throat had become. "That and your little pointer a matched set?"

Rourke lowered the beam until it pointed to the floor. Bosch looked around and saw the M-16 and his own gun side by side in the water next to the opposite wall. Too far to reach. He noticed that Rourke, dressed in a black jumpsuit tucked into rubber boots, held another M-16 pointed at him.

"You killed Delgado," Bosch said. A statement, not a question.

Rourke didn't speak. He hefted the gun in his hand.

"You going to kill a cop now, that the idea?"

"It's the only way I'll come out of this. The way it will look is Delgado gets you first with this." He held the M-16 up. "Then I get him. I come out a hero."

Bosch didn't know whether to say anything about Wish. It would put her in danger. But it might also save his life.

"Forget it, Rourke," he finally said. "Wish knows. I told her. There's a letter in Meadows's file. It ties you in. She's probably already told everybody up there. Give it up now and get me some help. It will go better for you if you get me out of here. I'm going into shock, man."

Bosch wasn't sure but he thought he saw a slight change in Rourke's face, his eyes. They stayed open, but it was as if they had stopped seeing, as if the only thing he was seeing was what was inside. Then they were back, looking at Bosch without sympathy, just contempt. Bosch braced his heels in the slime and tried to push himself up the wall into a standing position. But he had moved only a few inches when Rourke leaned over and easily pushed him back down.

"Stay there, don't fuckin' move. You think I'm going to take you out of here? I figure you cost us five, maybe six million, from what Tran had in his box. Had to be that much. But I'll never know now. You fucked up the perfect crime. You aren't getting out of here."

Bosch dropped his head until his chin was on his chest. His eyes were rolling up into their lids. He wanted to sleep now but he was fighting it. He groaned but said nothing.

"You were the only thing left to chance in the whole goddam plan. And what happens? The one chance something will happen, it does. You're Murphy's fuckin' Law, man, in the flesh."

Bosch managed to look up at Rourke. It was a terrible struggle. After, his good arm fell away from the shoulder wound. There was no more strength left to hold it there.

"What?" he managed to say. "Wh-wha . . . do you mean? . . . Chance?"

"What I mean is coincidence. You getting the call out on Meadows. That wasn't part of the plan, Bosch. You believe that shit? I wonder what the odds are. I mean, Meadows is put in a pipe we knew he had crashed in before. We're hoping maybe he won't be found for a couple of days and then maybe it takes two, three days for somebody to make the ID off the prints. Meantime, he gets written off as an OD, a no-count. The guy's got a hype card in the files. Why not?

"But what happens? This kid reports the body right off the fucking bat"—he shook his head, the persecuted man —"and who gets the call, a dipshit dick who actually knew the fucking stiff and ID's him in about two seconds. An asshole buddy from the tunnels of Viet-fucking-nam. I don't believe this shit myself.

"You messed everything up with that, Bosch. Even your own miserable life . . . Hey, still with me?"

Bosch felt his head raise, the gun barrel under his chin.

"Still with me?" Rourke said again, and then he poked the barrel into Bosch's right shoulder. It sent a shock wave of red neon pain searing down his arm and through his chest, right down to his balls. He groaned and gasped for air, then took a slow-motion swing with his left hand at the gun. It wasn't enough. He only got air. He swallowed back vomit and felt beads of sweat running through his damp hair.

"You don't look so good, buddy," Rourke said. "I'm thinking maybe I won't have to do this after all. Maybe my man Delgado did it right with the first shot."

The pain had brought Bosch back. It pulsed through him, leaving him alert, albeit temporarily. He could already feel himself fading. Rourke continued to lean over him, and he looked up and noticed the flaps hanging from the chest and waist of the FBI agent's jumpsuit. Pockets. He was wearing the jumpsuit inside out. Something clicked in Bosch's brain. He remembered Sharkey saying he saw an empty tool belt around the waist of the man who pulled the body into the pipe at the reservoir. That was Rourke. He wore the jumpsuit inside out that night, too. Because it said FBI on the back. He didn't want to risk that that would be seen. It was a bit of information that was useless now, but for some reason it pleased Bosch to be able to put it in place in the puzzle.

"What are you smiling at, dead man?" Rourke asked.

"Fuck you."

Rourke raised his foot and kicked at Bosch's shoulder but Bosch was ready for it. He grabbed the heel with his left hand and pushed upward and out. Rourke's other foot gave way on the slick bed of algae and slipped out from under him. He went down on his back with a splash. But he didn't drop the gun as Bosch had hoped. That was it. That was all there was. Bosch made a halfhearted effort to grab the weapon, but Rourke easily peeled his fingers off the barrel and pushed him back against the wall. Bosch leaned to his side and vomited into the water. He felt a new flow of blood coming from his shoulder, running down his arm. That had been his play. There was nothing else.

Rourke got up out of the water. He moved in close and put the barrel of the gun against Bosch's forehead. "You know, Meadows used to tell me about all that black echo stuff. All that bullshit. Well, Harry, here you are. This is it."

"Why'd he die?" Bosch whispered. "Meadows. Why?"

Rourke stepped back and looked up and down the tunnel before speaking.

"You know why. He was a fuckup over there, he was a fuckup here. That's why he died." Rourke seemed to be reviewing a memory in his mind and he shook his head disgustedly. "It was all perfect except for him. He held back the bracelet. Little jade dolphins on gold."

Rourke stared off into the darkness of the tunnel. A wistful look played on his face. "That's all it took," he said. "See, the plan relied on complete adherence for success. Meadows, goddammit—he didn't do that."

He shook his head, still angry at the dead man, and was quiet. It was at that moment that Bosch thought he could hear the sound of steps somewhere off in the distance. He wasn't sure if he had heard it or if it was what he hoped to hear. He moved his left leg in the water. Not enough to cause Rourke to pull the trigger, but enough to make the water slosh and to cover the sound of the steps. If they were even there.

"He kept the bracelet," Bosch said. "That was it?"

"That was enough," Rourke said angrily. "Nothing was to turn up. Don't you see? That was the beauty of the thing. Nothing would turn up. We'd get rid of everything except the diamonds. And those we'd keep until we were done with both jobs. But that fool couldn't wait until the second job was completed. He palms that cheap bracelet and pawns it to score dope.

"I saw it on the pawn reports. Yeah, after the WestLand job, we went to LAPD and asked them to send over their monthly pawn lists so we could check 'em out, too. We started to get 'em at the bureau. The only reason I made the bracelet and your pawn guys didn't was I was looking for it. The pawn detail has to look for a thousand things. I only looked for that one thing.

"I knew somebody had held it back. There was a lot reported stolen from that first vault that wasn't in the shit we took out of there. Insurance scammers. But the dolphin bracelet I knew was legit. That old lady . . . crying. The story behind it with her husband and all that sentimental value shit. Interviewed her myself. And I knew she wasn't scamming. So I knew one of my tunnel people had held the bracelet back."

Keep him talking, Bosch thought. He keeps talking and you'll end up walking. Out of here. Out of here. Someone's coming, my arm's humming. He laughed in his delirium and that made him vomit again. Rourke just went on.

"I bet on Meadows right from the start. Once on the needle . . . you know how that goes. So when the bracelet turned up he was the first one I went to."

Rourke drifted off then, and Bosch made more water noise with his legs. The water now seemed warm to him and it was the blood that ran down his side that was cold.

Rourke finally said, "You know, I really don't know whether to kiss you or kill you, Bosch. You cost us millions on this job, but then again my share of the first one sure has gone up now that three of my guys are dead. Probably even out in the end."

Bosch did not think he could stay awake much longer. He felt tired, helpless and resigned. The alertness had run out of him. Even now when he managed to reach his hand up and throw it against his torn shoulder, there was no pain. He couldn't get it back. He lapsed into contemplation of the water moving slowly around his legs. It felt so warm and he felt so cold. He wanted to lie down and pull it over him like a blanket. He wanted to sleep in it. But from somewhere a voice told him to hang in. He thought of Clarke clutching his throat. The blood. He looked at the beam of light in Rourke's hand and tried one more time.

"Why so long?" he asked in a voice no louder than a whisper. "All these years. Tran and Binh. Why now?"

"No answer, Bosch. Things just come together sometimes. Like Halley's Comet. It comes around every seventy-two or whatever years. Things come together. I helped them bring their diamonds across. Set the whole thing up for them. I was paid well and never thought otherwise. And then one day the seed planted all those years ago came out of the ground, man. It was there for the taking and, man, we took it. I took it! That's why now."

A gloating smile played across Rourke's face. He brought the muzzle of the weapon back to a point in front of Bosch's face. All Bosch could do was watch.

"I'm out of time, Bosch, and so are you."

Rourke braced the gun with both hands and spread his feet to the width of his shoulders. At that final moment Bosch closed his eyes. He cleared his mind of all thought but of the water. So warm, like a blanket. He heard two gunshots, echoing like thunder through the concrete tunnel. He fought to open his eyes and saw Rourke leaning against the other wall, both his hands up in the air. One held the M-16, the other the penlight. The gun dropped and clattered into the water, then the penlight. It bobbed on the surface, its bulb still on. It cast a swirling pattern on the roof and walls of the tunnel as it slowly moved away with the current.

Rourke never said a word. He slowly sagged down the wall, staring off to his right—the direction Bosch thought the shots had come from—and leaving a smear of blood that followed him down. In the dimming light, Bosch could see surprise on his face and then a look of resolve in his eyes. Pretty soon he sat like Bosch against the wall, the water moving around his legs, his dead eyes no longer staring at anything.

Things went out of focus for Bosch then. He wanted to ask a question but couldn't form the words. There was another light in the tunnel and he thought he heard a voice, a woman's voice, telling him everything was okay.

Then he thought he saw Eleanor Wish's face, floating in and out of focus. And then it sank away into inky blackness. That blackness was finally all he saw.

Part VIII
Sunday, May 27

Bosch dreamed of the jungle. Meadows was there, and all the soldiers from Harry's photo album. They stood around the hole at the bottom of a leaf-covered trench. Above them a gray mist clung to the top of the jungle canopy. The air was still and warm. Bosch took photographs of the other rats with his camera. Meadows was going into the ground, he said. Out of the blue and into the black. He looked at Bosch through the camera and said, "Remember the promise, Hieronymus."

"Rhymes with anonymous," Bosch said.

But before he could tell him not to go, Meadows promptly jumped feet first into the hole and disappeared. Bosch rushed to the edge and looked down but saw nothing, just darkness like ink. Faces came into focus, then slipped back into the blackness. There was Meadows and Rourke and Lewis and Clarke. From behind him, he heard a voice he recognized but couldn't place with a face.

"Harry, c'mon, man. I need to talk to you."

Then Bosch became aware of a deep pain in his shoulder, throbbing from elbow to neck. Someone was tapping his left hand, lightly patting it. He opened his eyes. It was Jerry Edgar.

"Yeah, that's it," Edgar said. "I don't have much time. This guy on the door says they'll be here anytime now. Plus, he's due to go off watch. I wanted to try to talk to you before the brass did. Would've been by yesterday but this place was crawling with silk. Besides, I heard you were out most of the day. Too delirious."

Bosch just stared at him.

"On these things," Edgar said, "I've always heard it's best to say you can't remember a thing. Let them put it whatever way they want. I mean, when you catch a round, there's no way they can say you're lying about re-membering. The mind shuts down, man, when there is traumatic insult to the body. I've read that."

By now Bosch realized he was in a hospital room and he began to look about. He noticed five or six vases of flowers, and the room smelled putridly sweet. He also noticed he had restraining belts across his chest and waist.

"You're at MLK, Harry. Um, doctors say you'll be all right. They still have some work to do on your arm, though." Edgar lowered his voice to a whisper. "I snuck in. Think the nurses have a change of shift or something. Cop on the door, he's over from Wilshire patrol, let me in 'cause he's selling and he musta heard that's my gig. I told him I'd take his listing for two points if he gave me five minutes in here."

Bosch still hadn't spoken. He wasn't sure he could. He felt like he was floating on a layer of air. He had trouble concentrating on Edgar's words. What did he mean about points? And why was he at Martin Luther King–Drew Medical Center near Watts? Last he remembered, he had been in Beverly Hills. In the tunnel. UCLA Med Center or Cedars would have been closer.

"Anyway," Edgar was saying, "I'm just trying to let you know what's going on as much as possible before the silks get here and try to fuck you over. Rourke is dead. Lewis is dead. Clarke is bad, he's on the machine, and I heard they were just keeping him going for parts. As soon as they line up people that need 'em, they'll pull the plug. How'd you like to end up with that asshole's heart or eyeball or something? Anyway, like I said, you should come out of this all right. Either way, with that arm, you can get your eighty percent, no questions asked. Line of duty. You're a made man."

He smiled at Bosch, who just looked at him blankly. Harry's throat was dry and cracked when he finally tried to speak.

"MLK?"

It came out a little weak but okay. Edgar poured a cup of water from a pitcher on the bedside table and handed it to him. Bosch unbuckled the restraints, sat himself up to drink it and immediately felt a wave of nausea hit him. Edgar didn't notice.

"It's a gun-and-knife club, man. This is where they take the gangbangers after the drive-bys. No better place to go with a gunshot in the county, leastwise those yuppie doctors over at UCLA. They train military doctors here. So they'll be ready for war casualties. They brought you in on a chopper."

"What time is it?"

"It's a little after seven, Sunday morning. You lost a day."

Then Bosch remembered Eleanor. Was she the one in

the tunnel at the end? What had happened? Edgar seemed to read him. Everybody had been doing that lately.

"Your lady partner is fine. She and you are in the spotlight, man, heroes."

Heroes. Bosch thought about that. After a while, Edgar said, "I gotta book on out of here. If they know I talked to you first, I'll get shipped out to Newton."

Bosch nodded. Most cops wouldn't mind Newton Division. Nonstop action in Shootin' Newton. But not Jerry Edgar, real estate agent.

"Who's coming?"

"Usual crew, I guess. IAD, Officer Involved Shooting team, the FBI is in on the act. Bev Hills, too. I think everybody's still figurin' out what the fuck happened down there. And they only got you and Wish to tell 'em. They probly want to make sure you two have the same story. That's why I'm saying, tell 'em you don't remember dick. You're shot, man. You are an injured officer. Line of duty. It's your right not to remember what happened."

"What do you know about what happened?"

"The department isn't saying shit. No scut going around on this at all. When I heard it went down I went out to the scene and Pounds was already there. He saw me and ordered me back. Fuckin' Ninety-eight, he wouldn't say shit. So I only know what's in the press. The usual load of bullshit. TV last night didn't know shit. The *Times* this morning doesn't have much, either. The department and the bureau, they look like they joined up to make everybody a valiant soldier."

"Everybody?"

"Yeah. Rourke, Lewis, Clarke—they all went down in the line of duty."

"Wish said that stuff?"

"No. She's not in the story. I mean, she isn't quoted. I 'spect they're keeping her kind of under wraps till the investigation is over."

"What's the official line?"

"The *Times* says the department says Lewis and Clarke and you were part of the FBI surveillance at that vault. Now I know that's a lie 'cause you'd never let those clowns near one of your operations. Besides, they're IAD. I think the *Times* knows something about it stinks, too. That Bremmer guy you know was calling me yesterday, seeing what I heard. But I didn't talk. My name gets in the paper on this and I'll get worse than Newton. If there is such a place."

"Yeah," Bosch said. He looked away from his old partner and became immediately depressed. It seemed to make his arm throb all the harder.

"Look, Harry," Edgar said after a half minute. "I better get out of here. I don't know when they'll be coming, but they will be, man. You take care and do like I told you. Amnesia. Then take the eighty percent line-of-duty disability and fuck 'em."

Edgar pointed a finger to his temple and nodded his head. Harry nodded absently and then Edgar left. Bosch could see a uniformed officer sitting on a chair outside the door.

After a while Bosch picked up the phone that was attached to the railing alongside his bed. He couldn't get a dial tone, so he pushed the nurse call button and a few minutes later a nurse came in and told him the phone was shut off, as per LAPD orders. He asked for a newspaper and she shook her head. Same thing.

He became even more depressed. He knew that both

LAPD and the FBI faced huge public relations problems with what had happened, but he couldn't see how it could be covered up. Too many agencies. Too many people. They could never keep a lid on it. Could they be stupid enough to try?

He loosened the strap across his chest and tried to sit all the way up. It made him dizzy, and his arm screamed to be left alone. He felt nausea overtake him and reached for a stainless steel pan on the bed table. The feeling subsided. But it jogged loose a memory of being in the tunnel with Rourke the morning before. He began remembering pieces of Rourke's conversation. He tried to fit the new information with what he had already known. Then he wondered about the diamonds—the cache from the WestLand job—and whether they had been found. Where? As much as he had grown to admire the engineering of the caper, he could not bring himself to admire its maker. Rourke.

Bosch felt fatigue overcome him like a cloud crossing the sun. He dropped back against the pillow. And the last thing he thought of before dozing off was what Rourke had said in the tunnel. The part about getting a larger share because Meadows, Franklin and Delgado were dead. It was then, as he slid into the black jungle hole that Meadows had jumped into before, that Bosch realized the full meaning of what Rourke had said.

The man in the visitor's chair wore an $800 pinstripe suit, gold cuff links and an onyx pinky ring. But it was no disguise.

"IAD, right?" Bosch said and yawned. "Wake up from a dream to a nightmare."

The man started. He hadn't seen Bosch open his eyes.

He stood up and left the hospital room without saying a word. Bosch yawned again and looked around for a clock. There was none. He loosened the chest belt again and tried to sit up. This time he was much better. No dizziness. No sickness. He looked over at the floral arrangements on the windowsill and the bureau. He thought that their number might have grown while he was asleep. He wondered if any of them were from Eleanor. Had she come by to see him? They probably wouldn't let her.

In another minute, Pinstripe came back in, carrying a tape recorder and leading a procession that included four other suits. One was Lieutenant Bill Haley, head of the LAPD Officer Involved Shooting squad, and one was Deputy Chief Irvin Irving, head of IAD. Bosch figured the other two for FBI men.

"If I'd known I had so many suits waiting for me, I would have set an alarm," Bosch said. "But they didn't give me an alarm clock, or a phone that works or a TV or a newspaper."

"Bosch, you know who I am," Irving said and threw a hand toward the others. "And you know Haley. This is Agent Stone and this is Agent Folsom, FBI."

Irving looked at Pinstripe and nodded toward the bed table. The man stepped forward and placed the recorder on the table, put a finger on the record button and looked back at Irving. Bosch looked at him and said, "You don't rate an introduction?"

Pinstripe ignored him and so did everybody else.

"Bosch, I want to do this quickly and without any of your brand of humor," Irving said. He flexed his massive jaw muscles and nodded at Pinstripe. The recorder was turned on. Irving dryly spoke the date, day and time. It was 11:30 A.M. Bosch had only been asleep a few hours. But he felt much stronger than when Edgar had visited.

Irving then added the names of those present in the room, this time giving a name to Pinstripe. Clifford Galvin, Jr. Same name, minus the junior part, as one of the department's other deputy chiefs. Junior was being groomed and doomed, Bosch thought. He was on the fast track, under Irving's wing.

"Let's do it from the top," Irving said. "Detective Bosch, you start by telling us everything about this deal since the moment you climbed in."

"You got a couple days?"

Irving walked over to the recorder and hit the pause button.

"Bosch," he said, "we all know what a smart guy you are, but we are not going to hear it today. I stop the tape only this once. If I do it again, I will have your badge in a glass block by Tuesday morning. And that's only because of the holiday tomorrow. And never mind any line-of-duty pension. I will see you get eighty percent of nothing."

He was referring to the department practice of forbidding a retiring cop to keep his badge. The chief and the city council didn't like the idea of some of the city's former finest floating around the city with buzzers to show off. Shakedowns, free meals, free flops, it was a scandal they could see coming a hundred miles away. So if you wanted to take your badge with you, you could: set nicely in a Lucite block with a decorative clock. It was about a foot square. Too big to fit in the pocket.

Irving nodded and Junior pushed the button again. Bosch told it like it had been, leaving out nothing and stopping only when Junior needed to turn the tape over.

The suits asked him questions from time to time but mostly just let him tell it. Irving wanted to know what Bosch had dropped from the Malibu pier. Bosch almost didn't even remember. Nobody took notes. They just watched him tell it. He finally finished the tale an hour and a half after starting. Irving looked at Junior then and nodded. Junior stopped the tape.

When they had no more questions, Bosch asked his.

"What did you find at Rourke's place?"

"That's not your business," Irving said.

"The hell it isn't. It's part of a murder investigation. Rourke was the murderer. He admitted it to me."

"Your investigation has been reassigned."

Bosch said nothing as the anger pushed its way into his throat. He looked around the room and noticed that none of the others, even Junior, would look at him.

Irving said, "Now, before I would go around shooting my mouth off about fellow law enforcement officers killed in the line of duty, I would make sure I knew the facts. And I would make sure that I had the evidence supporting those facts. We don't want any rumors being spread about good men."

Bosch couldn't hold back.

"You think you people will pull this off? What about your two goons? How are you going to explain that? First they put the bug in my phone, then they blunder into a fucking surveillance and get themselves shot. And you want to make them heroes. Who are you kidding?"

"Detective Bosch, it already has been explained. That is not your worry. It is also not your role to contradict the public statements of the department or the bureau on this matter. That, Detective, is an order. If you talk to the press about this, it will be the last time you do as a Los Angeles police detective."

Now it was Bosch who could not look at them. He stared at the flowers on the table and said, "Then why the tape, the statement, all the suits here with you? What's the point when you don't want to know the truth?"

"We want the truth, Detective. You are confusing that with what we choose to tell the public. But out of the public eye I guarantee and the Federal Bureau of Investigation guarantees that we will complete your investigation and take appropriate action where fitting."

"That's pathetic."

"And so are you, Detective. So are you." Irving leaned over the bed with his face close enough that Bosch could smell his sour breath. "This is one of those rare times when you hold your future in your own hands, Detective Bosch. You do what is right, maybe you find yourself back at Robbery-Homicide. Or you can pick up that phone—yes. I am going to have the nurse turn it on—and call your pals at that rag over on Spring Street. But if you do that, you better ask them if there are any career opportunities there for a former homicide detective."

The five of them then left, leaving Bosch alone with his anger. He sat up and was ready to take a swing with his good arm at a vase of daisies on the bedside table, when the door opened and Irving came back in. Alone. No tape recorder.

"Detective Bosch, this is unofficial. I told the others I forgot to give you this."

He pulled a greeting card out of his coat pocket and propped it upright on the windowsill. On the front was a busty policewoman with her uniform blouse unbuttoned to the navel. She was rapping her nightstick in her hand

436 | MICHAEL CONNELLY

impatiently. A bubble from her mouth said Get Well Soon or. . . . Bosch would have to read the inside to get the punch line.

"I didn't forget. I just wanted to say something private." He stood mute at the foot of the bed until Bosch nodded. "You are good at what you do, Detective Bosch. Anybody knows that. But that doesn't mean you are a good police officer. You refuse to be part of the Family. And that's not good. And, meantime, you see, I have this department to protect. To me, that's the most important job in the world. And one of the best ways to do that is to control public opinion. Keep everybody happy. So if it means putting out a couple of nice press releases and putting on a couple of big funerals with the mayor and the TV cameras and all the brass there, that's what we are going to do. The protection of the department is more important than the fact that two dumb cops made a mistake.

"Same goes for the Federal Bureau of Investigation. They will grind you up before they publicly flog themselves with Rourke. So what I am telling you is that rule one is you have to go along to get along."

"That's bullshit and you know it."

"No, I do not know it. Deep down neither do you. Let me ask you something. Why is it, you think, that Lewis and Clarke were pulled back on the investigation of the Dollmaker shooting? Who do you think reined them in?"

When Bosch didn't say anything Irving nodded. "You see, we had to make a decision. Would it be better to see one of our detectives dragged through the papers and brought up on criminal charges, or for him to be quietly demoted and transferred?" He let that hang there a few seconds before continuing. "Another thing. Lewis and Clarke came to me last week with the story about what you did to them. Cuffing them to that tree. Very brutal, that was. But they were as happy as a couple of high school cheerleaders after an evening with the football team. They had you by the balls and were ready to put the paper in right then. They—"

"They had me, but I had them."

"No. That's what I'm telling you. They came to me with this story about the bug in the phone, what you told them. But the thing is, they didn't drop the bug in your phone, like you thought. I checked it out. That is what I am telling you. They had you."

"Then who—" Bosch stopped right there. He knew the answer.

"I told them to hold back a few days. To watch, see what happened. Something was going on. Those two men were always hard to bridle when it came to you. They overstepped when they decided to stop that fellow Avery and then told him to take them back to the vault. They paid the price."

"What about the FBI, what do they say about the bug?"

"I don't know and I'm not asking. If I did, they would say, 'What bug?' You know that."

Bosch nodded and was immediately tired of the man. A thought was pushing into his head that he didn't want to allow in. He looked away from Irving to the window. Irving told him once more to think of the department before he did anything, then walked out. When he was sure Irving had made his way down the hall, Bosch lashed out with his left arm and sent the vase of daisies tumbling into the corner of the room. The vase was plastic and didn't break. The damage was just spilled water and flowers. Galvin Junior's ferret face momentarily poked in and then out of the room. He said nothing, but it tipped Bosch that the IAD man was posted outside in the hall. Was that for his protection? Or for the department's? Bosch didn't know. He didn't know anything anymore.

Bosch pushed away an untouched tray containing an institutional meal of turkey loaf with flour gravy, corn, yams, a hard roll that was supposed to be soft, and strawberry shortcake with flat whipped cream.

"You eat that, you might never get out of here."

He looked up. It was Eleanor. She stood in the open door, smiling. He smiled back. He couldn't help himself.

"I know."

"How are you, Harry?"

"Okay. I'll be okay. Might not be able to do chin-ups anymore, but I'll survive with that. How are you, Eleanor?"

"I'm fine," she said, and her smile just slayed him. "They put you through the Veg-O-Matic today?"

"Oh, yeah. Sliced and diced. The best and the brightest of my fine department—a couple of your pals, too—had me on the ropes all morning. There's a chair on this side."

She circled the bed but continued standing next to the chair. She looked around and a slight frown creased her brow, as if she knew this room and therefore knew something wasn't right.

"They got me, too. Last night. They wouldn't let me come see you till they were through with you. Orders. Didn't want us going together on the story. But I guess our stories came out all right. At least they didn't pull me back in after they talked to you today. Told me that was it."

"They find the diamonds?"

"Not that I've heard, but they aren't telling me much anymore. They've got two crews working it today, but I'm out of it. I'm on a desk till it cools off and the shooting team finishes up. They're still probably at Rourke's place looking."

"What about Tran and Binh, they cooperate?"

"No. They aren't saying word one. I know that from a friend who was on the interrogation. They don't know anything about any diamonds. Probably got their own people together in a posse. They'll be out on the treasure hunt, too."

"Where do you think the treasure is?"

"I don't have any idea. This whole thing, Harry, it's kind of thrown me. I don't know what I think about things anymore."

That included how she thought about him, he knew. He didn't say anything and after a while the silence became uneasy.

"What happened, Eleanor? Irving told me Lewis and Clarke intercepted Avery. But that's all I know. I don't understand."

"They watched us watch the vault all night. They must've gotten it into their heads that we were lookouts. If you start with the assumption that you were a bad cop, like they did, then you might come to the same conclusion. So when they see you turn Avery away and send the two uniforms home, they figure they know your game. They grab Avery at Darling's and he tells them about your visit the day before, and all the alarms this week, and then he lets it slip that you didn't want him to open the vault."

"And they said, 'You mean you can open the vault?' and the next thing is they are sneaking down the alley."

"Yeah. They had an idea about being heroes. Catching the bad cops and the robbers all at once. Nice plan until the payoff."

"Poor dumb jerks."

"Poor dumb jerks."

The silence came back then and Eleanor didn't wait for it to settle.

"Well, I just wanted to see how you were doing."

He nodded.

"And . . . and to tell you—"

Here it is, he thought, the kiss good-bye.

"—I've decided to quit. I'm going to leave the bureau."

"What about. . . . What will you do?"

"I don't know. But I'm going to leave here, Harry. I have some money so I'll travel awhile and then see what I want to do."

"Eleanor, why?"

"I don't—it's hard for me to explain. But everything that happened. Everything about the job has turned to shit. And I don't think I can go back and work in that squad room again after what has happened."

"Will you come back to L.A.?"

She looked down at her hands and then around the room again.

"I don't know. Harry, I'm sorry. It seemed like—I don't know, I'm very confused about things right now."

"What things?"

"I don't know. Us. What's happened. Everything." Silence filled the room again and it seemed so loud that Bosch hoped a nurse or even Galvin Junior would stick a head in to see if everything was all right. He needed a cigarette badly. He realized it was the first time today that he had thought about smoking. Eleanor looked down at her feet now, and he looked over at his untouched food. He picked up the roll and started to toss it up and down in his hand like a baseball. After a while Eleanor's eyes made their third trip around the room without seeing whatever it was she was looking for. Bosch couldn't figure it out.

"Didn't you get the flowers I sent?"

"Flowers?"

"Yes, I sent daisies. Like the ones growing on the hill below your house. I don't see any in here."

Daisies, Bosch thought. The vase he had knocked against the wall. Where are my goddam cigarettes, he wanted to yell.

"They'll probably come later. They only make deliveries up here once a day."

She frowned.

"You know," Bosch said, "if Rourke knew we'd found the second vault and were watching it, and if he knew that we watched Tran go in and clear his box, why didn't he get his people out? That really bothers me about this whole thing. Why'd he go through with it?"

She shook her head slowly, "I don't know. Maybe . . . well, I've been thinking that maybe he wanted them to go down. He knew those guys, maybe he knew it would work out that they'd go down shooting, that without them he'd get to keep all the diamonds from the first vault."

"Yeah. But you know, I've been remembering things all day. About when we were down there. It's been coming back, and I remember that he didn't say he'd get it all. He said something about his share being bigger now with

Meadows and the other two dead. He still used the word 'share,' like there was still someone else to split it with."

She raised her eyebrows. "Maybe, but it's just semantics, Harry."

"Maybe."

"I've got to go. You know how long they'll keep you?"

"Haven't been told, but I think tomorrow I'll take myself out. Thinking about going to Meadows's funeral over at veterans."

"A Memorial Day funeral. Sounds appropriate to me."

"Want to go with me?"

"Mmmm, no. I don't think I want anything more to do with Mr. Meadows. . . . But I'll be at the bureau tomorrow. Clearing out my desk and writing up status sheets on the cases I'll have to pass to other agents. You could come by if you'd like. I'll brew you some fresh coffee like before. But, you know, I don't really think they are going to let you out so fast, Harry. Not with a bullet wound. You need to rest. You need to heal some."

"Sure," Bosch said. He knew she was saying good-bye to him.

"Okay, then, maybe I'll see you."

She leaned over and kissed him good-bye, and he knew it was good-bye to everything about them. She was almost out the door before he opened his eyes.

"One last thing," he said, and she turned at the door and looked back at him. "How'd you find me, Eleanor? You know, in the tunnels with Rourke."

She hesitated and her eyebrows went up again.

"Well, I went down with Hanlon. But when we got out of the hand-dug tunnel we split up. He went one way in that first line and I went the other. I picked the winner. I found the blood. Then I found Franklin. Dead. And after that I was a little lucky. I heard the shots and then the voices. Mostly Rourke's voice. I followed that. Why did you think of that now?"

"I don't know. It just sort of came up. You saved my life."

They looked at each other. Her hand was on the door handle and it was open just enough so that Bosch could look past her and see Galvin Junior still there, sitting in a chair in the hallway.

"All I can say is thanks."

She made a shushing sound, dismissing his gratitude.

"You don't have to say anything."

"Don't quit."

He saw the crack in the door disappear, Junior with it. She stood there silently.

"Don't leave."

"I must. I'll see you, Harry."

She pulled the door all the way open now.

"Good-bye," she said, and then she was gone.

Bosch remained motionless on the hospital bed for the better part of an hour. He was thinking about two people: Eleanor Wish and John Rourke. For a long time he closed his eyes and dwelt on the look on Rourke's face as he crumpled and went down into the black water. I'd be surprised, too, Bosch thought, but there was also something else there, something he couldn't exactly identify. Some kind of knowing look of recognition and resolution—not of his dying, but of another, secret knowledge.

After a while he got up and took a few tentative steps alongside his bed. His body felt weak, yet all the sleep in the last thirty-six hours had made him restless. After he got his bearings and his shoulder made a slightly painful adjustment to gravity, he began to pace back and forth alongside the bed. He was wearing pale green hospital pajamas, not one of the opened-back smocks that he would have found humiliating. He padded around the room in bare feet, stopping to read the cards that had come with the flowers. The protective league had sent one of the vases. The others came from a couple of cops he knew but wasn't particularly close to, the widow of an old partner, his union lawyer and another old partner who lived in Ensenada.

He walked away from the flowers and went to the door. He opened it a crack and saw Galvin Junior still sitting there, reading a police equipment catalog. Bosch pulled the door all the way open. Galvin's head jerked up and he slapped the magazine closed and slipped it into a briefcase at his feet. He didn't say anything.

"So, Clifford—I hope I can call you that—what are you doing here? Am I supposed to be in danger?"

The younger cop didn't say anything. Bosch glanced up and down the hall and saw that it was empty all the way down to the nurses' station about fifty feet away. He looked at his door and noticed he was in room 313.

"Detective, please go back in your room," Galvin finally said. "I am only here to keep the press out of your room. The deputy chief thinks they will probably try to get in to get an interview with you, and my job is to prevent that, to prevent you from being disturbed."

"What if they use the sneaky method of just"—Bosch made a show of looking up and down the hall to make sure no one would hear—"using the telephone?"

Galvin exhaled loudly and continued not to look at Bosch, "The nurses are screening incoming calls. Only family, and I am told you don't have family, so no calls."

"How'd that lady FBI agent get by you?"

"She was cleared by Irving. Go back into your room, please."

"Certainly."

Bosch sat on his bed and tried to go over the case again in his mind. But the more he turned the parts of it over the more he got an anxious feeling that sitting on a bed in a hospital room was wasting time. He felt he was onto something, a breakthrough in the logic of the case. A detective's job was to walk down the trail of evidence, examine each piece and take it with him. At the end of the trail, what he had in his basket made or lost the case. Bosch had a full basket, but he began to believe there were pieces missing. What had he missed? What had Rourke told him at the end? Not so much in his words but his meaning. And the look on his face. Surprise. But surprise at what? Was he shocked at the bullet? Or shocked by where, and who, it came from? It could have been both, Bosch decided, and either way, what did it mean?

Rourke's reference to his share growing larger because of the deaths of Meadows, Franklin and Delgado continued to bother him. He tried to put himself in Rourke's position. If all his partners were dead and he was suddenly the sole beneficiary of the first vault caper, would he say, "My share has gone up," or would be simply say, "It's all mine"? Bosch's gut feeling was he would say the latter, unless there was still someone else sharing in the pot.

He decided he had to do something. He had to get out of this room. He was not under house arrest, but he knew that if he left Galvin was there to follow and report to Irving. He checked the phone and found that it had been turned on as Irving promised. No calls in, but Harry could call out.

He got up and checked the closet. His clothes were there, what was left of them. Shoes, socks and pants, that was it. The pants had abrasion marks on the knees but had been cleaned and pressed by the hospital. His sport coat and shirt had probably been taken off with scissors in the ER and either thrown away or put in an evidence bag. He grabbed all the clothing and got dressed, tucking his pajama top into his pants when he was done. He looked cloddish, but it would do until he got some clothes on the outside.

The pain in his shoulder was least when he held his arm up in front of his chest, so he began to put his belt around his shoulders to use it as a sling. But deciding that would make him too noticeable going out of the hospital, he put the belt back through the loops of his pants. He checked the drawer of the nightstand and found his wallet and badge, but no gun.

When he was ready, he picked up the phone on the bedside table, dialed the operator and asked for the third-floor nursing station. A woman's voice said hello and Bosch identified himself as Deputy Chief Irvin Irving. "Can you get Detective Galvin, my man on the chair down the hall, to come to the phone? I need to speak with him."

Bosch put the phone down on the bed and walked softly to the door. He opened it just wide enough to see Galvin sitting on the chair reading the catalog again. Bosch heard the nurse's voice calling him to the phone, and Galvin got up. Bosch waited about ten seconds before looking down the hall. Galvin was still walking toward the nurses' station. Bosch stepped out of the room and began walking quietly the opposite way.

After ten yards there was an intersection of hallways and Bosch took a left. He came to an elevator with a sign above it that said Hospital Personnel Only and he punched the button. When it came, it was a stainless steel and fake wood-grain affair with another set of doors at the back, big enough for at least two beds to be wheeled in. He pushed the first-floor button and the door closed. His treatment for the bullet wound had ended.

The elevator dropped Bosch off in the emergency room. He walked through and out into the night. On the way to Hollywood Station in a cab, he had the driver stop at his bank, where he got money out of an ATM, and then at a Sav-On drugstore, where he bought a cheap sport shirt, a carton of cigarettes, a lighter since he couldn't handle matches, and some cotton, fresh bandages and a sling. The sling was navy blue. It would be perfect for a funeral.

He paid the cabdriver at the station on Wilcox and went in through the front door, where he knew there was less chance that he would be recognized or spoken to. There was a rookie he didn't know on the front desk with the same pimple-faced Explorer Scout who had brought the pizza to Sharkey. Bosch held up his badge and passed by without saying a word. The detective bureau was dark and deserted, as it was on most Sunday nights, even in Hollywood. Bosch had a desk light clamped to his spot at the homicide table. He turned it on rather than using the bureau's ceiling lights, which might draw curious patrol officers down the hall from the watch commander's office. Harry didn't feel like answering questions, even the well-meaning ones from the uniform troops.

He first went to the back of the room and started a pot of coffee. Then he went into one of the interview rooms to change into his new shirt. His shoulder sent arrows of searing pain through his chest and down his arm as he pulled the hospital shirt off. He sat down in one of the chairs and examined the bandage for signs of a blood leak. There was none. Carefully, and much less painfully, he slipped the new shirt on—it was extra large. There was a small drawing of a mountain, sun, and seascape on the left breast and the words City of Angels. Bosch covered that when he put on the sling and adjusted it so that it held his arm tightly against his chest.

The coffee was ready when he was finished changing. He carried a steaming cup to the homicide table, lit a cigarette and pulled the murder book and other files on the Meadows case out of a file drawer. He looked at the pile and didn't know where to start or what he was looking for. He began reading through it all, hoping something would hit him as being wrong. He was looking for anything, a new name, a discrepancy in somebody's statement, something that had been discarded earlier as unimportant but would look different to him now.

He quickly scanned his own reports because most of the information he could still recall. Then he reread Meadows's military file. It was the slimmer version, the FBI handout. He had no idea what had happened to the more detailed records he had received from St. Louis and had left in the car when he went running toward the vault the morning before. He realized then that he had no idea where that car was, either.

Bosch drew a blank on the military file. While he was looking down at the miscellaneous paperwork in the back of the binder, the ceiling lights came on and an old beat cop named Pederson came in. He was heading toward one of the typewriters with an arrest report in his hand and didn't notice Bosch until he had sat down. He looked around when he smelled the cigarettes and coffee and saw the detective with the sling.

"Harry, how goes it? They let you out quick. Word around here was that you were righteously fucked up."

"Just a scratch, Peds. You get it worse from the fingernails of the he-shes you pull in every Saturday night. Least with a bullet you don't have to worry about the AIDS shit."

"You're telling me." Pederson instinctively massaged his neck where he still had scars from scratches inflicted by a transvestite hooker infected with the HIV virus. The old beat cop had sweated out two years of testing every three months but didn't get the virus. It was a story that was nightmarish legend in the division and probably the single reason the average occupancy in the TV and prostitute tanks at the station jail had dropped by half since then. Nobody wanted to arrest them anymore, unless it was for murder.

"Anyway," Pederson said, "sorry it went to shit out there, Harry. I heard the second cop went code seven a little while ago. Two cops and a feebee down in one shootout. Not to mention you gettin' your arm all fucked up. Probably some kind of a record for this town. Mind if I have a cup?"

Bosch gestured to the coffeepot. He hadn't heard that Clarke had died. Code seven. Out of service, for good. He still couldn't bring himself to feel sorry for the two IAD cops, and that made him feel sorry for himself. Made him feel like the hardening of the heart was now complete. He no longer had compassion for anybody, not even poor dumb jerks who screwed up and got themselves killed.

"They don't tell you shit around here," Pederson was saying as he poured, "but when I read those names in the paper I said, 'Whoah, I know them guys.' Lewis and Clarke. They were IAD, not on any bank detail. They called them two the great explorers. Always digging around, looking to fuck somebody up. I think everybody knows that's who they were but the TV and the *Times*. Anyway, that sure was curious, you know, what they were doing there."

Bosch wasn't going to bite on that. Pederson and the other cops would have to find out from another source what really went down at Beverly Hills Safe & Lock. In fact, he began to wonder if Pederson really had an arrest report to type up. Or had the rookie at the front desk spread the word that Bosch was in the bureau and the old beat cop been sent back to pump him?

Pederson had hair whiter than chalk and was considered an old cop but was actually only a few years older than Bosch. He had walked or driven the Boulevard beat for twenty years on night watch, and that was enough to turn a man's hair white early. Bosch liked Pederson. He was a silo of information about the street. There was rarely a murder on the Boulevard that went by without Bosch's checking with him to see what his informants were saying. And he almost always came through.

"Yeah, it's curious," Bosch said. He added nothing else.

"You doing paper from your shooting?" Pederson asked after settling himself in front of a typewriter. When Bosch didn't answer he added, "You got any more of those cigarettes?"

Bosch got up and carried a whole pack over to Pederson. He put them down on the typewriter in front of the beat cop and told him they were his. Pederson got the message. Nothing personal, but Bosch wasn't going to talk about the shoot-out, especially about what a couple of IAD cops were doing there.

Pederson got to work on the typewriter after that, and Bosch went back to his murder book. He finished reading through it without a single forty-watt bulb lighting up in his head. He sat there with the typewriter clacking in the background, and smoked and tried to think of what else there was to do. There was nothing. He was at the wall.

He decided to call his home and check the tape machine. He picked up his phone, then thought better of using it and hung up. On the off chance his desk phone wasn't a private line, he walked around to Jerry Edgar's spot at the table and used his line. He got his answering machine, punched in a code and listened as it played a dozen messages. The first nine were from cops and some old friends wishing him a speedy recovery. The last three, the most recent messages, were from the doctor who had been treating him, Irving and Pounds.

"Mr. Bosch, this is Dr. McKenna. I consider it very unwise and unsafe for you to have left the hospital environment. You are risking further damage to your body. If you get this message, would you please return to the hospital. We are holding the bed. I can no longer treat you or consider you my patient if you do not return. Please. Thank you."

Irving and Pounds were not as worried about Bosch's health.

Irving's message said, "I do not know where you are or what you are doing, but it better be that you just do not like hospital food. Think about what I told you, Detective Bosch. Do not make a mistake we will both be sorry for."

Irving hadn't bothered to identify himself but didn't

have to. Neither did Pounds. His message was the last. It was the chorus.

"Bosch, call me at home as soon as you get this. I have received word that you left the hospital and we need to talk. Bosch, you are not, repeat, not, to continue any line of investigation relating to the shootings on Saturday. Call me."

Bosch hung up. He wasn't going to call any of them. Not yet. While sitting at Edgar's spot he noticed a scratch pad on the table on which the name Veronica Niese was written. Sharkey's mother. There was also a phone number. Edgar must have called her to notify her about her son's death. Bosch thought of her answering the call, expecting it to be another one of her jerkoff customers, and instead it was Jerry Edgar calling to say her son was dead.

His thought of the boy reminded Bosch of the interview. He had not had the tape transcribed yet. He decided to listen to it, and went back to his place at the table. He pulled his tape recorder out of a drawer. The tape was gone. He remembered he had given it to Eleanor. He went to the supply closet, trying to calculate whether the interview would still be on the backup tape. The backup automatically rewound when it reached its end and then started taping over itself. Depending on how often the taping system in the interview room had been used since Tuesday's session with Sharkey, the Q-and-A with the boy might still be intact on the backup tape.

Bosch popped the cassette out of the recorder and brought it back to his table. He put it in his own portable, put on a set of earphones and rewound the tape to its beginning. He reviewed it by playing it for a few seconds until he could tell whether it was his voice or Sharkey's or Eleanor's, and then fast-forwarding for about ten seconds.

He repeated this process for several minutes before he finally hit the Sharkey interview in the last half of the tape.

Once he found it, he rewound the tape a bit so he could hear the interview from the start. He rewound too far and ended up listening to half a minute of another interview concluding. Then he heard Sharkey's voice.

"What are you looking at?"

"I don't know." It was Eleanor. "I was wondering if you knew me. You seem familiar. I didn't realize I was staring."

"What? Why should I know you? I never did no federal shit, man, I don't know—"

"Never mind. You looked familiar to me, that's all. I was wondering if you recognized me. Why don't we wait until Detective Bosch comes in."

"Yeah, okay. Cool."

There was silence on the tape then. Listening to it, Bosch was confused. Then he realized that what he had just heard had been said before he went into the interview room.

What had she been doing? The silence on the tape ended and Bosch heard his own voice.

"Sharkey, we are going to tape this because it might help us later to go over it. Like I said, you are not a suspect so you—"

Bosch stopped the tape and rewound it to the exchange between the boy and Eleanor. He listened to it again and then again. Each time it felt as if he had been punched in the heart. His hands were sweating and his fingers slipped on the buttons of the recorder. He finally pulled the earphones off and flung them onto the table.

"Damn it," he said.

Pederson stopped typing and looked over.

Part IX

Monday, May 28
Memorial Day Observed

By the time Bosch got to the veterans cemetery in Westwood, it was just after midnight.

He had checked a new car out of the Wilcox fleet garage and then driven by Eleanor Wish's apartment. There were no lights on and he felt like a teenager checking on the girlfriend who dumped him. Even though he was alone he was embarrassed. He didn't know what he would have done if there had been a light. He headed back east toward the cemetery, thinking about Eleanor and how she had betrayed him in love and business, all at the same time.

He started with the supposition that Eleanor had asked Sharkey if he recognized her because it was she who had been in the Jeep that delivered Meadows's body to the reservoir. She had been looking for a sign that the boy realized this and recognized her. But he didn't. Sharkey went on—after Bosch joined the interview—to say he had seen two people who he thought were men. He said the smaller of the two stayed in the Jeep's passenger seat and didn't help with the body at all. It seemed to Bosch that the boy's mistake should have insured his life. But he knew that it had been he who had then doomed Sharkey when he suggested hypnotizing him. Eleanor had passed that on to Rourke, who knew he couldn't risk it.

Next was the question of why. The money was the ultimate answer, but Bosch could not comfortably attribute this motive to Eleanor. There was something more. The others involved—Meadows, Franklin, Delgado and Rourke—all shared the common bond of Vietnam as well as direct knowledge of the two targets, Binh and Tran. How did Eleanor fit into this? Bosch thought about her brother, killed in Vietnam. Was he the connection? He remembered that she had said his name was Michael, but she hadn't mentioned how or when he was killed. Bosch hadn't let her. Now he regretted having stopped her when she apparently wanted to talk about him. She had mentioned the memorial in Washington and how it had changed her. What could she have seen that would do that? What could the wall have told her that she didn't already know?

He drove into the cemetery off Sepulveda Boulevard and up to the great black iron gates that stood closed across the gravel entrance road. Bosch got out and walked up, but they were locked with a chain and padlock. He looked through the black bars and saw a small stone-block house about thirty yards up the gravel road. He saw the pale blue glow of TV light against a curtained window. Bosch went back to the car and flipped the siren. He let it wail until a light came on behind the curtain. The cemetery attendant came out a few moments later and walked toward the gate with a flashlight, while Bosch got his badge case out and held it open through the bars. The man wore dark pants and a light-blue shirt with a tin badge on it.

"You police?" he asked.

Bosch felt like saying no, Amway. Instead, he said, "LAPD. I wonder if you can open 'er up for me."

The attendant put the flashlight on his badge and ID. In the light Bosch could see the white whiskers on the man's face and smell the slight scent of bourbon and sweat.

"What's the problem, officer?"

"Detective. I'm on a homicide investigation, Mr. . . . ?"

"Kester. Homicide? We got plenty dead people here, but these cases are closed, I guess you could say."

"Mr. Kester, I don't have time to go through all the details but what I need to do is take a look at the Vietnam memorial, the replica that is on display here for the holiday weekend."

"What's wrong with your arm, and where's your partner? Don't you guys travel in twos?"

"I was hurt, Mr. Kester. My partner is working on another part of the investigation. You watch too much TV in that little room of yours. That's TV cops stuff."

Bosch said this last part with a smile, but he was already getting tired of the old security guard. Kester turned and looked at the cemetery house and then back at Bosch.

"You seen the TV light, right? I figured that one. Uh, this is federal property and I don't know if I can open it up without—"

"Look, Kester, I know you're civil service and they haven't fired anyone since maybe Truman was president. But if you give me a bad time on this, I'm going to give you a bad time. I'll put a drinking-on-the-job beef in on you Tuesday morning. First thing. Now let's do it. Open it up and I won't bother you. I just need to take a look at the wall."

Bosch rattled the chain. Kester stared dull-eyed at the lock and then fished a ring of keys off his belt and opened the gate.

"Sorry," Bosch said.

"I still don't think this is proper," Kester said angrily. "What's that black stone got to do with a homicide anyway?"

"Maybe everything," Bosch said. He started walking back to his car but then turned around, remembering something he had read about the memorial. "There's a book. It tells where the names are on the wall. You can look them up. Is that up there at the wall?"

Kester had a puzzled look on his face that Bosch could see even in the dark. He said, "Don't know about any book. All I know is that the U.S. Park Service people brought that thing in here, set it up. Took a bulldozer to clear a spot on the hill. They got some guy that stays with it during proper visiting hours. He's the one you'll have to ask about books. And don't ask me where he is. I don't even know his name. You gonna be a while or should I leave it unlocked?"

"Better lock it up. I'll come get you when I'm leaving." He drove the car through the gate after the old man pulled it open, then up to a gravel parking area near the hill. Bosch could see the dark shine of the wall in the gash carved out of the rise. There were no lights and the area was deserted. He took a flashlight off the car seat and headed up the slope.

He first swung the light around to get an idea of the wall's size. It was about sixty feet long, tapering at each end. Then he walked up close enough to read the names.

An unexpected feeling came over him. A dread. He did not want to see these names, he realized. There would be too many that he knew. And what was worse was that he might come across names he didn't expect, that belonged to men he didn't know were here. He swept the beam around and saw a wooden lectern, its top canted and ledged to hold a book, like a church Bible stand. But when he walked over, he found nothing on the stand. The park service people must have taken the directory with them for safekeeping. Bosch turned and looked back at the wall, its far end tapering off into darkness. He checked his cigarettes and saw he had nearly a whole pack. He admitted to himself that he had expected it would be this way. He would have to read every name. He knew it before he came. He lit a cigarette and put the beam on the first panel of the wall.

It was four hours before he saw a name he recognized. It wasn't Michael Scarletti. It was Darius Coleman, a boy Bosch had known from First Infantry. Coleman was the first guy Bosch had known, really known, to get blown away. Everybody had called him Cake. He had a knife-cut tattoo on his forearm that said Cake. And he was killed by friendly fire when a twenty-two-year-old lieutenant called in the wrong chart coordinates for an air strike in the Triangle.

Bosch reached to the wall and ran his fingers along the letters in the dead soldier's name. He had seen people do that on TV and in movies. He pictured Cake with a reefer tucked behind his ear, sitting on his pack and eating chocolate cake out of a can. He was always trading for everybody's cake. The reefer made him crave the chocolate.

Harry moved on to other names after that, stopping

only to light cigarettes, until he had none left. In nearly four more hours he had come across three dozen more names belonging to soldiers he had known and knew were dead. There were no surprise names, and so his fear in that regard was unfounded. But despair came from something else. A small picture of a man in uniform was wedged into the thin crack between the false marble panels of the memorial. The man offered his full, proud smile to the world. Now he was a name on the wall. Bosch held the photo in his hand and turned it over. It said: "George, we miss your smile. All our love, Mom and Teri."

Bosch carefully put the photo back into the crack, feeling like an intruder on something very private. He thought about George, a man he never knew, and grew sad for no reason he could explain to himself. After a while, he moved on.

At the end, after 58,132 names, there was one he had not seen. Michael Scarletti. It was what he had expected. Bosch looked up at the sky. It was turning orange in the east and he could feel a slight breeze coming out of the northwest. To the south the Federal Building loomed above the cemetery tree line like a giant dark tombstone. Bosch was lost. He didn't know why he was here or whether what he had found meant a damned thing. Was Michael Scarletti still alive? Had he ever existed? What Eleanor had said about her trip to the memorial had seemed so real and true. How could any of this make sense? The beam of the flashlight was weak and dying. He turned it off.

Bosch napped a couple of hours in his car at the cemetery. When he woke the sun was high in the sky, and for the first time he noticed that the cemetery lawns were awash in flags, each grave marked by a small plastic Old Glory on a wooden stick. He started the car and slowly made his way along the thin cemetery roads, looking for the spot where Meadows would be buried.

It wasn't hard to find. Nestled on the side of one of the roads that wound into the northeast section of the cemetery were four vans with microwave antennas. There was a grouping of other cars as well. The media. Bosch hadn't expected all of the TV cameras and the reporters. But once he saw this crowd he realized that he had forgotten that holidays were slow news days. And the tunnel caper, as it had been dubbed by the media, was still a hot item. The video vampires would need fresh footage for the evening's broadcasts.

He decided to stay in the car, and watched as the short ceremony at Meadows's gray casket was filmed in quadruplicate. It was presided over by a rumpled minister who probably came from one of the downtown missions. There were no real mourners except for a few professionals from the VFW. A three-man honor guard also stood at attention.

When it was over, the minister pushed the brake pedal with his foot and the casket slowly descended. The cameras came in tight on this. And then, afterward, the news teams broke off in different directions to film stand-up reports at locations around the gravesite. They were spread out in a semicircle. This way, each reporter would look as if he or she had been at the funeral exclusively. Bosch recognized a few as people who had shoved microphones in his face before. Then he noticed that one of the men he had thought was one of the professional mourners was actually Bremmer. The *Times* reporter walked away from the grave and was heading to one of the cars parked along the access road. Bosch waited until Bremmer was almost next to his car before he rolled down the window and called to him.

"Harry, I thought you were in the hospital or something."

"I thought I'd come by. But I didn't know it was going to be a circus. Don't you people have anything better to do?"

"Hey, I'm not with them. That's a pig fuck."

"What?"

"TV reporters. That's what they call one of these gang-bangs. So, what are you doing here? I didn't think you'd be out so soon."

"I escaped. Why don't you get in and take a ride." Then indicating the TV reporters with his hand, Bosch said, "They might see me here and charge over and trample us."

Bremmer walked around and got in the car. Bosch took the driveway to the west section of the cemetery. He parked under the shade of a sprawling oak tree, from which they could see the Vietnam memorial. There were several people milling about, mostly men, mostly alone. They all looked at the black stone quietly. A couple of the men wore old fatigue jackets, the sleeves cut off.

"You seen the papers or TV yet on this thing?" Bremmer asked.

"Not yet. But I heard what was put out."

"And?"

"Bullshit. Most of it, at least."

"Can you tell me?"

"Not that it gets back to me."

Bremmer nodded. They had known each other a long time. Bosch did not have to ask for promises and Bremmer did not have to go over the differences between off-the-record statements, background statements and statements not for attribution. They had a trust built on prior credibility, going both ways.

"Three things you should check," Bosch said. "Nobody's asked about Lewis and Clarke. They weren't part of my surveillance. They were working for Irving over at IAD. So once you get that established, put the heat on them to explain what they were doing."

"What were they doing?"

"That you'll have to get somewhere else. I know you have other sources in the department."

Bremmer was writing in a long, thin spiral notebook, the kind that always gave reporters away. He was nodding as he wrote.

"Second, find out about Rourke's funeral. It will probably be out of state somewhere. Someplace far enough away that the media back here won't bother to send anybody. But send somebody anyway. Somebody with a camera. He'll probably be the only one there. Just like today's planting. That should tell you something."

Bremmer looked up from his notebook. "You mean no hero's funeral? You're saying Rourke was part of this thing, or he just fucked it up? Christ, the bureau—and we, the media—are making the guy out to be John Wayne reincarnated."

"Yeah, well, you gave him life after death. You can take it away, I guess."

Bosch just looked at him a moment, contemplating how much he should tell, what was safe for him to tell. For just a moment he felt so outraged he wanted to tell Bremmer everything he knew, and the hell with what would happen and what Irving had said. But he didn't. Control came back.

"What's the third thing?" Bremmer asked.

"Get the military records of Meadows, Rourke, Franklin and Delgado. That will tie it up for you. They were in Vietnam, same time, same unit. That's where this whole thing starts. When you get that far, call me and I'll try to fill in what you don't have."

Then all at once Bosch grew tired of the charade being orchestrated by his department and the FBI. The thought of the boy, Sharkey, kept coming to mind. Flat on his back, his head cocked at that odd, sickening angle. The blood. They were going to mop that one up like it didn't matter.

"There's a fourth thing," he said. "There was a kid."

When the story about Sharkey was finished, Bosch started the car and drove Bremmer back down the driveway to his own car. The TV reporters had cleared out of the cemetery and a man in a small front loader was pushing dirt into Meadows's grave. Another man leaned on a shovel nearby and watched.

"I'll probably need a job after your story comes out," Bosch said while watching the gravediggers.

"You won't be in it as an attribution. Plus, when I get the military records, they'll speak for themselves. I'll be able to scam the department's public information officers into confirming some of this other stuff, make it look like it came from them. And then near the bottom of the story, I'll say, 'Detective Harry Bosch declined comment.' How's that?"

"I'll probably need a job after your story comes out."

Bremmer just looked at the detective for a long moment.

"Are you going over to the grave?"

"I might. After you leave me alone."

"I'm leaving." He opened the car door and got out, then

leaned back in. "Thanks, Harry. This is going to be a good one. Heads are going to bounce."

Bosch looked at the reporter and sadly shook his head. "No they aren't," he said.

Bremmer stared uneasily and Bosch dismissed him with his hand. The reporter closed the door and went to his own car. Bosch had no misconceived notion about Bremmer. The reporter was not guided by any genuine sense of outrage or by his role as a watchdog for the public. All he wanted was a story no other reporter had. Bremmer was thinking of that, and maybe the book that would come after, and the TV movie, and the money and ego-feeding fame. That was what motivated him, not the outrage that had made Bosch tell him the story. Bosch knew this and accepted it. It was the way things worked.

"Heads never bounce," he said to himself.

He watched the gravediggers finish their job. After a while he got out and walked over. There was one small bouquet of flowers next to the flag stuck in the soft orange ground. The flowers were from the VFW. Bosch stared at the scene and didn't know what he should feel. Maybe some kind of sentimental affection or remorse. Meadows was underground for good this time. Bosch didn't feel a thing. After a while he looked up from the grave and toward the Federal Building. He started walking in that direction. He felt like a ghost, coming from the grave for justice. Or maybe just vengeance.

If she was surprised it was Bosch who had pressed the door buzzer, Eleanor Wish didn't show it. Harry had flipped his badge to the guard on the first floor and been waved to the elevator. There was no receptionist working on the holiday, so he had pressed the night bell. It was

Eleanor who opened the door. She wore faded jeans and a white blouse. There was no gun on her belt.

"I thought you might come, Harry. Were you at the funeral?"

He nodded but made no move toward the door she held open. She looked at him a long moment, her eyebrows arched in that lovely questioning look she had. "Well, are you going to come in or stand out there all day?"

"I was thinking we would take a walk. Talk alone."

"I have to get my keycard so I can come back in." She made a move to go back in and then stopped. "I doubt you heard this, because they haven't put the word out. But they found the diamonds."

"What?"

"Yes. They traced Rourke to some public storage lockers in Huntington Beach. They found receipts somewhere. They got the court order this morning and just opened them. I've been listening to the scanner. They're saying hundreds of diamonds. They'll have to get an appraiser. We were right, Harry. Diamonds. You were right. They also found all the other stuff—in a second locker. Rourke hadn't gotten rid of it. The boxholders will get their stuff back. There's going to be a press conference, but I doubt they will be saying whose lockers they were."

He just nodded, and she disappeared through the door. Bosch wandered over to the elevators and pushed the button while waiting for her. She had her purse with her when she came out. It made him conscious of not having a gun. And it privately embarrassed him that he momentarily thought that was a concern. They didn't speak on the way down, not until they were out of the building and on the sidewalk, heading toward Wilshire. Bosch had been weighing his words, wondering if the finding of the diamonds meant anything. She seemed to be waiting for him to begin but uncomfortable in the silence.

"I like the blue sling," she finally said. "How do you feel, anyway? I'm surprised they let you out of there so soon."

"I just left. I feel fine." He stopped to put a cigarette in his mouth. He had bought a pack from a machine in the lobby. He lit it with the lighter.

"You know," she said, "this would be a good time to quit those. Make a new start."

He ignored the suggestion and breathed the smoke in deeply.

"Eleanor, tell me about your brother."

"My brother? I told you."

"I know. I want to hear again. About what happened to him and what happened when you visited the wall in Washington. You said it changed things for you. Why did it change things for you?"

They were at Wilshire. Bosch pointed across the street and they crossed toward the cemetery. "I left my car over here. I'll drive you back."

"I don't like cemeteries. I told you."

"Who does?"

They walked through the opening in the hedge and the sound of traffic was quieted. Before them was the expanse of green lawn, white stones and American flags.

"My story's the same as a thousand others," she said. "My brother went over there and didn't come back. That's all. And then, you know, going to the memorial, well, it filled me with a lot of different feelings."

"Anger?"

"Yes, there was that."

"Outrage?"

"Yes, I guess. I don't know. It was very personal. What's going on, Harry? What has this got to do with . . . with anything?"

They were on the gravel drive that ran alongside the rows of white stone. Bosch was leading her toward the replica.

"You said your father was career military. Did you get the details of what happened to your brother?"

"He did, but he and my mother never really said anything to me. About details. I mean, they just said he was coming home soon, and I had gotten a letter from him saying he was coming. Then, like the next week, you know, they said he had been killed. He didn't make it home after all. Harry, you are making me feel . . . What do you want? I don't understand this."

"Sure you do, Eleanor."

She stopped and just looked down at the ground. Bosch saw the color in her face change to a lighter shade of pale. And her expression became one of resignation. It was subtle, but it was there. Like the faces of mothers and wives he had seen while making next-of-kin notification. You didn't have to tell them somebody was dead. They opened the door; they knew the score. And now Eleanor's face showed that she knew Bosch had her secret. She lifted her eyes and looked off, away from him. Her gaze settled on the black memorial gleaming in the sun at the top of the rise.

"That's it, isn't it? You brought me here to see that."

"I guess I could ask you to show me where your brother's name is. But we both know it's not on there."

"No . . . it's not."

She was transfixed by the sight of the memorial. Bosch

could see in her face that the hard-shell resistance was gone. The secret wanted to come out.

"So, tell me about it," he said.

"I did have a brother, and he died. I never lied to you, Harry. I never actually said he was killed over there. I said he never came back, and he didn't. That is true. But he died here in L.A. On his way home. It was 1973."

She seemed to go off on a memory. Then she came back.

"Amazing. I mean, to make it through that war and then to not make the trip home. It doesn't make sense. He had a two-day layover in L.A. on the way back to D.C. to the hero's welcome we were going to have for him. There was a nice safe job, arranged through Father at the Pentagon. Only they found him in a brothel in Hollywood. The spike was still in his arm. Heroin."

She looked up at Bosch's face and then looked away.

"That's the way it looked, but that wasn't the way it was. It was ruled an OD, but he was murdered. Just like Meadows so many years later. But my brother was written off the way Meadows was supposed to have been written off."

Bosch thought she might be beginning to cry. He needed to keep her on track, telling the story.

"What's going on, Eleanor? What's it got to do with Meadows?"

"Nothing," she said, and looked back along the trail they had walked.

Now she was lying. He knew there was something. He had the dreadful feeling in his gut that the whole thing revolved around her. He thought of the daisies she had sent to his hospital room. The music they had played at her apartment. The way she had found him in the tunnel. Too many coincidences.

"Everything," he said, "it was all part of your plan."

"No, Harry."

"Eleanor, how did you know there are daisies growing on the hill below my house?"

"I saw them when I—"

"You visited me at night. Remember? You couldn't see anything below the porch." He let that sink in a little. "You had been there before, Eleanor. When I was taking care of Sharkey. And then the visit later that night, that wasn't a visit. That was a test. Like the hang-up phone call. That was you. Because it was you who put the bug in my phone. This whole thing was. . . . Why don't you just tell me?"

She nodded without looking at him. He could not take his eyes off her. She composed herself and began.

"Did you ever have one thing that was at your center, was the very seed of your existence? Everybody has one unalterable truth at their core. For me, it was my brother. My brother and his sacrifice. That's how I dealt with his death. By making it and him larger than life. Making him a hero. It was the seed that I protected and nurtured. I built a hard shell around it and watered it with my adoration, and as it grew it became a bigger part of me. It grew into the tree that shaded my life. Then, all of a sudden, one day it was gone. The truth was false. The tree was chopped down, Harry. No more shade. Just the blinding sun."

She was quiet a moment and Bosch studied her. She seemed all at once to be so fragile he wanted to rush her to a chair before she collapsed. She cupped one elbow with her hand and held the other hand to her lips. It dawned on him what she was saying.

"You didn't know, did you?" Bosch said. "Your parents . . . nobody told you the truth."

She nodded. "I grew up thinking he was the hero my mother and father told me he was. They shielded me. They lied. But how could they know that one day a monument would be made and they would put every name on it. . . . Every name but my brother's."

She stopped, but this time he waited her out.

"One day a few years ago I went to the memorial. And I thought there was some kind of mistake. There was a book there, an index of the names, and I looked and he wasn't listed. No Michael Scarletti. I yelled at the parks people. 'How could you just leave someone's name out of the book?' And so I spent the rest of the day reading the names on the wall. All of them. I was going to show them how wrong they were. But . . . he wasn't there, either. I couldn't— Do you know what it's like to spend almost fifteen years of your life believing something, to build your beliefs around one single, shining fact, and have . . . to find that all that time it actually was like cancer growing inside?"

Bosch smeared the tears on her cheeks with his hand. He leaned his face close to hers.

"So what did you do, Eleanor?"

The fist against her lips squeezed tighter, her knuckles as bloodless as a corpse's. Bosch noticed a park bench farther down the walkway and he took her by the shoulder and directed her there.

"This whole thing," he said after they were sitting. "I don't understand, Eleanor. This whole thing. You were the—You wanted some kind of revenge against—"

"Justice. Not revenge, not vengeance."

"Is there a difference?"

She didn't answer.

"Tell me what you did."

"I confronted my parents. And they finally told me about L.A. I went through all my things from him and I found a letter, his last letter. I still had it in my things at my parents' house but I'd forgotten it. It's here."

She opened her purse and pulled out her wallet. Bosch could see the rubber grips and the handle of her gun in the purse. She opened her wallet and pulled out a twice-folded piece of lined notebook paper. She delicately unfolded it and held it open for him to read. He didn't touch it.

Ellie,

I'm getting so short here I can practically taste the soft-shell crabs. I should be home in two weeks or so. First I have to stop off in Los Angeles to make some money. Ha Ha! I have a plan (but don't tell the OM). I'm supposed to drop off a "diplomatic" package in L.A. But there might be a way to do something better with it. When I get back, maybe we can go up to the Poconos again before I have to go back to work for the "war machine." I know what you think about what I'm doing but I can't tell the OM no. We'll see how it goes. One thing's for sure, I'm glad to be leaving this place. I've been in the bush for six weeks before getting some R & R here in Saigon. I don't want to go back, so I'm having them treat me for dysentery. (Ask the OM what that is! Ha Ha.) All I had to do was eat some of the restaurant food in this town and got the symptoms. Anyway, that's all for now. I'm safe and I'll be home soon. So get those crab traps out of the shed.

Love,
Michael

She folded the letter carefully and put it away.

"The OM?" Bosch asked.

"The Old Man."

"Right."

Her composure was coming back. Her face was taking on the hard look Bosch had seen the first day he met her. Her eyes dropped from his face to his chest and his arm in the blue sling.

"I'm not wired, Eleanor," he said. "I'm here for myself, I want to know for myself."

"That's not what I was looking at," she said. "I knew you wouldn't be wired. I was thinking of your arm. Harry, if there is anything that you believe about me now, that you can believe, believe me when I say no one was supposed to get hurt.

"No one. . . . Everybody was to lose. But that was all. After that day—at the memorial, I looked and I searched and I found out what happened to my brother. I used Ernst at State, I used the Pentagon, my father, I used whatever I could and I found out about my brother."

She searched his eyes but he tried not to reveal the thoughts behind them.

"And?"

"And it was like Ernst told us. Toward the end of the war, the three captains, the triad, were taking an active part in the transport of heroin to the States. One conduit was Rourke and his crew at the embassy, the military police. That included Meadows, Delgado and Franklin. They would find short-timers in the bars in Saigon and proposition them: a few thousand dollars to take a sealed diplomatic package through customs. Nothing to it. They could arrange for them to receive temporary courier status, put them on a plane, and somebody would be waiting for the package in L.A. My brother was one of those that accepted. . . . But Michael had a plan. It didn't take a genius to figure out what they were carrying. And so he must have thought he could get over here and make a better deal with somebody else. I don't know how far he thought it out or had it set up. But it didn't matter. They found him and they killed him."

"They?"

"I don't know who. People working for the captains. For Rourke. It was perfect. He was killed in a way that the army, his family, just about everybody, would want to keep quiet. So it was quickly tidied up and that was that."

Bosch sat next to her as she told the rest of the story and did not interrupt until it was done, until it had come out of her like a demon.

She said the first one she found was Rourke. He was, to her astonishment, in the bureau. She called in her markers and transferred from D.C. out to his crew. She had a different last name than her brother had. Rourke didn't know who she was. After that, Meadows, Franklin and Delgado were located easily enough in prisons. They weren't going anywhere.

"Rourke was the key," she said. "I went to work on him. I guess you could say I seduced him with the plan."

Bosch felt something tear loose inside, some final feeling for her.

"I clearly insinuated that I wanted to make a score. I knew he would go for it because he'd been corrupt for years. And he was greedy. One night he told me about the diamonds, how he had helped these two guys out of Saigon with boxes full of diamonds. It was Tran and Binh. From there, it was easy to plan the whole thing. Rourke recruited the other three and pulled some strings, anonymously, to get them early releases into Charlie Company. It was a perfect plan and Rourke actually thought it was his. That's what made it perfect. In the end, I was going to disappear with the treasure. Binh and Tran would be robbed of the fortune they had spent their lives collecting and hoarding, and the other four would taste the biggest score of their lives and have it taken away. It would be the best way of hurting them the most. But no one outside the circle of guilt was to get hurt. . . . Things just happened."

"Meadows took the bracelet," Bosch said.

"Yes. Meadows took the bracelet. I saw it on the pawn lists that got sent over from LAPD. It was routine, but I panicked. Those lists go to every burglary unit in the county. I thought it would get noticed by somebody, Meadows would be pulled in and spill the story. I told Rourke. And he panicked, too. He waited until they were pretty much done with the second tunnel, and then he and the two others confronted Meadows. I wasn't there."

Her eyes were fixed on a point far away. There was no emotion in her voice anymore. It was just a flat line. Bosch didn't have to prompt her. The rest just came out.

"I wasn't there," she said again. "Rourke called me. He told me that, you know, Meadows died without giving up the pawn ticket. He said he'd made it look like an overdose. The bastard actually said that he knew people who had done it before, a long time ago, and gotten away with it. You see? He was talking about my brother. When he said that, I knew I was doing the right thing . . .

"Anyway, he needed my help. They had searched Meadows's place and couldn't find the pawn stub. That meant Delgado and Franklin were going to break into the shop and get the bracelet back. But Rourke wanted my help with Meadows. The body. He didn't know what to do with it."

She said she knew from Meadows's record that he had been busted for loitering at the reservoir. It wasn't difficult for her to convince Rourke it was a good place to leave the body.

"But I also knew that the reservoir was Hollywood Division, that if you didn't get the call you would at least hear about it and probably take an interest after Meadows was ID'd. See, I knew about you and Meadows. And now I knew Rourke was out of control. You were the safety valve, in case I needed to bring the whole thing down. I couldn't let Rourke get away with it again."

She swept her gaze across the stones and absentmindedly raised a hand and dropped it in her lap, a small show of resignation.

"After we put his body in the Jeep and covered it with the blanket, Rourke went back in to make a last sweep of the place. I stayed outside. There was a tire iron in the back. I took it and hit his fingers with it. Meadows's fingers. It was so somebody would see it was murder. I remember the sound so clearly. The bone. So loud I thought Rourke might even have heard. . . ."

"What about Sharkey?" Bosch asked.

"Sharkey," she said wistfully, as if she were trying the name out for the first time.

"After the interview, I told Rourke that Sharkey didn't see our faces at the dam. He even thought I was a man, sitting in the Jeep. But I made a mistake. I mentioned how we discussed hypnotizing him. Even though I stopped you and trusted that you wouldn't do it without me, Rourke didn't trust you. So he did what he did with Sharkey. After we were called out there and I saw him I . . ."

She didn't finish but Bosch wanted to know everything.

"You what?"

"Later, I confronted Rourke and told him I was bringing the whole thing down because he was out of control, killing innocent people. He told me there was no way to stop it. Franklin and Delgado were in the tunnel and out of reach. They turned the radios off when they brought the C-4 in. It's too unstable. He said there was no stopping it without more spilled blood. Then the next night you and I were almost run down. That was Rourke, I'm sure."

She said that the two of them played an unspoken game of mutual distrust and suspicion after that. The burglary of Beverly Hills Safe & Lock continued as planned, and Rourke steered Bosch and everybody else away from going underground to stop it. He had to let Franklin and Delgado go through with it, even though there were no diamonds left in Tran's box. Rourke could not risk going underground to warn them, either.

Eleanor finally ended the game when she followed Bosch down into the tunnel and killed Rourke, his eyes staring at her as he slid down into the black water.

"And that's the whole story," she said quietly.

"My car is over this way," Bosch said as he stood up from the bench. "I'll take you back now."

They found his car on the driveway, and Bosch noticed her eyes linger on the fresh soil on Meadows's grave before she got in. He wondered if she had watched from the Federal Building as the casket was put in the ground. As he drove toward the exit, Harry said, "Why couldn't you let it go? What happened to your brother was another time, another place. Why didn't you let it go?"

"You don't know how many times I've asked that and how many times I didn't know the answer. I still don't."

They were at the light at Wilshire and Bosch was wondering what he was going to do. And once again she read him, she sensed his indecision.

"Are you going to take me in now, Harry? You might have a hard time proving your case. Everybody's dead. It could look like you were part of it, too, You going to risk that?"

He didn't say anything. The light changed and he drove down to the Federal Building, pulling to the curb near the garden of flags.

She said, "If it means anything to you at all, what happened between you and me, it wasn't part of any plan. I know you won't ever know if that's the truth, but I wanted to say—"

"Don't," he said. "Don't say a thing about it."

A few uneasy moments of silence passed between them.

"You're just letting me go here?"

"I think it would be best for you, Eleanor, if you turned yourself in. Go get a lawyer and then come in. Tell them you didn't have anything to do with the murders. Tell them the story about your brother. They are reasonable people and they'll want to keep it low profile, avoid the scandal. The U.S. attorney will probably let you plead to something short of murder. The bureau will go along."

"And what if I don't turn myself in? You will tell them?"

"No. Like you said, I'm too much a part of it. They'd never go with what I'd tell them."

He thought a long moment. He didn't want to say what

he was going to say next unless he was sure he meant it. And could, and would, do it.

"No, I won't tell them. : . . But if I don't hear in a few days that you went in, I will tell Binh. And I'll tell Tran. I won't need to prove it to them. I'll just tell them the story with enough facts that they'll know it is true. Then, you know what they'll do? They'll act like they don't know what the hell I'm talking about and they'll tell me to get out. And then they'll come after you, Eleanor, looking for the same kind of justice you got for your brother."

"You would do that, Harry?"

"I said I would. I'll give you two days to go in. Then I tell them the story."

She looked at him, and the pained expression on her face asked why.

Harry said, "Somebody has to answer for Sharkey."

She turned away, put her hand on the door handle and looked out the car window at the flags flapping in the Santa Ana breeze. She didn't look back at him when she said, "So, I guess I was wrong about you."

"If you mean the Dollmaker case, the answer is yes, you were wrong about me."

She looked back at him with a wan smile as she opened the door. She quickly leaned over and kissed him on the cheek. She said, "Good-bye, Harry Bosch."

Then she was out of the car, standing in the wind and looking in at him. She hesitated and then closed the door. As Harry drove away he glanced once in the mirror and saw her still at the curb. She stood there looking down like someone who had dropped something in the gutter. After that, he didn't look back.

Epilogue

T he morning after Memorial Day, Harry Bosch
checked back into MLK, where he was severely
chastised by his doctor, who seemed, to Harry at
least, to take a perverse pleasure in ripping the home-
applied bandages away from his shoulder and then using
a stinging saline solution to rinse the wound. He spent
two days resting and then was wheeled into the OR for
surgery to reattach muscles that had been torn from bone
by the bullet.

On the second day of his recovery from surgery, a
nurse's aide dropped off a day-old *Los Angeles Times* for
him to while away a few hours with. Bremmer's story
was on the front page, and it accompanied a photograph
of a priest standing before a lonely casket at a cemetery
in Syracuse, New York. It was FBI Special Agent John
Rourke's casket. Bosch could tell from the photo that
more mourners—albeit members of the media—had been
at Meadows's funeral. But Bosch tossed the front section
aside after scanning the first few paragraphs of the story
and realizing it wasn't about Eleanor. He turned to the
sports.

The next day, he had a visitor. Lieutenant Harvey Pounds told Bosch that when he was recovered, he would report back to Hollywood homicide. Pounds said that neither of them had any choice in the matter. The order came from the sixth floor at Parker Center. The lieutenant didn't have much else to say, and didn't mention the newspaper article at all. Harry took the news with a smile and a nod, not wanting to show a hint of what he felt or thought.

"Of course, this is all contingent on you being able to pass a departmental physical when you're released by your physicians here," Pounds added.

"Of course," Bosch said.

"You know, Bosch, some officers would want the disability, retire at eighty percent pay. You could get a job in the private sector and do very nicely. You'd deserve it."

Ah, Harry thought, there is the reason for the visit.

"Is that what the department wants me to do, Lieutenant?" he asked. "Are you the messenger?"

"Of course not. The department wants you to do what you want, Harry. I'm just looking at the advantages of the situation. You know, just something to think about. I understand private investigation is the growth market of the nineties. No trust anymore, you know? Nowadays people are secretly getting complete backgrounds—medical, financial, romantic—on the people they are going to marry."

"That doesn't sound like my kind of work."

"You'll take the homicide table, then?"

"Soon as I pass the physical."

He had another visitor the next day. This one was expected. She was a prosecutor from the U.S. attorney's office. Her name was Chavez and she wanted to know about the night Sharkey was killed. Eleanor Wish had come in, Bosch knew then.

He told the prosecutor that he had been with Eleanor, confirming her alibi. Chavez said she just had to check to be sure, before they started talking a deal. She asked a few other questions about the case, then got up from the visitor's chair to go.

"What's going to happen to her?" Bosch asked.

"I can't discuss that, Detective."

"Off the record?"

"Off the record, she's obviously going to have to go away, but it probably won't be long. The climate is right for this to be handled very quietly. She came forward, she brought competent counsel and it appears she was not directly responsible for the deaths involved. If you ask me, she'll get out of this very lucky. She'll plead and do maybe thirty months tops up at Tehachapi."

Bosch nodded and Chavez was gone.

Harry, too, was gone the next day, sent home for six weeks recuperative leave before reporting back to the station on Wilcox. When he arrived at the house on Woodrow Wilson he found a yellow slip of paper in his mailbox. He took it to the post office and exchanged it for a wide, flat package in brown paper. He didn't open it until he was home. It was from Eleanor Wish, though it did not say so: it was just something he knew. After tearing away the paper and bubbled plastic liner, he found a framed print of Hopper's *Nighthawks*. It was the piece he had seen above her couch that first night he was with her.

Bosch hung the print in the hallway near his front door, and from time to time he would stop and study it when he came in, particularly from a weary day or night on the job. The painting never failed to fascinate him, or to evoke memories of Eleanor Wish. The darkness. The stark loneliness. The man sitting alone, his face turned to the shadows. I am that man, Harry Bosch would think each time he looked.